"I'd like to do a few nude shots."

Jess had tried everywhere to get a job, but there was no work to be found. She had only one thing of value to sell . . .

Now he wanted to see all of her.

She knew it was going to happen this time, it was going to change her forever. Part of her thought "All right, get it over with;" and another part cried out, "Please don't" . . .

And it was then that she remembered her dying father, her baby sister, and reached for the buttons on her dress . . .

Charlotte Vale Allen's
PROMISES

Promises

Charlotte Vale Allen

BERKLEY BOOKS, NEW YORK

This Berkley book contains the complete
text of the original hardcover edition.
It has been completely reset in a type face
designed for easy reading, and was printed
from new film.

PROMISES

A Berkley Book / published by arrangement with
E. P. Dutton

PRINTING HISTORY
E. P. Dutton edition published 1980
Berkley edition / June 1981
Second printing / June 1981
Third printing / July 1981
Fourth printing / July 1981
Fifth printing / August 1981

ISBN: 0-425-04843-8

A BERKLEY BOOK® TM 757,375
Berkley Books are published by Berkley Publishing Corporation,
200 Madison Avenue, New York, New York 10016.
PRINTED IN THE UNITED STATES OF AMERICA

ACKNOWLEDGMENTS

I would like to thank my brother Bill and our dear friend Dorothy Hollingsworth for sharing their memories of the city with me. Also, I am grateful to another dear friend, Beverley Beetham, who so kindly raided the shelves to provide me with numerous reference books on Toronto.

I thank Liza Hatcher for her many hours spent on this manuscript and finally, I offer my gratitude to Tom Congdon, from whom I have learned so much.

For Tana Raikes

Promises

ONE

New York & Vermont

1936

◇ One ◇

It was like a ladder, she thought. They'd started very close to the top and then had slowly descended one rung at a time, with a little less to carry on each level. Until Father died. After that, there was nothing at all left, except a few bits of clothing, hers and Tillie's.

This morning, still numbed with grief a month after her father's death, Jess traveled between the kitchen and the bedroom looking for something, anything of value she might have missed in her previous searches. But there was nothing.

Tillie, relatively unaffected once past her brief-lived burst of sorrow, sat on the edge of the bed they shared and watched Jess go back and forth, waiting expectantly, positive Jess would think of something. She always did. She knew Jess would take care of her, and it never occurred to her to think of who might take care of Jess.

"You're going to be late for school," Jess said suddenly, stopping. "Hurry up, Till! Have you got your lunch? Good. All right. Hurry now! You'll be late!"

Tillie went off, casting doubtful backward glances as she started down the five flights of stairs, skirting the garbage piled on the landings. Jess stood at the top, looking down into the stairwell, waving reassuringly as Tillie paused at every landing

3

and looked up to make sure Jess was still there. The front door
closed finally, and Jess went back into the empty flat and shut
the door to stand staring at the emptiness, a panicky thumping
inside.

The last of their food had gone into Tillie's lunch bag, and
unless she did something there wouldn't be an evening meal.
She closed her eyes for a moment, thinking back to family
dinners, meals taken at the polished mahogany table that had
occupied most of the space in the dining room. There'd been
just enough room for the eight chairs and sideboard. Only six
years ago. Gladys carrying in the tureen, the heady aroma of
sherry spooned into the consommé at the last moment. The
Limoges china, Mother's wedding-present china—sold, one
of the first things to go. And the solid silver Sheffield carving
set—sold, too. All of it gone. The table, the chairs, the sideboard. Each room of the apartment was emptied one after the
other, until the apartment too was gone and they had moved
to that place on Fifty-third Street. Then to West Eighty-fifth.
After that, to West Sixty-seventh. And then to cold-water flats,
where they could only stay a week or two until the money ran
out. Then in the night she and Father and Tillie carried their
bags tiptoe down the stairs, out into the street, with Father
smiling, making a game of it for Tillie's benefit, saying, "Try
to guess where we're going this time, Till! Try to guess!" Of
course, she couldn't, but she went along eagerly, caught up
in Father's games. He and Jess made light of their clandestine
moves in order to shelter Tillie from the knowledge that everything they'd had was gone.

Now, Jess was deeply frightened. Surprisingly, more for
Tillie's sake than her own. She was eighteen, capable of sur-
viving somehow. But Tillie was not yet twelve; she had to
depend upon her older sister to provide food and shelter. And
Jess had promised her father she'd look after Tillie. She
wouldn't let them take Tillie away and put her in an orphanage.
No one was going to separate them! The idea of it filled her
with horror.

I've got to do something, she decided.

But what?

She'd tried everywhere to get a job. There was simply no
work to be had. Former executives in once-good suits were
standing in bread lines. People panhandled on every corner,
and on every other corner, once respectable women solicited
strangers, selling themselves. Selling themselves.

The idea came to her slowly. And it wasn't as horrible as it might have been, say, last year, or the year before. Because Father was no longer with them to see or know. The only one who'd have to know was Jess herself. She actually came close to smiling as the novelty of the thought occurred to her: She did have one last thing of value to sell—herself.

She'd never given very much consideration to herself. She'd been far too concerned with her father's failing health, his dreadful, crippling depressions, and their constant moves here and there, running to stay ahead of that pack of invisible creditors close on their heels.

It really wasn't too terrible to contemplate.

She placed her hands over her breasts, trying to imagine some strange man's hands laying claim to her, to all the parts of her. She couldn't imagine it and went to look at herself in the small mirror near the empty icebox, wondering how she might appear to others.

It was the sight of her own face in the mirror that brought fear crowding into her. Some man, perhaps old or ugly, would buy his way into her, buy the right to touch her in any way he chose. She turned away from the mirror, hoping to see something she might have missed in her earlier inspections of the two rooms. But there was nothing. Deeply distressed, she looked again at the mirror and the reflection there of the stark, vacant room behind her, faded wallpaper bending away from the walls and cracked, filthy linoleum on the floor. Cockroaches were lurking there, and water bugs; silverfish, too. Stained, torn curtains covered the window that looked out on the airshaft, and a large section of plaster was missing from the wall in the other room, revealing the brick underneath. Realizing that there were no choices left, Jess was full of fear. She was going to have to do this thing. And quickly, before Tillie returned home from school.

She stepped out through the front door feeling as if everyone who saw her knew her squalid destination, could see the aura of her imminent debasement clinging shadowlike to the hem of her skirt. She was clad in her last few decent items of clothing; her dress was almost four years old, very much out of fashion, and too tight under the arms.

She went down the front steps of the brownstone, a six-story building on East Nineteenth Street near Second Avenue, a block from the El, one of a long row of ugly, scarred buildings on what she thought of as the dark side of the street. The sun never seemed to shine here, the noise of the trains never ceased.

Her shoes pinched. They'd been her mother's: It would have been wasteful to throw away practically new, scarcely worn shoes, even though they pinched. The too-small black pumps reminded her with each step that she was on her way . . . to what? She hadn't any real idea of where to go or how to set about doing this thing. She supposed she'd simply have to find some street corner or doorway and approach men, or allow them to approach her, until one (or more—she'd have to do this many more times than once, she realized, attempting to swallow the sudden obstruction in her throat) accepted the offer of her body in return for money. But how much? She didn't know what to ask.

As she crossed Second Avenue, heading toward Third and her vague destination, she wondered how she might appear to strangers. They'd see an eighteen-year-old girl, somewhat taller than most, with thick, unruly black hair. Well-defined, arching eyebrows over deep-set brown eyes. Her nose was unspecial, her mouth too wide, her skin too white, and her chin too assertive to complete the oval of her face. She thought her neck was too long, and her body far too thin, really, for the weight of her breasts; especially in view of her almost complete lack of hips. Her legs were thin and straight, with ankles she thought looked as if they might be easily broken. A misstep taken in these fancy high-heeled shoes and her ankles might snap like pencils in the fist of an angry man.

She crossed Third Avenue, under the El, and came to a stop, at last, in a doorway. What do I do now? she wondered, scanning the street, watching as a car went past, heading downtown. So little traffic, so few people. The pulse of the city was very slow. An old woman was carefully sorting through the trash in a nearby garbage can, examining the contents, refolding a newspaper before placing it in a paper sack on the ground by her feet. Then, as if feeling Jess's eyes, the woman raised her head. Embarrassed, distraught, Jess quickly looked away, edging back into the doorway.

I don't want to be here, she thought. I want it to be the way it was, the way it used to be. I don't want anyone to touch me, give me money for touching me. I'm so scared! What if someone comes . . . if some man . . . what'll I do?

He might have walked past, but the composition was so perfect, the play of light and shadow so arresting, that he had to stop and take the photograph. He couldn't resist the street scenes these days. They were like some narcotic he had to have, these images of the people, the times.

He didn't like the small, new cameras. But the photographs he took with them often served as references, visual notes for later works with the appropriate equipment. Even so, on several occasions in the near-recent past, the prints from this small camera he was using today had been excellent, really excellent.

He did three exposures and started to move on, then stopped again, realizing that the woman had turned and was looking at him with large, eloquent eyes.

He'd assumed she was older than he now saw she was. Her posture and the downtilt of her head had suggested a hopeless passivity he'd usually witnessed in far older people. And he'd taken the posture to be representative of the woman. But this female wasn't in the least passive. Rather, she was like a magnificent, wearied animal that had paused to rest and, in resting, had given the false impression of defenselessness.

She was scarcely a woman, he thought, judging by the lineless fluidity of her face. Her body, though, was the essence of womanliness and he had an instant desire to capture that child-woman's face so incongruously atop that very mature body. What an extraordinary mix of qualities she seemed to possess.

Looking again at her face, he saw that her eyes had tracked every movement of his. And her eyes, he noted, were very alive and filled with a strong intelligence that was now quietly, alertly waiting, studying him.

What does this old man want? she wondered, prepared to fight if necessary. She could feel, suddenly, the danger hidden in every doorway, along every street of the city she'd known and loved all her life. This new awareness caused her muscles to tense, turned the palms of her hands damp.

He approached her. "Would you like to earn five dollars?" He was upset by the way the question emerged, its crudity, but he was always at a loss dealing with strangers and, especially, women.

Here it is! she thought, feeling as if she'd placed her hands on a live wire. What she'd come out into the streets for. She nodded, noticing his very blue eyes; unable to decide if he was old or young. The mustache and beard made it difficult to tell. But his clothes were good and his hands were clean, the fingernails starkly white against the black of his suit. Looking at his hands, she thought, I don't like you, and wondered how it was possible to dislike someone she didn't even know. She didn't want this man to touch her.

He indicated she should accompany him, and he moved along the sidewalk. "It isn't far," he said, "just a few blocks."

He was tall, well over six feet. Despite the paunch swelling out the front of his trousers and jacket, he appeared rather thin. She decided he must be rich. Very few people had custom-made suits anymore. If he was rich and willing to pay her five dollars, she must successfully pretend to like him, because he might want to see her again, another time.

She stole a sidelong glance at him. His hair was a whitish-gray aureole wildly framing his head. What if he was crazy? No. Crazy people didn't go around offering women on the streets five dollars. Did they? But if they were crazy, then perhaps they did. He walked rapidly, and she had to take small, quick steps to keep up with him. Her feet hurt inside the stiff shoes.

"Why did you take my picture back there?" she asked, out of breath.

They were moving quickly, along past deserted buildings and areas that had been abandoned in mid-construction; past sullen, gray people, shadows shifting in doorways. Weeds grew up through cracks in the sidewalk, creeping upward over piles of rubble. She saw it all, her eyes briefly connecting with those of the people they passed, wondering if they knew, if they could tell why she was with this man. Small, dirty-faced children sat on the curb with their feet in the gutters, staring dully into space.

He didn't answer. He was too busy deciding on just how he'd photograph her; anxious to see if his instinct was right this time. It usually was. A feeling, a sensation of *yes* invariably overcame him when the subject and the light and the texture were all perfectly attuned. He hoped to God she was right because he could feel the images he wanted, could see them clearly in his mind. And the *yes* was all but shouting at him as he—nearly forgetting her presence in his absorption with photographing her—strode rapidly toward the house on Twenty-fourth Street that contained his studio, the darkroom, and his living quarters.

Following him through the door, she experienced a moment of terror. Suppose he really was crazy and intended to murder her. The house was dark and seemed menacing as she looked down the hallway toward the rear of the ground floor.

He climbed the stairs and she went up behind him, thinking both the house and the man were strange. But perhaps, she told herself, it was her fear that made everything appear sinister. She couldn't seem to put her thoughts into any reasonable order.

They arrived at the top of the house and entered a large, startlingly sunny room. She stood just inside the door waiting to be told where to go, what to do. He threw off his jacket and began fussing with a camera on legs. Obviously, this stark room, with curtainless windows and scrubbed, bare floorboards was a studio. Light flooded down through a skylight cut into the roof. Her eyes came to rest on an ornately scrolled, velvet-upholstered chaise lounge that seemed out of place in this austere room. She had a terrible impulse to laugh, and held it down as she looked over at the far wall. Unlike the others, which were white-painted plaster, this wall was brick.

He ducked under the black curtainlike cover at the rear of the camera and she watched, wondering if he somehow intended to photograph the two of them while he did it to her. Again, she had that impulse to laugh. Because if that was his intention, then maybe he really was crazy. It was certainly peculiar that he wasn't telling her what to do, not even talking to her. Maybe he expected her to know, to get undressed and get on with it. She moistened her lips, asking, "Is there somewhere...I mean...Could I...?"

Misunderstanding, thinking she wished to use the bathroom, he waved indefinitely toward the far end of the studio. "Through there," he said. "Just please hurry. I don't want to lose this light."

She went through the door and found herself in a bedroom, a very spartan one furnished only with a bed, a chest of drawers, a table, and a chair. The far wall was completely covered from floor to ceiling with photographs that at once captured her interest and attention. The man might be crazy, but if he'd done these he was crazy in a very special way. They were like fine paintings, works by Old Masters she'd seen years ago when Father had had the time and money to take her to art galleries and museums. Moving closer, she saw how the grain of the paper enhanced each image. The faces and figures were lit dramatically, yet naturally, to highlight them compellingly.

He called to her to hurry. She began nervously removing her clothes, forcing herself to study the photographs in a failing effort to take her mind off what was going to happen; she wished she could just remain in here, taking the time to examine all these images.

She looked down at her naked arms, breasts, and felt her mouth going dry. Oh, God, I don't think I can do this. I really don't. . . .

"Please!" He tapped at the door.

She jumped, turning to stare at the closed door between them. "I'll be right there." She again wet her lips as she stepped, without her underclothes, back into her dress, holding it closed with one hand as she opened the door.

He hurried over and took her by the arm. The touch of his hand on the bare flesh of her arm shocked her. Despite her nervousness and fear, his hand touching her caused an expectation to begin taking form inside her. He directed her over to the window and left her there while he almost ran back to the camera.

He watched her—upside down in his lens—as she lowered the dress slightly to free one arm, then the other, keeping the dress clutched like armor to her breasts. What was she doing?

The voice in her head told her, You've got to take off the dress! You've got to! Wishing she could die or disappear, ashamed and frightened, she forced her hands to lower the dress, uncovering her breasts. She blinked back tears, refusing to cry.

It wasn't right, not what he'd wanted. Yet the *yes* was there and he said, "Don't move! Just raise your eyes! Look here, here!" He squeezed the bulb, withdrew the plate, warned her, "Don't move! Not at all!" and quickly reached for another plate, slipped it in, and counted off the seconds required to expose it. She stood unmoving except for the lift and fall of her breasts as she breathed.

"Turn a bit!" She turned. He could see she was right. She knew instinctively how to stand, how to maintain an attitude. Nevertheless, he wanted to tell her to put her clothes back on, tell her that having her half-naked there, reversed to his eyes, was excruciatingly arousing, upsetting. He didn't do nudes, didn't buy women, which was what, he suddenly realized, she'd assumed he was doing. He forced himself to continue working, but the idea, once in his brain, of making love to her was almost overpoweringly attractive. He was addled, unable to understand the perversity of that insistent *yes* mixed with his lust for her.

He made sixteen exposures, then covered over the camera, straightened up, and looked down the room at her for a long moment. Then he slowly walked the length of the studio. His eyes were like the unreadable open camera lens. His every step sounded loudly in her ears, causing her breathing to quicken in renewed fear and expectation. He placed his hands over her breasts and she was again shocked by her body's reaction to his touch. This man—with his rather prissy way of speaking, this man with perspiration glistening on his face and with eyes that might be signposts to the fanatic inside—put his hands on her. She was made dizzy, made soft by the contact; she couldn't understand her reactions. It seemed as if her body had all at once assumed a separate identity, complete with responses and desires that were entirely strange.

He moved his hands on her breasts. "To know the feeling," he explained enigmatically. His voice and manner of expressing himself made her want to scream at him to remain silent. He was shaping her flesh with his hands, each slight movement sending light shimmers across her vision. He was no longer speaking. Good. If she didn't have to listen, didn't have to hear the carefully enunciated words or see the shape of his mouth forming them, she could withdraw altogether from the necessity of having to think and could instead revel solely in the surprising sensations he was generating inside her.

He pulled away from her abruptly and pressed the promised five dollars into her hand. "Come again Wednesday morning at ten-thirty."

She was stung by his curt dismissal of her as if she had no importance as a human being, and strangely disappointed, too. She'd been dismissed. But intact. And in possession of a subtle but powerful feeling in her body she'd never felt before.

"I've got a job," she told Tillie, serving up the dinner. "Everything's going to be fine now."

Tillie did wonder where the food had come from, and if regular jobs gave you money after just one day's work. But something told her not to ask questions. She might get answers she didn't want to hear. If she didn't ask, wasn't told, then she didn't know and couldn't be blamed. Except that something was definitely different about Jess and she did want to ask about that. But if she asked about one thing, she was bound to ask about another. So it was best simply to nod and say, "This is really good, Jess," and smile at her older sister.

◇ Two ◇

Jess couldn't sleep. Her thoughts ticked away relentlessly, reviewing the events of the day, and she slowly understood for the first time that she held a place in the world, no matter how small. I'm someone, she thought, not just Tillie's sister. I did things today I didn't know I could do.

It was strange that the old man had dismissed her, especially after the way he'd touched her and the things he'd said. It was unpleasant to think of him touching her when his face and voice and the hinting obsessiveness in his eyes faintly repelled her. Why hadn't he gone ahead and done what he'd so obviously wanted to do? His eyes had probed hers during those few moments when his hands had caressed her. It was repellent, the recollection of perspiration, slightly bulging eyes, and wet-looking mouth. Yet there was something kind about him, too. And he'd given her the money, asked her to return. That meant five more dollars she could be sure of. Money, right now, was more important than her feelings. Never mind whether or not she liked him. She couldn't afford feelings, couldn't afford to acknowledge how much she'd actually wanted him.

Turning carefully so as not to disturb Tillie, she stared into the darkness and examined the feeling that had gripped her during those moments of his touching her; the giddy, anticipatory rush that had swelled her lungs. How was it possible that she'd actually enjoyed his caress? Somehow, the instant his hands had come into contact with her skin, some new Jess had emerged. She'd felt it happen, felt her body assume control of her.

What sort of person am I really? she wondered, wanting, with a new and painful longing, to have someone to take care of her, to look after her, see to her well-being and relieve her of the onerous responsibility of keeping her promise to look after Tillie.

Keeping her promise to her father was going to force her into new and dangerous areas of life. It was already happening; what had happened today felt dangerous. She wasn't afraid of the old man so much as she feared her very strong reaction to his touching her.

She needed someone, she thought. But why would anyone want to involve himself with her? Still, the dream of being cared for was potent, rich with detail; so potent it felt very like a battle between the day- and nighttime halves of herself: The daytime self coming up hard against facts and reality over and over, while her nighttime self dreamed and dreamed. Just the way Tillie did, she thought, smiling in the dark. Tillie with her fanciful fairy-tale images of handsome princes, castles, and limitless pleasures. I don't want that much, she thought. Only something to look forward to.

That was the thought that brought the tears—the idea of being accepted, loved just as she was. She wanted to be the way she'd been that morning before going out into the street. Yet, if she was to keep Tillie with her, she'd have to return to that house on Twenty-fourth Street come Wednesday.

I don't want to go, a child's voice cried inside her, but the newly resigned adult sighed and admitted that she'd go back. There were no choices. She felt trapped and terrified, a small panic beating hard inside her chest.

Tillie turned over, taking most of the blankets with her. Jess reached out to touch Tillie's hair, then gently eased the blankets back over herself, experiencing the familiar grip of love squeezing her lungs. This baby, this little girl, this sister.

No one would ever separate them. She would never allow that to happen.

Wednesday morning, filled with dread, she set out to walk to Twenty-fourth Street. Perhaps, she thought, she could learn to like this man. He was a little eccentric, but not unkind. She could make herself like him. She could try.

But upon her arrival, he smiled at her and she realized he hadn't actually expected her to return. It upset her to think he'd assumed she was someone irresponsible. She wanted to explain that she always kept her word, but found herself unable to speak, too aware of the small dots of perspiration on his upper lip, bothered by them and by his evident uneasiness.

"I have coffee made," he said almost solicitously. "And rolls. Are you hungry?"

He made her sad because he was trying so hard to be pleasant and to make her like him. Because she couldn't, she felt an odd tenderness toward him and wanted to put her arms around him and say, "I'm sorry. I wish I could, but I can't like you. But don't feel badly about it, please don't." Instead, she smiled and forced herself to meet his eyes, saying, "Thank you very much."

He decided she was shy, and felt reassured. He was as intimately familiar with shyness as he was with the bottles of chemicals in his darkroom, knowing each by feel, by smell. He knew too well the groping uncertainty and the hesitance, the refusal of interior confidence to surface and cloak the awful superficial awkwardness.

As she stood by the window gazing out, a cup in one hand and a piece of sweet roll in the other, her expression was so complex, her features possessed such intelligence, her aura was so intensely sexual that he had to shift the camera—nearly deafened by the *yes!* roaring in his ears—and photograph her there.

"What's your name?" he asked.

"Jess," she answered, still in the clutches of that strange feeling of tenderness toward him. "Jessica Greaves."

For a second or two, he thought she'd said, "Jessica grieves," and found that fascinating. Then he shook himself mentally, half-smiling at his ludicrously literal brain. Greaves, not grieves.

"What is your name?" she asked, wondering if he'd intentionally not told her, perhaps because he considered her merely a girl from the streets and not anyone important enough to know his name. She wanted very much to tell him that not so very long ago she'd had a mother, and a father, and a lovely life. Not long ago at all, but it seemed very far in the past.

"I really must be getting old." He smiled. "I thought I'd told you." He shook his head and readjusted the tripod legs before glancing up at her and saying, "Jamieson Land. I'll give you my card today before you go."

It was a famous-sounding name, one that made her think she'd heard it before. Had she? Or was it simply the old-fashioned, solid quality of it? The name itself had character and dignity, making her feel guilty for having had such negative and suspicious thoughts about him. After all, he was a splendid photographer. She'd seen that wall overlaid with photographs in the bedroom. Beautiful pictures with great depth and sensitivity. She was, all at once, curious to see the photographs he'd taken of her, anxious to know how he saw her.

"My father was a stockbroker," she said quietly. "And my mother's family came to New York in the late eighteenth century . . . from England."

He looked up, interested.

"My, ah, mother died almost seven years ago. And my father . . ." She stopped, thinking it sounded like a plea for sympathy and not the explanation she'd intended.

"Your father?" he prompted.

"He died. Last month." She felt the anguish in her throat, as if it were happening all over again and she was once more going to the sofa to awaken him, finding him dead; crying out, "*Daddy!*" It had been years since she'd called him anything but "Father," yet she'd cried out like a small child at discovering his stiffened, cold body; overwhelmed by fear and sorrow.

"I'm sorry," Land said.

His expression of sympathy made her want to close her eyes and find herself being held and soothed, stroked gently while a voice claimed to love her. But that wasn't what she was here for, what he was paying her for. Not love.

"Is it time for me to undress?" she asked, her hands icy, her body rigid with reservation.

"I don't think that'll be necessary," he said, then loudly cleared his throat. "I would like you to put this on though, if you will."

A frilly robe. Confused, she accepted it from him. He did want her undressed if he wanted her in this. She went to his bedroom to put on the robe, wishing she hadn't told him about her parents. It made her feel too vulnerable. She emerged clad in the robe, holding it closed with both hands, all the things she'd been taught to believe still in her head, warring against the actions she was now performing. She remembered very clearly conversations with her mother in the course of her mother's long soaks in the tub, dialogues having to do with holding one's self highly and preserving one's purity for a suitable marriage. She wondered if some invisible form of her mother, some spirit perhaps, could see her and knew what she was doing now. Silently she apologized to the possible presence of that spirit. But what else could she do? she asked of that unseen presence.

He wanted her to stretch out on the lushly upholstered chaise longue, wanted some sort of facial expression she couldn't seem to give him. Nor did he seem able to put it into words.

She could see that he was becoming frustrated, his hands lifting and falling in gestures of futility as he gave her directions. "Let your head fall back more. More. Yes, like that. No, it isn't right." It increased her nervousness. If she failed to satisfy him, he might tell her to leave, he might not pay her. She wanted to cry.

The *yes* was gone and didn't seem to want to come back. He stepped from behind the camera to cross the room and arrange her hair, then her arm, signaling to her to recline more fully and turn slightly so that her hips were at a sharp angle, creating a deep curve at her waist into which the white georgette gown fell in soft folds. The pose caused her stomach to round out somewhat and her breasts to billow into the opening at the neckline. He returned to the camera only to straighten at once, shaking his head. "It *still* isn't right." What was wrong? he asked himself, knowing but unable to accept it. There was no photograph to be taken here. He wanted the woman. But that wasn't why he'd asked her to come back. And she was too rigid on the chaise, too...frightened. He approached her again, and bent toward her, asking, "You're not afraid, are you? Of me, I mean?"

"No," she lied, afraid of everything. Especially the feeling he'd managed to generate inside her at their first meeting, created by his hands on her breasts.

"Are you a virgin?" he asked, astonishing them both; neither of them had believed him capable of asking so direct and intimate a question.

"No," she lied again, dangerously close to tears, but determined not to break down in front of him.

"Then there's no need for you to be so apprehensive," he said gruffly, wanting to take his hand gently over the curve of her cheek. "Try turning just a little bit more toward me. And relax your legs, let the top one come forward slightly."

The gown slithered open, revealing her naked belly and thighs. She wanted to reach over and draw the gown closed, but couldn't. Perhaps this was the way he wanted it. She closed her eyes for a moment, casting about for the courage she needed to get through this.

He hurried back to the camera and looked through the lens, wanting nothing more now than to return to the far side of the studio and lose himself in her nakedness. Instead, he took what he knew would be a technically excellent exposure but was too distraught to listen for the *yes* or to hear anything but his own insistent mental voice telling him to leave her alone. He was somewhat alarmed by the determination and hints of what looked to be anger in her eyes and wondered if it might really be fear he was seeing.

She held the pose until he signaled to her to relax, then sat on the side of the chaise with the gown wrapped safely around her, feeling as if she'd been violated. She wished she could like him, that he cared for her and would put his arms around her and say everything was all right, he'd look after her. She lifted her eyes to look at him, trying to imagine why he or anyone else would want to say or do any such thing. She wasn't even pretty, or friendly, or given to smiles and able to chatter away like Tillie. Tall and skinny and frightened, why would anyone want her?

He said, "Why don't you get dressed now?" and, both relieved and bewildered, she went to put on her clothes.

He gave her a five-dollar bill and said, "I'll be going up to Vermont next week, to my summer place there."

Her disappointment was so strong it was like something bitter inside the cave of her mouth. "I see," she said, thinking of finding herself back on some street corner. She realized she'd hoped to return to this place. It wasn't so dreadful having him photograph her, not nearly so bad as it would be out there on the streets.

"You live alone?" he asked, tilting his head so that the afternoon sun came through the electric halo of his hair, capturing her eye.

"No. With my sister, Tillie. She's eleven, almost twelve. Will you be away for long?" Please don't go, she thought. Or take me with you. I'll make myself like you. I'll pose any way you want me to. I don't want to go out on the streets. I'm afraid.

"Not long," he said slowly, studying her face intently. She looked suddenly younger, touchingly young. "A week. Just to see what condition the winter's left the place in."

"I see. Will you want me to come again next week?"

"In June," he went on, as if he hadn't heard her, "I move up there. Friends come. To work, talk. I do some of my best work there." He wished suddenly to have her with him, to photograph her at the lake and in the house.

She wet her lips, feeling anxious, and opened her mouth to speak when he said, "Come Friday morning next week." She started to ask about his place in Vermont, but his eyes had shut down like lights being turned off inside a house at night. She decided he wasn't interested in her. Why should he be? Grateful, though, to have been given at least one more opportunity to return and earn five more dollars, she said, "Thank you," and hurried away before he could possibly change his mind.

"What kind of job is it?" Tillie asked, dragging a bit of bread across her plate, sopping up the last of the gravy.

"Working for a photographer. Have you got homework, Till?"

"I did it while I was waiting for you. What *kind* of work do you do for him?"

"Posing."

"Posing?"

"That's right." It didn't sound right, Jess thought, or else Tillie wouldn't have looked so instantly inquisitive. She'd have to be careful what she said to Tillie from now on. She didn't want to reduce herself in Tillie's eyes. "And helping out in the studio," she added, to make it sound more like a proper job.

"Doing what?" Tillie asked.

"Oh, this and that. I'll put water on so you can have a bath. Your hair needs washing, too." She was afraid Tillie might want to pursue the matter. Jess was dreadful at lying, and silently begged Tillie not to ask more questions. Absently touching her own hair, she said, "Mine could use washing, too," and thought longingly of the creamy shampoo her mother used to buy, and the scented bath oils; the silk nightgowns and silk underwear she'd worn. She could see her mother—tall and frail with tiny breasts, narrow feet, and alarmed eyes—sinking into a tubful of frothy, perfumed water with a sigh. Her mother had enjoyed taking long baths and liked company at these times; she had encouraged Jess to come sit on the small stool beside the tub and talk, their voices small, insubstantial within that large, high-ceilinged room with the oversized tub, the gleaming tiles, the soft thick towels and furry bath mat. Damp strands flattened on the nape of her neck, her mother had lazily lifted an arm to lather it, then a leg. Her thin, blue-veined inner thighs had made Jess weak with sadness because her mother was so delicate, so ethereal that she might simply slip away, disappear along with the froth and liquid as they slithered gurgling down the drain. She'd died, finally, in almost that way: just closing her eyes and sliding away. They'd called it consumption. Tillie had had her fifth birthday three weeks later and had become twelve-year-old Jessica's baby, because, Father had explained, "We must stay very close to one another now."

She'd never questioned the fairness of it, but simply accepted the responsibility to please her father, to show him how worthy she was of the small power he'd placed in her hands. Look after your little sister, Jess, while I put patches on our life and try to keep us all from going under.

Unlike the majority of his stockbroker associates, he hadn't overextended himself financially by buying on margin. He'd bought some stocks, of course. But he'd also contributed regularly to savings accounts—for the children's education, for the real estate he liked to invest in, for luxuries for his wife—in the event that anything should happen to him. There were insurance policies, and some dividend-yielding utilities stocks,

and a decent amount of cash. When it all fell apart on The
Street, he wasn't tempted to leap out the window or put a gun
in his mouth. The panic would blow over. The government
would step in. If he simply sat tight, he'd weather this.

But the Market became a graveyard in winter and the banks
began to fail. Mother was expensively ill and the cash steadily
flowed out until, at a considerable loss, he sold off his properties, withdrew the cash values accumulated within the insurance policies, let the staff and servants go one by one, and
gave up his office. Then Mother was dead and it was just the
three of them alone in the sprawling Seventy-second Street
apartment. He burned his fingers, as well as the food, trying
to prepare meals for himself and the two girls; making a joke
of it as he smeared butter on his seared fingertips, apologetically serving up hastily scrambled eggs and pieces of blackened
toast. Making a further joke, he'd treated it lightly, but gratefully when Jess—with a natural aptitude—took over the preparing of meals.

In time, sleek, self-satisfied people came to offer laughably
low prices for this piece of furniture and that one, and with
shock and insult enlarging Father's eyes, he'd accepted the
demeaning packets of cash and told the girls, "We'll celebrate,
ladies!" Then they always went to the ice cream parlor for
sodas. Perhaps, Jess always thought, he also needed that bit
of sweetness to take the sting out of the disappointments.

It took four years before they found themselves living in
just two of the twelve rooms of the apartment. The gas was
cut off, and the telephone was a distant memory. A grayish
pallor to their father's face, he set off each morning, freshly
shaven and neatly dressed to find the job he was sure he could
get through the friend of a friend who'd been a classmate at
St. Paul's. Or the friend he'd roomed with at Yale. Or the
fellow he'd known on The Street who'd managed to start up
a small business. He'd returned every evening looking that
much grayer and older, until the evening when he'd announced,
"I've got a big surprise!" and tried to make a celebration ceremony out of the fact that the apartment, their home, had been
sold. They were going to move. "You'll like it," he'd told
them, his eyes begging Jess to make enthusiastic noises for
Tillie's benefit.

And so it went. Jess left school just before graduation in

order to look after Tillie full time until Tillie started school again the next autumn.

Then, Jess set out to find some sort of work. She knew how to type and went off armed with the morning paper, positive she'd find a job, return home, and surprise her father. She wanted to please him with her initiative, her success. But the lines of women waiting for jobs stretched almost out of sight, and after standing in several of them, listening to conversations among the women, hearing them proudly reciting their qualifications, she knew she hadn't a chance. Then she applied at restaurants, small stores, factories; anywhere, everywhere. Each time, someone had always been there just ahead of her and got the job. Or they'd just been forced to let someone go. Sorry, sorry. She skirted the bread lines on her way home, hurrying past with fear growling like hunger at the bottom of her stomach, always frightened she might, one afternoon, see her father standing in one of those lines.

She cut down some of her dresses to fit Tillie, who went off to school each day spick and span in neat, clean clothes, hair gleaming, with a nourishing lunch in her bag. She looked after Tillie's hair, insisted she brush her teeth, not slouch, do her homework. And, meanwhile, Jess wondered how her father managed to fill all the days he spent away from the apartment.

What destroyed him, at the end, was the job he took as a laborer, digging up roadbeds. He was a man whose muscles—particularly his heart—had never been strenuously tested. When he brought home his first week's pay, he was dressed as always in suit and tie and hat, but with a telltale, touching residue of dirt beneath his fingernails. He had smiled tiredly, yet wanted to celebrate. He'd offered to take the girls out for ice cream, but Jess had been alarmed by his grayish-looking skin and the sunken flesh around his eyes, and had insisted upon preparing a small meal, then going out to fetch a pint of the strawberry ice cream he was so partial to. He didn't wake up for work on Monday morning.

There was just enough cash value left to the insurance policies to bury him. No one came because no one knew. Rather than spend the money on an obituary notice in the *Times*—as she knew her father would have liked—she used it to pay another week's rent on the flat. Now she was totally alone with the awesome responsibility of Tillie's welfare. She'd promised.

"If anything happens to me," he'd said, "look after your sister."
She used Tillie's bathwater to wash her own hair.

Something about her absolutely fascinated him. In part, it
was her aura of sexuality. He was certain she was utterly
unaware of it, but it did shine off her. It was in her slender
ankles, her long neck, her thick, wild hair and haunted eyes;
in her fragile-looking pure-white skin and her long-fingered
hands. He studied the dripping prints trying to pinpoint the
source of his fascination, but he couldn't.
Had she simply been a slim girl with small breasts, her
appeal would have been considerably less. But those large
breasts lent her an overpowering vulnerability. Something
about her cried out to be tended to, and recognizing this, he
was lost to a sudden, almost violent longing to ignite her
smouldering sexuality and watch as it blazed, knowing intuitively that she'd have great difficulty coming to terms with her
own desires. She was intelligent and sensitive, a shy, gentle
girl; and reliable—a quality found too rarely. He wanted, studying the prints again, to assault her, and had an image of himself
plunging into her. Her startled, heated responses were so real
he could almost see and feel them.
But when she came the following Friday, he was, as before,
intimidated simply by her presence, by her complete contain-
ment within herself. Photographs were not reality, he reminded
himself, but simply fragments of it, their depths and dimensions
real only within his perceptions. This child-woman, this Jessica
had a reality that she carried about with her, as permanent as
her flesh and bones. And he could not capture that, or the
uncertainty, and fear he'd glimpsed in her. He could only
visually underscore certain moments representative of her entire reality. He could not invade more than her time, which
was why, it occurred to him, he would have to photograph her
hourly, daily for the remainder of his life in order to attain any
cohesive series of moments indicative of the woman.
He wanted her nude this time, needing, finally, to see all
of her. Capitulating to his need, he summoned up the bravado
to tell her, "I'd like to do a few nude shots today." Seeing the
apprehension appear at once in her eyes, he hoped she'd refuse.
But she said, "All right," and went off to the bedroom to
undress. Mortified but determined, she returned holding her
dress in front of her. The air in the studio was thick and tense.

She knew something was going to happen this time, and part of her thought, All right, get it over with; and another part thought, Please don't. Don't hurt me or make me do this. She relinquished her dress at his signal, feeling that somehow her entire life and its future course hinged on what happened here today.

He studied her naked buttocks, the secret cleft of hidden flesh; the skin stretched thinly over ribs that seemed too insubstantial to support the weight of her breasts. That same determination mingled with fear gleamed out at him from her eyes, so that he felt diminished for having given in to his desire to look at her, a desire having nothing to do with the *yes* that was haughtily ignoring him today because of his prurience. In the stunning absence of that *yes*, he told himself he was wasting his time photographing her, trying to capture something so elusive and tentative it might be nothing more than his own imaginings. Yet he couldn't stop. He posed her here and there, moving her so that the light fell across half her body, highlighting it; catching a dull glow from the shadowed half of her face. It exhausted both of them. She held herself in the poses, with each new change of stance feeling less and less like herself; feeling as if she was being torn away from everything about herself that had been familiar, even comforting. His eyes and his camera were stripping her beyond her skin, all the way to her bones, making her feel utterly isolated and ugly. Not even thoughts of Tillie could salvage or detain any of her parting feelings for herself. She would never be the same, she thought. Whatever happened here was going to change her forever. Perhaps from the outside, she thought, it looked as if she didn't mind. But inside, she was protesting. She didn't want to hate herself any more than she already did, and thought desperately, At least care about me. If you will, even if I can't like you, I'll have something left of myself.

"When will you be leaving for your summer house?" she asked hesitantly, her eyes fixed on the floor. She couldn't risk looking at him.

"Sunday," he answered, tinkering needlessly with the tripod, wondering how so many of his friends were able so effortlessly and casually to seduce the women they did. He felt clumsy and inept, wanting only to hold this girl in his arms and whisper praise in her ear. She was so young, so shy.

"I see," she said.

He watched her, his hands arrested mid-motion.

Ask him! her interior voice dictated. But it was so hard to have to ask a stranger for anything. She lifted her head and met his eyes. "Could I come with you?" she asked. "I could help. Clean. Cook. And Tillie's such a good little girl, no trouble at all. You wouldn't even have to pay me if you ... It would be ... Just to get away from the city."

She was begging and it was awful. If he said no, she didn't know what she'd do. *We went every summer,* she remembered. *Mother under a parasol, in a yellow lawn dress and sun hat, walking barefoot along the beach at Narragansett, while I splashed at the water's edge, studying the swell of my mother's belly and the slow, careful way she carried herself. It was Tillie I watched being carried so cautiously along the beach. I'm so glad you're not alive to know about this, that you can't hear or see me begging this man to help me keep my promise to look after Tillie.*

She returned to the present and realized he was staring at her, his hand stroking his beard, his eyes disturbed.

"What I mean," she went on doggedly, determined to see it through to the end, "is that it's been such a long time. And the city's so ... for a little girl. She's never had a chance to be in the country ..." Why was he letting her go on begging this way? Why didn't he say something? She struggled not to cry in front of him.

It was awful. Partly, he wanted to dismiss her summarily, pay her and let her go. But mainly he was filled with awesome craving for everything about her he could never permanently capture. He simply couldn't respond. He could see how costly an effort she was making to stand there that way, her eyes glossy with unshed tears. His senses and feelings responded to her need and to his own completely unexpected desire to offer her shelter, to hold her protectively. He pushed past his considerable reserve to reach out for her.

The instant his hands came into contact with her flesh, everything inside her went berserk. At the same time something in her brain was calmed and comforted. She couldn't breathe, suspended in curiosity and a ravening hunger to be held and stroked and to have the dreadful act of begging erased from her memory. His arms around her were so unexpectedly strong and reassuring. Eased somewhat and grateful, she wound her arms around his neck, her eyes tightly closed, to have him kiss her deeper and harder. She opened her mouth to his in a sudden frenzy of needing to be wanted that closed down her astounded brain and caused shock waves of pleasure inside her. Her body twisted wildly under his searching hands and suddenly she was willing to do anything to perpetuate both the pleasure and the sense of security that came with being held and caressed. A tiny unheeded voice in her head was chanting love me, love me, please love me.

The irony of it made him clench his jaws so tightly that his head ached for hours after. He wanted so desperately to see that look of ecstasy he was sure would be on her face, yet he was unable to bear the possible reproach in her eyes. So he sat on the edge of the chaise with his trousers and shorts caught around his ankles and drew her—she came so willingly, even frantically—down on his lap with her back against his chest, sparing himself having to see her eyes. He held her spread securely across his lap with his left arm while his right hand opened her, and he fed himself slowly into the exquisitely tight, moist core of her body. Then, cupping her hard, heaving breasts, he quickly satisfied his terrible hunger; aware of her stiffening, of one startled cry at the outset, her surprised-sound-ing gasps and then her stillness. Once it was done, a painful loving welled up inside him. Understanding belatedly, he was deeply reluctant to release her, knowing she'd lied and he'd been fool enough to believe her.

His body began slowly penetrating hers and she went rigid, thinking, My God, this is how it is! It's actually happening! There were a few seconds of tearing pain that dragged a cry from her throat, and then the pain gave way to something that promised to be pleasure. She went with it, able only to con-centrate on trying to get to the pleasure, bracing herself against him in order to reach it. But it was suddenly over. And once it was, all of her quickly cooling, she wanted to get up and run away home, grief-stricken. She was dismayed at having gone so completely out of control, at having, for those few minutes, behaved with such total abandon. How could she have done that? she wondered, trying to catch her breath as she remained astride his lap, gazing at the unlocked studio door, praying no one would come in and find the two of them this way. She awaited some sign from him that she could go, that it was indeed over, or that there was to be more; still she was reassured by his hand gently smoothing her breast, over and over. She wondered fearfully if she'd get pregnant now and prayed that wouldn't happen, terrified of the implications of what she'd allowed to take place. But, oh, to be held! She closed her eyes for a few more moments, relishing it. His enclosing arms and stroking hand were so comforting. She wished recklessly that he'd do it all again, do it over and over.

He shifted his knees slightly. It was the signal she'd been awaiting. A cry escaped her involuntarily at the pain of his withdrawal. She got up—her stomach hurt the way it did when she was having a period—and walked across the studio, quietly closing the bedroom door after her. She shivered, crying soundlessly as she reached for her clothes. There was a dull pain inside her, accompanied by an insistent, expectant throbbing. The two discordant feelings pulled against each other. She delayed returning to the studio as long as possible, trying to stop crying. In a state of shock and renewed fear, she wadded her handkerchief between her legs to catch the blood and stop it from staining her clothes. Now that she'd done this, he mightn't have any interest in taking her and Tillie with him to Vermont. Quaking, her hand on the doorknob, she felt as if she might throw up the coffee and roll he'd given her earlier. Finally, she opened the door to see him fully dressed and involved in adjusting his camera lens.

"Your money's on the table," he said without looking up, making her believe he was sending her away after all. She blinked rapidly, fighting off a return of the tears. She hadn't the right, after all, to make demands or requests of him. She wasn't important, she thought. Not even her body was important. She felt deadened, and wanted to be away from this place, from this man, as quickly as possible. She wondered if she had the courage to face the streets, risk the danger out there. She swallowed, lifting her head, knowing she'd try again. She had no choice.

"There's some extra," he said uncomfortably. "Get a few new things for yourself and your sister."

She stared at him. He wasn't sending her away. She couldn't believe it. He was a kind man, she thought, again feeling that tenderness for him; speechless in the face of his kindness.

"Be here Sunday, eight in the morning," he said, looking up at last because of her prolonged silence.

She was standing just beyond the bedroom door, her hands clasped tightly in front of her. "You won't be sorry, I promise," she said thickly. "I'll work very hard for you."

All in a moment, he understood several things, the most important being her failure to recognize or understand his caring for her. She seemed to think that he was being charitable, when, in fact, he thought it was she who was. Why would this lovely young girl want to spend her time with an old man like him? But obviously she didn't see it that way. She said, "Thank you," in that same husky voice and went, leaving him feeling guilty but not unhappy.

He listened to her footsteps descending the stairs, heard the quiet closing of the front door, then sat down abruptly on one of the chairs, feeling ill. A virgin. He'd never have done it if she hadn't lied, but he could understand why she had. He could too easily imagine the price she had paid each time she'd come here and taken off her clothes, suffered his eyes and his camera, and now his intrusive touch.

While it had lasted, though, he'd felt something so close to joy he'd been elevated to a new plane of existence. Now he asked himself, What am I doing, taking on this stranger and her sister? Yet all he really wanted was to keep this girl, cherish and take care of her.

She went home shaking, feeling totally, irrevocably altered, and alarmed by her newly discovered interest in sexual pleasure. It was an interest so large it might easily overwhelm her. Simply thinking of what had taken place, she wanted to have it happen to her again. But how, she wondered, could she derive pleasure from a man she only barely liked?

She was a woman, a grown woman. There were no secrets left to her now. This was the way the world was, the way life was, the way she was. Perhaps she wasn't pretty, but she did have something to give. Did that, in turn, give her value? Or did it make her something that had an ugly name?

She looked at the men she passed on the street, studying their faces, considering their potential, and her own. She could do it, she decided. If necessary, she'd do whatever had to be done to survive and keep on going. She could feel herself quickly filling out, growing to fit her new role as an adult woman. What I do is not what I am, she thought. She was still herself, still had the same thoughts; she wasn't bad or evil. She wasn't!

By the time she arrived back at the flat, she was in control

of herself, although her brain was still jolted each time she
thought about what had happened. She'd do whatever needed
doing, she told herself over and over, trying to diminish the
force of her own reactions.

When Tillie returned home from school, Jess found herself
filled with an even greater love for her. It would be years
before Tillie had to face any of what Jess had faced today.
Years. And she'd never allow Tillie to go through any of this.
She'd have the best life Jess could provide for her.

"We're going to go away for the summer!" she told Tillie
excitedly. "To Vermont! Isn't that wonderful! I know you'll
adore it. Vermont's so green. I remember it very clearly. And
for the whole summer."

"How?"

"With Mr. Land. To his summer house."

"But I thought you worked for him..."

"Well, yes, I do."

"But how can you work for him if we're going to Vermont?"

"A photographer can work anywhere, Till. Aren't you
pleased?"

Tillie's fair brows pulled together doubtfully, somewhat
suspiciously.

"What'll we *do* there?" she asked.

"You'll be able to play outdoors, have good fresh fruit and
vegetables. . . . I thought you'd be so pleased." Oh, God! she
thought tiredly. Please be glad about this! You've got to be
glad. Otherwise, what was it all for?

"Oh, I am. I just don't understand how it can be a job and
a summer vacation, too."

"It will be a vacation for you," Jess explained. "I'm still
going to be working, helping around the house, posing." Why
was she being so difficult, demanding explanations? Why
couldn't she just accept it? "You'll have a wonderful time,
angel. Wonderful." It all sounded so empty suddenly, like a
rock dropped in a metal trash can.

"What's he like anyway?"

"Quite old. And very busy. He's an important man, you
know." Why was she telling Tillie this? she wondered. Or was
she saying it to make herself feel better?

"Important how?"

"He's a famous photographer. You'll see," she said. "It'll
be wonderful." She felt suddenly drained from this effort to

convince Tillie. *I'm paying for it all, Tillie. You've got to want it.*

"Why are you working for him if you don't like him?" Tillie asked.

"I didn't say I don't like him," she answered, taken aback by this astute observation.

"You didn't say you did, though, either."

"It's a job, Till. We need the money. It's also a chance for us to get out of here." She looked around the dismal, near-empty room.

"Why're you getting so mad at me?" Tillie asked, hurt.

Jess put her arms around her saying, "I'm not mad at you. I guess I'm just tired. I love you more than anything in the world, you know that. It's just that I was hoping you'd be pleased."

Tillie couldn't say anything. She was trying to understand why Jess seemed different, as if she were changing a little more every day. And yet she was the same Jess. Wasn't she?

Jess walked back and forth in the darkened bedroom, her arms wrapped around herself, while Tillie slept. She was frightened by Tillie's unpredictable reactions. If Tillie didn't approve, then everything she'd done was for nothing.

Stopping, she leaned against the wall and stared out the window at the deserted street below, watching a newspaper blow down the pitted roadway and out of sight. She allowed herself to be caught up in the old standby dream of someone to care for her. If only Land was the right one. But he wasn't and never would be. She felt like a parasite, willfully attaching herself to him because he had the money and the interest in her to allow himself to be persuaded. She felt more tired than she ever had in her life, so tired her eyes stopped moving. She stared at the broken window in the building across the street where a rag of curtain limply drifted with the breeze.

◊ Three ◊

"She's certainly exotic," Flora said, a little grudgingly. She'd been hoping the girl would be merely commercially pretty. She should've known better; Jamie didn't go for commerciality. "I'll grant you that," she went on. "But wasn't it enough to take her on without taking on her little sister to boot?" She went through the prints slowly, turning them over one by one.

"She's not a tramp, if that's what you're thinking," he said defensively, somewhat irrelevantly. Flora looked over at him with interest. "The family lost everything in The Crash."

"I've heard it before, Jamie."

Huge, immovable, like a soft boulder, Flora—of the irreverent tongue and unlikely talent—sat on the edge of the chaise longue in the studio. She worked in miniature, capturing insects and the hidden hearts of flowers; the world beneath the world. Within her enormous bulk was another Flora, with the same flaming red hair and brilliant green eyes, but small and nearly weightless. This other Flora moved effortlessly among the grasses without disturbing them. In reality, however, she lowered herself, heaving and grunting, to her knees and then down onto her stomach, where she lay for hours at a stretch moving nothing but her eyes and hands as she shot roll after roll of film. Done, she'd turn onto her back with a mighty effort, and slowly pull her three hundred-odd pounds upright.

The photographs that resulted from these stints of motionless watching and waiting were as odd and unexpectedly attractive as the woman herself: drops of dew glistening on a spider's web, blades of grass bending under the weight of raindrops, a beetle caught in his dignified progress through a landscape of small stones, a cluster of budding buttercups. All were enlarged in their stark clarity against a blur of background so that their definition assailed, then charmed the eye. There was an elf, an artist-sprite housed within those pounds and pounds of excess meat that had turned the Flora of fifteen years before into the Flora of now. The weight was like a victim she dragged around, confronting the world with her crime, daring it to take note of the obvious. No one was willing to condemn her, except herself. Few people could resist her generosity, her depth of caring.

She and Jamieson had been friends for more than fifteen years and, from the first, she'd assumed a protective, motherly attitude toward him, even though she was eight years his junior. It was through Flora that he'd found friends, acceptance, and even success. He loved her as he would have loved the sister he'd never had, the mother who hadn't had time for him.

Her most recent project, on which she'd been working for close to two years, was a series she called The Destructive Force; shots of praying mantises eating their young, of red ants battling black ants, of one insect fighting another to the death, of a spider weaving its web around a captive fly. For all her preoccupation with the minor forms of violence among the smaller species, she was, once secure within a given friendship, or in a genial environment such as Jamie's, unselfish, gentle, and sympathetic.

Occasionally, her comments and observations seemed to shriek of some barely contained rage, yet what anger she did have she reserved primarily for herself, cursing her gargantuan appetites—both for food and for people.

"This girl," Jamie said simply, wanting and needing Flora's approval, "is unusual. And not just physically. There's something about her. A quality I admire."

Her attention now well and truly caught, she set down the last of the prints, quietly asking, "What quality?"

"I'm not altogether certain I can put it into words." He lit a cigarette, holding the match absentmindedly until it singed his fingers, then dropped it into the ashtray. Looking at the tips of his fingers, he said, "She's reliable, for one thing. I know, I know." He waved his hand impatiently in the air between them. "Lots of reliable people around. She's responsible. She's been taking care of a younger sister for six years, nearly single-handedly." Almost to himself, he added, "I'm curious to meet the little sister."

"You're taking along a child you've never laid eyes on?" she asked doubtfully.

"I have to." He raised his eyes to hers. "Have you ever seen someone . . . ? Those narrow ankles, high-heeled shoes. That darkness behind her eyes. Tall and . . ." He shook his head, unable to express the powerful mix of feelings Jess aroused in him.

"I think you're in love with this girl, Jamie," Flora said gently. She sat back expecting him to argue, to deny it. He drew thoughtfully on his cigarette before answering, "It might be that. I'm not sure I'd call it love. All I do know is I can't seem to let her go. At least, not yet."

Poor Jamie, she thought, knowing too well how it felt. Hadn't she spent the last fifteen years eating her way through the misery, trying to forget? Still, she felt hurt and a little jealous. She'd gone along hoping he might, one day, find he loved her, just as she'd discovered it growing inside her for him. Silently berating herself, she wondered why she'd thought he'd take any interest in a whale of a once-pretty woman like her when there was this young, slender, dark-eyed girl with a really quite wonderful body. Jess was exotic, no question of it; someone you'd find either ugly or beautiful. Flora could easily believe that Jamie saw beauty. Being truthful, she could see it herself.

"I'm still invited, aren't I?" she asked, smiling to cover her sudden uncertainty. Some people in love chose to exclude everyone but the object of their love.

"Of course." He smiled back at her, erasing at least ten years from his creased features. At forty-eight, he looked sixty, and acted it most of the time, too. But when he smiled, the boy he'd once been emerged and she was heartened. He was

so special, so difficult to really get to know. She hoped this
girl didn't let him down.

"I don't think I want to go," Tillie said doubtfully, watching
Jess hurriedly packing the last of their things.

Oh, God, *please*! Jess thought. "Once we're there, you'll
like it," she said. Surely after seven solid years in the city, the
child would leap at an opportunity to leave it for a while. Jess
could clearly remember her own excitement when the time
approached for the family to move out of the city for the
summer—to Rhode Island, or Vermont, or the half dozen other
places they'd visited before Mother had died.

Tillie, at almost twelve, was blond and very pretty and
endowed with an intelligence that was still doing battle with
her more childish wants. She was capable of sometimes seeing
clearly the underside of situations. Right now, she couldn't
help feeling that there was something going on she hadn't been
told about, and it didn't seem right that Jess would make
decisions for her without consulting her. So, to exercise her
own ability to say no, to display her independent will—of
which she was only newly aware—she was trying them out on
Jess.

Actually she wanted to go. But she was bothered by Jess's
sketchiness about this mysterious job she'd managed to find
with this supposedly famous photographer. Well, maybe he
was famous. That wasn't important. It was this different Jess,
her new way of holding herself, of walking, that bothered
Tillie. Without consciously making the connection, the differences in Jess made Tillie very curious about this Mr. Land.
And curious, too, about what happened to change Jess. What
Tillie really wanted, more than anything else, was to keep
things the way they were. Not the way they lived, being poor
and all that. But her and Jess together, the way they'd always
been.

Catching sight of herself in the little mirror in the kitchen,
she watched herself as she said, "I don't think I've ever heard
of a job where you got to go away for the summer and take
your family along." Not really thinking about what she was
saying, she was concentrating on the way her mouth moved
when she spoke, liking that as well as the way she looked with
her hair down. She wished her sister would, just this once,
forget to put it in pigtails. Tillie thought she looked so much

older, so much more grown up with her hair down.

She turned away from the mirror when Jess failed to respond, a little alarmed by the unhappy expression on Jess's face as she picked up the comb and brush. Jess wasn't changed so much that she was forgetting things like pigtails. "Do I have to?" she groaned as Jess approached.

Tiredly, Jess said, "You'll be hot with it hanging. And anyway, little girls don't go around with their hair hanging down. Unless there's no one around to make sure their hair's done the way it's supposed to be. And I'm here to make sure."

As she brushed Tillie's hair—calmed by the act and pleased, as always, by the fine silken consistency of it—she found herself close to tears. She felt brokenhearted by Tillie's continuing lack of enthusiasm for the trip to Vermont. A heavy sense of futility was descending on her.

"Come on, Jess!" Tillie craned around. "You're taking so long. . . ." She was stopped by Jess's expression. She hadn't seen her sister cry since Daddy died. "What's the matter?" she asked, scared Jess was actually going to start crying now.

"I wanted you to be happy," Jess said, trying to get herself under control, not wanting Tillie to feel responsible for making her cry. "I'm just disappointed, that's all."

"I *want* to be happy about it," Tillie protested. "But what am I going to do up there with no one to play with?"

She couldn't bear another moment of Tillie's arguments, wrapped her arms around her and held her close and hard, whispering, "I love you so much, Tillie. Please try to be happy and stop fretting. You'll have a fine time. I know you will." She held her, pressing her cheek against Tillie's solid, unyielding shoulder, feeling the familiar painful surge of loving. "I'm just as nervous about this as you are, Till," she admitted. "So we'll look after each other, won't we? You know I'd never do anything I thought would upset you."

Tillie hated it sometimes when Jess started all this. It made her go all red and hot and angry and she had to force herself to stand still until Jess finally stopped carrying on, let go of her and finished doing the pigtails. "I love you, too," she said automatically, wondering why you always had to say that when somebody said they loved you and why you couldn't just say nothing. But she couldn't do that because then Jess's face would go all hurt and hollow the way it just had.

She'd never make her children say what they didn't want

to say, she promised herself. And they wouldn't have to wear pigtails, if they didn't want to. Why shouldn't someone nearly twelve wear her hair down if she felt like it? It was all so silly, rules grown-ups made to get you to do the things they wanted you to do.

She went off to wait downstairs on the stoop while Jess started carrying down the first of the bags. Leaning her elbows on her knees, chin in her hands, she looked at a family across the street who stood on the sidewalk surrounded by all their furniture. They were looking at each other with funny blank expressions, as if they couldn't believe what was happening to them. Tillie knew all right. Evicted. That's what. It'd never happen to her. Jess would never let that happen to her. The little boy was looking over at her, to see if she was looking back. Well, let him! *She* wasn't being thrown out on the street with all her things because they couldn't pay the rent. Someday, she thought, when she was rich and living in a great big house, maybe that same little boy over there would come knocking at the door asking for a job and she'd hire him to drive her limousine, or maybe to take care of her garden. No. Instead, she'd say, "My sister will see to it." And she'd get Jess to give him some kind of job. Because she'd be too busy to worry about hiring people to take care of all the things she'd have.

Jess lurched through the door and put down the big suitcase with a sigh, saying, "Look after this, Till. I'm just going back up to get the other one."

Tillie didn't hear. She was thinking about the penny in her pocket. She could run up to the corner real fast and get a good hard candy, a jawbreaker that would last, if she was careful, all the way to Vermont. She jumped up, skipped down the steps, and walked quickly to the corner store. She could already taste the candy. She spent several minutes walking back and forth in front of the glass-fronted display case, studying the jelly babies and jujubes and peppermints before finally saying she'd like a jawbreaker, please. She was polite to show she wasn't someone who got evicted. She placed her penny carefully on the counter, picked up the jawbreaker and slid it into her cheek where she could run her tongue over every so often to taste it, and went out of the store, making the bell in back jingle as she opened, then closed the door.

The suitcase was gone. She stared at the empty stoop, her heart beating funny, telling herself Jess must've moved it back inside. Jess came through the door with the other bag and looked at the empty place, then down at Tillie on the sidewalk with her cheek bulging, asking, "Where's the bag, Tillie?"

"I don't know." Her throat was working, the big jawbreaker hurting her cheek. "It was right there. Somebody must've taken it."

"I asked you to watch it," Jess said, her arm muscles straining from the weight of the bag, unable to look away from the telltale swelling in Tillie's cheek, her anger growing again.

"I was only gone for a minute, just up to the corner."

"Oh, *Tillie*!" She put the bag down. "All my things, everything was in that bag. Everything I *own*. I haven't any clothes ... Why didn't you stay and watch the bag?"

"I'm sorry. But he was supposed to watch it," she lied, turning around to look across the street, seizing up inside at seeing only the tired furniture sitting on the sidewalk. The family and the little boy were gone. Why did I lie? she asked herself frantically. Why did I say that?

"Who?" Jess asked sharply.

"I knew I shouldn't have trusted him!" she said indignantly, trapped now into the lie, glaring over at the boy who wasn't there. "I just knew I shouldn't."

You're lying, Jess thought, wanting for the first time ever to strike her sister, to hit her just as hard as she could. She was suddenly filled with the unshakable conviction that if there were no Tillie, there'd be no problems.

"Tell the truth, Tillie," she said quietly, with tremendous effort. "You went to get yourself some candy and didn't even stop to think about the bag. You *know* people steal things around here! You know that!"

"It *is* the truth!" she lied staunchly, unable to be truthful now. It was too late for it. "I asked him to watch and he didn't do it." Her eyes swimming, she was stung by the idea that Jess didn't believe her. Even if it was a lie, Jess should've believed her.

What should she do? Jess looked up the street, then down at Tillie, pushing away her anger. They'd be late if they didn't leave now. But how could she spend three months with one dress and one pair of shoes, and not even a nightgown?

She reached to pick up the suitcase, changed her mind and, instead, fastened her hand around Tillie's upper arm, still keeping her voice very soft. "Don't you ever lie to me again! I don't care what you do, just don't lie to me. You're my sister and I'll always love you and take care of you. But don't ever, *ever* lie to me!" Her eyes drilled into Tillie's for several long seconds and Tillie's throat hurt with the intensity of the moment. Then Jess released her and picked up the suitcase. "He said eight o'clock sharp. I wouldn't want him to leave without us." She went down a step, then turned back. "Do you understand me, Tillie?" she asked, thanking God she hadn't put the money in the suitcase.

"But I didn't lie. . . ." She gave it one last feeble try.

"You did," Jess said flatly. "Now, let's go or we'll be late."

Defeated, Tillie went down the steps after her, thinking Jess ought to have looked after the bag herself. I'm only a little girl. I can't do everything. Tillie was considerably more respectful of Jess in the awed aftermath of her anger. She never used to be someone who got so mad about things, Tillie thought. She wondered if it was going to be this way from now on.

There was a moment during the ride when Jess turned to look back at Tillie in the rumble seat, knowing that not only was Tillie unconcerned that Jess had lost everything she'd had, but she didn't know how much it meant. She told herself she was wrong, that Tillie loved her and would've done what Jess was doing had their positions been reversed. But even as she thought it, she knew Tillie would never sell any part of herself for anyone, and felt a new regard for her younger sister. Tillie would grow into a woman of inflexible conviction. Once she decided, it would be all but impossible to move her. And maybe, Jess thought, that's not such a bad way to be. She simply wished she could be clearer about her own uncertain moves through the world.

He hadn't doubted for a moment that she'd come, and so felt it was unnecessary to say anything in the way of welcome when she arrived with the little sister in tow. He hurried them both into the already-loaded Ford coupe and they set off.

He'd expected Tillie would be a smaller version of Jess and was surprised therefore by Tillie's fair hair and large gray eyes, her picture-perfect good looks. She was a bit too storybook perfect for his liking, almost disturbingly so, he decided, watching her make herself comfortable in the rumble seat.

The contrast between the two girls predisposed him even more toward Jess, particularly when, without wheedling, she explained to him about the stolen suitcase.

"Don't worry about it," he said, his voice rough with unaccustomed caring. "I'll see to it you get new things."

"That isn't why I told you," she said, nonetheless pleased by his offer.

"You can't spend the summer in one dress," he said reasonably, liking the idea of being able to do something for her.

"You're very kind," she said, studying his profile. It was true. "Very kind," she added.

Tillie couldn't hear what they were saying but, studying their faces, decided Jess had told him about the suitcase and he was maybe saying that he'd get her new things. At least that's the way it appeared. She looked at her sister, deciding Jess looked beautiful. Sometimes she did. And sometimes she looked almost ugly. But this was one of her pretty times, the sun catching hints of red in her hair. She wanted all at once to say, Don't take anything from him, Jess. I am sorry. I didn't mean it. Don't take anything from that old man. I don't like him.

The house was beautiful, a place Jess loved at once, a home that only someone with a lot of money could maintain. For the first time, she began giving serious consideration to Jamieson Land's money. He could afford to be generous. If he wished to extend his generosity to include her, then she'd accept whatever he chose to offer. After all, she was willing to give him what he wanted. It was a fair exchange.

The house was so in keeping with everything she'd once known: large, of white clapboard with black shutters, a sprawling carefully tended lawn that, in back, ran down to the edge of Echo Lake, with a vast, slightly lopsided barn that served as Jamieson's summer studio. A local woman came daily from Ludlow to help with the cleaning and cooking, the running of the place. A deep porch ran around the front and sides of the house, with white-painted wicker rockers and a glider. Flowers and shrubs grew close up against the base of the porch. Inside, the big airy rooms were nicely underfurnished: hooked rugs, polished maple furniture, plain white curtains on the windows, jugs and pots of flowers everywhere.

Tillie took a quick look at the bedroom she'd been given, then said, "I'm going down to have a look at the lake."

"Take your hat," Jess cautioned. "You don't want to get too much sun on your first day."

Tillie grabbed the hat, then turned and ran off eagerly. Jess stood for a moment watching her go, then set the suitcase on the bed and began unpacking Tillie's things, hanging her dresses in the closet and placing her other things in the dresser drawers. That done, she went to her own room. She put her handbag down on the bed then went over to the window and opened it, allowing the fresh, scented air to set the curtains dancing. She saw Tillie, hatless, running off beneath the trees. Smiling, she turned to take in the details of the room. One door gave onto the hallway. Two more were side by side to her left, another to her right. A room much taken up by doors, she thought. She went to open the one to her right and drew a deep, gratified breath at the sight of the large, spotlessly clean bathroom. How splendid it would be to have a bath without having to go out into the hall, hoping vainly that the other tenants might have left a little hot water. After her first few forays at their last place into the distressing filth left by others, she'd given up and heated pots of water on the stove so that first Tillie and then she might bathe in the tin bath in the kitchen, near the warmth of the stove. But this! A bathroom entirely to herself. She'd almost forgotten the delight of such luxuries.

The first door on the left opened into a closet, and the second into a very spacious bedroom that was, she knew instantly, his. Mrs. Holloway, the woman who came daily from town, was unpacking his bags. She paused to smile at Jess, asking, "Like it?"

"It's a wonderful place. I hadn't expected it to be so big."

"Won't seem all that big to you, another week or two when they all start coming up from the city. Fill up every bedroom in the house. Ten, twelve, fifteen for meals sometimes. I'll be glad of your help, for a fact."

"I'll help," Jess confirmed, stifling her sudden feeling of anger at the realization that she was here as an employee. She'd managed to forget it for a few minutes; now this woman brought it sharply home to her. She was no damned servant, she thought hotly. She shouldn't have told him she'd help around the house. He'd have been just as happy. Well, it was too late to do anything about it now. And it wouldn't kill her.

Seeing that Mrs. Holloway was watching her, she offered

to hang some of the clothes in the closet, wondering as she did what Mrs. Holloway thought about his having assigned Jess the bedroom adjoining his.

"Your sister, is it?" Mrs. Holloway asked.

"That's right. Tillie."

"Pretty little creature. Up to all kinds of mischief, I'll warrant. She's at the age."

"Oh?"

"Starting to reach into being a woman, not knowing which way to act most of the time."

"I suppose," Jess said noncommittally, privately accepting that what the woman said made good sense. Of course that was what was happening. Tillie was starting to grow up. She looked again at Mrs. Holloway to find the woman covertly inspecting her.

Look at me if you like, Jess thought defiantly. Think whatever you like. I'll help because I said I would. But I'm not a servant and never will be. I've had servants and because I have to do what I'm doing now doesn't mean it'll always be this way.

Abby Holloway wasn't quite sure what to make of this girl. She helped readily enough but didn't seem especially friendly. But upon further inspection Abby decided—as Jamieson had— that she wasn't so much unfriendly as shy. No easy thing, she thought, being shy as well as so tall and gawky, so pale in the face and with such a tangle of black hair. She sensed, though, the pride that kept Jess's spine fiercely erect. Have a hard row to hoe with that kind of pride, Abby thought compassionately.

"New places make you nervous?" she asked.

"Sometimes," Jess admitted. "Who are all the people?" she asked, helping unpack, placing things where Mrs. Holloway directed. "The ones who'll be coming, I mean."

"His friends. Photographers and writers, a couple of them paint and one or two do I don't know what. Between you, me, and the gatepost, not very much, those odd few."

"I see."

"There's also Miss Ogilvie, of course. You'll like her." Mrs. Holloway smiled, as if the thought of this Miss Ogilvie had managed to brighten the day for her. "She's something, is Miss Ogilvie. Biggest woman I think I've ever seen."

"Big, you mean fat?"

"That. Though she's big other ways, too. I think that about

does it here. If you'd care to, I'd be glad of a hand with the lunch. I'll put the kettle on, we'll have a cup of tea first."

"I'd like that."

"What do folks call you?" Mrs. Holloway asked as they went side by side down the hall.

"Please call me Jess."

"Abby," Mrs. Holloway said. "It's what they've always called me."

"Abby," Jess repeated.

Jess got a fairly sunburned Tillie settled in for the night, then returned down the hall to her room and through to the bathroom to start the water running in the tub, looking forward to a bath. Undressing while the water was going, she pinned up her hair. She was dismayed that she didn't have a nightgown. She'd have to sleep in her slip. Reviewing the suitcase incident again, she felt unusually vexed with Tillie. First the suitcase, then the self-satisfied look on her face when they were driving up. She was probably just flustered by the change in the routines of their life. Children didn't like big moves.

She turned to look at that second door to her left, noticing there wasn't a key. The door didn't lock. Nor, she saw, was there one for the bathroom door. It didn't matter, she decided, and sank into the hot water, sighing with pleasure.

After a few minutes, she sat up and began to wash, looking out to her bedroom and at the door leading to his room. She really should have closed the bathroom door. If he came in, he'd see her. But that didn't matter either. He'd see her in any case, sooner or later. No, it bothered her. She stood up and leaned far out of the tub to swing the door shut, then hummed tunelessly as she finished bathing. When she returned to her room she saw that his door now stood ajar, a gap of several inches. Her heart jumped. Obviously, he expected her to come in. She unpinned her hair, eyes fixed on the door, then stepped back into her slip. Her heart was rapping as she went across the room.

He was in bed reading, the blankets neatly folded back across his middle. His chest was bare and broader than she'd thought—not at all the chest and arms of an old man. She remained on the threshold and he put down his book, removing his wire-framed reading glasses to look at her.

The sight of her was a shock every time. She came over

and sat down gingerly on the side of the bed, holding her hands together in her lap; anxious for him to touch her, hold her, make her feel the excitement she had felt the first time; anxious to have him do all that so she wouldn't feel guilty about his buying her new clothes, or for asking him to continue paying her the five dollars a week. Money was essential. The more she was able to save, the more secure hers and Tillie's lives would be.

"Mr. Land," she began.

"Jamieson," he corrected.

"Mr. . . . Jamieson, I'm afraid I'm going to have to ask you for the five dollars a week after all. You see . . ."

He stopped her. "I had every intention of paying you. I always pay my models."

"Thank you." She at once lost her train of thought as his hand reached out and tilted her head up. His touch, as before, jarred her senses, brought her body into control of her.

"I'd like to do a portrait of you with your sister," he said.

Without thinking, too filled with the expectation of pleasure, she said, "If you like. Should I turn out the light?" She could hardly speak, scarcely think; his hand on her throat was like a rope slowly strangling her.

"If you don't mind," he said, "I'd prefer it on."

"I don't mind," she said truthfully. She stood up and took off her slip, pleased by his reaction, the flush of color rising into his face. He folded the blankets down further and she sat again beside him, engulfed anew by that inexplicable tenderness for him as she confronted his eyes. She felt physically strained by her own intense desire, as if she'd been placed on a rack and was being gradually stretched to the point where she'd tear apart.

His hand settled on her shoulder. She wanted to close her eyes, to faint. Her body was hot and cold; the hair on her arms stood on end. The voice in her brain whispered, love me, love me, look after me.

"God!" he whispered, sounding choked.

No time for talking, listening. She slid down slightly, offering her mouth to his, her breasts to his hands. Instantly on fire, her body melted into him. She was taking short, gasping breaths as he urged her down, his mouth on her nipples, first one then the other. Her quivering responses heightened his already enormous appetite for her. Closely studying her face,

he stroked between her thighs, seeing a certain madness overtake her as he caressed her, causing her to writhe beneath
his delicately but insistently probing fingers. He was caught
up in the profoundly proprietory knowledge that she'd known
no other man. His hand flatly traveled over her breasts, down
her belly, back between her legs. Her eyes round and out of
focus, she blindly stroked him as her thighs parted more, more,
her breasts heaving with the effort of breathing under the weight
of her suffocating lust; her slender legs spread tautly white.
The invitation of her limbs and shallow breathing prompted
him to do something he'd never done before. He lowered his
head to taste the unbearable sweetness of her, tightly closing
his eyes to better appreciate this unique embrace. He was
startled by the increasing ferocity of her reactions. Her body
was like oil running over him. And he knew all at once that
Flora was right, that he was in love with this child, this woman,
whoever she was. This realization so overwhelmed him that
he was only distantly aware of her heated, reciprocating caresses.

Moving on top of her, he held her face between his hands
and kissed her searchingly as she opened her knees, sighing
shudderingly as he entered her. Clutching him to her, she thrust
herself up to take more, all of him, deep deep. All wet sliding
hard, nothing ever as good or better than this. Each inward
thrust delivered a stab of rippling pleasure; her body had gone
over to his, no longer belonging to her. She was dependent
upon him for everything, everything.

He heard a chorus of *yes, yes* in his skull as her mouth
opened and her body danced under him, clinging; again again,
until it passed, left her; then returned, captured her again.

Oh, God, she thought, Jesus God, I could die of this.

Tillie couldn't sleep. Her sunburn was stinging and the bed
was too hard. She kicked off the blankets and turned to one
side, then to the other. It was too quiet—there was only some
kind of buzzy humming insect and the breeze pushing through
the leaves, making them rustle and slap against each other. No
cars, no buses, no El, no night sounds, no street sounds. She
couldn't sleep. She'd go get into bed with Jess, she decided;
let Jess tell her one of those good stories she could always
make up. She got up and walked over to the door and out into
the dark hallway, down to Jess's room. Cautiously, she opened

the door and poked her head around just in case Jess was
already sleeping. But the lights were on and Jess's bed was
still all made up. She went through to the bathroom. Empty.
Then turning, she stopped, hearing the funniest sounds, a creak-
ing kind of noise and, over that, a high-pitched moaning.

She went toward the partially open door to look through
into the room beyond, her hand gripping the doorknob, her
mouth dropping open at the sight of Jess all the way naked
with that old man on top of her doing something, bumping
against her, his bottom going up and down, and Jess with her
head turning back and forth, her arms all around him, her hands
holding onto him while she kept on making those moaning
sounds. In horror, Tillie saw that the old man had that part of
him inside of Jess and was doing something, going faster until
Jess made a choking noise and her whole body shook and
jumped.

Tillie couldn't move, and remained standing there until she
slowly became aware of herself, of where she was. Then she
closed her mouth, unstiffened a little, and took several steps
back away from the door. She held her clenched fists in front
of her as she glared, hate-filled, at the open door, wanting to
scream and scream; hating Jess and that old man and what they
were doing. I hate you! she screamed inside her head, her eyes
bulging as she gaped at the door. I hate you both! You'll be
sorry. I'll make you sorry. Telling me you were doing it for
me. But it isn't for me, it's for you, so you can do that horrible
thing with him. You're horrible! And he's horrible, too! She
felt as if she were going to vomit.

The hatred abruptly let go of her and she ran back down
the hall to throw herself on her bed, sobbing. Jess! Don't do
that, Jess! I don't want you to do that. I know you don't like
that awful old man. Why are you doing that? So ugly and
horrible. As long as she lived she'd never let anyone do something so disgusting to her! Never!

The tears passing, she rolled over onto her side, her knees
tucked up, her hands clasped and folded under her cheek,
feeling scared, lost. Was that what all grown-ups did? Probably, she thought. I'll never grow up if it means having some
man do that to me! she vowed. And Jess wasn't even really
a grown-up. She wasn't nineteen yet. And they weren't married
or anything like that. The idea of Jess being married to that
old man was the most terrible thing that had ever entered her

mind. Could Jess actually like him? If that was the truth and she did, did it mean Jess would stay on with him? I don't want to stay, I don't like it here. Jess! I don't like it here! How can you let him do that to you, how can you?

There were so many things he wanted to say to her, holding her secure in his arms, stroking the thick, springy hair back from her damp forehead. He might say, I love you, have my children, I never thought I'd have any—it's late in the day for me, but maybe not too late, dear God but you're beautiful. But he couldn't say anything at all. Unable to give voice to his many thoughts, he kissed her lingeringly instead, continuing to stroke her; deeply happy to have witnessed that radiant glow on her features. Woman, pure woman. One morning very soon, he'd bring her here to his bed, they'd make love and, afterward, he'd take the picture he'd finally been privileged to view.

She felt exquisitely exhausted, utterly satisfied; an un-dreamed-of lassitude weighting down her limbs. She didn't care about anything at all, and drifted down beneath the weight of her satiation, only to awaken some hours later to his hand lightly smoothing her arm. She opened her eyes, immediately ready to enter into all of it again.

". . . best if you go back to your own room now, Jess." His hand lingered a moment, then went away; the contact was broken.

"Yes, all right." She got up quickly, chagrined at being treated like something to be hidden away in the dark. How dare he treat her so casually? She'd let him touch her every-where, in ways she'd never dreamed existed, and now it didn't seem to mean anything at all to him. The fondness she'd been feeling for him disintegrated in the face of his capacity to dismiss her.

"Goodnight, Jess," he said wearily.

She sat down on the side of the bed and took hold of his hand, asking, "Would it be all right for me to go into town tomorrow?" She'd make him pay for treating her so indiffer-ently, sending her away when she'd felt so safe.

"Of course," he agreed and reached for his billfold on the bedside table. Extracting several bills, he handed them to her, saying, "Get whatever you need."

"Thank you." She smiled, bent to kiss him on the lips, then said, "Goodnight," and switched off the light before tiptoeing

to her room to climb between the fresh cool sheets, the money
safely under her pillow. He'd soon enough stop sending her
back to her own room. Yet she lost a good measure of her
angry determination as she recalled her contentment in being
held close. She'd spend the nights with him and return to her
own room when she chose, not when she was ordered to.
Having decided this, she sank back into sleep.

◊ Four ◊

He'd done a number of head shots of the two sisters, but somehow they contained very little, certainly no affirming *yes*. Perhaps, he thought, something of a more intimate nature—the sisters bathing in the lake, say—might evoke the feeling he wanted. And if the girls were nude, there would, he hoped, be still more mood to the pictures.

Tillie absolutely refused. "I won't do it!" She presented a face of stone to her sister, daring Jess to get angry.

"Tillie," Jess said quietly, "I'd like you to do this for Mr. Land."

All too aware of the old man hovering close by with his camera, Tillie pulled harder into herself. "I'm not going to do it, no matter what you say."

He wanted to step in and say it wasn't important. He didn't want the child—or anyone, for that matter—to do something so obviously against her will. But this was a matter solely between the sisters and he didn't know how to go about separating them in order to tell Jess to let it be. Perhaps, though, if he discreetly removed himself, Jess might be better able to settle it. "I'll just nip back to the house for my hat," he said. "It's hotter than I'd realized."

Their silence held until he was well out of earshot. Jess, her sense of honor and obligation working full tilt, felt that since he'd asked very little of either of them, the least Tillie could do was stand for a few photographs. Clad in the ridiculous frilly robe that had somehow managed to find its way up here, she'd been prepared to begin posing at once, expecting Tillie's full cooperation.

"What's the matter, Till?" she asked, still quietly. "Would you please tell me what's bothering you so I can do something about it?"

There's nothing you can do about it, Tillie thought, except take us both away from here and go back to being the Jess you used to be.

"How could you do it?" she asked. "Taking off your clothes for that horrible old man." She said "taking off your clothes," but what she meant and wanted Jess to understand was that she knew about the other business, and wished to know how Jess could do that. But Jess didn't seem to hear the underlying question, which made Tillie wonder, for a few seconds, if she'd actually seen what she had, or simply dreamed it. But she couldn't have dreamed something like that, she told herself. Never!

"Sometimes," Jess said thoughtfully, "people have to do things they don't really want to do."

"Are you saying you're here, taking your clothes off and *everything*, but you don't really want to?"

"Something like that. It isn't easy to explain. There are some things that just have to be done." Tillie looked over at the water's edge, searching for words. "Look at me, Tillie," Jess said persuasively. Tillie's head turned. "This isn't the way I ever dreamed my life was going to be. But there's a Depression going on. No jobs, no money. We need to eat. Please," she begged, her tone turning desperate. "Let him photograph you. He isn't going to touch you or harm you in any way."

"Do you love him?"

"*Love him?*" Flummoxed by the question, Jess could only stare at her.

"Well, do you?"

"No," she answered firmly.

"Then how *can* you?"

"How can I what?"

"How can you do what you're doing?"

Jess still didn't seem to be getting it and Tillie, looking into
her eyes, knew she was going to have to do it. Because there
were things people had to do, even when they didn't want to.
She'd do it because Jess wanted her to so badly, for some
reason Tillie couldn't begin to comprehend. As far as Tillie
could see, her sister had lots of choices but just wasn't recognizing them. Jess was like that sometimes: seeing only one
way when there were lots of others if she'd just stop and look
around for them. I'd never do these things for someone I didn't
love, Tillie thought, and silently told Jess she ought to know
better. This wasn't the only place in the world for them. There
were other places, other people who'd pay her to work for
them. And they wouldn't make us take off our clothes, either,
she added recriminatingly. None of this made any sense. Unless
Jess wasn't telling the truth and really did love him but just
didn't want to admit it to Tillie for some reason.

He was coming back. Tillie could hear him moving across
the grass. His footsteps seemed to move the ground right under
her. She stood up, dusting off her dress, not saying anything.
But Jess, watching, understood that Tillie was going to give
in, and wondered what had caused her to change her mind.

"Are you all right, Till?" she asked in an undertone, her
arm going around Tillie's shoulders.

"Oh, Jess." She hid her face for a moment against Jess's
arm. "I hate it here," she whispered. "I . . ." She pulled away,
unable to trust herself or the situation sufficiently to say more.

While he was setting up the camera, the girls walked to the
edge of the lake. Jess shrugged off the robe and bent to help
Tillie unfasten her dress, trying to smile encouragingly, succeeding only in making her face look strange. "We'll go for
a swim after," she coaxed, feeling as if she'd betrayed both
Tillie and the feelings she had for her.

"You know I can't swim," Tillie said aggrievedly, moving
away. "I can do it myself," she insisted, hating her sister and
that man, telling herself she wouldn't let him see her. She kept
her back to him and his stupid camera, looking instead at Jess's
breasts, feeling broken down, somehow, by the sight of them,
and studied instead the thin, tight-looking flesh of Jess's middle, while Jess pinned up Tillie's hair. The back of her neck
cooled where the air was now able to get at it. She risked
turning her head slightly, to see what he was doing.

It was precisely the shot he'd wanted: Jess concentrating

on pinning up the little one's hair, and Tillie daring to peek
over her shoulder at him. No question it'd be a good shot. A
quietly sibilant *yesss* sighed to him. Then, hand in hand, the
girls took several steps into the stony-bottomed, clear-watered
lake.

"Turn slightly to the right," he told them. "Look just to the
right. That's it."

Jess's hand went to Tillie's shoulder, directing her. Another
good one. *Yes.* The contrast was marvelous. He could already
see the exhibition, knew the phenomenal response it would
get. There was a mood finally to all this; a softness and tone,
a dimensional thrust he loved even though he could feel the
waves of disapproval, even hatred, emanating from Tillie. But
he was too caught up in the technicalities, and too charmed
by Jess's dark, slender height beside Tillie's fair, rounded little-
girlishness, to try to deal with the emotions of a small girl. He
was bothered, in any case, only peripherally by the knowledge
that the child hated him. He couldn't understand what he'd
done to inspire such a feeling in her, but he couldn't spare the
time to analyze the matter.

He'd grown up here, in this house, the only child of two
people so happy with each other that they had all but excluded
the nearsighted boy they had bred almost accidentally, certainly
only incidentally. He spent his childhood studying their fascination with each other as well as indulging his own bur-
geoning fascination with the rapidly progressing science of
photography. They financed his interests—it allowed them
even more time together—and sent him off to the best schools,
for the best possible education, when all he ever truly wanted
was to wedge his way between them and cloak himself in the
heat of their obsession with one another. He'd hoped they'd
see and find in him the ultimate mirror of their separate selves,
but it never happened. They lived and died absorbed only in
each other, paying only minimum attention to their son, leaving
him shy, inept with strangers, comfortable only behind the
reversed images of the world he saw through the lenses of his
various cameras, and in possession of an image of love he
never thought to realize.

There'd been no unpleasantness, no dissension ever during
his childhood and youth. Each time one or the other of his
parents addressed him, he had the distinct impression that the
eyes of the one were joined, above his head, to those of the

other. He photographed them hundreds of times, hoping to please them by successfully capturing their many moods of involvement. They simply smiled approvingly, mouthed words of encouragement, accepted his offers of framed prints, and continued on their way; he couldn't be a part of them. After spending a year at home following his graduation from Harvard, he gave up hope, packed his clothes, books, and cameras, lenses and prints, and moved to New York. There was nothing for him in the house on Echo Lake. Perhaps there would be in New York.

It took a long time to happen. A silent, preoccupied, lonely man who could never manage to present himself to others with the ease he'd have liked, he was in his early thirties when he met Flora. Between his desire to belong and his ability to communicate stood a wall of disenchantment that others interpreted as indifference. But Flora understood at once, and she made it all take shape for him. Through her he met other photographers, writers, and artists, people who intrigued and puzzled him, people who claimed to find great merit in his work. He created a second family, surrounding himself carefully with people whose praise he knew to be genuine, whose work he admired, and whose warmth seeped through to thaw his frozen feelings.

His parents died within a year of each other, because, he was convinced, they couldn't live without each other. They left him a wealthy man. He kept the house and moved his new, surrogate family in each summer in order to relish the proximity and open interest of these brothers and sisters, these sets of parents he'd managed to locate in a world he rarely understood but had an endless compulsion to photograph. He always believed he might one day—even inadvertently—take a photograph that would suddenly explain life to him.

He'd had very little to do with children, except for his classmates at Groton, and he'd made no friends there. He'd known very few little girls, and no one remotely like Tillie. From a safe distance he admired her. She'd have an interesting, difficult life, he was sure, and was curious to know how it would evolve. But for the most part, she simply frightened him. There was a raging sense of self-importance inside the child, and he wondered if Jess was aware of how dynamic Tillie actually was. Jess seemed fairly oblivious to a lot about her sister, seeming to concentrate solely on her responsibility to look after the child. He wanted to warn Jess, tell her she was doing too much for Tillie, tell her to stop and allow the girl to grow. No one could mature properly when someone else was doing all the work. But he couldn't say anything since he wasn't really sure how much Jess actually did see and know. He might be judging mistakenly on the basis of the externals as he perceived them.

So he said nothing at all. He took his pictures, packed away the camera, and wondered how Flora would respond to the sisters. He was quite confident she would see in Jess all he saw, and was anxious to know her reactions to Tillie.

Tillie got her clothes back on, then confronted Jess.

"Don't you *ever* make me do anything like that again!" she warned a bewildered Jess. "You don't want me to lie to you. Okay, I won't. You do the things you want to do, but don't expect me to do them, too. I'm not you. I'm not like you and I happen to think there *are* choices, even if you don't."

"I didn't *make* you, Tillie. You decided for yourself."

"Oh, yes, you did so make me! Because you know I don't want you to be mad at me."

"Tillie...!"

But Tillie was already running away from her across the grass.

Flora wanted to dislike her, but just couldn't. Jess was too unpretentious, too uncomplicated and direct, too on edge. Jamie's photographs had, from all the prints Flora had so far seen, failed to capture properly her large, magnificent eyes. Her hand was lean, her grip firm and forthright, her eyes unhesitatingly meeting Flora's so that Flora smiled instinctively, clapping her arms around the girl, swallowing her up in an embrace, laughingly exclaiming, "Hell, come give me a hug! I've heard so much about you, seen so many pictures I feel I already know you." The instant she spoke she realized that she knew of this girl only what Jamie knew: the surface, and the parts Jess allowed others to see. It was, Flora could now tell, all too easy to be misled by Jess's surfaces. There was undoubtedly a great deal underneath.

Jess enjoyed the feel of the woman's arms, her substance, and the potential of friendship, even shelter, being offered. How nice she was! Jess thought. To someone she didn't even know. She wondered how nice Flora might be if they actually knew one another. These few moments made Jess aware of how much she missed the few friends she'd once had.

"You *are* beautiful!" Flora said appraisingly, ending the embrace and holding Jess at arm's length for a moment before letting her go. "So, how d'you like it here? Pretty swell place, huh?"

"It's lovely," Jess agreed, unable not to smile at this woman. Flora had a truly beautiful face and Jess was astonished to think that someone who looked like Flora could ever think Jess beautiful. Compared to Flora, Jess thought, she was positively ugly.

"C'mon in here, sit down and talk with me. I don't do too well on my feet, but on my backside, sweetheart, I can go for days." She laughed loudly and Jess, curious and disarmed by Flora's immediacy and unstinting warmth, went along with her into the living room. She was saddened in advance at the prospect of losing Flora's friendship. It seemed inevitable somehow that she would. Since the episode at the lake with Tillie, there seemed to be a strong, daily-growing sense of finality about everything. Tillie was doing her damnedest to talk Jess away—from this house, and from Jamieson Land and his money, his security. Why couldn't Tillie just be satisfied?

"So," Flora huffed, settling her bulk into one of the larger armchairs. "What d'you think?"

"About what?"

"Anything, everything. Having a good time?"

"I like it here very much. I'd be quite happy to stay."

I'll bet you would, Flora thought. There was a homeless, motherless look to Jess, a searching quality to her eyes, as if seeking someone or some place that might offer her permanent shelter. "And how," she asked leadingly, "are you getting on with Jamie?"

Jess's eyes left hers for the first time. She'd never wanted to speak truthfully quite so much as she did now with this woman. "Fine," she replied, wondering if he'd told all his friends about her, told them he'd bought himself a girl who not only slept with him but also fetched and carried. She shouldn't be thinking this way, she warned herself. He'd been kind, very kind. And none of his friends had seemed in the least surprised to find her there and hadn't, any of them, treated her as other than an equal. But maybe that was because he brought a woman here with him every summer. "He's very generous," she said guardedly. "And I like his work very much."

"Really? What do you like about it?" Flora lit a cigarette and offered one to Jess while trying to absorb the subtler meanings of this girl. She was aware of Jess's sudden tenseness when asked about Jamie.

"No, thank you. I don't smoke. I like the portraits," she said, giving the matter thought. "And the street scenes."

"Yes, but *why* do you like them?"

Jess's eyes came back to hers. "Because they make me feel good to look at them, make me want to say, 'Yes, that's right. That's just the way so and so looks, or the way that is.' And the . . . depth to them, the feeling that they're not photographs but something I'm really seeing. Of course, I don't know very much about these things."

"You know all you need to. What're you afraid of?" she asked quietly.

"I don't know," Jess said openly. "A lot of things."

"What kind of things?"

Jess looked down at her hands, then back at Flora. "Being alone. Being poor. I suppose that sounds silly."

"Doesn't sound silly to me," Flora said feelingly. "Sounds about like what most of us're afraid of."

Dropping her guard completely, Jess admitted, "Sometimes I think it would be so good to have a place where I know I belong, a place that's mine. Not just rooms. But . . ." She stopped, unsure of herself or her audience.

"I know about that," Flora said. "Don't be embarrassed 'cause you talked about it."

"But we don't even know each other," Jess said, feeling endangered by her admissions.

"Sure we do." Flora smiled. "Anyway, where's your sister?"

Jess looked over at the doorway as if Tillie might be standing there. She was concerned about Tillie, feeling that they were all too quickly growing apart. The existence of Jamieson Land seemed to be placing more and more distance between them. "I'm not sure," she answered slowly. "I think she's gone for a walk with Mrs. Holloway's granddaughter. Tillie seems to like babysitting Elsa. Elsa's only eight, you see. I think it makes Till feel grown up to be in charge of her."

"Does Jamie know you're going?"

She recoiled as if Flora had struck her. "I beg your pardon?"

"Does he know yet? Have you told him? Or haven't you realized it yourself?"

"But I'm not—"

"You are, you know," Flora said with calm confidence. "I can see it all over you."

"What are you trying to do?" Jess asked imploringly. "Are you trying to . . . upset things . . . me . . . somehow?"

Surprised, she said, "Heavens no! I like you. And I'm not in the habit of going around trying to upset other people's applecarts."

"Then why do you say that . . . about going?"

"Don't honestly know. Just something I felt about you the moment I mentioned Jamie's name. I could be wrong. God knows, I've been wrong often enough before. But I don't think I am this time. It has to do with your sister, huh?"

"Tillie?" She couldn't think clearly. But, yes, it did have to do with Tillie. "I don't want to leave," she said, again looking at her hands. "He's very good to . . . to us. Very kind. But Tillie . . . she doesn't like him. I wish," she said with sudden candor, "I could love him. I've tried so hard. But I can't. I don't know what I'm going to do. I'm afraid . . ."

"Just don't hurt him," Flora said, looking unhappy at the prospect. "Try not to do that. Whatever your feelings, he doesn't deserve it."

"Oh no!" Jess agreed quickly, perplexed. "He doesn't." Flora was right, she thought. She was going to have to leave him in order to keep Tillie. Which meant that once they left here, she'd have to take Till back to New York, get settled somewhere and start all over again trying to find a way to keep the both of them fed and clothed. The very idea of it was horribly fatiguing. Jamieson had spoiled her, allowed her to become reaccustomed to certain luxuries that would be denied her if they left. Why the hell couldn't Till learn to appreciate what he was doing for them?

"Don't let me scare you." Flora smiled. "I'm really not all that scary, just a forty-year-old fat lady who sees a little too much for everyone's good."

"Why do you talk about yourself that way?" Jess asked

sharply. "You're very pretty; you have beautiful hair."

"I *was* pretty," she amended. "Twenty years ago, my God, but I was pretty." She spoke of her past beauty as if referring to a dead friend, and Jess wanted to stop her. "I'll show you pictures sometime," Flora went on, thinking Jess probably wouldn't be there long enough for that. The younger one didn't like Jamie, although Jess apparently liked him enough to want to stay. But Jess's loyalty was plainly to her sister and the sister would break it up, one way or another. It was too bad, she thought. Jess didn't appear to have the strength to go against her sister. Or was it that? That, she decided, and something else she couldn't quite put her finger on, something having to do with the way she'd responded to Flora's embrace.

"Sweetheart," she said softly, "would you let your little sister move you out of a place where you're pretty happy?"

"You don't understand," Jess said, a plaintive note in her voice. "Tillie's all I have. I don't *have* anyone else."

The front door opened, footsteps sounded and Jamieson appeared in the doorway, looking happy, contented. Jess quickly redirected her gaze to the window, while Flora summoned up a smile and hefted herself out of the chair, lumbering across the room to throw her arms around Jamieson, happily saying, "Jamie! It's been one hell of a long month!"

"Good to see you." He smiled one of his rare, beatific smiles. "I see you've met Jess," he said proudly, his eyes filling with tenderness and caring. Jess felt uncomfortable. And Flora felt uncomfortable for her. Poor Jamie, she thought. He didn't handle his feelings very well.

"Met her and crazy about her." Flora grinned. "Now I'm waiting to meet the little sister."

"You'll make Jess think we're all judging," he said.

"You know better, don't you?" she asked Jess.

Jess agreed soberly. It was true. She knew intuitively that Flora was someone who didn't judge but simply saw things as they were.

The two of them chatted and Jess sat listening, observing the change wrought in Jamieson by Flora's presence. He was more open, more relaxed, more eagerly expansive than she'd seen him with any of his other friends. She'd heard him have very serious, knowledgeable-sounding conversations with the two photographers who'd arrived the week before. She'd seen him critically inspect the works-in-progress of the water-colorist who'd been there two weeks now. And she'd also noted how respectfully he'd listened to the evidently ongoing debate between the two writers who'd come up together almost three weeks earlier. With them, Jamieson had interjected occasional comments, but generally refrained from inflicting himself or his views.

The two photographers seemed to want the world to know what they were and dressed accordingly in what appeared to be a uniform of baggy dark trousers with suspenders, open-throated collarless white shirts, full beards, wire-frame glasses, straw hats, and a fogged air of perennial distraction. Jamie had laughed when she'd commented on this, telling her, "We're all trying to be Steichen or Stieglitz."

The painter was an intense, nervous little man who always wore long sleeves in order to cover the red scaly patches of psoriasis on his forearms and who, Jamieson had told her privately, had had shingles at least three times due to his extreme nervousness. "He doesn't think he's good, wants to be good, is, and can't deal with it."

The pair of writers were loud, argumentative, and given to sudden lengthy silences intersticed by just as sudden shouting matches. The one was at work on a WPA project having something to do with reeducation. The other was a journalist on the *Herald Tribune*. They argued mainly about some crazed Austrian named Hitler who'd taken over politically in Germany and was going to create another World War. The WPA man called the idea "nuts" and the journalist rolled his eyes back, waved his fists around, and shouted, "You dumb son of a bitch! Tell me it's nuts when the whole fucking world's busy fighting! Come tell me that a couple of years from now, you insufferable cretin!" They were inseparable friends. And Jamie displayed his usual tolerance and generosity toward them.

But with Flora he seemed to step out from beneath the many layers of himself, emerging from the protective armor of silence and tactful withdrawal to offer her his thoughts and opinions, his seldom-seen sense of humor and his considerable affection. All of which was, for the most part, a relief for Jess to see. But confusing, too. She couldn't understand why he hadn't involved himself with Flora, who seemed infinitely better suited to him than herself. Still, it was good to know there was someone around who cared for him and was capable of eliciting so much of his best. She'll look after him, Jess thought, allowing herself to contemplate Flora's earlier remarks. The woman *was* right. If it came to choosing between Jamieson and Tillie, she'd have to choose her sister because she didn't love this man. She was sometimes fond of him, strongly attracted to what he could offer her, but she'd promised to look after Tillie, and Tillie was growing more vocal daily in her discontent.

She silently cursed Tillie and her unhappiness, which was going to deprive Jess of the first comfort and sense of belonging she'd had in years. If she closed her eyes, she could project herself into a warm, secure future with Land. Without Tillie, there'd have been no question at all of leaving. When they did go, it was bound to hurt Jamieson because he cared for her and she knew it. Even if she couldn't reciprocate his feelings, she did derive pleasure and comfort from their nights together, not to mention the weekly money he gave her. In time, she might even have learned to care for him. But because of Tillie, she'd never have that chance. She felt like screaming. She'd have to go back to New York, with no job and no money. And if she was going to continue providing for her sister, she'd have to try the streets again, a thought that made her feel sick.

A few days later, Flora invited her to come out for a walk up the road after dinner, and Jess went gladly, hoping they'd talk.

"What's Tillie got against Jamie?" Flora asked, right to the point. "She looks at him like he's got a highly contagious disease."

"I don't know," Jess said thoughtfully, fearfully. "I think she might have guessed about us."

"Oh!" Flora lit a cigarette. "That'd do it, I suppose."

"And I forced her to pose for him. She swore she'd never forgive me for that. I probably shouldn't have made her do it."

"Probably not," Flora agreed.

Jess looked up at the sky—deep blue prior to the dark—and clenched her fists at her sides, feeling torn. "I didn't know what else to do," she said. "After all, he could've said no, not brought us with him. But he did. And I didn't want to upset him. I thought he might be because Tillie was refusing. I was wrong. I know I was. Now, I keep waiting for her to...say or do something. And then, when she does, I know it'll mean we have to leave and I don't really want to go. I really don't. He's already talking about the fall, the things we'll do when we get back to New York, and I listen to what he says, wanting all of it so much, but knowing it'll never happen because Tillie won't *let* it happen."

"What'll you do?"

"I don't know," Jess sighed.

"What would you like, sweetheart?"

"Like? Now, you mean?"

"For your life."

"Oh, God! For my life. Not very much, really. Just enough to live on without having to be terrified when Friday comes around and there's no money to pay the rent. A job of some sort. Someone to belong to." She wanted to cry, needing so badly to belong. In an unsteady voice, she went on to say, "Not to be treated like a servant, or ordered around."

"You're not treated that way now."

"No, not now," she agreed. But at the beginning, the way he'd awakened her night after night, sending her back to her room until she'd had to ask him to let her stay because she felt most afraid when she was all alone at night. She'd never again, as long as she lived, ask any man for anything.

"What were you doing when you met Jamie?" Flora asked.

It was almost dark now. Grateful that they couldn't see each other, Jess said, "Trying to pick up men on the streets."

"Jesus!" Flora exclaimed softly. "Came to that, huh?"

"There was nothing left," she explained. "Nothing. We had so much and it all went. *So much,*" she said longingly. "I thought," she admitted, "that Jamieson was going to...buy me."

Flora laughed and reached out to tousle Jess's hair. "You sure didn't know your customer," she said. "Jamie wouldn't have the nerve."

"No. I know that now. Anyway, it didn't happen. I mean, I didn't have to stay on the streets."

But you'll go back again, Flora thought, chilled by this insight. "You've got a lot of moxie," she said.

"I haven't," Jess countered.

"Yeah, you do," Flora disagreed. "Just make sure you know

what you're doing when you do it."

"I don't know," Jess said again.

"You could, you know, always tell your sister to lump it, let her live with it."

"I couldn't!" Jess shook her head.

"No, I guess you couldn't. Too bad. For everyone."

"How come you got to be so . . . big?" Tillie asked, crouched on the grass, watching Flora on her belly in the underbrush, fussing with the aperture on her Graflex, setting up her equipment for a morning of shooting.

"Fat, you mean?"

"I didn't want to say that," she said, admiring Flora for knowing she was fat. "I mean, it isn't polite to say things like that to people."

"Depends on who you're saying it to, I'd guess. And how much politeness matters to you. Hand me that mirror there, will you?"

Tillie looked down, saw the foot-square mirror, picked it up, and presented it into Flora's surprisingly slim, long-fingered hand.

"Thanks."

"Was there a reason or something?" Tillie persisted, highly intrigued by this woman.

"Sure was," Flora wheezed, pausing to wipe the back of her hand over her mouth and forehead. "Gonna be a scorcher today," she observed. "What it was," she said, positioning the mirror carefully at an angle—she was hoping to shoot into the mirror and thereby create mixed and double images—"I fell in love with someone, twenty years ago. And, for a time, it was the best thing in the whole world. Nothing's better than being young, being crazy in love. But it went sour and then I got hungry. I've been hungry ever since."

"Hungry? For food, you mean?"

"I guess you could put it that way. Filling up something that was too empty. Come on down here," she invited. "I'll show you what I'm trying to do."

Tillie flopped down on her belly, listening closely as Flora explained. "See, if I shoot into the mirror at this angle, I get my subject and the background, as well as the immediate foreground. So—at least, I hope—it'll have a three-dimensional effect. Or, if I shoot the subject seeing itself in the mirror, I get a double-image effect. Follow any of that?"

"I think so."

Flora put out a hand and briefly caressed Tillie's hair. "Good girl."

Tillie actually didn't mind Flora doing that.

"You and Mr. Land been friends a long time?" she asked, fascinated by the deftness of Flora's fingers as she rearranged individual blades of grass.

"Long time."

"Twenty years?"

Flora laughed loudly, a huge, booming sound. "Some head you got on those shoulders," she roared appreciatively. "About fifteen years," she said.

"Is he in love with you?"

"Don't I wish! But, no. Only woman I know of Jamie's been in love with is your sister."

"He *is*?"

"I'd definitely say so."

"And is she," Tillie asked cautiously, suddenly very afraid of the answer Flora might give, "in love with him, do you think?"

Flora sensed it would be unwise of her to attempt to answer this question. Jess struck her as someone who was fulfilling an obligation, but her feelings, Flora thought, didn't enter into it.

"Do you think she is?" Tillie asked again, feeling that everything hinged on Flora's answer to this vital question.

"Can't say," she said at last.

"But if she is," Tillie said rashly, dissatisfied with the response, "what about me?"

"What about you?"

"What'll happen to me . . . I mean . . ."

Flora turned to take a sharp, hard look at the girl, quickly sizing up the dimensions of the problem. "What d'you imagine's going to happen to you if she is?"

"I don't know, but . . . I don't know."

"I wouldn't worry myself about it, I were you."

"You don't think so?" Tillie asked with almost pathetic hopefulness.

"I think not."

Tillie then felt really quite close to Flora as they lay side by side in the tickly grass, with the sun hot, and the air heavy and alive with cricket songs. She put her arm around Flora's shoulder, grateful that Flora hadn't confirmed her worst fear: that Jess really did love the old man. If Jess didn't love him, then they wouldn't have to stay here.

◇ Five ◇

Tillie got up out of bed and went to sit in the chair by the window. Gazing out, she tried to think. There was a chill in the air. It was starting to turn cold. Mrs. Holloway had told her it got very cold up here in the winter. "Comes early," she'd said. "Round about the start of November, we can look out for the first snows. And, once they come, we're in then for the real cold."

It was almost September. If things kept on as they were, she and Jess would be going back to New York with *him*. Jess seemed fairly content to keep things as they were. Tillie couldn't let it happen, couldn't believe Jess wanted to be with him even if she did do all those things in his room. She just couldn't—no matter how hard she tried—make herself believe Jess really wanted to stay.

She slipped off the chair and sat on the floor, leaning against the windowsill, staring out. She was finally accustomed to the nighttime silence and thought miserably of going back to the city, not wanting that. She wanted to go somewhere exciting and new where the two of them could start fresh, some place where things would be different. She'd have to talk to Jess, get her to see that if they were going to make a move, they'd have to make it soon. Otherwise, it'd be too late. It'd be too cold, for one thing. And for another, the old man would start getting ready any time now to move back to the city.

She doesn't love him. I'd know it if she did. And that's what's important: She doesn't love him. We've got to talk it over, make a plan. We've got to run away, leave without letting anyone know. Because if Jess has a chance to talk to the old man, he'll talk her out of it. She hates upsetting people, even ones she doesn't like. So if she tells him we're going, he'll get all upset and ask her not to go, and she'll stay. I've just got to make her do it my way. Or else we'll end up going back to New York with him and Jess'll probably stay with him forever, or as long as he tells her he wants her to stay. I can't let her tell him we're going. She'd break down and agree to stay, and then she'd come back to me all sorry and upset and say we weren't going after all. I've just got to convince her to run away.

She fell asleep with her head on her folded arms on the windowsill. The rain splashing on her face woke her up. Stiff and unhappy, she got up, leaving the window open. She didn't care if it rained all over everything and ruined his whole stupid house. She climbed into bed determined to find a time to talk to Jess.

"*Do* you love him, Jess?" she asked in an impassioned whisper. The two of them were in Tillie's bedroom.

"I told you no."

"Then listen!" Her hands fastened to Jess's arms. "We've got to run away, Jess! We've *got* to!"

"What do you mean?" Jess looked alarmed.

"It's going to be winter soon, and he'll be closing his house and going back to New York. Do you *want* to go with him?"

"I don't know, Till. He takes care of us . . ."

"You don't *love* him. There's no reason for us to stay. I hate him! I won't go back to New York with him. We've *got to run away!*"

"We can't!"

"We can, too! It'd be easy."

"Oh, God, Tillie. I need time to think about this. I can't just decide . . ."

"Listen!" Tillie interrupted. "We don't have a whole lot of things to carry. And it's only five miles to the highway. We can walk it easily. Once we get to the highway, we'll get a ride and be on our way. That's all there is to it."

"To where?"

"Somewhere. I know! Canada. We'll go to Canada."

"Tillie, this is crazy! We can't just run away to Canada."

"Sure we can. Why not? It's no good here, it's no good in New York. And it isn't even very far. If we get a ride with somebody going north to the border and just keep on getting rides, we'll be in Canada in no time."

Jess looked at her, seeing in Tillie's eyes the promise of renewed closeness; impressed by Tillie's imagination and resourcefulness, but confounded by this idea of running away. What was the point to it?

"Why do we have to talk about that? If we want to leave, no one's going to stop us."

"Oh no!" Tillie argued fiercely. "You'll let him talk you out of it. I know you. If you don't do this, I'll run away! I will! I'll go where you'll never find me and then you'll be sorry!"

"*Tillie!*"

"You'll see!" she threatened hysterically. "I won't stay here, and if you tell him we're going, I'll run away. I'll *know* if you tell him. I'll know and I'll do it!"

"You're being unreasonable. I know you're not happy, and I'm sorry. But there's no *reason* for us to do something so silly. Mr. Land isn't going to force us to stay if we don't want to. I don't *understand* this, Tillie!"

"I don't trust you!" she cried. "If you tell him, he'll talk you out of it. I heard him talking to Flora about boarding schools. He thinks he'll send me off to some boarding school and you'll stay with him. If you talk to him, he'll convince you. I know he will, and I won't go to any boarding school. *I won't go!*"

"You don't know that he was talking about sending you away to school. You don't know anything of the sort. He might have been talking about the school he went to."

"Oh, yes, I do so know! I heard them talking."

"Why do you hate him so much?" Jess asked, keeping her voice lowered. "He hasn't done anything to you."

"No! But you, you made me do that. Taking your clothes off and making me do it, too. And he'll get you to make me do other things. *I'll run away!*" Her face had turned dark red and the words crowded into her mouth. She wanted to shout about the things she knew the two of them did in his room and had to clench her teeth to keep herself from admitting she knew.

"Tillie," Jess whispered, putting her arms around her, unnerved by Tillie's rigidity. "Listen to me, angel."

"I won't listen! I won't!"

"All right," Jess sighed. "All right."

"All right what?" Tillie asked suspiciously.

"All right, we'll go." She got to her feet and stood looking at Tillie, thinking it was all wrong. But she believed Tillie would do something dangerous if she didn't agree. I've got to talk to Flora, she thought. She had to get away from Tillie and try to think.

"I love you, Jess." Tillie wound her arms around her sister's waist. "That's all that's important, isn't it?"

"I love you, too," Jess responded mechanically, unwinding Tillie's arms, close to hating her for forcing her into this, but too afraid Tillie would carry out her threats to do further battle with her. Her brain was suddenly busy with images of Tillie running off, getting herself picked up by some man, raped perhaps. "Go to sleep now."

She got Tillie tucked in, turned off the light and went down the hall. Every part of her had gone tight and hard in protest against Tillie's threats and her insistence upon the two of them running off, like criminals. She went past her room to knock at Flora's door.

Flora was seated against four large pillows on the bed, going through a sheaf of photographs.

"Could we talk for a moment?" Jess asked from the doorway, dry-mouthed.

"Sure, sweetheart. C'mon over here and sit down." She made room for Jess on the side of the bed. "What's up? You look a little blue."

"It's Tillie. She says if we don't run away together, *she'll* run away from me, from here."

"Run away?"

"I know. It's ridiculous. But she insists. If I talk to him, she says she'll go. She doesn't want me to tell him because she thinks he'll talk me out of leaving."

"She's right, though, huh?" Flora said sympathetically.

Jess nodded, unhappily. "I don't want to go," she said,

about to cry. "But if she runs away..."

Flora reached out and dragged Jess over against her, stroking her hair.

"Listen to me," Flora said. "You listening?" Jess nodded against her shoulder. "She's got you cornered. And it was me, I'd believe her, too. Because she's got a hell of a mind of her own, your kid sister. It was me, though, I'd do it all differently. But it's not me, it's you. So, I guess you've got to do it. I just want to ask you one thing."

Jess sat away from her. "What?"

"You planning to spend the rest of your life doing what your sister wants and not what you want?"

"No, of course not."

"Don't be too fast with your answers," Flora cautioned. "Think about it."

"Flora, if she ran off... I'd die. It would be all my fault if anything happened to her. I promised my father I'd take care of her. We don't have any close family. Tillie's the only person in this world who really belongs to me. If I loved him..."

"I know. That'd be a whole other story."

"The thing is," Jess said, feeling shy all at once, "I'm going to miss you, Flora. And I've got to say good-bye now, I guess. If I say anything tomorrow, she'll know I've told you and..."

"When will you go?"

"I don't know. Tomorrow night, I suppose. What difference does it make? I'd better get back. He's waiting for me."

It was a big mistake, Flora thought sadly. *You let her run you this way now and she'll wind up running your whole life.* But maybe not. Maybe Jess would find someone to belong to and get some distance from her sister. She believed Jess had the decency to tell Jamie the truth.

"How're you fixed for money, sweetheart?"

"I have some," Jess said, studying Flora's face as if attempting to memorize it. *I love you,* she thought, stricken, choking up. "I'll never forget you, Flora." She got up and hurried out, down the hall to her own room, quickly throwing off her clothes in order to bathe before going in to Jamieson.

He was so gentle and kind. He made her feel so good and had given her such a lot. She just couldn't walk away without saying something, but didn't know how to say it and, instead, to her chagrin, began to cry, which at once upset him.

"What's wrong, Jess?" he asked.

"We've got to go," she murmured, getting herself back into control. "Please listen and don't say anything for a minute. All right? Tillie's miserable and she's threatening to run away unless I run away with her. I know it's stupid. I know that. But she's my sister and I . . . So we're going to do it. Except I can't just go without saying good-bye. You've got to do something for me, though. You've got to pretend you don't know, that I haven't said anything to you."

"You're going to carry out this charade?" he asked disbelievingly. "Pretend you're running off to pacify your sister?"

"I've got to. Please understand."

"You don't have to go, Jess."

"But I *do*. I don't want to. I really don't. You've been so good to me. Please don't try to talk me out of it. You could, and I'm so afraid of what she might do."

"I love you, Jess. Don't go."

"Please don't do this!" she begged. "It's so difficult for me."

"You're right," he said very quietly. "It is stupid. Why are you so afraid of her?"

"Please! Just give me your word you'll go along, pretend you know nothing about it."

He looked at her closely, seeing how torn she was and yet how determined. "There's no reason on earth, Jess," he said reasonably, "why the two of you can't simply leave in broad daylight."

"She doesn't want you to know," she explained. "And if we do that—of course I want to do that—she'll know I've told you. She'll . . . make my life miserable. Please," she said helplessly, "do this for me."

"Where will you go?" he asked, finding it hard to accept any of this.

"I don't know. Canada. I don't know."

"Wait awhile. At least until times are better."

"I can't. I said I'd do it."

"Jess!" he said angrily, his voice rising. "It's sheer idiocy!"

"I know, I know."

"Nothing I say is going to change your mind, is it?"

"No. I'm sorry. No."

He sighed and sank back against the pillows, very slowly

saying, "I would give anything in the world to have you love me the way you love your sister."

"I have to go. I promised."

He shook his head. "You're so young. You've got everything confused. Canada." He shook his head again. "I think you'd better go back to your own room now, Jess."

Miserable, she nodded and moved to get up. Dismissed. She hated it. It made her feel like a worthless fool. All because of Tillie. Damn her! Damn her!

"You'd better take this," he said, and reached for his billfold to pull out several notes and pushing them at her. "You're going to need it."

She wanted to refuse but couldn't, wished she had the courage not to accept his money, but took it and said, "Thank you," galled by her weakness, her powerlessness.

"Go on, go to bed!" he said sharply.

Sick with shame, she returned through the connecting door to her room, to sit on the side of the bed clutching the twenty-five dollars he'd given her, sobbing helplessly, thinking, *We're quits now, Tillie. I'll always love you, but I'll never forgive you for forcing me into this.*

She fell asleep finally and dreamed of running through the darkness in a downpour, searching through the underbrush for a Tillie she'd lost through her own negligence and needs; screaming into the darkness, "Come out! I'll kill you! Come out! I'm afraid! Come out and stop doing this! Don't do this to me!"

At breakfast, Jamieson announced he was driving into New York for several days. Tillie, at Jess's side, watched him closely, looking for any hint that Jess might have told him, prepared—if she saw any evidence—to run off at the first possible moment; keeping a close watch, too, on Jess, waiting to catch her eyes connecting with the old man's.

At last, he got up to go. Jess rose to walk out with him. Tillie started to say something and Jess grabbed hold of her by the arm and marched her into the downstairs bathroom, where she held her hard against the wall, whispering, "Stop this! If you don't stop watching me like some kind of jailer, I swear to God I'm going to kill you! I'm doing what you want. We're sneaking out of here tonight like a pair of damned idiots. You've *got* what you wanted. Now leave me alone! I'm going out to say good-bye to him. He'll expect me to because he doesn't know I've been stupid enough to let you talk me into this whole mess. Go play somewhere and *leave me alone!* And don't think for one minute that I'm so dumb I don't know what you're doing. I know! The only reason I'm going, aside from having promised to look after you, is because I don't love him enough to stay. I hate you right now, Tillie. So, just get out of my sight and stay out until it's time for us to leave!"

Cowed, Tillie nodded. Jess released her, flung open the door, and ran through the house in time to see Jamieson driving away down the road, going far too fast for her to catch up and say good-bye. I've hurt him, she thought. I've hurt him terribly. I'm sorry. I'm so sorry.

Conspicuously minus Jamieson, they were all in the living room after dinner. Jess was fidgeting, frustrated by this demented plan of Tillie's. Flora was chain-smoking, drinking neat brandy, and passing around prints of some shots she'd taken several days earlier. Jess sat looking at her, thinking with a pang how deeply she was going to miss her. Flora's warmth and interest were lavished unstintingly on people she liked, and she'd chosen to favor Jess with large quantities of both. A few days earlier, she'd asked Jess to pose. "I don't usually do people," she'd explained, "but I'd like a few shots of you for myself." Jess had gone with her, clad only in a thin nightgown and coated liberally with citronella against the mosquitoes and gnats, into the overgrown area down near the lake to pose while Flora took one picture after another, going very quickly through several rolls of film. Unlike Jamieson, who took many minutes, sometimes even as long as an hour to set up every shot, Flora had instructed her to move here, move there, all the while clicking away, moving with surprising speed and grace for a woman her size. Posing for Flora hadn't been the aching strain it was with Jamieson. And the prints, she now saw, accepting a sheaf of them to look at, seemed far more arresting, far more like her than any Jamieson had done.

"May I have this one?" she asked Flora of a backlit shot of herself by the morning-damp willow at the water's edge. "I like this very much." The photograph would help her remember Flora and the way she'd looked taking these pictures, the captivating purity of her concentrated features as her eyes—

like the camera lens—had fixed on her. The knowledge that she'd probably never see Flora again made her feel sick.

"Sure, sweetheart," Flora agreed expansively, with a smile. "I've got half a dozen prints. You like that one, huh?"

Jess took a second, longer look at the photograph. "It looks like me," she said simply. And Flora smiled her agreement. She was right. It did look like her and more than that, it had managed to capture the contradicting look of Jess's physical frailty—the backlit body very slender through the nightgown—opposed to the awesome determination in her eyes and the set of her jaw. The shot, like the girl herself, was winsome, enticing; the image of a homeless child desperate for a place where she belonged, Flora thought, yet resolved not to show it to the world; so desperate to belong she'd allow herself to be coerced into an imbecilic flight into the night by the one person alive she cared for. It was all so sad and silly, this business of Tillie blackmailing Jess into running away. She hoped fervently that Jess wouldn't wind up selling her soul for the sake of the child, because if it was left up to Tillie, Jess just probably might. Don't be intimidated, Flora wanted to tell her. You've got the strength to deal with her if you'd just stop and see it. But no, she thought. Jess was too young and insecure, too in need to risk forfeiting the one sure love she had.

At last, people started to go off to their rooms. Flora was one of the first. Jess said good-night to the remaining few in a voice that sounded unnaturally loud to her own ears, and then she went upstairs.

Tillie had fallen asleep, although she'd insisted she'd stay up and wait. Jess had to shake her several times to rouse her.

"Come on, Tillie. We're going."

"What time is it?" she asked, yawning, her cheeks flushed from sleep.

"Just after eleven. We can leave any time now."

"I've got to go to the bathroom." Tillie got up and went out dopily.

While she was gone, Jess went back to her room to gather up her few things and give the place a last look-around to make sure she hadn't forgotten anything. Then she went back down the hall to Tillie's room, holding her breath, her eyes stealthily checking every door, prepared to have one or all of them fling open and people pop out laughing at her. Nothing happened.

She set her things down just inside the door to Tillie's room, then double-checked in there, too. Finally, she went to stand by the window to wait for Tillie to come back. She was taking ages and it made Jess nervous. If they were going, she wanted to get on with it.

It was windy and very dark, with only a thin, pale quarter moon. The heavy boughs of the firs lurched in the gusts. She was glad she'd bought Tillie the new sweater in town the week before. She'd need it tonight. It was bound to be cold walking. What was taking her so long? One more minute and to hell with it, they wouldn't go. She looked at the door, debating whether or not to go after her, when Tillie let herself in, appearing to be on the verge of either laughter or tears.

"It's happening!" she announced momentously, wide-eyed.

"What's happening?" Jess asked impatiently, still furious with her.

"*It*," she said meaningfully, looking quite unlike herself.

"It?" Jess stared at her for a moment, then understood, and all her love for her sister came rushing back. "Oh, Till," she sighed, embracing her. "You scared me half to death."

"It scared *me*," Tillie said, clinging atypically, not sure whether or not to cry. "Took me a few minutes to figure out what was happening."

"Well." Jess took a deep breath. "It's a big day. I guess we'd better get you fixed up."

"Oh, that's all right," she said, regaining her composure. "I've got everything. I've been waiting, you know."

"No, I didn't know." Tillie was prepared for every eventuality, Jess thought, awed; while she herself was prepared for very little. "How do you feel?"

"Kind of a little stomachache, but I'm all right," Tillie said, dropping to her knees to peer under the bed. "I lost a sock and can't find it."

"It doesn't matter. You'd better put on your sweater." Jess moved toward the door, looking down at her own feet. She was wearing low-heeled, comfortable shoes and a plain cotton dress, with her hair drawn back in a ribbon; all set for a long walk. She picked up Tillie's suitcase, signaling to Tillie to carry Jess's smaller, lighter bag, then switched off the light, opened the door, and looked out into the hallway. Not a sound. With Tillie behind her, they tiptoed along the landing to the stairs, avoiding the risers they knew creaked, holding their breaths going down.

In the front hallway, Jess paused beside the old oak coat-rack, hesitated a moment, then lifted down the ancient sweater Jamieson liked to wear in the evenings. She draped it over her arm and opened the door. He wouldn't miss it and it wasn't really like stealing. Once outside on the porch, she turned to discover Tillie wasn't with her. Her heart seemed to stop beating as her mouth fell open. What was happening now? She heard a skittering, whispery sound, and then Tillie came hurrying through the door waving the flashlight she'd taken from the kitchen.

They were well away from the house before Jess dared speak. "Don't ever do a thing like that again without telling me! You nearly gave me heart failure."

"But we needed the flashlight," Tillie countered sensibly. "We'll never be able to see where we're going without it."

Knowing she was right, Jess swallowed her upset and smiled thinly saying, "Just don't turn it on until we get a little farther away from the house."

Sitting in bed having a last cigarette and yet another look at the prints, Flora heard a slight noise and was instantly alert. She sat very still, listening. It was definitely the sound of a door being opened and closed, not the typical, matter-of-fact sounds of someone moving about the house, but a subtler not-meant-to-be-heard sound followed by another, heavier one— a closing door. The front one this time. With a grunt, she got up and made her way over to the window. Unable to see anything outside, she lumbered back to the bedside table to turn off the light, then went again to the window. Now she was able to distinguish two forms moving quickly away from the house.

So that's it, she thought. There they go. She felt an immeasurable sadness that there was to be no final good-bye. Poor Jess. Take care of yourself and don't let that kid take you over a hundred percent. Poor Jamie. He'd be brokenhearted. It was just as well she was there, she thought, going for another cigarette. He'd need someone to help him get over this.

Sitting on the side of the bed with the light on again, she wondered where they'd end up and wished she knew where

they were going so that contact wouldn't be lost altogether.
She'd have to deal with the problem of Jamie's reactions, but
there'd be all the time in the world for that. What a pity Jess
couldn't have loved him. *It's a rare thing to be so well loved
in this world. And he does love her.* Was Jess someone capable
of valuing the love she inspired? Flora wondered. Was she
even aware that she inspired it? Flora didn't believe she was.
Jess didn't think she was lovable.

She looked back toward the window as if those two slight
shadows might still be moving about below, already missing
Jess, knowing she'd think about her for a long time to come.
Funny to think of missing someone who was loved by the man
you loved. But that's the way I am, she thought, smiling wryly,
the ash from her cigarette dropping unnoticed to the floor. Fat
Flora, the pushover, the human sponge. Absorb anything.

Jess set down the bag while she pulled on Jamieson's
sweater. It smelled of him. She felt suddenly dizzy, breathing
in everything familiar she was abandoning. The night was cold,
as she'd expected, and she hadn't anything else that was as
warm. Her eyes filled with tears as she bent to retrieve the
suitcase. Tenderness for the man swept over her as it had so
often in the months she'd spent with him. She grieved over
the absence of good-byes, of the shabby aspects to this ludicrous departure she'd been badgered into. Taking Tillie's hand,
she said, "This is the first and last time you'll ever pull anything
like this. We're not going to talk about it. I just want you to
know that you've made me do something I'm very ashamed
of. Don't *ever* try this again, Tillie. Because next time you do,
I'll let you run away."

◊ Six ◊

What they hadn't anticipated was the lack of traffic on the highway. A secondary road, it was used in the summer mainly by tourists—those few with sufficient money to run a car—and by the locals the rest of the time, with occasional trucks passing through.

They waited by the roadside for close to two hours, and saw only two cars and one truck go by. Tillie was beginning to complain of being tired and of having a stomachache, and sat on her suitcase with her head in her hands, half-asleep, while Jess stared down the road in the dark thinking, angrily, that this was the stupidest thing she'd ever allowed herself to be talked into. She wanted to drag Tillie by the hair back to the house, throw her into her bed, and then go peacefully to sleep. Instead, she continued gazing down the dark road, trying to decide if there mightn't be some advantage to this feeble attempt at running away that she'd so far failed to see. The only one she could think of was that the Depression mightn't be so bad in Canada and there might actually be jobs to be had there.

"Let's keep on walking," she said, at last, going over to pick up Tillie's suitcase, starting off with a grumbling Tillie tripping along after her. Every step Jess took simply served to convince her this was a lunatic mistake. She turned, prepared to tell Tillie they were going to go back, when she heard something approaching and turned to see the yellow glow of headlights in the distance. She stopped so abruptly that Tillie—all but sleepwalking—marched right into her and came to with a jolt, exclaiming, "Don't do that!"

"There's something coming," Jess said, setting the bag down, deciding that if they didn't get a ride now, they were going back.

The headlights picked out two girls standing by the edge of the road. A little one maybe twelve, and an older one eighteen or so, maybe younger, maybe older. Hard to tell. The older one had her thumb out. René wasn't going to stop, but as he drove past, he took a quick look at the older girl. Plain-faced, hair tied back, a too-big cardigan over a cotton dress. Their eyes connected for a second. He wanted to keep on going but his foot was already hitting the brake and, glancing into the rearview mirror, he could see the two girls running toward him. Jesus-damned thing to do! he cursed himself. He didn't have no time for picking up passengers. He had to get the damn apples up to the canning factory outside Trois Rivières, get the truck unloaded, pick up the next load and head west for Toronto with the new consignment. Could be anything from tins of salmon to peanut butter or lumber. He never knew, didn't care, just kept on schedule, delivered when promised, and went out after the next job; had to, otherwise he'd never finish paying for the damn truck that was already falling apart. Should've known better than to trust Marie's brother-in-law. That man, he'd steal the communion wafers from a priest's hand, he thought he could make fifty cents.

He reached across to open the cab door and the older one helped the little one inside, saying, "Thank you so much. We've been trying to get someone to stop for hours. My sister's exhausted and I was beginning to think we'd have to . . . spend all night out here." She'd never admit that she'd been prepared to give up and go back.

"Where you going, eh?" He checked the rearview mirror automatically to see if any traffic was coming up on them. Of course there wasn't. It was why he always traveled this road: because he could make such good time. They didn't have the police to sit out at night waiting for speeders.

"Canada!" Tillie announced. Having revived, she bounced into the middle of the seat as Jess climbed in and closed the door.

He lit a cigarette before putting the truck in gear, and took another quick look at the older one. It hit him right in the gut and he couldn't figure it out. No great beauty, for sure. Except—taking yet another quick look—she seemed to look better every time he set eyes on her.

"Where you going in Canada?" he asked Tillie, working the gears to get to top speed fast, hoping to make up for those few lost minutes stopping to pick them up. "Big country, eh, *petite*?"

"I suppose it is," Tillie agreed thoughtfully.

"Toronto," Jess said. Her soft, husky voice fell like an invitation, a caress against his ears.

"Toronto, eh? You want a smoke?"

"No, thank you." Jess smiled, trying to make herself unaware of the smell of him. It wasn't a very big truck and the cab seemed crowded with the three of them in it, even though Tillie took up little room.

"Comin' from where?" he asked.

"New York," Tillie said quickly, lying so effortlessly and adeptly that Jess stared at her for a moment or two, wondering how many times Tillie had managed to lie to her in that same skillful fashion.

"One fine place, New York, eh?" he said, rolling down his window to tip out his ash. The fresh air displaced his potent male smell inside the cab. "I been down there one time with a load of Canadian whiskey. Back nineteen-twenty. Crazy place, those days." He laughed happily and Tillie joined in. Jess smiled, enjoying the way he talked. His accent was sing-song, thick as glue; the words ran up and down in musical cadence.

"You're French?" Jess asked, causing him to laugh again.

"*Oui, oui*," he answered, a flat nasal quality to the vowels making the words sound like "way way." "Come from Trois Rivières. You know it?"

"No," Jess said.

"Three rivers," he translated. She smiled again, not knowing why. "Hey!" he said, startling Tillie who'd been on the verge of falling asleep. "You want some apples? You're hungry?"

Tillie said, "Yes, please," and he reached behind to the shelf at the rear of the cab, feeling around before coming up with three apples held in one huge, darkly tanned hand. "Go on!" he urged, holding them out. "Good. Not the ones from back there." He jerked his head rearward indicating the load behind them. "Macs, these. Good, sweet apples."

Tillie said thank you and took one. Then his hand reached past her to Jess, who felt obliged to take one although she didn't want it. He set the remaining apple in his lap, at the top of his thighs. Jess looked away out the window. He finished his cigarette, flipped the butt out the window, and began eating the apple in huge bites; a big man with big hands and a big appetite.

Her apple half-finished, Tillie fell asleep against Jess, who eased the apple from her hand and settled her more comfortably, then sat back waiting for whatever would happen. He seemed a kind enough man, a good-natured one. He wouldn't hurt them. And what would it matter if he expected her to pay for this ride?

"Are you going back to Trois Rivières now?" she asked after a time.

He nodded, his eyes on the road, aware peripherally of her breasts and her narrow knees, trying not to be.

"And after that, where do you go?"

"I pick up a load, eh? Go on down to Toronto." He turned to look at her, a slow examination that kept his eyes off the road for such a long time she was afraid they'd have an accident. But finally, when the pressure of his eyes was reaching unbearable proportions, he redirected his gaze to the road, saying nothing for several minutes.

"How long," she asked, "will you stay in Trois Rivières before starting out for Toronto?"

"One night. I go on home, see Marie and the kids, clean up, sleep some, start again day after tomorrow." See Marie, get rid of this big need he suddenly had.

"Marie is your wife?"

He grinned, showing splendid teeth. "Twenty-one years," he said proudly.

"You don't look old enough to have been married that long," she observed truthfully, without intending to flatter.

"Thirty-seven years old. I marry at sixteen."

"Sixteen? How old was your wife?"

"Fourteen."

My God! Jess thought. It sounded like something that happened in the hill country of Tennessee or maybe in Appalachia. "How many children do you have?"

"Eleven," he stated, even more proudly.

"*Eleven?*"

"You think that's a lot?"

"Well, yes, I suppose I do."

"Hah!" he said so loudly she thought Tillie might wake up, but she didn't. "Eleven, that's nothin', eh? Me, I got the fifteen brothers and sisters. And Marie, she got thirteen. Her sister, Clothilde, she got seventeen kids already."

She couldn't imagine it. "You must like children," she said lamely, appalled by the idea of having such huge families to look after.

"Good kids," he said seriously. "Good family. This little one, she's the only sister?"

"Yes, that's right."

"And where's Mama and Papa, eh?"

"They're dead." The words fell heavily, echoing inside her head.

"Oh! This is too bad. So now you take care of the little one?"

"That's right."

"And you think you go down to Toronto. What you gonna do in Hogtown, eh?"

"Hogtown?"

He smiled again, his teeth very white in his dark face. "It's what they call it."

"My father used to say it was a very beautiful city. He was there once, on business."

"Not beautiful like Montreal or Quebec," he said. "But it's not so bad. She sleeps real good, eh?" He tilted his head at Tillie and Jess's stomach clenched. It was bound to happen soon now. Her breasts felt burned by his eyes, her body wanted to take control of her. She fought herself, and kept her eyes away from the sight of his strong-looking, muscular thighs.

"She's tired out. It's been a big day for her." It had been an important day, she thought, tenderly stroking Tillie's hair. Till wasn't a little girl anymore and it felt strange to think of that.

Skinny woman, he thought, watching her long hand stroking

the little one's hair. But real nice up on top, and not so plain in the face after all. He struggled to ignore his body, but as the miles slid away under them, it was becoming increasingly difficult to do.

She dozed off, lulled by the motion of the truck.

The girls were so worn out, he hated the idea of having to wake them, and as they approached the border he decided he'd wait, see who was on, it might be someone he knew. Luckily, it was Marie's second cousin, Claude, and Claude was happy to get a sack of apples to take home.

"Who're the girls?" Claude asked, leaning to peer past René at the sleeping sisters.

"Cousins of Marie, eh? You know her sister, Clothilde?"

Claude nodded, unable to keep track of all the cousins and their children.

"The little one's Mathilde, and the big one's Jacqueline. They been down picking the apples. A favor to Clothilde, I bring them home."

And that was that. Claude said, "Okay," and thanked René for the apples and René drove on. A few miles into Canada, he stopped to fill up with gas, relieved himself out back of the boarded-up café, then took off again.

She came awake to his hand on her arm and opened her eyes asking, "Where are we?"

"Comin' on to Waterloo," he whispered.

"Are we in Canada yet?" she asked, wondering why they were whispering until she realized the truck's engine had been turned off.

He nodded, whispering, "Come on," as he lifted Tillie's head off Jess's lap. "She sleeps good, eh? Come, we talk."

Talk? Feeling resigned and yet anticipatory, she got the cab door open and climbed down. Her legs were stiff after all the hours cramped inside the small cab. The truck, she now saw, was parked at the side of the road, well in under the trees. She looked up to see the thin sliver of moon hidden behind gathering clouds. It was very dark and she stood for a few seconds trying to adjust her eyes.

He made a sound between his teeth and she followed it around to the rear of the truck. He'd opened the gate and climbed up, then turned to reach for her, lifting her as if she were weightless up into the back with him. He sat down on the tailgate and she sat, too, leaning back against the banked

sacks of apples. The wind had risen and the leaves on the trees
made a dry rattling noise as she sat very still, waiting, her
heart beating too quickly so that she felt suddenly quite warm.
She expected him to make some move or gesture toward her
and she waited, the tart-sweet, starting-to-rot smell of the apples filling her nostrils. A match flared and he lit a cigarette.
She exhaled slowly. He wasn't going to touch her.

He was so tempted it was like a pain in his throat, and for
a minute or two he thought recklessly that the truck and Marie,
the kids, the whole world could go to hell, he'd just stay here
forever parked by the side of the road sitting beside this girl.
But that was crazy, he told himself.

"What'll you do, eh, you get to Toronto?"

"I don't know," she answered softly.

"You tell the truth. What you think you gonna do?"

"Whatever I have to do," she said hoarsely.

"That's what I'm thinkin', eh?" He shook his head. "Some
times, some bad times we got."

"I don't want to leave my sister alone. She might wake up
and be frightened."

"Me, I'm thinkin'."

"About what?"

"Hard times. Maybe I help you."

"Help me how?"

"Don't know yet. I'm thinkin'," he repeated.

They sat silently side by side for several minutes. Now that
she knew he wasn't going to touch her, she was no longer
afraid. And realizing this, she wondered what it was she'd
feared. Not this man, she decided. No, not him. He was kind
and unhurried. It was herself she feared, her body's ability to
take her over. But it hadn't happened and she was able to relax
at René's side, feeling safe in his presence.

He flicked away a cigarette, then jumped down and stood
with his arms extended to help her to the ground. Holding
her—her body so small under his hands—he thought how easy
it would be, how easy . . . but no. Releasing her, he said, "You
wanna wait one night, I take you and the little one with me
to Toronto."

She said, "Yes, all right. Thank you very much," and hurried up front to the cab, to lift Tillie back on her lap, wrapping
Jamieson's cardigan around Tillie to keep her warm. She turned
to look over as he climbed into the driver's seat, feeling an

affinity toward him. After a moment, she turned away to look out the window at the graying dawn sky, sudden sadness like a rock in the center of her chest. Why did he have to be married and have all those children? Why couldn't he be single and free to see to her needs? Still, he'd get them to Toronto and it wouldn't cost anything. And that was something. She felt very respectful of him for not having made any move toward her.

She was aware of towns whose signs they hurried past in the dawn: Roxton Falls, Vale, Wickham, Drummondville, a sizable city. Ste. Brigitte, Ste. Monique. Then they crossed the St. Lawrence River to arrive, finally, at the outskirts of Trois Rivières.

He pulled the truck over in front of a weather-beaten, dreary-looking cabin court near the highway, saying, "I get a cabin for you. The two of you eat, sleep. I come in the morning, six o'clock. You be ready, eh?"

She paid a dollar for a cabin with damp-feeling bedclothes and cobwebs decorating the rough-raftered ceiling. There was a bathhouse with a toilet out back, and just up the road, a sad diner, empty but for the owner and his wife, who served them a surprisingly delicious breakfast of pancakes and fried apples for twenty cents a plate. Tillie ate like a robot, her eyes gritted half-shut with sleep. Jess steered her out of the diner, back down the road, took her to the bathhouse and got herself and Tillie showered, then helped Tillie change the pad, mystified and awed by the sight of Tillie's blood. It made her sister seem someone quite new and different to her, someone no longer attached to her in quite the same way as before. At last, they climbed into the sagging old metal bed and fell asleep.

Jess awakened just past midnight to creep carefully from the bed and stand looking out the window at the highway, trying to understand her life and the things that were happening. She thought about the truck driver, his generosity and warmth. He hadn't touched her. He'd wanted to, she knew, but he hadn't, as if she was someone he considered special. It made her want to cry.

She'd wanted him.

Tillie slept unmoving as Jess got dressed and decided to go up the road to the diner to pick up some food and bring it back. In a few more hours they'd be on their way again, to Toronto.

She walked up the road, thinking about wanting him, wondering, Is this the way women are? Do they live hiding the way they feel about men, about the things they like to do with them? Hurrying back down the road to the cabin with the paper sack of food, she tried to picture her mother with her father, knowing with certainty that her mother hadn't ever felt the way Jess did. There had to be something very wrong with her, she decided. A perfectly nice man, he'd been good to Tillie and her and she kept thinking about lying down under him. Was it a sickness? It felt like one.

At four-thirty, she roused Tillie, made sure she ate both the sandwiches from the bag and drank all the milk, then—still feeling impatient and angry with her, and guilty for it—escorted her with the flashlight out to the bathhouse to use the toilet. While she waited for Tillie to get washed, she tried to sort through her feelings, but couldn't, and gave up trying. By five forty-five, they were sitting on the front steps of the cabin waiting when he rolled up in the truck.

"Hey!" He laughed, still jovial and good-natured, darkly tanned with a mouthful of stunningly white teeth, exuding health and well-being. "You sleep good, eh?"

Tillie said, "Hi," as if he were an old family friend, then climbed up into the cab as if she'd been doing it all her life.

Smiling apologetically, he put his hand on Jess's arm, saying, "I am René."

The spot where his hand lay on her arm throbbed and the little voice in her head began to chant, love me, love me, love me. "My name is Jess," she said, then turned and got in beside Tillie, distraught by her immediate and powerful desire for this man.

Nicolet, Louisville, Maskinonge, Berthierville, L'Assomption.

He was thinking. "When you get there, eh, and maybe things they don't go so good?"

Tillie turned toward Jess.

"Yes?"

Tillie turned toward René. Jess asked him with her eyes not to speak of the things she might have to do in order to live. His eyes answered that it was too bad, but he understood and wouldn't talk in front of the little one.

"Maybe I think of something," he said, then fell silent.

Laval. Bypassing the outskirts of Montreal. Pte. Claire. Vaudreuil. Alexandria.

"We come into Ontario now." He smiled at Tillie, then lifted his eyes to Jess's.

"How much longer will it take to get to Toronto?" Tillie asked.

"By morning," he told her. "We stop to eat in a little while." He looked at his pocket watch. "Couple hours."

What *would* they do when they got there? Jess wondered, facing up to the logistics for the first time. They'd have to find a place to live, and that would cost money. She couldn't afford to keep them in a hotel for more than a few days. But, providing costs weren't too different from New York, she'd be able to get a small flat, get Tillie enrolled in school, and then . . .

"Is it just as bad up here as it is in the States, the Depression?" she asked him.

"Bad everywhere, eh? I dunno about Toronto. Maybe pretty bad from what I see but not so bad as Montreal."

Kemptville, Smiths Falls, Perth, Arden, Kaladar.

Tillie seemed deeply asleep. Jess and René crept out of the cab and around to the rear of the truck, to sit while he smoked a cigarette and she waited out his thoughts.

Finally, he said, "I know a man. He's the boss, eh? Maybe I can do something." It didn't feel good, what he was thinking. He didn't like the idea of sending this girl to Cotton, but Cotton had the money and he liked the girls. And René couldn't think of anyone else who didn't beat the girls, then kick them out with no money. Cotton paid. But still, to send this girl to any man . . . It bothered him. He hoped maybe things would go good and she wouldn't go see Cotton.

Jess said, "All right. Thank you very much."

And for a few seconds, René hated the world, hated everything that was happening, that forced people like this girl to do anything to keep alive. He wished he'd never picked her up, never had to know and like her. Then he wouldn't have had to care what was to become of her.

Tillie sat up and looked around. Finding herself alone, she was afraid. She listened to the whispers coming from the back of the truck and told herself they were just talking, that's all, talking. She closed her eyes, curled into a tight little ball on the seat, and slept again.

Tweed, Peterborough, Oshawa, Pickering.

"I know a hotel downtown," René said. "Not so good, eh, but not so bad either. I take you there."

Toronto seemed like a very big city. "'Cause of the lake," he explained. "They build out to the east and west, up north."

They traveled through the outskirts for some time before at last moving into the downtown area. He pointed out things, but both girls were so dazed from lack of sleep they scarcely noticed, and only came awake when he stopped the truck in front of a small, seedy-looking hotel. A hobo, asleep in the dawn in the doorway, looked like a bundle of discarded rags.

"I come right back," René told them, going into the hotel and returning a few minutes later, smiling, saying, "All set! I got you a good price. You stay here, sleep an' I come see you before I go. You wait, eh? I come back later."

Jess paid two fifty, was given a heavy brass room key with a large oval brass tag attached and told to take the elevator. Neither of them had the strength to do more than put down their bags and struggle out of their clothes before crawling into the bed. Jess's dreams were filled with motion and black roadbeds slipping past beneath her. She came awake to the sound of tapping at the door and told Tillie to go back to sleep as she pulled on a cotton robe, pushed the hair out of her eyes, and went staggering over to open the door a crack. René was there, summoning her out into the corridor.

"You get dressed, eh? We eat, talk."

"All right."

He waited in the corridor, feeling anxious. She was just a kid, he thought. Maybe she'd get work and keep away from Cotton. It bothered him even to think about giving her Cotton's name. Not that Cotton was a bad man. From what he knew of him, René didn't think he was so bad. But to send this girl . . .

Jess threw on her clothes and went to the door. Tillie slept soundly.

Downstairs in the coffee shop, he ordered coffee, hamburgers, and chips for both of them. Then he lit a cigarette, took out a piece of paper and, looking reluctant, handed it to her. "This is Mr. Cotton, eh? And this is where you go to.

You get the streetcar right out there on the corner of Dundas, and you ask the conductor to let you off at this here street. You find it real easy. You call up this number, talk with him, say you come. You say my name and he knows about you."

"Knows about me?" she asked, confused.

"Me, I talk with him, eh?" He felt bad now and couldn't look at her, but stared down at the tabletop. "He pays five dollars," he said quietly. "An' he got plenty of friends. He pays good for good girls. An' he don't hurt you," he added, looking at her again. "Anybody ever hurt you, you let me know."

She wanted to swallow but couldn't and sat watching him finish his hamburger in four big bites.

"Maybe it's like insurance, eh?" he said sadly. "Things they don't go so good, you go see Cotton. But maybe they go good, you don't have to see him."

"No, I'll get a job."

"Me, I hope so." He paused, looked down at his empty plate, then slowly back up at her. "I give you the address, you let me know how you are?"

"Yes," she agreed and watched him print out his address on the reverse side of the paper with Cotton's number on it. She didn't want him to leave, but if he had to go, she wished he'd take her and Tillie with him.

"Marie," he said, "she don't know English. So you send to me a letter, say how you are. Okay?"

"Okay."

"I gotta go. Gotta truckload bacon to go to Montreal by mornin'. You say good-bye to the little one, eh? And me, I see you soon again."

She nodded, staring at the piece of paper in her hand. "Thank you so much, René," she said, unable to breathe properly. "For everything."

He got up and stood beside the counter close to her and she knew he wanted to touch her, say something important. But he shook his head, then smiled, said good-bye, and hurried away.

Her voice still unusually deep, she called out, "Good-bye," then jumped up and hurried back to the room.

Tillie was sitting on the bed, her arms folded around her knees. "Where'd you go?" she asked. "You've been gone for ages, you know." Her tone was accusing, her eyes filled with suspicion.

"I was downstairs talking to René about a friend of his who might have a job for me."

"What kind of job?"

"I don't know," she said shakily, wanting to run after René and beg him not to leave. "Tomorrow," she announced, drumming up a smile, "we'll go out and find a place to live."

She *would* get a job! She wouldn't be a whore! There had to be a job she could do, had to be. God! She didn't want to be on the streets.

All the way to Montreal, he thought about her, trying to shake the bad feeling he had from giving her Cotton's number and telling Cotton about her. She'll be okay, he told himself. A smart girl, and strong, she'd find some work to do. Anybody hurt her, though... He didn't know what he'd do. The idea of anyone harming her made every muscle in his body go tight. Funny thing, he thought. In his mind, she stood real small. And the little one, she stood real big. It didn't make no sense.

TWO

Toronto

1936–1944

◇ Seven ◇

From the outset, Jess loved the city. It was impressively clean and, on the surface, gave few hints of the Depression that was, she all too soon discovered, bad here, too. There were no tall buildings to speak of, certainly nothing in the way of sky-scrapers, no brownstones, no bright lights, no glare of bars and late-night restaurants, no sudden and alarming night noises, and few sleazy districts. Everything seemed intentionally un-derstated, even drab, but she found it appealing. The single-family brick houses, each with its meticulously tended front garden, and the trees lining residential streets lent the city the air of a continuous suburb rather than that of a large metropolis. She and Tillie walked about the city, getting some sense of the place and Jess found herself more hopeful of establishing a life here for the two of them. It seemed to be an extraordinarily safe place where, she was certain, no harm could come to her; there was something old-fashioned and secure about the city and the people she saw, and a lack of the anger, even violence that she'd become accustomed to in New York. There were no spontaneous and bloodthirsty fights on the streets, no drunk-en displays of outrage. On one occasion when she saw a drunk on the street, within a minute or two, two policemen arrived and discreetly escorted the man away. The street was again quiet and people continued on their way as if the man had never existed.

Within a week, she'd managed to find a pleasant, relatively inexpensive flat in a huge old house on Palmerston Boulevard just below Harbord. The street looked like a vintage film set, its huge, gracious houses set well back from the sidewalk and its globe-topped standards lining both sides from College at the southernmost end to Harbord at the north. Every house had flowers and shrubs and the windows gleamed.

Their flat consisted of two adjoining rooms on the third floor, with a kitchen and bathroom a few steps down the hall. The rooms were large and joined by sliding doors that slid silently closed, separating the bedroom from the living room and offering Jess privacy in the evenings once Tillie had been put to bed.

With Tillie enrolled in school, Jess set out in search of work. She bought copies of the Toronto *Star* and *Telegram* and folded them open to the want ads. The ads took her all over the city and as she rode the streetcars, gazing out the windows and absorbing the details of what she saw, she promised herself she would, once she landed a job, take time to walk these streets at her leisure.

There was a feeling about the city she couldn't articulate, something peaceful and yet quietly exciting; it seemed to be a growing place, one where she, too, might grow. When she had to ask directions, she was warmed by the politeness of the policemen she encountered. They were very reassuring and contrasted startlingly to their shabby New York counterparts. She came to realize that all the policemen were at least six feet tall, although they looked even taller in their English bobby hats; all were of either Canadian, English, or Scottish extraction, and all were unfailingly courteous.

She also discovered that the city had all sorts of rigid rules about drinking, business hours and, primarily, about Sundays. Everything except churches was closed up tight on Sundays. Like some deserted model town on a drafting table, the city with its neatly laid-out grid of streets was empty on this day except for the new Canadians who chose to go out walking. It was impossible to buy even an ice-cream cone. Movies were closed, there were no Sunday newspapers, not even drugstores were open if one needed some emergency medication. Sunday, all too plainly, was a day of enforced rest. One either went to church or walked through the parks or simply stayed at home and waited for Monday.

Beneath the facade of prosperity the city was suffering from the Depression. For Jess, this was all too frighteningly evident in the lack of jobs. Applying first for the clerk-typist positions, she stood in long lines of men and women. She told herself she had just as good a chance as any of these others and wasn't going to be scared off by the crowds of people.

The first four places asked her name and address, her typing speed, and her experience, then shook their heads when they discovered she hadn't worked before and dismissed her, calling out, "Next!" She tried three more businesses before deciding it was hopeless.

Next she tried the factories. The lines were even longer. On the sixth day of trying, she was told by the dour-looking man in charge of hiring to step to one side and fill out the form he handed her. She was going to get a job. Giddy with excitement, she completed the form and gave it to the woman the man had indicated. The woman took her to the personnel department, where they sat across from each other at a desk while the woman read over the application. When she arrived at the line marked place of birth, the woman stopped, asking, "You're American?"

"Well, yes," Jess said.

"You've worked in Canada before?"

"No, I haven't. We just arrived, you see."

She was a round, pleasant-faced woman and seemed genuinely apologetic when she said, "I'm sorry, dearie. Even if you'd worked for years, I couldn't give you a job. You'd be lynched by the crowd in line or by our employees who've got friends and family out there. I'd like to help you. I'm sorry."

"But I've got to work. I've got to eat just the same as they do."

"Of course," she commiserated. "But this *is* their country, after all, isn't it?"

Jess tried the downtown restaurants, going into every one of them from Bay and Adelaide all the way up to Yonge and Bloor, asking for anything—a waitressing job, even dishwashing. There was nothing.

By the afternoon of the fourteenth day, she was desperate. In a diner, a cup of coffee in front of her, she sat down to

examine her options. Her money was all but gone. She
wouldn't be able to pay this week's rent, or buy food. She
stared at the cup of coffee, able only to think about her father
and how it must have been for him. A successful businessman—not someone inexperienced like her—who had gone out
day after day, for months, years, hearing, "No, sorry," time
after time. It was that constant rejection that had killed him,
she now understood, destroyed his pride, his self-esteem, and,
finally, his life. After two weeks of it, she'd already lost what
little self-esteem she'd had, and all of her optimism.

She was too much of a coward to keep on this way, she
admitted to herself, stirring sugar into the coffee, stirring mind-
lessly, the spoon making whirlpools in the liquid. Why couldn't
there be someone to look after her, instead of her having always
to look after Tillie?

Coward, coward!

She found the paper with Cotton's number in her bag and
sat studying René's careful printing, thinking about him and
how kind he'd been. Like insurance, she thought grimly, leaving the untasted drink on the counter and going to the telephone.

He was in his middle fifties, fat, with a very red face. He
wore a gray pinstripe suit and a white shirt with a collar so
tight it seemed to be choking him. His expression altered oddly
when he opened the door to her, but then he seemed to quickly
regain himself and smiled, saying, "You're gonna have to get
a telephone."

As he locked the factory door, his hands were trembling.
He was remembering Melinda Richmond for the first time in
forty years and feeling the hatred welling up inside him. He
was a little boy again, playing in the kitchen of the big house
in Rosedale, while his mother—her face flushed and damp—
hurried back and forth between the stove and the table, preparing the Richmond family's dinner. Melinda was standing
in the doorway, blond and shiny, looking as if someone had
polished her, and saying, "Mummy says to say there'll be four
more this evening." Then, having delivered her message to the
cook, she looked over at the cook's little boy, Stosh, asking,
"Want to come up and play?"

Elated, he'd raced across the kitchen toward her. She was
so beautiful and he loved her. He loved her smooth, glossy
blond hair and her shining skin, her beautiful clothes and her

small, perfect features. She'd taken hold of his hand and led him through to the front of the house and up the stairs to her pink and white bedroom where she'd made him play the patient while she played the doctor. He'd loved her.

Then they were both fifteen and she was tall and beautiful and very cool with her delicately pointed nose and uptilted chin. He was standing before her with his hair wet-combed and his best clothes on and she was laughing at him and exclaiming, "Me? Go out with you? You don't know your place." The laughter gone, her face suddenly ugly, she'd said, "I wouldn't be seen on the street with you. I'd be embarrassed." And he'd stared at her, trying to understand. They'd been friends always, had played together year after year in her pink and white bedroom. But no, they'd never been friends—she'd simply used him. The understanding came in a rush of hatred and he stormed away.

Now, here was Melinda again. She had black hair, not blond, but she was the same girl, looking down her nose at him with that same rich-bitch attitude, thinking too much of herself by far. Well, he'd see about that, he thought, almost drunk with the thought of revenge. "Don't like mixing my business with pleasure," he said, smiling. "Midday's better, too. Always works, taking long lunches. New in town, eh?"

"Yes, that's right." She didn't like it there, didn't like him. He scared her. There was something about him, about the way he looked at her.

"C'mon, we'll go in the back." He led the way through to a small storage room containing half a dozen metal filing cabinets, a battered old leather sofa, and a small table holding an ashtray overfull of cigarette butts. He saw the distaste she couldn't hide and thought, Think you're too good for it, eh? We'll get past that soon enough, fix you up so you never think you're better than anyone. He despised her aristocratic bearing and what he thought of as her condescending height.

"It's okay with you," he wheezed, removing his jacket and placing it carefully on one of the cabinets, "you'd better be on top. Too fat," he said, grinning, "for the other." He'd be able to watch her while she did all the work, the skinny, uppity bitch.

So this was how it was going to be, she thought, setting her handbag on another of the filing cabinets. Her insides had turned to lead, fear pulsed in her throat, her temples. She thought about Tillie, hoping that this wouldn't take long and that she could get home before Tillie did.

He looked her over, licking his lips as if she were a pork roast he was about to devour. She couldn't bear the sight of him, clad in his shirt and tie, naked from the waist down, white like a slug, still wearing his shoes and socks. He sprawled on the sofa with his head propped up on the arm, indicating with an unmistakably crude gesture what he wanted her to do. She didn't think she could do it and took as long as she could removing her clothes. She felt chilled, her stomach was churning, and fear pounded now in her ears. When she was finally naked, his hand took hold of her wrist and forced her nearer, down on her knees on the floor. She closed her eyes as he roughly fondled her breasts, hearing him murmur, "Beautiful tits. Goddamned beautiful pair of knockers. C'mon, honey. I haven't got all night. Let's have a little help getting started, eh?"

Do it, bitch! he thought, feeling a rare sense of complete power.

She looked down knowing what she was going to have to do, positive she couldn't. His hand squeezed her shoulder, then her breast. Hard. Then it came back up over her shoulder, along the length of her neck and around, pressing her head down. She closed her eyes again, opened her mouth. He pushed, hitting the back of her throat, and she gagged, her eyes filling with tears.

He allowed her to stop at last, saying, "C'mon, get up here," reveling in the shock dulling her eyes as she got unsteadily to her feet, knowing she'd never done a bit of it before. He wanted to see her cowering, wanted to see her reamed out like one of the old Jarvis Street pros, wanted to break her spine; hating her for being one of the ones who, just because they'd had some money once upon a time, thought they could lord it over everybody else, thought they could still do it even when they didn't have a pot to piss in and lived eight to a room in shacks in Cabbagetown. Well, the tables had turned and he had the money now. No skinny snob bitch was gonna think she was better than Stanley Cotton.

With powerful, bruising hands, he held her thighs open and touched her in a way that made something at the very center of her being go cold. His eyes and mouth wet, he watched himself aiming into her. Then his entire face creased with satisfaction as his hands on her hips brought her down on him. Roughly, he directed her up and down, then, having established the rhythm, he fastened his hands to her breasts with painful strength. He smiled, his eyes on her face. "C'mon now, harder."

He made her work, made her feel shame so deep and thick it seemed to clot her blood and stop her heart. And when she thought perhaps he might be finished, that she might be free to leave this place with some small remnant of feeling left for herself, he said, "Stop a minute now and turn around."

"What?"

"Same thing, just turn around."

Her chest constricted with unshed tears, she turned so that she was staring at his feet as he once again took hold of her hips and thrust himself back into her. Then he did something that made her mouth open around a scream she didn't dare to emit.

"Just you relax now, honey," his too-soft voice told her. "You go all tight 'n' you'll just hurt yourself. Okay now. Okay." His free hand clutching her breast, he sent her back into motion.

"Wanna learn how to relax," he went on, glorying in this, "get used to it. Lotta the boys're ass men.".

It hurt, it burned, it would never end. But she wouldn't cry. All of them wouldn't be like this. She'd just do it until times got better and when they did, she'd never do it again. She'd get a job, make herself forget she ever allowed anything like this to happen to her.

It was over at last. He patted her on the hip, moved her off him, and wiped himself with his handkerchief before pulling on his clothes. Then he sat on the sofa waiting for her to get dressed. She had more guts than he'd thought. Breaking her down was going to take some doing. A party might do the trick. Five or six of the boys for one hell of a party.

She wanted to kill him, to tear his face off. As she got dressed, he watched and raved about her breasts and how she'd have to learn to take it any way it came, otherwise the competition would put her out of business. She couldn't listen, refused to. He stood up, gave her five dollars and his card saying, "You let me know right away when you've got a tele-

phone, eh? I'll put the word out with the boys. Always on the
lookout for a good girl for a party. You'll do just fine so long's
you remember to relax."

Mute with loathing, she pushed the card and money into
her bag and fixed a smile on her mouth. She wasn't sure why,
but she was determined not to allow this man to see her anything
other than composed, in control, and dignified. She was aware
that her straight shoulders and unflinching eyes somehow antagonized him. Why? Hadn't she done everything he'd wanted?

"You know how to get back?" he asked.

"Yes, I do. Thank you very much."

Her politeness, too, galled him. A party for sure, he decided. Fix your damned ass for you.

She left the building, at once got her bearings, and headed
back toward the streetcar stop, feeling desperate to bathe, to
wash him off her body, to soothe her damaged flesh.

She sat at the rear of the nearly empty streetcar and cried
soundlessly almost all the way to her stop, trying to think how
she could possibly do this for a living, and wished despairingly
there were some other way, knowing there was nothing else.

It didn't take long. Inside a year, she'd managed to establish
herself, discreetly distributing her telephone number and building a small clientele of regulars. She despised herself. Slowly,
steadily, she turned off her feelings until she arrived at the
point where her performances were strictly that, nothing more.
She set off for each appointment with a lump in her stomach,
playing a game in her mind that revolved around the tale that
this wouldn't be forever, that the Depression was bound to
end, and when it did, she'd get a proper job and forget all this.

Because she was both constantly frightened and by nature
sensible, she limited the number of her clients, keeping it
always at a dozen or so. She set down firm rules, making it
clear from the outset that she was available only during Tillie's
school hours and that she would not accept telephone calls
from clients after four P.M. She had a horror of Tillie's inadvertently answering a call from one of her men, or of her
coming face to face with one. They were never invited into
her home.

She worked Monday through Friday, not accepting more
than two appointments on any given day, two being sufficient
to push her to the self-hate level without sending her right over

the edge. At first, she was able to earn between fifty and eighty dollars a week, depending on the generosity and pleasure of the men. She refused to state a price. To her mind, her refusal to discuss money or ask for it made a difference in her status; it allowed her to play at believing she simply received gifts of money in return for certain favors. To her somewhat bitter amusement, her clients accepted this little eccentricity as a sign of her "quality."

In the evenings and on weekends, she erased from her mind all knowledge of her work, and either concentrated on fixing up the flat or shopped for new clothes for herself and Tillie. With her sister in tow, she investigated the city. She discovered Shopsy's and an acquired taste for kosher food, and Laura Secord chocolates, and Murray's Restaurants, where a decent meal could be had very inexpensively.

Sometimes, to escape reality for a couple of hours, she went to Shea's to see a movie. The first time, she was surprised to find the huge, rococo theater almost full. It seemed she wasn't the only one seeking escape. She'd shrugged off her coat and settled back, becoming aware that the people around her were speaking in different languages. As the theater darkened, she turned first to one side, then the other, hearing Italian to her right, French to her left, and, directly in front, some Asian language. Being surrounded by so many other foreigners made her feel less of a stranger and she relaxed. An organ rose out of the floor before the stage and a spotlight picked out the organist, who was filling the place with "Let Me Call You Sweetheart" in booming tones. Then the spotlight went off, *News of the World* appeared on the screen, and the organ vanished down through the floor.

After the news came a short, three cartoons, and, finally, the feature began. She came out of her involvement with the film when one of the characters on screen mentioned Toronto. A self-conscious titter ran through the audience. Even the non-English-speaking people reacted. She couldn't understand why; back in New York there was never a bit of audience reaction to the mention of New York in a film. But Toronto had been named, and everyone in the audience was reacting as if his name had been announced over a microphone.

In the months following and over the years she again saw displays of this self-consciousness and came to cherish the rather childlike enthusiasm of the people who lived here. They

appeared sophisticated and cultured, but every so often something would happen and they'd act like excited children at a
garden party, exclaiming ingenuously over some matter of local
pride, or some Canadian's success in "The States," as they
called it, or overseas. She found this endearing.

She was particularly enchanted with the Allan Gardens and
happily spent entire afternoons wandering through the greenhouses and admiring the flower beds along the paths. She
ignored the occasional "rubby-dub"—as the locals called
them—stretched out on the park benches, sleeping off a drunk.
Nothing could diminish her pleasure in the park and it seemed
to her something of a gift that in the heart of the city there
should be thirteen acres of grass and flowers. But it bored
Tillie. She wasn't interested in that, or in the Art Gallery, or
the Museum, or Fort York which had been recently restored,
or the Parliament Buildings with their gray stone and roofs
gone to green, or the masses of flowers and trees lining the
broad boulevard of University Avenue. Nor was she interested
in MacKenzie's house on Bond Street, old and very English;
or in the University of Toronto campus and its winding paths
and colleges of stone with their elaborately arched entryways
and leaded glass windows. And the "rubbies" offended Tillie.
The sight of one of them shambling toward her sent her into
an angry panic that had her grabbing at Jess's arm and crying,
"Don't let him come near me!"

"He's harmless," Jess told her again and again. But Tillie
reacted with indignation and fear each time she saw one.

As for the evenings out, Tillie merely tolerated the excur-
sions to Hart House, where she squirmed through the Hart
House string quartet's selections. She was put to sleep by the
plays Jess insisted she come along to see at the Royal Alexandra, with its Old World charm and its balconies and red
plush seats.

Tillie did, however, adore Sunnyside Park. Clutching a
handful of tickets, she'd ride the merry-go-round again and
again and, when Jess refused to accompany her, went alone
on the Flyer—a white-painted, alarmingly rickety-looking
roller coaster—and came off begging to be allowed to go on
again. For an entire afternoon, she went from one ride to the
next, pausing only to consume two cones of chips and an ear
of corn before asking if she could, please, ride the Flyer one

last time. Throughout, Jess sat on one bench or another waiting for Tillie to return.

Tillie was also delighted when, on a bitterly cold Saturday morning in November, they stood on Queen Street with thousands of others watching Eaton's Santa Claus parade, applauding the elaborate floats and tapping their feet to the music of the many marching bands all smartly turned out in uniforms ranging from Scottish kilts to brown military.

It seemed to Jess that, at twelve, Tillie should have been somewhat more sophisticated in her tastes. But having failed to inspire in Tillie an interest in music and the theater, Jess gave up and left her to her favorite radio shows, and began going out alone once or twice a month. Frequently, she went for long solitary walks. She could go for miles, for hours, and encounter only buildings and monuments and houses that pleased her eye and satisfied something inside her that had been searching for a permanent place to settle. She intended to make her home here.

Her feelings about her "professional" life, however, were deeply dark. The only good aspect was her freedom from worrying about money. She had it, saved it, and used it to treat herself to good clothes and evenings out. Money was what her life was all about: cash to pay the rent, to keep herself and Tillie well fed and clothed. She'd grown completely dependent upon her work as the means of maintaining their new standard of living. And when Tillie announced that she hated the local high school and would die if she couldn't go to Branksome Hall, an exclusive girls' school, Jess gave up any immediate hope of being able to exchange this mode of earning for some other. She wanted Tillie to go to a good school, wanted to cloak the surfaces of their existence in respectability.

If Tillie ever wondered how Jess was able to provide them with all they now had, she never mentioned it. She simply accepted the changes as they occurred and concentrated on her new circle of friends, on her growing passion for expensive clothes, and on her cache of secret dreams for her future. When tempted—rarely—to speculate on Jess's daytime activities, she reminded herself of how they'd lived in New York, and was able to avoid any need for speculation. Jess was taking care of her as she always had and always would. Yet in a remote place in her brain, she did accurately suspect in just what fashion Jess was managing to provide for them; to stop herself thinking about it, she'd leave the house to go shopping, or get together with her friends. Anything not to have to think about it. Jess was doing what she was supposed to do: taking care of her.

Jess, on the other hand, was compelled daily to face the dangers of her life, not just its illegality, but also its continuing erosive effect on her feelings for men and for herself. She adhered unwaveringly to the rule that her clients provide the accommodations, in that way ensuring that she didn't come to the regular notice either of the authorities or of hotel staffs. She was fanatically careful, all too aware both of the scandal that would arise from her arrest, and of the disastrous effects her public exposure would have on Tillie. She knew that were she ever found out, Tillie would be taken away from her. And she couldn't risk that happening; she lived in constant fear of it.

She felt a certain very real power over the majority of the men she serviced, combined with a sense of disgust and contempt for them. And she'd been right about one thing: No man had been more frightening and hateful than Cotton. She would never forgive him for the party he'd arranged, the most horrifying experience of her life. Still, when he called her, which he did regularly, she made a great effort to be firm but most polite in declining. "I think not," she said each time. "But thank you for calling." She knew that he was enraged by her refusals despite the fact that he kept his voice soft, his manner unctuous.

The only man for whom she had any real feeling was René. She saw him two or three times a year when he had a truckload of something or other that brought him into the city. She'd come to think of him as a friend, her only one, someone she could talk with, to whom she could express her fears. Even though he knew how she earned her money, he still treated her as he had from the start: as someone special and worthy of his respect. René would hold her arm on the street when he took her downtown to a steamy little Italian restaurant on Dundas Street. He would always introduce her to everyone in the place as "my Yankee friend." There would be Chianti, the smell of Parmesan cheese, and steaming platters of rigatoni, or fettucini, or spaghettini. The owner, a small man wrapped in a white apron, would hold out a chair for Jess, smiling. "Come, you sit down, we get you the peppers, uh? You still like the peppers?" Everyone in the place would smile at her.

With René she developed a deeper fondness for the city and for the people who made it, sometimes, such a warm, happy place. With René she was able to pretend there was someone in her life who cared. Alone at home at night, she conceded that it was all a game, nothing more. But René kept a small part of her feeling for herself intact, because he held her arm, removed a cinder from her eye, smiled at her and said, "You keep on sending me the letters, eh?" and because he hugged her at each visit's end and said, "Me, I love you. You take good care." Whether or not he meant it was of no consequence whatsoever. She needed someone to say the words.

She had a list of regulars with whom she played another, different pretending game, learning the rules as she went along, making them up to suit each situation. There was the law professor from Osgoode Hall, the banker from the Royal Bank of Canada, the surgeon at St. Michael's hospital who, in return for rather odd favors rendered, provided her with free, improvised medical checkups in hotel rooms. There was the alderman, and the public school principal from New York, and the owner of a clothing factory on Spadina. There was the optometrist, the lawyer, and the jeweler who specialized in cutting diamonds. Her regulars. The majority of them were generous. She, in turn, detached herself from the hateful reality of what she'd become and catered diligently to their sexual interests, never revealing her loathing for them and for herself. Her feelings safely placed to one side, she imagined that these men were just one man, someone who loved her and would, in time, take her out of this life. At the start of each encounter, she formally told new clients, "I have only one rule. You have to say you love me." And, to humor her, all of them did. They thought she was a little mad but only slightly embarrassing in her bold requests for declarations of caring. She didn't care about their embarrassment or what they thought of her as long as she was able, at some point, to close her eyes and hear a male voice whispering, "I love you." It enabled her to go on.

To compound the pretense, she arrived for each appointment fresh from the bath, perfectly groomed and carefully made up, dressed in the best clothes she could afford. She insisted there never be an unseemly rush to bed but rather an initial brief period of conversation and then an exchange of caresses that led to bed. She achieved no physical satisfaction from these encounters and at most felt only that peculiar, remote tenderness she'd felt for Jamieson Land. She was able to be tender out of guilt because she couldn't like them—they were contributing to her self-hatred. She had to apply vaginal jelly before leaving the house for an appointment because her body had lost its lubricity. She bathed several times a day but never felt quite clean. She felt, finally, like a tenant in her body.

Despite the high cost of Tillie's tuition, after three years of careful saving, she had enough money to make a down payment on a small house on Brunswick, just north of Bloor. It was an unpretentious little place, with two decent-sized bedrooms upstairs and three rooms down. At the rear was a tiny grassed area, and in front were the expected flower beds. The rooms were sunny in the morning, rather dark by afternoon, and somewhat gloomy at night. Still, she'd managed to get them a place of their own. She and Tillie moved. The telephone number remained the same.

With the start of the war, there were visible differences in the city. The Island Airport was called Little Norway in reference to the Norwegian exiles who'd taken up residence on the island and who were training there to fly Tiger Moths and Ansons. There were blackouts that took place only after everyone had been advised well in advance that they were to occur. People seemed more in need of alcohol than before and many of Jess's clients appeared with a bottle of bootlegged liquor tucked in their briefcases. Jess heard them complain, endlessly it seemed, about the idiocy of the liquor permits, the restrictions, and the foolishness of having to stand in line for an hour at some Liquor Control Board outlet waiting to get one stinking bottle and then having their permits checked and punched.

There was some talk of police brutality and the joking rumor that there was a Jew on the police force but no one was able to find him. There was rationing of butter, sugar, meat, and gas. There were no new tires, and few canned goods to be had. Nevertheless, the economy improved and Jess's income rose accordingly.

She prevailed upon Harry Allenby, her lawyer client, to

assist her in naturalization proceedings and by the end of 1941, with Canada well into the war, she and Tillie were both Canadian citizens, despite some small initial difficulties arising from their having arrived in the country without proper documentation. Harry was more than happy to accept a year's "visiting" privileges in return for his efforts.

Occasionally, she'd stand at her bedroom window looking down at the gardens of her neighbors, sometimes seeing someone at work on a Victory Garden, carefully weeding and watering; she wished she had the time to do something as simple and gratifying as tending to a garden. She felt there was far more between her and her neighbors than just a few panes of glass and low fences. And although she heard her own laughter upon occasion and felt herself smiling, her smiles and laughter seemed to emanate from some mechanical source within her that operated independently of her brain.

She took note of the increasing number of uniforms to be seen on the streets and even accepted the odd serviceman as client when one of her regulars was unable to keep his appointment. The uniforms in no way altered her feelings about the men, or about herself.

By 1943, at twenty-five, she wanted to stop. She could feel herself slipping steadily and could think of only one way to save herself: to go out of business before her self-hatred ate her sanity. Late at night while Tillie was upstairs asleep, she spent hours gazing into the living-room fire trying to think of some way out. But there wasn't any, not with Tillie due to start at the University of Toronto come September, fully expecting Jess to foot the bill.

One afternoon she tried to remember how to type, using Tillie's portable Remington, and gave up feeling frustrated when her fingers refused to find the keys. She sat down with the want-ad sections of the papers every evening for a solid week, looking at the jobs offered, and going salaries. At forty dollars a week—the wages for a top secretary, which she was not—she wouldn't be able to keep Tillie in school for a month, let alone provide for both of them and meet the mortgage payments.

She gave up. A victim now to her own fondness for comfort, for fine clothes, for good cuts of steak, and silk underwear, she saw that the only way to keep on having them was to continue cultivating her clients and their preferences. She began considering, quite objectively and coldly, various means of taking her life, going over them all as a kind of mathematical exercise, plotting down to the last detail how she'd do it, under what circumstances, and calculating how many more months she'd have to wait before the twenty-five-thousand-dollar life insurance policy she'd taken out would cover suicide and pay the money to Tillie.

She still daydreamed about someone coming along to rescue her, yet she knew full well that no respectable man went about affiancing prostitutes, however well-bred they might once have been. It was particularly true in this city where such store was placed on appearances. No matter if there were rot and maggots underneath, so long as the surface was polished and healthy, everything was just fine. Marriage would never happen, but she couldn't stop thinking about it. Her daydreams took place on a level where her onetime fondness for men remained intact and she had some measure of feeling for herself. The fantasy was the only thing remaining between her and death. There was nothing else. She felt she'd fulfilled her obligations to Tillie, made good the promise. Tillie was old enough now to take care of herself. And the insurance money would safely see her through until she got married or started some career. Her love for Tillie was still there and flared up occasionally, causing her to believe that, whatever the cost, it had all been worthwhile. Tillie was grown. She was pretty and well-groomed and on her way into her future.

On other occasions, she looked at Tillie and felt nothing at all for her. At those times she saw her sister as the one responsible for her evolution into a whore, responsible, too, for the loss of Jamieson Land and of Flora, the one female friend she'd had in her adult life. She continued to think about Flora and miss her with something very close to pain. Sometimes she even held mental conversations with her, trying to supply for herself Flora's good sense and warmth. In part, she sustained herself on the memory of that brief friendship.

She was finding it close to impossible now to face herself in the mirror and had developed the trick of focusing solely on that part of her face she was making up, unable to regard the whole for fear she might finally let go of the string of her sanity and put her fist through the glass. It was only a matter of time, she thought resignedly, before it all ended one way or another.

At eighteen, Tillie had essentially two things on her mind: first, to get into the university as fast as she could so that, second, she could get married. It was all she wanted, and she had an image of the perfect man that she carried about with her, ready to recognize him anywhere, under any circumstances. The scenario of their romance was written in her brain, down to the last detail, complete with flowers and gifts and the surging admiration this young dream-man would have for her because she was Tillie and unlike any other girl he'd met. She was more than pretty and knew how to dress to perfection, how to present herself to her best advantage. She was neither unduly vain, nor particularly ruthless. She was simply ready and waiting to be found by love, to play according to all the rules, as she understood them, and to win herself a husband, home, and family.

It did occur to her to wonder—on that daytime, innocent level where Jess's real occupation had neither place nor identity—why Jess continued to remain single, why she never dated and always went to her concerts and plays alone, or with Tillie because Tillie didn't happen to have anything better to do. But when she tried to discuss it with her, Jess was always vague, invariably saying, "Eventually I'll probably get married."

In mid-September 1943, Jess received a telephone call one afternoon from what she assumed was a new client. She listened as a deep, well-modulated voice explained that he'd secured her number from Harry Allenby and asked if she might be free that same evening for dinner.

"I'm sorry," she said, "I'm never free in the evenings or on weekends."

"I think you misunderstand me," the voice said with a hint of humor. "I do mean *dinner*. I've heard some interesting things about you and it would be my great pleasure if you'd come out to dinner this evening. Unless," he added, "you have other plans."

She wanted to say no, but something made her accept. And the voice then sounded very warm, pleased.

"Shall I pick you up?" he asked.

"I'd prefer not. If you'll tell me where, I'll meet you."

"The Imperial Room at the Royal York, at eight. My name," he told her, "is Woodrich. Sanford Woodrich. I'm looking forward to this evening."

The Royal York? It seemed so public. Confused and a little mystified, she went upstairs to look through her closet, trying agitatedly to decide on an appropriate dress. She chose a very plain, very expensive black crêpe de chine floor-length dress with enough of a neckline to show a bit of cleavage without being in poor taste. Luckily, Tillie had a date, so there was no need to feel she might be neglecting her in going out for an evening.

A friend of Harry Allenby's. She fingered the fabric of the dress, thinking. The name Sanford Woodrich sounded familiar but she couldn't connect it to anyone or anything. She looked ahead to the evening with trepidation and misgivings.

Tillie, out on her first date with Prescott Ames, decided almost at once that he was the one she wanted to marry. In the final year of study for his master's degree, he was very good-looking, intelligent, witty, and charming. He also came from a fine family and lived at home with them in Rosedale, a neighborhood of splendid houses, many of them with large grounds; an area that had been a secluded bastion of wealth and propriety since the mid-nineteenth century. Everything about Press, especially the family in Rosedale, was perfect.

While they were still on the streetcar, on their way down to Chinatown for a meal, she was already visualizing their children, the house they'd have, the parties they'd give and the people they'd know. People met and fell in love every day, she mused, admiring his cleanly honed profile, and now it was their turn.

As if he sensed the direction of her thoughts, he turned, smiled, and took hold of her hand. She felt thoroughly gratified. It was all going to work out exactly to plan.

"What will you do after you graduate?" she asked, basking in his presence.

"I'll be going into the family business," he said. "It's been arranged for ages."

"What sort of business?"

"Stockbroking."

"Oh! You're going to be a stockbroker?"

"Someday. I've got to start in on the ground floor, work my way up, of course."

"Of course," she agreed, mentally complimenting him on his practical nature as well as on all his other obvious attributes. Stockbrokers made a lot of money, she reflected.

"What're your plans?" he asked.

"I'll teach," she said, giving her standard, practiced lie. If all went well, they'd be married in no time and she wouldn't have to do anything but be a wife and a mother.

"Anything in particular?"

"English, probably."

"Oh!" He looked thoughtful for a moment, then smiled, giving her hand a tug, saying, "This is our stop."

It was such fun being out with a handsome young man when there were so few around nowadays. There were at least twenty-five girls to every boy at the university, and most of the boys who were around were either boring grinds or misfits of one sort or another. She wondered why Press, who was so evidently in good physical condition, wasn't off in the army.

"I was asthmatic as a kid," he explained, as they walked downtown after dinner, trying to decide which movie to see. "They wouldn't take me because of it."

"That's too bad," she said sympathetically, privately delighted. "Is it serious? I mean, do you still have it?"

"Haven't had it in years."

"Did you want to go overseas and fight, all of that?"

"Sure," he said quickly. "It's embarrassing, always having to explain to people why I'm not over there." He changed subjects adeptly, with a smile, saying, "Tell me about Matilda Greaves. I don't know a thing about you except that you're about the prettiest girl I've seen lately at the old U. of T."

"Well, I was born in New York. My parents died when I was little and my sister Jess has been looking after me ever since. We came up here almost seven years ago. That's about all there is to it."

"How old's your sister?"

"Twenty-five."

"And what does she do?"

"Do?"

"Work at, you know."

"Oh. She doesn't." Adept herself, she now changed subjects

in order to avoid the question. She'd found it safer and easier,
through a few innocent allusions, to allow people to believe
she and Jess were living on inherited money. By saying nothing
and wearing a properly sedate expression, she left others to
draw their own conclusions. And since she was such an obviously dignified and well-brought-up young woman, not to
mention a graduate of Branksome Hall, they quickly came to
the conclusions she'd intended them to.

"What did your father do?" he asked.

"He was a stockbroker."

"Well, no kidding! Isn't that a coincidence?"

"Isn't it?" she concurred happily.

They decided not to bother with a movie after all and walked
hand in hand through the crowds of Yonge all the way up to
St. Clair, then cut across over to Spadina Road to have a look
at Casa Loma at night. They walked slowly past the older,
elegant houses of the area and then on home. Knowing Jess
was out for the evening and feeling very mature and in control
of the situation, Tillie decided to invite him in for coffee—this
being something self-possessed women did with men in movies
and which she'd never before had an opportunity to do.

"Sure, okay," he accepted.

He was highly complimentary about the house and the furnishings, making straight for the photograph of Jess on the
living-room wall near the bay of the front windows, asking,
"Is *this* your sister?"

"That was taken just before we came here," she told him,
embarrassed as always by the picture, wishing she could convince Jess to take the damned thing down and stick it up in
her bedroom or someplace where people couldn't see it. And
never mind Jess's saying that the photograph reminded her of
Flora.

"You don't look at all alike, do you?" he observed, unable
for several moments to look away from the portrait.

"No."

"She's very . . . different-looking, isn't she?"

"I suppose she is," she said, bored by the topic of Jess.
"She's funny. Sometimes she can look really beautiful. And
other times she looks almost ugly."

"I know what you mean," he said, finally turning away.
"I've known a few people like that. They're fascinating."

"I'll make the coffee," she said, dismayed at the idea of his finding Jess fascinating.

"I'll come with you, keep you company. I like kitchens."

"So do I," she lied with a smile, leading the way. "Isn't that something?"

They sat in the kitchen drinking their coffee, chatting. Then he looked at his watch, pushed his empty cup away, and as an afterthought got up to put it in the sink. "Hate to, but I'd better push off."

She walked with him to the front door hoping he wouldn't leave without asking for another date, unsure of herself for the first time all evening.

"Thanks for the coffee," he said. "It's been swell. And I like your house. Your sister's got really good taste."

"Thank you for the dinner," she said, wishing he'd shut up about Jess, thinking she'd die if he didn't ask for another date.

"I'll talk to you during the week." He gave her a quick kiss on the lips and was gone. All her dreams of their perfect future together collapsed around her as she went back to the kitchen to clear away the coffee things. What had she done wrong? she wondered, reviewing the evening, unable to find a fault. But he had said he'd talk to her during the week. It wasn't as if he'd gone off without saying anything. Plus a good-night kiss. He hadn't tried to go any further than that, either, like a lot of the other boys she'd dated. No, she hadn't done anything wrong. You just couldn't rush these things, she told herself, going upstairs to get ready for bed. By the time she turned out the light, she was back to arranging the furniture in their house in Rosedale.

"This is very kind of you," he said, upon her arrival at the table. The headwaiter discreetly moved off. "On such short notice."

"I had no plans," Jess said with formality, wondering why she was there.

"To be candid," he said, "I saw you at the Royal Alexandra a few months ago. You were with another girl, a fair-haired one."

"My sister."

"She's very pretty. Jess—you don't mind if I call you by your first name?"

"No."

"Good. I have to confess I was very intrigued by you."

"Intrigued?"

"The way you carried yourself, your clothes. I'm impulsive at times. I went to quite some lengths to find out about you."

"Why?" she asked, frightened.

"I liked the look of you. I was curious." She was frightened, he realized. She thought he planned to harm her. He was going to have to go more slowly than he'd thought. But how beautiful she was, and the sound of her voice, the look of her hands. "Will you have something to drink?" he offered.

"I . . . some tea, perhaps?"

"Of course." He signaled to the waiter.

"Is there some reason for tonight?"

"Only pleasure," he answered. "To talk and get to know one another."

"You know who I am, what I do?"

"That is *not*, most definitely, why I invited you out tonight."

"No?"

"No." He smiled. "I thought we'd have dinner, talk, dance if you like." He nodded in the direction of the bandstand. "A date," he summed it up.

"A date," she repeated, completely at sea as she, too, looked over at the band, then allowed her eyes to trail over the faces of the people dancing before turning back to his eyes.

"To get to know one another," he said simply.

"I don't care to dance," she said tentatively, her hands cold, her body hot.

He laughed. "Fine! We won't dance. Let me order your tea."

He gave the waiter their order and the waiter bowed slightly, gave Jess a thin smile, and stiffly moved off. He seemed, Jess thought, like dethroned royalty in his erect bearing.

Lighting a cigarette, he said, "There's nothing sinister about any of this, I promise you. I have the impression you think there is."

"You're a friend of Harry's?"

"More of an acquaintance, really. We've run into each other here and there. He was the only one I knew who knew you. I asked a number of people about you."

"God!" she exclaimed softly, feeling even more overheated in the black dress.

"It really is all right," he assured her.

Her eyes were again on the waiter, following his progress as he directed an underwaiter bearing a silver tray with tea things toward their table. Glancing again at this man opposite, she decided he reminded her of René. An older, smoother, infinitely more sophisticated version, but with a similar magnetism and aura of good health and benevolence. She began relaxing slowly, believing he'd meant what he'd said. They'd talk, get to know one another. He seemed, like René, to be truthful. For several seconds, she imagined him taking her out, lavishing attention upon her. It was a fairy tale, but so pleasant. She looked at his hands, pleased by the size and shape of them, then raised her head. He began again to speak.

◇ Eight ◇

Uncertain of what she'd respond to, Sanford decided to remain in the safe area of his background and began speaking of that.

Born in 1891 just outside Guelph, the second son and fourth and last child of a struggling dairy farmer, he'd left home at fourteen and made his way to Toronto, determined to be more and do better than his father. He'd taken a job in a small grocery store on Dundas, unloading new stock, delivering groceries, serving behind the counter, sweeping up, cleaning the scales, washing the two front windows, and, when required, shoveling coal into the furnace in the basement under the store. In return for his fifteen-hour workday, he was given his meals by the grocer's wife, was allowed to sleep on a cot at the rear of the store—thereby also serving as night watchman—and was paid three dollars a week, with Sundays off.

He used his free time learning his way around the city, or reading. He had an appetite for books, especially success stories, and identified with young heroes who struggled their way out of impossibly dreary situations to arrive, in early manhood, at independence and financial security. These characters, he gleaned, all had imagination, boldness, the willingness to take risks, and the gift for creating their own luck.

He wasn't given to daydreaming. The son of a farmer and on firsthand terms with long, hard days, he knew that to become successful he had to learn. His lack of education might hold him back and it might be many years before he'd be able to educate himself beyond the eight grades he'd completed before leaving home. He also suspected that he had some as yet undefined talent he could feel waiting inside him.

After a year with the grocer, he'd approached the man with an idea: "Open a second store and let me run it for you. With the profits, we'll be able to hire other people and in a couple of years get a third store started, and then a fourth."

"And how," asked the amused grocer, "do you suggest I'm going to pay for this second store?"

"You go to the bank and put the store as collateral, let the bank give you the money. It won't take that much. I've got it all worked out." He produced several pieces of paper on which he'd set out the figures—the rental prices of three properties, the initial cost of setting up and stocking the second store, and the projected outlay and income. "I'll work for no salary at all," he proposed, "until the store turns a profit. But when it does, then we'll split all the profits and, from then on, we go into partnership."

It had taken some convincing but Sandy's effortless charm and integrity prompted the grocer to agree, despite his misgivings. Half-believing himself to be some kind of fool, the grocer went along, and in time, the success of the two men became something of a legend in Toronto business circles. The little grocery store on Dundas had become, by the onset of the Depression, a small chain of stores and was competing strongly with the city's other chains of markets. There were fourteen good-sized stores under the Riverwood name all over the city, each turning a healthy annual profit.

In the Depression, the stores suffered, as did most other businesses. Sanford proposed to carry their regular customers on credit—each store manager would know the people and use his discretion as to which ones to carry—if they couldn't afford to pay. "If we help them out now when things are bad," he said, "they'll remember it and give us their business when times get better." The paying customers managed to balance the nonpaying ones and, through clever management and careful purchasing, they came through the Depression still intact, very short of cash but rich in goodwill.

Old Riverton died in 1940. Sanford became president and sole owner of the company, buying out Riverton's heirs, and began branching out nationally. He also entered into the production of a number of Riverwood Brand products—bread, jams, an inexpensive line of canned goods—that managed to compete successfully with the house-brand lines offered by other stores. By the time he invited Jess out to dinner, Sanford was a millionaire and had been a widower for almost three years. His wife, after two miscarriages, had died delivering a second stillborn child.

He'd married finally, at the age of forty-one, because he wanted to have children who would, he hoped, one day move into the company and continue on with it after he was gone.

"Bess," he said, without expression, "was a woman trained to listen and not interrupt with silly questions if a man was speaking; a woman bred for dependency, with no real mind of her own, and spirit only when it came to making babies. She died determined to fulfill her role—as she saw it—as a woman. Trying to have a baby; dispensing with the diaphragm and ignoring the warnings not to attempt another pregnancy. It was a complete waste. Nothing I ever said or did made much of an impression on her. She saw herself as intended solely for motherhood and playing out her part as a wife. She had very little to say. About anything.

"Still," he said philosophically, "we all fall into habits and I miss having someone around to relax with, talk to. Then, there's the matter of the children . . ." He paused and smiled. "You look a little lost," he said gently. "I want to be completely truthful with you, Jess. I know as much about you as there is to know. I had you thoroughly investigated. Now, please, don't be alarmed," he added quickly, seeing her stiffen. "I'm not trying to frighten or upset you. I was curious, and satisfied my curiosity. It really is that simple." He picked up his glass and held it before his mouth for several seconds, looking at her intently, hoping he wasn't going to scare her off; taking advantage of the moment to enjoy the sight of her, thinking she seemed to sit behind a carefully constructed barrier of self-control that might have been invisibly welded into her character. He admired her poise and self-discipline. Despite the fact that she was patently shaken by his remarks, she remained perfectly still and managed to keep her movements graceful. He took a swallow of water, then returned the glass to the table. There were all sorts of things he wanted to say to her and it took a concerted effort for him to maintain the tone he'd set for the evening. "Would you like to tell me about yourself?" he invited, wishing it were possible to produce the perfect set of words that would render her receptive and trusting.

"What's the point," she countered softly, "if you already know all there is to know?" She looked up to see that the regal-looking waiter was staring at her. She stared back at him for a moment, then turned away.

"The facts I've learned don't really tell me much about *you*," Sanford said, "about how you feel, your thoughts and hopes."

"I don't think I can do this."

"We won't rush it," he said caringly. "There's time."

Time? What did that mean? she wondered, defeated by his talk of not rushing, of time, as if the two of them had some sort of future.

"Is the food to your liking?" he asked, caught for a moment by the sight of her long tapering fingers bent around the water glass, her unpainted fingernails.

"It's fine, thank you."

"Will you come out again next Saturday?"

"Another 'date'?"

"If you like."

She lowered her eyes thoughtfully, reaching for her cigarette, not knowing why she was smoking when she didn't even like the taste of tobacco. But it did give her something to do while she tried to sort through her reactions.

He looked at her shoulders, at her breasts, then again at her hands, thinking how much more of a lady she was than the supposed ladies of the city. He wished he could point-blank ask her to close down and go out of business for good. But it was too soon. And he wanted her to be the one to choose, to want to put up the "Closed" sign and get her telephone number changed.

She raised her head and allowed herself to meet his eyes. He seemed to be silently urging her to accept this second invitation, as if it were some sort of life-rope he was offering.

"Yes, all right," she said at last. "Next Saturday."

She allowed him to drive her home. Parked in front of the house, he extended his hand and she placed hers in it, asking herself if he didn't feel contaminated knowing that her hand had too intimately touched dozens of men, if he didn't feel slightly soiled simply being in her company.

"You're beautiful," he said quietly. "And I've enjoyed the evening. I hope you have. I'll pick you up at eight next Saturday."

Without a word, and before he could get out to open the door for her, she was out of the car, up the path, and letting herself into the house. He sat for several moments watching the lights go on in the lower half of the house, thinking that words on paper, detectives' reports, contained few elements of the truth of this woman; certainly none of her beauty and intelligence, her sensitivity, dignity, and grace. He willed her not to go out in the coming week. Stay at home and wonder about me, about what it is you think I want of you. He wanted to feel that she'd be thinking of him. Because he'd be thinking about her, just the way he'd thought about her day and night for months.

Monday morning, Cotton called.

"How about this afternoon?"

"I am sorry, but I'm not accepting any invitations this week. But thank you for calling. Perhaps next week."

Bitch! he thought, carefully replacing the receiver when he'd have preferred to slam it down in her goddamned snooty ear. He'd fix her. One way or another, one fine day, he'd see her down there where she belonged. She was no goddamned better than anybody else and he'd prove it to her.

Tuesday afternoon, she went along to the King Edward to keep her regular appointment with the Osgoode Hall professor. Feeling decidedly peculiar and more than usually removed as she allowed herself to be put on her hands and knees and braced to bear his weight, she found herself imagining Sanford Woodrich, his hands, his arms, his body thrusting back and forth against hers. Forgetting herself, she was becoming aroused. The professor noticed and, trying to coax her further out of her usual nonreactive state, succeeded only in reminding her of who and what she was, thereby returning her to her typical numbness.

While she was dressing—the professor had already dressed and gone so that they wouldn't be seen leaving the hotel together—she decided to make good what she'd told Cotton the previous day and see no more clients this week. She had the idea that she'd like to appear before Sanford Woodrich come Saturday without any trace of other men upon her. She didn't know why. Perhaps it was simply because, like René, he treated her as worthy of respect and she wanted, even if only once, to live up to that.

This man was, to her mind, clean. By contrast, she felt fouled. Spending that evening with him had brought back an entire segment of childhood memories, all having to do with the visits to her parents' apartment of important people. Prior to the arrival of those visitors, the atmosphere at home had been electric with excitement. Even the staff had seemed infected by it as they'd hurried back and forth, polishing the already-gleaming furniture with tight-lipped attention, setting out small scalloped silver dishes of cashews and almonds. Her mother and father would emerge from their bedroom splendidly dressed. And on those occasions when she'd been allowed to make an appearance, Jess had bathed and then suffered the maid's clumsy ministrations while she washed Jess's hair at the bathroom sink. Her damp hair already curling wildly out of control, she'd return to her room to put on clean underwear, new white socks and black patent-leather shoes, a white organdy dress with a pink ribbon sash. God, the feeling! she thought, remembering with a distant smile. The momentousness of the occasion and her privilege in being allowed to enter into it, shaking hands with the guests, being expected to offer around the silver dishes of nuts.

Once past her initial distrust and skepticism, the evening with Sanford Woodrich had taken on much of that same feeling, so that she wanted now to go to their next meeting possessed of the scrubbed-clean presentability she'd known at ten.

She experienced a monstrous anxiety coupled with childlike anticipation, doubting his credibility and her own, knowing with certainty that she could never again have that cleanliness of spirit she'd once had. Yet Saturday stood in her mind like a significant portal through which she could pass and, once on the far side, find herself in a state of grace, suspended for a time above the grimmer realities of her life.

Ready early, she noted this time that he not only had a car and the gasoline to run it but an expensive foreign one, black and gleaming. At the sight of him getting out of the car, coming up the walk carrying his hat and gloves, she felt a jolt of

excitement. Smiling, she put on her coat and went to the front
door.

"You look wonderful!" he said, admiring her flushed features.

She thanked him, thinking this really was a fairy tale, a
magnificent fantasy, and she wanted it to last as long as possible. She was relieved and grateful that he made no attempt
to touch her, because as long as he didn't, she could indulge
wholeheartedly in the luxury of this dream.

For his part, he had to remind himself constantly not to
touch her or admire her too effusively. It would surely put an
end to the small, tentative trust he could feel he was creating
in her. And, above all else, he wanted her to trust him.

They went to La Chaumière, a French restaurant occupying
a converted house on Charles Street, with many small, dimly
lit rooms and an hors d'oeuvres cart that offered sumptuous
little tidbits.

"I was thinking," she volunteered while they awaited their
entrées, "of the way it was when I was a child and my parents
were having guests. The fuss and how the staff rushed about.
I loved our home," she said, her eyes caught by a laden dessert
trolley near the doorway of the cozy room in which they were
seated. "The way it smelled and the shine on everything. My
mother and the feeling I'd get seeing her all dressed up for the
evening. Do you know what I mean?"

He shook his head. "I can imagine it, but it wasn't part of
my life. Tell me about it," he coaxed.

He'd been poor, she suddenly remembered.

"Don't be embarrassed, Jess. Your parents had money, mine
didn't. Neither of us is responsible for what our parents had
or didn't have. Tell me," he said again. "I like hearing you
talk about it."

She looked to one side of the restaurant as if deciding, and
he watched her, wishing her features revealed more than they
did. Yet her very unpredictability captivated him. He'd come
close to disliking Bess; it had bored him that he'd known what
she'd say before she said it, that she'd come to him with every
decision needing to be made, expecting him to make it for her.
With satisfaction, he thought that Jess was a person who made
her own, and was aware of the risks that went along with
making decisions.

"It's hard," she said more quietly, her eyes drifting back

to his, "to put that part of my life . . . What I mean . . . It's like a film, a movie I saw once that's become real. The feelings I remember and the things we did . . . but there's so much in between then and now, I . . ." She stopped. "Why," she asked awkwardly, "do you want to be with me? What's the point? You know all about me, what I am, do. . . . Why?"

"Has it occurred to you," he asked, "that if you're unhappy with your life it's your right to change it?"

"Changing it isn't going to change *me*."

"Nonsense! Of course it will."

"And what else would I do? Take a job selling notions at Simpson's?"

"Why not, if it makes you feel better about yourself?"

"You assume I'm not happy with myself."

"It's not an assumption," he said a little sadly. "It's a fact, isn't it? And there's no reason for you not to make changes if you want to."

He had such strength, such persuasiveness and conviction that, for a moment, she was overwhelmingly tempted to place herself in his hands and allow him to tell her what to do, and how, and when. But it was only a moment. A man with his kind of personal power might be dangerous.

"You don't understand," she argued.

"Then explain it to me," he said patiently. "I want to understand."

"I . . ." There it was again, the temptation. "No. Tell me about growing up on a farm. I'd like to hear about that."

He smiled, the concession made. "Not wonderfully picturesque," he said, with a bit of a shrug. "What I remember most is Saturday-night bath time. The old tin bath and kettles of water heated up on the wood stove. We always had our baths in the kitchen because it was the only warm place in the house. We went in order. Youngest first, oldest last. So I got the clean water, the scalding water that made me howl and refuse to sit down." He chuckled, remembering. "Finally, of course, I sat down. I liked to dig my fingers and toes in the bottom of that galvanized tub. There was a layer of something—probably the accumulation of years of soap and bodies. I can remember so damned clearly the feeling, being in that tub. Then not wanting to come out because I was warm by then and the air was colder than hell. So I howled coming out, too. My mother used to say Saturday nights were the only times she could get a sound out of me. Spanking didn't do it. I recall being five or six, maybe seven, deciding they could spank me till they broke their hands but they'd never get the satisfaction of hearing me make a sound, never mind cry."

"Were you happy?" she asked almost inaudibly, able to see through the man to the boy he'd been.

"Not happy. We were all too busy to be happy, busy trying to beat the weather, the bank, time. Up at five to do the chores. Happiness never entered into it," he said consideringly. "Except a Christmas or two I remember. Popcorn balls and a few sprigs of holly, a skinny roast duck. We each got two thin slices with a lot of fat, but we ate slowly to make it last. I recall that as a happy time. We weren't unhappy, I don't think. Just poor. Being poor doesn't allow very much time for consideration of whether or not you're happy."

"But doesn't it seem strange to you now," she asked, caught up in the images he'd drawn for her, "to have such a lot, to be..." She looked at his mouth and lost her words, had to look away.

"Not strange," he answered, as if she'd completed her question. "The one thing I've learned over the years is not to look back. Except when looking back gives you the perspective you need for dealing with now, but for any other reason, it can be damned unhealthy."

He said little more during the rest of the meal, and at the end she felt let down. She had hoped, she realized, for more; perhaps to go on talking, exchanging thoughts and memories until morning. It had been a very long time—since those months in Vermont with Flora—since she'd had the opportunity to talk freely.

He did not extend another invitation. When they arrived back at her house, he shook her hand as before, then said, "I'll get the door," and got out to walk around to her side of the car. "Thank you for coming," he said, not offering to help her out as he'd have liked but instead allowing her to emerge unaided from the car. She looked anxious, he thought, as she hurried from him and into the house.

In the darkened living room, she peered through a crack between the curtains to watch him return to the driver's seat, then drive away.

That week, afraid of missing his call, she accepted no clients, waiting, hoping he'd get in touch with her. Nothing happened. She walked her way through the weekend, was in bed before nine both Saturday and Sunday nights, and on Monday morning made several appointments and went along only to find her former disgust still very much intact and her body as numb as ever to sensation. What had happened? she wondered repeatedly. Had she, in some way, offended or upset him?

When she didn't hear from him the second week, she tried to make herself forget him, almost ready to believe it had actually been a dream, that those two evenings hadn't really happened. But his face and their conversations haunted her sleep, interfered with her thoughts and nagged at her. As abruptly and unexpectedly as it had begun, it had ended. And she didn't know why. His continuing silence moved her out of her long apathy. She could not keep on as before. The negative feelings being generated inside her by each additional assignation were becoming stronger, more focused. Finally, she started very seriously examining her suicide plans. She had, for a few hours, known something akin to normality, to simple pleasure, and she couldn't now go on making herself available to these men. Her awareness had been so heightened that it was no longer possible for her to pretend about anything.

He spent the first Saturday evening with Barbara, a woman he'd been seeing periodically for six months or so. At first, he was bothered by the coarseness of this woman after Jess. But when he took her to her home and into her bedroom, suddenly she *was* Jess, and he was expressing himself lovingly, as he'd never done with Barbara before. Afterward, while he was dressing, he saw that this woman could never be Jess.

He wanted to go directly home and telephone her. Instead, he made himself wait out another week, convinced now that his initial instincts had been right. She was the one he wanted and he wasn't going to be satisfied until he had her.

His call sent her soaring. She agreed to dine again with him at the Royal York on the coming Saturday, then rushed through the house with restored energy, aimlessly moving from room to room—pausing from moment to moment to stare at the furnishings—until some of the excitement had been dissipated.

She had no idea what she was doing. Two weeks with only three clients meant she'd soon be dipping into her savings. But she'd been waiting for the sound of his voice, his words of invitation. Why? she asked herself, the sudden burst of energy gone, leaving her flat. What was she hoping for? She sat tiredly on the sofa, elbows on her knees, without an answer. She only knew that he'd called her again and she wanted to dig back into the past to retrieve feelings like gems she'd once owned in order to offer herself cleanly renewed for his approval. She wanted to be her best possible self—for someone about whom she knew little, who might choose never to see her again. Was it possible that he derived some perverse pleasure in being with her and hoped for revelations about her occupation? God, don't let him shame me, she thought.

A pulsing parcel of impossible hopes and expectation, she met him at the door. He looked so serious and adult compared to the somehow childish men she serviced, admirably self-possessed and confident. His smile came slowly, as if in some way she'd startled him beyond thought.

"Beautiful," he said huskily, and stood aside so that she could come through the door. As they walked to the car, he said, "You look lovely," thwarted by the inadequacy of words that said too little about the feeling the mere sight of her created inside him, and for a second or two it enraged him to think that she'd been handled by so many men. Yet, perversely, the fact heightened her appeal for him.

He wouldn't wait, he decided; fearful of the potential pitfalls of wasted time, he couldn't. He'd always been a patient man, willing to see to it that time and his own efforts would reward him. But with this woman he seemed to have lost his old attitudes.

"Jess," he said, positioning his water glass carefully between the fingers of both hands, "I have something I'd like to say. I hope you'll do me the kindness of hearing me out."

"Of course." She followed the movements of his hands, alarmed. Would he now state his reasons for seeing her?

"Is your dinner all right?"

"It's fine, thank you."

"Good. Now,"—he smiled, distracted—"where was I?"

"A proposition?" she reminded him, selecting the word with care.

"Not that. A proposal actually. I'd like you to marry me."

She looked up at the low ceiling, then at the walls of the

vast, oak-paneled dining room, a buzzing in her ears. Taking small, shallow breaths, she glanced at the people at nearby tables, wondering if they could overhear this conversation. Two tables over, there was a handsome couple and she looked at them for several moments, studying the man's white hair and black dinner jacket and the woman's carefully upswept silver-blue hair; two elegant, older people talking quietly. Do we look ordinary to them? she wondered. Everything in her that had lifted so hopefully when he'd finally telephoned now dropped, leaving her cold. This had to be some cruel sort of joke.

He followed her reactions—more visible than any he'd so far been witness to—aware that he was scaring her, making her feel the butt of a joke.

"To come right to the point," he went on, "I'd like a child. Or several. Are you able to have children, Jess?" He wanted to smile at the image he had all at once of several small children with her fine, pale features and thick black hair.

So stunned she hadn't any room in which to be offended, she answered, "As far as I know, I am." She'd been asked far worse questions in the past seven years.

"Good. What I have in mind is a formal agreement, something I think you'll feel comfortable with."

"I don't understand." She was suddenly terribly tired, as if she'd been to a party and stayed too long.

"If there's a child, I'm prepared to make a very generous settlement on you. But, if for some reason, we don't have children, I'd still honor our agreement. I'm also willing to buy a house to your liking and, of course, furnish it." Then, in the same tone of voice, he said, "You don't care very much for men, do you?"

The question itself didn't surprise her so much as its placement smack in the middle of all he was purportedly offering. She could feel his power wrapping itself around her and was again tempted to say "yes" to everything and allow him to direct her as he chose. She had to concentrate hard in order not to do that. "I'm fond of a few," she said.

"I'd like to think you could learn to be fond of me," he said. "I'm already more than fond of you."

She looked up to see that his eyes were slightly widened in an earnest expression as he awaited her response. "I don't know," she began, then stopped, the pulse in her throat beating hurtfully. "What are you trying to do to me?"

He took a swallow of his water, then slowly set the glass down. "I'm proposing you go out of business. You're not happy with it, obviously. And I'm not happy living alone. I'm hoping the alternative I'm suggesting will solve both our problems."

"But why?"

"I want you," he said. "It isn't terribly complicated."

"My God!" She was trembling, her voice reduced to a near-breathless whisper. "This is crazy! You don't have to marry me for that and you know it. What are you trying to *do* to me?"

"I'm trying to offer what I think you need."

"You have *no idea* what I need!" she argued, badly shaken.

"I think I do," he said with smugness.

Astounded, she stared at him. The expression in his eyes hadn't changed. He still looked earnest.

"Let me give you the rest of the details, then we'll set it aside and enjoy the dinner and whatever comes after."

After? Did he mean, finally, to make love to her? She found herself completely willing on one level and utterly unwilling on another. Why did it feel as if she had no options left? The band was putting down their instruments and leaving the stand. The volume of the conversations all around them increased. It might not be too terrible to accept him, she thought cautiously. Don't lie to yourself! her interior voice said sharply. He wasn't in the least terrible: a most attractive man, an inch or two over six feet, with abundant gray hair, large, strong features, and very clear hazel eyes. He was impeccably dressed in a hand-tailored suit of dark gray, with a white silk shirt, a pale gray tie, and a red silk paisley handkerchief pushed with artful carelessness into his breast pocket. His only jewelry was a slim Swiss wristwatch. His hands. She quickly looked away from them, aware of his cologne.

After several minutes, he said, "I'm willing to include your sister in our plans and provide for the continuation of her education, as well as her maintenance." He smiled so that she was able, as before, to see the boy he'd once been. "We'll sign a contract. You'll receive an annual sum to be placed in a trust fund with the income paid you in monthly installments, as well as a lump sum upon our marriage. If and when we have a child, there'll be an additional cash settlement as well as the establishment of a second trust. The same follows for any additional children. At my death, you'll receive a final settlement as well as the residue of your trust. The remainder of my estate would go to our children. If there are none, the estate in its entirety would come to you."

"What," she asked, her throat dry, "will you do if my 'occupation' becomes known?"

"You've been very discreet," he said, unruffled. "Most of your clients are men who could no more afford scandal than I. I see very little risk involved and I'm willing to take whatever risk there is."

"Why me?"

"I've already told you. I want you. You're independent, intelligent, and beautiful. I enjoy your company. And you *are* discreet. I'm not overly interested in how you've earned your money. It's not the life you were intended to live."

She laughed—a harsh, discordant sound. He was either a fool or a liar.

"I hope I'm not making this sound too much like a business arrangement," he said in a softer tone.

"Oh, but that's precisely what it is, isn't it?"

"In one sense, I suppose. The truth is I don't want to be alone, Jess, and I'm attracted to you. Do *you* want to be alone?"

Did he know how much she feared that? she wondered, admitting, "No," in a whisper.

"I don't like being so cold-blooded and clinical about this and I apologize for it. But I'm fifty-two years old and I've learned what I can live with. I could live with you."

"What if you're wrong?"

"I'm not wrong," he said adamantly.

"I can't make sense . . . I've got to think about all this."

"That's not true, though, is it? You made up your mind ten or fifteen minutes ago, didn't you?"

He was alarming in his perceptiveness. Or was she more transparent than she'd suspected? "Doesn't it bother you that I've had sex with so many men?" she asked bluntly.

"I think it bothers you," he countered cleverly, "that it *doesn't* bother me."

He was absolutely amazing, she thought, and had no idea what to make of him, yet believed every word he spoke. "How are we to go about . . . arranging all this?" She'd play it through to the end, she decided, wait for him to deliver the punch line, and then go home.

"I think the first step will be for you to get a new, unlisted telephone number."

She continued to stare at him.

"And then," he went on, "in three months or so, say January, we'll get married. Judge's chambers, I think. Keep it quiet. No point to making any unnecessary splash."

"You really do mean all this," she said, finding it more and more difficult to breathe. "You're serious."

"Completely."

"Then you're crazy!" she declared.

He laughed, shaking his head.

"There is nothing," she said, trying to get him to see sense, shock him into it if need be, "*nothing* I haven't done, or had done to me. Nothing! I'm not *clean*! Get the joke over with and let me go home, please! This isn't amusing."

"I'm anything but amused," he granted. "But let me ask you this: Is it possible you could accept someone else's view of you?"

"I think . . . I think . . ."

"What?" he prompted quietly, willing her to believe him.

"Why do all this for something you can buy for twenty-five dollars?"

"Because," he said with finality, "what I want from you no one could buy at any price." He wanted to know what allowed her to hold herself as she did, to hear her tell of her childhood and the way life had been when it was something she enjoyed. He wanted her to offer herself trustingly into his life and his arms and find pleasure in the act. "Say yes!" he urged. "It isn't a joke. What are your alternatives, Jess?"

"Don't be unfair!" she pleaded. "Talking about alternatives as if I had them when we both know I don't."

"I don't mean to be unfair. But I think we're both aware that you're not going to receive too many offers of marriage."

"So you'd take me on out of some warped sense of . . . what? I don't even know what to call it . . . some sense of Samaritan duty?"

"Look, I've given you my reasons and I plan to say nothing more about it this evening. Let me know your decision when you're ready. Shall we order dessert?"

She swallowed with difficulty as she watched him open the menu and begin reading. Was this real? He looked and sounded real to her, but, God! he had to be mad offering to marry her.

She had nothing to give him. Was he, perhaps, someone who needed to live with an example of how wrong a life could go in order to feel the thrust of his own accomplishments? She wouldn't be that, not to anyone! She loathed her life and herself, yet here he sat telling her not to think about it, as if that were simple to do.

"You're serious?" she asked.

"Completely." He looked up at her, lowering the menu.

"All right," she said, then bit her lower lip.

"Good, Jess." He smiled sweetly. "That's very good."

"You believed all along I'd agree."

"No. I hoped you would, but I had doubts."

"Am I so easy to read?"

"Not in the least. The opposite, if anything."

"You confuse me," she admitted.

"What intrigues me about you," he said, leaning closer to her, "is that on the surface you seem to be one thing, but underneath you're very different. I found a prism when I was a child. Probably a stray bit of some chandelier one of my brothers or sisters had found somewhere and decided to have as a toy. I spent hours turning it this way and that, watching the light being bent and rainbows take shape. Few things in my life have fascinated me as much. But you do."

"So, you'd like to turn me this way and that, watch me change."

He nodded. "Something like that."

"Do you have to have everything that fascinates you?"

"I don't buy people. And the woman in you isn't for sale. No one could buy that."

He claimed to see what she'd almost lost sight of herself: the essential self who'd held herself away from everything bad that had happened. It made her want to cry both in gratitude and from fear. But he did see. And so she agreed.

Tillie was astonished. "Sanford Woodrich? I can't believe it! I didn't know you knew him. How long . . . When did you meet him?"

"Some time ago," Jess answered evasively.

"My God!" Tillie laughed excitedly. "I just can't believe it! You're actually going to marry him?"

"That's right."

"When?"

"In January."

"Where did you meet him? Tell me *something!*"

"I met him. Does it really matter where?"

"I guess not. But... Isn't he awfully old, Jess?"

"Not awfully. Fifty-two. He doesn't look it."

"But that makes him twenty-seven years older than you."

"That's right."

"Do you love him?" Tillie asked.

"No. But I'm... I like him very much."

Tillie looked flabbergasted. "How can you marry someone you don't love?"

"I like him and feel comfortable with him." It was the biggest lie she'd told so far. A good half the time he made her feel as if she were sitting naked in a glass cube, on display at the art gallery.

"Has he been married before?"

"He's a widower."

"But you don't love him," Tillie persisted.

"Love isn't everything, Till. I like him. I'm content with that."

"You talk like *you're* fifty-two and this is the only chance you're ever going to have," Tillie accused.

"Perhaps it is. I could certainly do far worse."

"And why," she asked obtusely, "did we have to have the telephone number changed?"

"We were getting too many wrong numbers," Jess said smoothly, having prepared her answer to this question. "I was getting tired of it."

"How long have you known him?" she asked, narrowing her eyes slightly, sensing too many things wrong with this completely unexpected announcement and with Jess's answers.

"Some time," Jess gave another intentionally vague response.

"Some time," she repeated. "How *much* time? A few weeks, a month?"

"Don't interrogate me, please. I don't care for it."

"Well, what'm I supposed to do, just say, Oh, okay, you're getting married to a man whose name I've never heard you mention until today? None of this makes any *sense*, Jess."

"Perhaps not, but it's what I'm going to do."

"You never used to be this way," Tillie said unhappily. "You've changed. You're so... And where are we going to live? Am I supposed to find a place of my own or what?"

"Of course not. We're going to buy a house and I'll take care of you just as I always have."

Tillie shook her head, again saying, "I don't *believe* this! When do I get to meet him?"

"Soon. Perhaps we'll have dinner, the three of us, this weekend."

"Not Saturday," she said quickly. "I've got a date." Press had called, after many anxious nights of waiting and hoping on her part, on Wednesday.

"I'll bear that in mind."

"You're not yourself one bit!" Tillie's eyes, like a cat's, seemed to dilate. "There's nothing wrong, is there, Jess?"

"Absolutely nothing. I'll see if Sanford can make it Friday night."

"The Riverwood Stores. He must be a millionaire, at least."

"At least," Jess said a bit sarcastically, disliking this talk of his money.

"You'll probably get to live in Rosedale."

"I have no idea where we'll live."

"You're not even excited or anything."

"I'm not an especially excitable person, Tillie. You know that."

"It's because," she said darkly, "you don't love him. If you did, you'd be positively on cloud nine."

"I don't think there's a man alive who could do that for me, whether I loved him or not."

"Jess!" Tillie looked horrified.

"It's not such an awful thing to say. It's just the truth." She had a sudden overwhelming desire to tell Tillie all the truth, and said, "I'll tell you the real reason I changed the telephone number, if you'd truly like to know."

"I don't think . . ."

"You *know*, Tillie. You've known for years."

"Don't tell me!" She covered her ears with her hands. "I don't want to know. *Don't tell me!*"

"All right," Jess said softly, relenting and taking Tillie into her arms. "All right."

"It's just that I can't," Tillie whispered, allowing herself to relax inside her embrace, closing her eyes. "I can't!"

"I know and it's all right. I love you, Till. You're the only one in the world I'll always love."

"Oh, just wait till you have kids and all the rest of it. You'll change your mind."

"I'll still love you."

"Well," she sniffed and eased herself away. "Do I at least get to help you buy a trousseau or something?"

"Something." Jess smiled.

"What'll we do with this place?" Tillie looked around the living room.

"Sell it, I suppose. Or keep it and rent it and someday I'll give it to you for a wedding present."

"Give it to me?"

"Would you like that?"

"It's very generous of you," Tillie said doubtfully, "but I don't think . . ."

"Then we'll sell it. And when you do get married, I'll give you money for a down payment on a house."

Tillie was most impressed by Sanford: by the way he treated Jess, by his clothes and manners and speaking voice, by almost everything about him. Her only disappointment was that Jess didn't love him, because he seemed to think very highly of her. It would have been perfect, she thought, if only Jess loved him.

She went off to bed and Jess sat downstairs in the living room with Sanford.

"I admire your taste," he complimented her. "I'll enjoy seeing how you do up the house."

"Thank you." She gazed down at her hands trying to make herself believe this wasn't some elaborate, insane game, that she'd go ahead and actually marry this man. "You're the first one who's ever been inside the house," she said meaningfully, feeling defenseless.

"I understand, and I'm honored. I want to touch you, Jess," he said quietly.

The words set off an inner siren. She could only hope to God he wouldn't touch her. If he did, she'd be unable to look at him again, let alone talk to him.

"It upset you," he said, "my saying that."

She nodded.

"I'm starting to understand you," he said, getting to his feet. "I'll be going now."

"I'll see you to the door."

Once there, he turned and she tensed, prepared for him to satisfy his desire to touch her. But he made no move. "The ring will be ready at the end of next week," he said. "The announcement's set to go into the papers a week from Saturday."

"Yes, fine."

He looked at her throat, very white against yet another black dress. "I'll talk to you at the beginning of the week."

"Thank you for dinner." She was stiff with wanting him to go, needing time alone.

"Tell me something," he said, drawing her eyes. "Have you ever wanted any of the men you've slept with?"

She shook her head.

"I want you to want *me*. Good night, Jess." He opened the door and let himself out.

◊ Nine ◊

Prescott Ames was neither as easy nor predictable as Tillie had thought he'd be. From the beginning, she was anxious to have him make some commitment to her, but at the end of each date he promised nothing more than to call during the next week. The result was she felt she was living suspended in midair, and couldn't concentrate on anything. Press had become the ultimate challenge, and winning him her only goal. She was convinced he was in love with her; it showed in so many ways: the deferential manner in which he treated her, his increasingly prolonged kisses and attempts to fondle her breasts, the way he held her hand and talked to her, looked at her. He was exactly what she wanted, but she couldn't find a way to get him to admit to caring for her.

He dated other girls, a fact that was like slow-acting poison in her bloodstream. She believed he did it to make her jealous. And he was succeeding, intentionally or not. On the two occasions when she saw him on campus in the company of other girls, she was so demoralized and angry she simply walked off and went home for the balance of the day.

She felt angry, too, with Jess for being so busy with Sanford Woodrich that she failed to pay Tillie the attention she felt she

should have. Everything about Jess's involvement with Woodrich struck Tillie wrong: the large, diamond solitaire set in
platinum that constantly caught Tillie's eye, and her endless
list of appointments—to look at houses, to buy new clothes,
to meet with Sanford's attorney—seemed something that had
little to do with a pending wedding. She wondered why Jess
was marrying this man. The entire venture seemed coldblooded
and unexciting; Jess wasn't even impressed by Sanford's
wealth.

To Tillie, she seemed taller, more erect, and more than ever
like a woman of fifty in her calm acceptance of the complicated
arrangements, lawyer's documents hand-delivered for her sig-
nature, and the regular, very uninspired-sounding telephone
calls from Sanford. It was as if Jess were in the process of
shedding all her previously recognizable qualities in order to
appear mature and in control both of herself and the situation.

Her demeanor did, however, belie a certain agitation she
exuded every time she prepared for another evening out with
Woodrich. They saw each other two or three times a week,
and it all seemed to Tillie the way a couple about to be married
might behave, yet the utter lack of any feeling but Jess's
strange, almost palpable tension removed what was happening
from the realm of romance and placed it squarely in the arena
of business. Tillie had regular visions of striking both her sister
and Sanford, seeing herself flying into their sedate midst and
stunning the two of them into human reactions.

Much of the time, she felt like screaming, and fought off
the constant temptation to telephone Press and shout at him for
being too thick to see how much she loved him; she fought,
as well, the urge to march downstairs and yell at Jess for being
willing to throw her life away on someone she didn't love, and
who was so much older; for settling herself into middle age
at twenty-five.

Instead of doing any of it, after the second time she saw
Press with another girl, Tillie stayed in her room, looking out
at the small grassed area at the rear of the house, between their
driveway and garage on the one side, and the fence belonging
to the neighbors on the other. She gazed at a row of evergreen
bushes planted in front of the fence, intended by the previous
owners to hide the fencing. The bushes—green green against
the gray-grimed snow—held her attention so fully that without
stopping to examine the impulse, she unearthed an old water-

color set, found some paper, and began painting the bushes and fence. She ran out of green paint, and, determined to finish, grabbed her bag, threw on her coat and boots, and tore down to Cole's on Bloor to buy two more watercolor sets.

She worked at the painting for hours, oblivious to everything, including Jess's several calls to come to dinner. Startled, she felt strangely guilty when Jess appeared in the doorway of her room asking, "What are you doing, Till? I've called you three times. Dinner's ready."

Flustered, she tried to hide the page, but Jess was already looking at it, saying, "This is *very* good, Tillie," sounding surprised. "Really! It's so good. The way you've done every branch . . . I don't think I've ever actually looked at the garden," she said, turning to look at it now.

"It's just . . . nothing," Tillie said dismissingly. She was mildly gratified by Jess's praise, yet nevertheless began to crumple the page.

"Don't do that!" Jess exclaimed and rescued the picture. "If you don't want to keep it, don't destroy it. Let me have it." She stood looking closely at the still-wet painting. "I can't tell you how good I think this is," she repeated. "You ought to be studying art, Tillie."

"That isn't art," Tillie argued, getting up and switching off the desk light. "That's just . . . doodling."

"Maybe art *is* doodling. Whatever you want to call it, you've got talent."

"I'm starved." Tillie walked past her and out of the room.

"I'll be down in a second," Jess said, going to put the watercolor safely in her own room, bewildered by her sister's having put so many hours and effort into something she was afterward willing to destroy. Studying the painting for another moment, Jess was awed by the angry, vivid life of it.

The wedding was to take place in judge's chambers on the first Saturday in January. After, there would be a small dinner with Sanford's older brother and vice-president of the company, Edward, who had joined the business five years earlier and who in no way resembled his younger brother; Edward's wife, June; Charlie Bocken, Sanford's solicitor and closest friend, and his wife; and Tillie and her date.

Press kept Tillie waiting almost until the last minute before agreeing to accompany her to the wedding. When he finally did call to say he'd be happy to go, she wanted to tell him to forget it, he'd kept her waiting so long she'd gone ahead and asked someone else. But her nerve failed and she simply said, "Good," and went on to give him the details.

Jess was busy with the house on Gleneden Road, a winding, tree-lined street with formal-looking houses of a variety of styles ranging from mock-Tudor to Georgian. Typically, the gardens were laid out with care and, in spring, the lawns would be very thick and green. She preferred Forest Hill Village to Rosedale only because the houses were not quite so enormous and the streets less confusingly roundabout. And she was taking a good deal of pleasure in supervising the painting and papering. She'd ordered new furniture to coordinate with those pieces of her own and Sanford's they'd agreed to keep, and was enjoying selecting drapery fabrics and new appliances for the kitchen. She loved the house. Large and stately, it sat at the top of a circular drive and had lawns, front and rear, that comprised almost half an acre of land. Inside, the rooms all had ten-foot ceilings and wide, multi-paned windows. At the apex of the shrub-lined side drive stood the triple garage with an apartment above that was in the process of being renovated to accommodate the staff.

Sanford had hired two women, both of middle age, who were friendly, capable, and well referred. Polly Ferguson, a recent widow and childless, was to look after the house, and Olga Polaski, also widowed but with a grown daughter in Winnipeg, was to cook. The two women met and agreed happily to occupy the staff quarters over the garage once they were ready.

In the weeks before the wedding, Sanford gave his brother Edward substantially more responsibility in the running of the business so that he could be free to accompany Jess on several shopping trips and inspection tours of the house. He went along only to be near her, feeling no need to approve of her purchases, and stood to one side in Simpson's while Jess selected a pair of chairs, fascinated by her carefully coiled hair, from which one curling tendril had escaped to hang enticingly against the nape of her long neck.

He admired her apparent disregard for current fashion, but deciding her clothes needed some sort of lift, he called a jeweler friend and had a pin of gold and diamonds set in a lazily looped open-ended circle made for her. When he presented it to her over dinner on the Saturday evening three weeks before the wedding, he was pleased to see her lose a large measure of her composure. Color brightening her face, she held the pin in her hand, saying, "Until now, this all seemed . . . make-believe. But this . . . this makes it real somehow." She looked up at him, something almost childlike and hesitant in her expression, very softly saying, "I wish I had something to give you. It doesn't feel right to accept so much."

"Don't be silly, Jess. It gave me the greatest pleasure having that made for you. I enjoy giving gifts." His voice was melodious, richly promising. The more quietly he spoke, the more aware she was of his power.

"But why?" she asked, feeling agonized at waiting week after week for him to make some move.

"Don't you believe you deserve gifts?" he asked, knowing she thought herself of no value.

"No."

"For God's sake, why not?"

She couldn't answer that.

"Because of what you've been," he answered for her. "Isn't that right?"

She nodded, her eyes again on the pin, remembering her father fastening a necklace around her mother's throat. She could see her mother's bent head and her father's hands and the flush of pleasure rising into her mother's face as she raised her head to look at herself in the mirror. A sudden flurry of motion and then her mother had embraced her father, kissing him. The diamonds holding her eyes, Jess had a sudden fierce desire to kiss Sanford, to feel his arms around her.

"Why not accept yourself?" he suggested. "People do what they must to survive."

"I know that." She looked at him, the pulse in her throat pounding painfully. "I said the same thing to Tillie, years ago. But that doesn't make it right or wipe it out. It doesn't make me . . ."

"What?"

She shrugged. "You can't tell me you haven't had thoughts on the matter."

"I'll tell you something interesting," he said. "Our mutual

friend, the lawyer who shall remain nameless,"—he smiled at this little joke—"told me, when I first asked about you, that you were someone it was almost shocking to find could be bought. He also said that you were quite the technician but one of the coldest women he'd ever encountered. I, personally, don't find that to be the case." Allenby simply hadn't understood, he thought. Jess was far too complicated to be readily understood by someone like Allenby who thought that his dollars bought him access to more than a woman's body.

"I don't want to hear," she said, uncomfortable.

"Jess," he asked, "how did you think of yourself, begging love from strangers?"

"Please don't do this," she whispered.

"It was the saddest damned thing I've ever heard," he said, again seeing Allenby's smile as he'd told about Jess's rules. "'You've got to say you love her before she'll let you put a finger on her. Beats the band, eh?'"

"Please!" she said again.

"All right, I'll stop. But one day," he said earnestly, "I'd like to get to the bottom of you, find out what's really there."

"Nothing's there." She watched the maître d' lead a young couple to a table in the far corner.

"Oh, yes, there is. Most definitely. Put the pin on," he coaxed. "I'm anxious to see how it looks. Is there some reason why you wear such dark clothes?"

"I don't look good in bright colors. They make me look sallow." She fastened the pin onto her dress just above her left breast, acutely aware of her cleavage and his eyes. She hadn't the faintest idea how to deal with this man. From the moment she'd accepted his first invitation, he'd been in complete control. Now, she alternated between feeling relaxed and comfortable with him, and utterly vulnerable and totally defenseless. She lived anticipating his making love to her and wished he'd go ahead, make his move and get it over with so she could settle into her feelings without having to wait for the time when she could begin hating him.

He looked at the deep shadow between her breasts, then at the diamond brooch, and, at last, at her face. For several moments their eyes held and he wanted to reach across the table and gently slide his hand down her cheek and across her shoulder, down the neckline of her dress and into the soft

warmth of her breasts. The longing to touch her was so strong
it wanted to take him over and he had to look away.

Tillie's frustration had her doing more watercolors. She
spent hours trying to reproduce a small vase of dried flowers
on the windowsill, or make a satisfactory rendering of her own
foot. She sat drawing her hand, trying to capture its depth and
substance on paper, failing. She was failing, too, in her studies,
so preoccupied with Press and dreams of their future together
that she couldn't do more than fiddle away at drawings and
paintings, killing time until something happened.

Two weeks before Jess's wedding, they were out for a
Sunday afternoon walk when Tillie confronted him, asking,
"Don't you care for me at all?"

"Of course, I do," he said, wide-eyed with surprise to think
she didn't know. "I thought you understood that." He looked
around, relieved no one seemed to be taking any notice of
them.

"You thought I *understood*? How was I supposed to 'understand' that?"

"Well, I mean I'm with you all the time, for one thing. And
we talk on the phone almost every night."

"You are *not* with me all the time," she argued, feeling
herself coming loose at the edges. "And we talk on the telephone maybe once or twice a week. I don't know what you're
talking about! *All the time*. And you go out with other girls,
too!"

"You're the only one I see regularly. Why're you getting
so mad, Tillie?" Two women passing turned to look at them
and he glanced down at the sidewalk, embarrassed.

"We spend one night a week together, talk on the 'phone—
if I'm lucky—twice a week, and in your head that's 'all the
time.' I wish I had that kind of a brain."

"I guess," he acknowledged, "it's only because I think about
you a lot, so it feels as if we're actually together."

"Why haven't you told me that? Don't you think it's something I'd like to know?"

"I'm telling you now," he said, looking baffled, as if she
were raving at him in a foreign language. "What is it you want
me to do?" he asked helplessly, wishing she hadn't chosen to
start a scene outdoors where they could be seen and overheard.

"I love you!" she cried, giving way. "And you don't even

care!" She began to cry, for the moment giving up playing games, too miserable to be concerned with them.

"Sure I care about you," he said, trying to put his arm around her, mortified that she'd picked the middle of a Sunday afternoon right in front of three churches to start this argument. He was glad services were over and there were few people about.

"If you do care, why don't you say so? You're driving me crazy!"

"Tillie, I didn't know you felt so...strongly. Come on, let's go back to the car. We'll talk."

An advance graduation present from his parents, the car was a nearly-new red Ford convertible he drove only on Sundays due to the gas rationing. He got Tillie installed on the front seat, then ran around to the driver's side. He was so thrown by her behavior that he flooded the engine and had to turn off the key to let the plugs dry out. "We'll have to wait before I can get it started," he said.

"I don't *care!*" she cried. "I don't give a damn about your car. And I probably shouldn't give a damn about you! You act like a baby!"

"I'm no damned baby!" he said hotly. "What the hell do you want from me anyway?"

"Tell me how you *feel* about me! I want to know right now!"

"We've only known each other a couple of months..." he began.

"What does that have to do with it?" she cut him off.

"It takes time to get to know people."

"Oh, hell! Either you care about someone or you don't! *Do* you care about me or *not*?"

"Of course I do. I've already told you that."

"How much?" she challenged, red-eyed, her face tear-stained.

"A lot!" he declared.

"You don't love me!" Her voice broke again threateningly. "I want to go home! I've made a fool of myself. Take me home!"

"I do...love you." He met the challenge, said the words, and felt a little sick. "But, Tillie, you're just eighteen, and I won't be twenty-three for another couple of months. We're too young for all this."

"Age doesn't have anything to do with it and neither does time."

Defeated, he fell silent, his fingers itching to try the ignition key again, get the car started, take her home and forget the whole silly business. He was getting in way over his head just because he thought she was pretty and sexy, too, in kind of an unsexy way. Here they were, talking about love and all that. He didn't know anything about love. The air inside the car was charged with anger, filled with the echoes of their raised voices.

"I really do love you," she said very quietly. "And I've never been so unhappy in all my life. Please take me home."

He turned to look at her, taken aback by the sudden alteration in her tone. Her face seemed blurred, as if someone had taken a huge eraser and tried to rub out her features. She looked like a sad, lost, little kid. In that moment, looking at her, something inside him cracked open and he fell in love. He could feel it happening as he drew her into his arms, feeling at once tremendously strong and protective as he stroked her slippery, silken hair and murmured, "Everything's going to be okay, Till. I guess I've been a little slow on the uptake, but I do love you. I can't imagine not being with you." Every bit of it was suddenly true. He eased her away but kept his arm around her as he turned the key, pulled the choke and the engine turned over. "Let's take a drive, calm down a little." He felt years older, as if this confrontation had thrust him prematurely but irretrievably into adulthood.

He drove downtown heading for the lakefront, got on Lakeshore Drive and started toward Sunnyside. As usual, being Sunday, icy roads or no, people were out for their Sunday drives and traffic was pretty heavy. He drove with care, his arm holding Tillie secure at his side. Her sobs ebbed until all that remained was a little-girlish hiccoughing he found amusing and endearing. His arm tightened reflexively around her and he smiled, thinking he actually did love her. He really did.

He pinned her that evening after dinner with his parents, placing his frat pin on the shoulder of her dress. She was so happy then that nothing else mattered. He was going to love her and look after her and life would be just as she'd always dreamed it. In the dark safety of the car, parked beside the house on Brunswick—Jess was out for the evening—she returned his open-mouthed kisses eagerly, not liking them particularly but anxious to reward him. She even allowed him to unfasten her dress and unhook her brassiere so that he could put his hands on her naked breasts. He sighed ecstatically as his kisses became more intense and his breathing turned thin and gaspy. He whispered, "Oh, Jesus, Tillie, I'm so crazy about you," as his hands squeezed her breasts like small pillows that gave him unimaginable comfort, and his tongue pushed into her ear. She wanted to shove him away, straighten her clothing and tell him to stop acting like a fool. But this was it: love. And it really was romantic, if she let herself think of this as a scene from a movie. She felt quite tender toward him, almost like a mother, as he panted and pressed and irritatingly twisted her nipples between his fingers so that they went all shivery and hideously puckered, and she waited it out, hoping he'd soon stop. But he didn't. He took hold of her hand and directed it down over the substantial bulge in his trousers. And that was going too far.

"I'd better get in," she said, trying to withdraw her hand. "It's getting late and Jess'll be home any minute. I've got to get up early, too, to help with the packing. The movers are coming Monday," she reminded him.

"In a minute," he said, holding her hand in place, kissing her wetly on the side of the neck.

She laughed, a wild jangled sound meant to hide her growing fear at losing control of the situation. "Come on, Press." She again laughed stridently. "I really do have to go in."

With a groan, he pulled away and sat with his head in his hands, his elbows on the steering wheel, wondering for a few seconds what the hell any of it meant. She seemed to place more store in being able to go with his family to church on Sunday than she did on a chance at their being alone together. But, hell, he reminded himself, she was only a kid and he had nearly five years on her, not to mention some experience, which she obviously didn't have. "Okay," he said. "I got kind of carried away there. You're right to stop me. Jesus! I really almost couldn't stop."

Feeling soiled, she fixed her clothes, letting her fingertips rest for a satisfied moment on his frat pin on her shoulder before drawing her coat closed, asking, "Have you ever thought how many children you'd like to have?"

"I don't know," he said distractedly, as he cleaned the misted windshield with his handkerchief. "Three, I guess. Someday."

"Me, too," she said, able to see three small faces in the darkness before her. "I love you." She smiled, placing her hand on the back of his neck. He seemed so upset she felt a bit guilty and wanted to cheer him up.

"I know," he murmured, getting the car started. "Me, too." For some reason, he found himself thinking about that near-naked portrait of Jess in the living room, in that nightgown with her nipples showing through and a dark shadow at the top of her thighs. It was a warm image of a well-ripened woman, while he sat out in the cold with a little girl. He shook it away and got out to see Tillie inside.

On Sunday, a week before the wedding, Jess and Sanford went to make a final inspection of the house. It had snowed the previous night and the driveway hadn't been cleared, so they had to leave the car on the street and make their way on foot up the drive to the house. He took her hand to help her through the deep, top-crusted snow and she turned to look at him, at once very aware of him through his hand, firm and strong, enclosing hers. Her heart began to beat rapidly in her throat and she realized she hadn't been touched by a man in close to four months. Her system seemed purged. Was this, too, part of his overall plan for her? she wondered. She could feel an empty twisting inside and studied his profile for several seconds, wanting him, yet afraid. If he did touch her, she'd come apart in dozens of small pieces and later, when the pieces were reassembled, she'd despise him just as she had the other men who'd bought and paid for her. It was what he was doing, after all: purchasing sole and exclusive rights to a whore. Did it give him some bizarre feeling of pride?

The house seemed to be waiting expectantly, as if for its interior life to begin, the white-painted brick very fresh in contrast to the black roof and shutters. The wide front door with its polished brass fittings seemed to invite a human touch. As he opened the front door, she freed her hand from his, thinking for the first time since it happened of that terrifying party Cotton had arranged shortly after her arrival in the city.

She'd gone along to the address he'd given her, to find him

in the company of four other men, all anticipating a party, rightly enough, and she was it. It had started out amicably, with quite a number of bootlegged bottles of rye and the air thick with cigarette smoke, bantering, and blue jokes she'd pretended to find amusing. But then it had all turned to business and she'd accommodated each of them, one after the other, with Cotton acting as ringmaster, directing the show with such a look of malevolent glee that she'd had to keep her eyes carefully averted from the sight of him.

She'd tried to tell herself not to think about it, just suffer through it and then escape. Her body had closed down after a time and gone dead, but still they'd wanted more. Variations and multiples. And she hadn't known how to escape. They'd made her do painful, degrading things she hadn't believed her mind or body could absorb; as if engaged in the common goal of her destruction, they'd used her relentlessly. It went on and on for hours until she'd arrived at the point where she'd believed herself incapable, finally, of ever caring for any man.

Drunkenly, they'd patted her—like a good horse, she'd thought—and slobbered final good-byes, caressing her as they paid their hundred dollars, while Cotton, the only sober one, watched slit-eyed from one side. For weeks afterward, she'd been unable to walk properly or go to the toilet without pain and blood. Her body had evolved into something repugnant yet pathetically dear to her, in need of her tenderest ministrations. She felt sorry for her body, as if it were something that had been left in her charge and which she'd allowed to be abused.

She'd refused Cotton's invitations from then on; the man deeply frightened her. His persistence and many telephone calls came to be like constant reminders of her weakness as well as of her failure to take proper care of the body that had been given into her charge. He'd called three and four times a week knowing she wouldn't see him, but still he'd kept on, saying, "How about it, eh?" with a hinting obscenity in his tone of voice and labored breathing. Repeatedly, she'd politely said no, her fear of him in no way diminished.

What frightened her most about the incident was her refusal to give in. And, thinking it through, she wondered if perhaps it was her stubbornness and determination that so angered Cotton.

Sanford stood watching her for several moments, seeing her

eyes go blank as she examined something that plainly upset her. It was a little alarming to see and he asked, "Is there something wrong, Jess?"

She returned to the present to see his face filled with concern.

"Are you all right?" he asked again.

She looked at him and wanted all at once to share her thoughts and fears with him, to have him assure her that his power would extend to include her and that she need not ever be afraid again. He was tall and strong and seemed to care. "I'm sorry," she said, trying to smile. "I was just thinking about something."

"It couldn't have been too pleasant, judging from your expression."

"It wasn't important." She moistened her lips, becoming increasingly aware of him.

He wanted to hold and comfort her, but smiled instead and turned, saying, "You've done a hell of a job! The place is beautiful." He admired the dining room she'd done entirely in white, with the only touch of color a dried-flower arrangement on the sideboard. The living room, with its pale green walls and green-printed curtains and matching upholstery, was cool and summery. She'd managed to make the rooms inviting, despite their monochromatic decor, by touches here and there of colored accessories and flower arrangements. "It's absolutely beautiful," he said again.

It took her a few seconds to respond. Her eyes had fastened to the back of his head and her mouth was working but she couldn't speak. He turned, asking, "Are you sure nothing's wrong?"

"No, really. I'm fine. Would you like to see upstairs?"

In silence, they climbed the stairs and again he complimented her decorating. Tillie's room, done in shades of peach with matching curtains and bedspread, and the carpeting a deeper, almost orange color, seemed perfectly suited to the girl, he thought. The guest room, in pale gray with white trim, was elegant, but not forbidding. "I very much like what you've done," he said, once more watching her closely.

"Thank you," she said stiffly, wishing he'd stop staring at her.

"Are you frightened of me, Jess?" he asked.

It reminded her of Jamieson Land, and she saw Land briefly on the screen of her memories, as if she'd known the man dozens of years earlier. She felt very old as she answered, "No. I'm not frightened of you," and made herself smile.

◊ Ten ◊

He kissed her at the end of the very brief ceremony in the judge's office and, to her dismay, everything inside her lifted in anticipation of further kisses, significant caresses. Forgetting their small audience, their eyes met for a few seconds to exchange a look fraught with unspoken questions on both sides. It happened several more times in the course of the celebration dinner in the private room at the small French restaurant downtown. She had to force herself to pay attention to Sanford's brother, Edward, whom she could not like—he was too wet-mouthed, too round and loud and ill-spoken, too ominously reminiscent of Cotton with his big-man's clumsy gestures and rasping voice—and his wife, June, a small, pleasant woman who seemed crimped in every way, from her hair to her too-small feet. Charlie Bocken, familiar to her now after months of explaining and having her sign documents, was warm, even affectionate and she could understand Sanford's fondness for him. His wife, though, was a lushly pretty peroxide blonde who had very little to say and seemed anxious only to get herself as drunk as possible as quickly as possible. Tillie, looking radiant, was lavishing her attention on Press, who seemed content with that.

There was well-prepared food and bootlegged champagne, everything to turn the occasion festive. Yet it wasn't. The air was tense, as if everyone were waiting for something more to happen. The conversations were awkward, directionless. It felt far more like a wake than a wedding and Jess couldn't help wondering if she were responsible. She turned to look at Sanford to see if he felt it too. Again, their eyes met. Would it happen, finally, tonight, when they were together for the first time in that house?

The evening passed her by in a multicolored swirl of motion, occasional moments moving in and out of focus. She was conscious primarily of her agitation and of her body inside the beige silk dress Sanford had selected at Holt Renfrew. It had too many tiny silk-covered buttons on the sleeves and down the bodice and Tillie had had to help her dress because her hands had balked after the second button with its reluctant little loop.

The others got up to dance to the music of the hired trio and Sanford reached across the table to take her hand. His hand a magnet to the iron in her system, he drew her up and into his arms, close against him. Unable to locate her coordination, she staggered against his enclosing arms and inescapable body, dragging air into her lungs in long breaths, her eyes fixed on the collar of his shirt. She wanted to cry. Here she was being led around the floor by this man she'd actually married. Raising her eyes fractionally, she looked at the rings weighting down her finger: the solitaire and the matching platinum wedding band. Everything was signed, registered, done. The others were watching them, murmuring their approval. What a fine-looking couple. Why had she done this? she asked herself.

He couldn't help being aware of her rigidity, her refusal to look at him, and in an undertone asked, "Are you regretting it now, Jess? Have you decided it's a mistake?"

Would it matter? she wondered. It was too late to change any of it. They'd both lifted the pens and put their names to the documents.

"No," was all she could manage to say. His hand was burning through the dress, making its impression on the bare flesh of her spine. She felt dizzy, faint.

"Perhaps you'd rather sit this one out," he suggested diplomatically, hating to see her suffer. She nodded and let him lead her back to the table, where he kept hold of her hand a moment longer, leaning close to whisper, "Everything will be all right. You have my word." Then he released her and summoned the waiter over to refill the glasses. She lifted hers and drank deeply while he watched, determined not to become the object of her hatred. From the outset, he'd sensed her awesome capacity for hating, recognizing how adeptly she cloaked it in good manners, kindness, and thoughtfulness. Not that those qualities weren't real, but she used them to hide her true feelings.

Tactfully, Tillie said good night and went off to her room.

Jess let Sanford take her coat, then remained in the foyer waiting to learn what he expected.

"You look worn out," he said solicitously, closing the closet door. "Come on, I'll see you up."

At the bedroom door, he stopped to lift a wisp of hair away from her face. "Sleep well, Jess," he said, and left her there.

Confused and a little drunk, she went into the bedroom where, with difficulty, she managed to get undressed and into a new white silk nightgown, all the while watching the door, thinking he'd return at any moment. In the too-bright bathroom she removed her makeup, then washed. He didn't come. She turned out the bathroom light and stood in the middle of the bedroom. Daunted, she looked at the vast expanse of bed with the pale blue blanket cover edged in lace and the paler blue pillow cases and sheets. He wasn't going to come. She went into the dressing room to look through his things, reassure herself they were indeed there. Everything was just as it had been that afternoon: a pack of Player's sitting on his chest of drawers, and a book of matches. She lit one of the cigarettes and got into bed, sitting stiffly against the headboard, waiting, smoking. She became more nauseated with each puff and, about to vomit, crushed out the cigarette, put off the light, and lay down.

She slept very badly, her night taken up with dreams of Sanford pursuing her, naked, from room to room, finally catching her in the front hall closet where he shoved her hard against the wall and became five huge Sanfords who used her over and over until blood was gushing down her thighs and her sanity was leaking from her eyes like tears.

At seven, bathed and dressed, she went downstairs to find Sanford in the midst of his breakfast. Olga Polaski appeared to ask, "Will you be having breakfast, Mrs. Woodrich?"

Wetting her lips, Jess turned to look at the woman. "No, thank you. Just coffee." She sat at the far end of the table, watching as he finished reading *The Financial Post*. He put aside the newspaper and smiled, asking, "Did you sleep well?"

"Not very. I drank too much champagne."

"Perhaps you'll do better tonight. I have an appointment this evening and won't be home for dinner. I'm sorry, but it's business and can't be switched to another night." He looked, she thought, genuinely apologetic.

"That's quite all right," she said, as Mrs. Polaski set down a cup and saucer and poured coffee from a silver pot. "Thank you," she said, and Mrs. Polaski gave her a warm smile.

"More coffee for you, sir?" the woman asked Sanford, whose eyes clicked off Jess and onto her.

"Thank you, Olga." He slid his cup toward her.

After Mrs. Polaski had gone back to the kitchen, Sanford lifted his cup with both hands, his eyes again on Jess. There were faintly purple circles under her eyes that were not merely, he decided, from fatigue. He'd known one or two other women with complexions like hers. A need for sexual release was responsible for casting those telltale circles under her eyes. He smiled at her, saying, "I give you my word I'll keep this next week clear."

"I have quite a lot left to do," she said, staring at the coffee, feeling too weak to lift the cup. "Some work needs to be done in the staff apartment. There's a leak somewhere . . . a plumber . . . And curtains for the second guest room."

"It's Sunday, Jess," he reminded her. "Today you can relax. Or go to church. Funny, I don't believe I've asked you about that."

"About church? I don't go, don't believe."

"Neither do I."

"You have a business appointment on a Sunday evening?" she asked rashly, without thinking.

"From out of town. Ottawa. He's on his way to Winnipeg, then Vancouver. I really am very sorry."

"I didn't mean to question you. *I'm* sorry." He seemed to feel very at home here, she thought, looking around the bright, white dining room. She knew this room, this house. Why did she feel so out of place?

"I didn't think you'd be up so early," he said, setting the newspaper down on the far side of his plate. "I was trying to catch up on last week's reading." He tapped the paper with his finger. "I've got quite a bit of catching up to do at the office, too."

She could feel tears building, and thought she'd never forgive herself if she wept in front of him like a disappointed schoolgirl. She made herself pick up the cup and take a drink of coffee, hoping to dissolve the clot in her throat. She swallowed. It went down wrong and she began to choke, coughing, too quickly putting down the cup so that the coffee sloshed over her hands and the tablecloth as she gagged, trying to catch her breath, tears flooding from her eyes.

He jumped up, ran around the table, yanked her to her feet, spun her around so that her back was against his chest and with his hands on her diaphragm, instructed her to, "Breathe out! Breathe out! Slowly! Don't cough, Jess! Try not to cough! That's it! Breathe out slowly, slowly."

After a minute or so, she was able to take a breath, then another, and he eased the directing pressure of his hands. Finally, he freed one hand to present her with his handkerchief. She reached for it, at the same moment seized by another, lesser coughing spasm, then held it to her eyes.

He looked at the downy nape of her neck, felt her breast against his hand and had to take a deep breath before saying, "You'll be all right. The best thing you can do now is sit down and slowly drink the rest of the coffee. You're all right?"

She nodded, forgetfully retaining the handkerchief. He returned to his chair and watched as she lifted the cup, took a small sip, swallowed, then took another sip. Her hair had become disarranged and half of it now hung over her shoulder. He thought she looked exquisitely beautiful.

"Aren't you hungry?" he asked. "You should eat breakfast."

Her hand lifted to touch the hair at her shoulder, then drifted back to the cup.

"Leave it," he said. "I like it. You look like one of those half-blasted statues they're forever digging up on Greek islands."

She gave him a small smile that quite suddenly grew larger. "I thought you were . . ." she stopped.

"I know," he said, reading her thought, elated by her smile.

She was about to say something more when Tillie bounced in, declaring, "I'm famished! Good morning, everyone," and took her place at the table as if she'd been dining with the two of them all her life. She sensed at once that she'd interrupted something, especially in view of the fact that Jess stayed only a few moments longer, then excused herself, saying, "I'll go up and try to get the stain out of my sleeve before it sets."

After she left, Tillie took in the spilled coffee on the table-cloth, and asked, "What happened?"

"Your sister swallowed the wrong way."

"Oh!" Tillie smiled as Mrs. Polaski came in, and asked for "lots of breakfast." Then she sat back to steal a look at Sanford, who'd returned to reading *The Financial Post*. In tan trousers, a matching V-necked cashmere sweater over a beige-and-white checked shirt, he was elegant, she thought. Press would be too, when he was as old as Sanford.

Tillie was going out with Press. "Ice-skating," she told Jess. "Then I'm having dinner with his parents. This is the big night when we tell them we're engaged."

"I'm happy for you." Jess smiled up at her from the depths of the blue armchair by the bedroom window where she'd been sitting, trying to read, but thinking longingly of a nap. Her body ached with fatigue. "He's a lovely man. And he thinks the world of you."

"I know. I think the world of him, too," she said glibly. "I won't be late," she promised, and left.

A short time later, Sanford knocked at the door and came in. Why, she wondered, did he feel he had to knock? Or had he no intention of sharing this room with her? This would be her second married night alone.

"The stain come out all right?" he asked. "May I?" he said, as he settled himself in the twin armchair.

"Yes, it did." She looked down at the sleeve of her light brown dress.

"I like this room," he said, reaching into his shirt pocket for his cigarettes. "It's the most comfortable in the house. Not," he added, "that the other rooms aren't. But this is the most inviting somehow." It came out sounding ambiguous, but he decided to let it stand.

"I like it, too," she agreed, her eyes traveling over the light-blue walls as if she'd never seen the place before. Snow-white trim, royal-blue carpeting, and blue-figured curtains with a white background, gracefully swagged. Their two armchairs were positioned either side of a low, round table, upon which sat a plump brass lamp with a white linen shade. Everything meshed in the blendings of blue and white. Her eyes came to rest for dangerous seconds on the now made-up bed with its half-moon curve of brass headboard and heavy white spread.

"Have you plans for the day?" he asked. He dropped his lighter back into his trouser pocket, extending his leg toward her to do so.

"Plans? No."

"Well, good. How about a walk?"

"Yes, all right. Now?"

"Why not?"

He was so polite, treating her like an elderly maiden aunt, or a visiting dignitary; knocking on doors, asking about her plans, taking her arm to escort her down the front steps. He kept hold of her arm once they were on the slippery sidewalk and heading out of the Village, south towards St. Clair. He had long legs and walked quickly. She silently admired a gracious, sprawling red brick house with white shutters and, next to it, a starkly black and white mock-Tudor.

"What do you like to do, Jess?"

"Do? In what way?"

"Do you like to swim, or play tennis, golf? It's never occurred to me to ask you that, either."

"I like to swim. But I'm afraid I don't know any games." Father had promised her tennis lessons; she was to have had them that summer of The Crash. "Tillie and Press are going to announce their engagement to his parents tonight," she said, anxious to take the conversation away from herself.

"What do you think of that?" he asked.

"I'm happy for her, of course."

"Tell me what you really think."

"I don't know what you mean."

"Of course you do, Jess. Sometimes you're so deliberately obtuse I'd like to shake you." He smiled and touched the crown of his hat to two elderly women passing.

"I think," she said cautiously, "that Press will end up badly hurt by her. I hope I'm wrong, but I don't think so."

"Why?"

"Because," she said, savoring this new freedom to air her thoughts in complete confidentiality, "Tillie believes so totally in 'love.' She's romanticized it out of all proportion. I don't think she actually loves him, or even knows what it is."

"No?" He turned to say, "Good day," to a couple who smiled and returned the greeting.

"He loves her very much. She's bound to hurt him, I think, because he can never live up to her expectations."

"I tend to agree. And what about you? What do you think of love?"

"It's how you feel about brothers and sisters, your mother and father, your children."

"And that's all?"

"I've always been . . . Well, not always . . . I don't believe in other kinds of love." Her eyes were caught by two small children tumbling in the snow, their cheeks very red from the cold.

"Yes, you do," he disagreed.

"You don't know that." Her eyes left the children and she looked down at the icy sidewalk.

"It shows," he said. "It's in the way you treat people, even the ones you think you hate."

"What are you trying to say?" She turned against the biting wind to look at him, noticing as she did that two girls on the opposite side of the street were watching them.

"I'm not *trying* to say anything. I'm just stating my observations."

They waited for a streetcar to pass, and then crossed St. Clair and started through the park, toward the reservoir. After about fifty yards, he stopped, asking, "Are you too cold? Are you enjoying this?" Were they both crazy? he wondered. Maybe this whole thing was crazy: going after a woman because of one viewing, and a sudden burning need to be free to see her face daily, hourly, if he chose. This was impossible. You couldn't force someone to be the way you wanted her to be. Perhaps he was endowing her with qualities she didn't have.

"I am cold," she said, bothered by the hard, penetrating light of his eyes.

"I'm sorry. I forget sometimes . . ." He didn't go on to complete the explanation as he steered her back over the snow-covered grass to the sidewalk. As they stepped down to recross St. Clair, he stopped her again, bringing her back onto the curb by taking hold of both arms under the elbows so that she was forced to look up at him. He seemed so sober all at once and his grip on her was so powerful, that for a moment she felt frightened.

"You looked so damned beautiful this morning," he said angrily. "Sitting there with your hair half up, half down and your nose running, your eyes red from coughing and crying. You looked *real* for the first time since we met. Have you any idea at all who you are, Jess?"

"I don't . . . what . . . ?"

"For God's sake, I'm scaring you." He let go of her arms and allowed his hands to fall to his sides. "You look like a woman, dress yourself like one, but I keep seeing a frightened little girl looking out at me through your eyes. And every time I do, I have an awful feeling I'm not sure I know which of the two is really you. I hope it's the woman."

"What do you *want*?" she asked beseechingly.

"I refuse to live with anyone's contempt, Jess. We can keep walking, or we can go back to the house, if you'd rather."

"I think I'd like to go back, if you don't mind."

"Fine." The light changed and they crossed. He didn't trust himself to take hold of her arm again and plunged his hands deep into his overcoat pockets. "Ever heard of the Brooke Bond Company?" he asked.

"I'm not sure," she answered, thrown by this altogether unexpected shift from personal matters to business.

"It's a British-owned tea company. They came into the North American market in Thirty-two when they acquired Red Rose Tea."

"Oh!"

"I'm trying to get them to produce and package a Riverwood Brand. I'm also trying to get a house brand of cheddar. Aside from that, I've got a supply contract with the government for a number of east-coast canteens. Business is very good, but Edward has none of the flair for it I'd hoped he would. He resents 'taking orders' from his younger brother, so I'm battling him most of the way; but he likes the money well enough to stay in line. We've got a lot of irons in the fire. Once the war's over, I want to build up the company, branch out even more. Right now, we're held back because most of the best men are in the service, but once the war's out of the way, I'll really start building, make it something important to leave behind."

He was talking about dying and she didn't want to hear about that when they'd only spent two days together and he'd yet to touch her. She half-listened as he elaborated on his plans, wondering when, if ever, he intended to get into bed with her.

Something feral and needy inside her shouted at him to shut up and just go ahead and take her. He'd paid for it, why not have it?

She sat in the living room listening to the news while he went to change for his meeting. When he reappeared in the doorway, his topcoat over his arm and hat in hand, she got up to turn down the volume.

"I'm sorry to have to do this," he said again.

"I understand." She took several steps across the room and stopped. He looked dignified and unapproachable, the light from the foyer catching the silver in his hair. A warm air current brought her the subtle scent of his cologne and she breathed deeply.

To hell with it! he thought and came across the room to stand in front of her. The full impact of his presence swept over her like a sudden rise in temperature and she thought back to that morning and how he'd pulled her up and dragged her against him, how his hands had pressed in under her breasts, forcing her to breathe slowly.

"I'll probably be late," he said, shifting the hat to his other hand, the newly freed one lifting past her shoulder and over the back of her neck. He brought her forward, their eyes locked, until his mouth covered hers and he kissed her deeply, then abruptly let her go. He started to say something, changed his mind, took a step away, then turned and strode out. Leaving her then was one of the single most difficult things he'd ever done.

She stood where he left her, slowly raising her hand to touch her wet mouth, wanting to run after him. After a minute or so, she adjusted the volume on the radio, then went back to the sofa, carefully crossing her legs and smoothing her skirt before picking up a copy of *Saturday Night* and lifting the cover. Her hands were trembling uncontrollably.

Three days later, he telephoned mid-morning from the office to say, "Come down and have lunch with me."

Treating all his requests like demands, she agreed to meet him at twelve, then went upstairs to change and call a taxi.

As she waited for the taxi, she found herself playing at planning suicide and wondered why, when it seemed as if she had everything she'd ever wanted, she couldn't enjoy it. The

answer was because Sanford wouldn't come to her. Did he
think of her as a whore? A ceremony and a set of rings didn't
elevate her above that.

The taxi honked. She pulled on her gloves and went out.

He showed her his wood-paneled office before introducing
her to the staff. She suffered through it with her spine stiff and
her chin uplifted, trying to decide if it was in his mind to
humiliate her in some subtle fashion. But no, he actually
seemed proud while making the introductions, and watched
with a fond expression as she shook hands with the secretaries
and clerks and receptionist. Then he held open the door before
escorting her out into the elevator.

"You hated every second of it," he said, his eyes on the
floor indicator. "Why?"

"I find it difficult meeting new people."

"I see," he said, unsatisfied.

In the restaurant, Jess looked around, freezing at the sight
of Cotton in the company of three executive types at a table
directly across the room. When his eyes connected with hers,
she looked away at once, peripherally seeing him whisper
something to the man to his right. She could feel all four men's
eyes on her and stared at the tabletop, wishing she could disappear.

"What is it?" Sanford asked, lighting a cigarette.

In a whisper, she explained briefly about Cotton. Sanford
glanced over, then looked back at Jess, taking hold of her hand.
"Don't hang your head and hide," he said. "I'm not ashamed
of you. Pay no attention to them."

"But he knows," she whispered, drowning in shame. "How
can you *bear* this?"

"For a long time to come, you and I are bound to run into
men who knew you. I won't allow you to feel this way."

"I'm a coward. Didn't you know?"

"Nonsense! You're no more a coward than I am. You're
bothered because you think I am, and I assure you I'm not.
You're a beautiful woman and I'm happy to be seen with you."

He meant it. She lifted her head and met his eyes. He smiled
encouragingly. She sat up straighter. His smile broadened and
he gave her hand a squeeze.

She said, "Thank you," and managed to eat a small portion
of the lunch.

Later, Sanford put her into a cab, saying, "I'll see you this evening," and then walked off. She watched him go, feeling as if she'd just sustained a severe beating, but reassured by what he'd said. Perhaps he'd come to her tonight, she thought, and sat back against the seat with her eyes closed, hands numbed inside her gloves, wanting to believe in miracles, thinking of those men all looking at her and whispering. Part of the price of the dream was humiliation, but it was too late to go back.

Delighted with the coincidence and the extraordinary good luck of having selected this particular restaurant on a day that brought the bitch and her new husband here, Cotton sat back lighting a White Owl, letting the conversation go on without him, thinking. She'd been upset as hell, he knew. Any fool could tell that from the way Woodrich had been talking to her and the way she'd slowly straightened.

Nothing to do about it at the moment, he concluded, having carefully gone back over the incident. But her having married this guy, there'd be something in that. Sooner or later, she'd get the comeuppance she deserved. And I'm a mighty patient fellow, he thought, puffing contentedly on the cigar. I can wait.

◇ Eleven ◇

Each night for two weeks, Sanford kissed her good night, told her to, "Sleep well," then took himself off to one of the guest rooms. She spent the nights hovering on the edge of sleep, waiting for him to come and make his claim upon her. She couldn't understand the game, or his rules, and refused to ask. So she moved through each day in an increasingly exhausted state, completely at sea, wishing he'd say or do something that would finally enable her to understand.

The week she was due to return to classes, Tillie announced, "I've decided not to go back."

Distressed, Jess asked, "You're quitting school?"

"I'm switching over to the Art College. I think maybe you were right. I'm not doing so well...got off to a bad start. Anyway, I'm going down there today to see if they'll let me start mid-term."

Now that they were engaged, Tillie felt secure enough about Press not to have to see him every day on campus. She also thought that a bit of distance might make him more eager for an early marriage. He was talking about getting married, "...in a couple of years, when I've really got my feet wet downtown." She had no intention of waiting that long, but he seemed quite immovable. If increased distance failed to accomplish what she wanted, then she'd have to think up something else. The "something else" was sickeningly clear to her, and she didn't want to have to do *that* unless there were no alternatives.

"What about Press?" Jess was asking. "I thought you liked seeing each other for lunch and so on."

"I've decided maybe that's been a mistake. It'll be better for both of us if we don't see each other quite so much."

"It's a game," Jess said tiredly. "You're playing with him."

"No, it isn't!" She looked offended. "It isn't at all."

"You don't think so, but it is. Do all the girls do it?"

"Do what?"

"Set their sights on some boy and then maneuver him until he capitulates?"

"That's not how it is!"

"That's the way it looks. I honestly don't see the point."

"The point? There *is* no point, not the way you mean. I love him and he loves me. I'm just doing..." For one glaringly lucid moment, she could see that Jess was right. It *was* a game, and she was playing it with a vengeance. But what other way was there? You found someone to love, got married, and lived together happily ever after. "I don't want to end up with no one to look after me, no one for me to care about. And that's the only other way."

"I don't think so."

"You don't think so," Tillie argued, "but you married Sanford. Why, if it wasn't because you didn't want to be alone?"

For you, Jess thought. So I could continue giving you the things you need. And for me because I couldn't keep on with that life.

"There are other ways, Tillie. You've got talent. You could do such a lot with it, be someone in your own right. If I had your talent... Why do you feel you have to tie yourself up in Press? I remember the day you told me we had to run away. In Vermont, remember? You insisted that I had choices but was never willing to see them. *You* have choices, far more than most people. And talent, too."

"I don't know what you're talking about," Tillie said crossly, privately agreeing with the part about Jess's lacking talent, but mainly annoyed at Jess's trying to run her life. "I suppose you'd like me to end up an eccentric old maid giving art classes somewhere and selling my dear little watercolors at local art shows with a bunch of other old fools."

"It might not be all that bad," Jess said thoughtfully. "At least you'd be doing what you wanted, and beholden to no one."

"People weren't *meant* to live all by themselves," Tillie reasoned. "We were meant to live *together*, to have families."

"Who says so?"

"Everybody! That's the way it gets done."

"So the story goes," Jess gave up, finding it hard to think clearly. She was too weary to sustain any line of thought for very long.

"You're talking like some kind of fanatic!" Tillie accused. "I mean, here you are with this house—six damned bedrooms, four bathrooms, formal and informal dining rooms, this room and that one, and those platinum rings, and a millionaire husband, and you're lecturing at me that there's some other way and *I'm* playing *games*? Don't you think that's just a little hypocritical?"

"I didn't mean it that way. I'm thinking about you, Tillie, and your future happiness."

"You don't look deliriously happy yourself, you know, sitting there like a zombie, for Pete's sake!"

"That hasn't anything to do with what I'm trying to tell you."

"You're saying you don't think Press can make me happy?"

"I didn't say that."

"Well, you're thinking it."

"No, I wasn't thinking it." They'd both be happy for a time, she thought. Until Tillie began to see that neither Press nor the love she claimed to have for him were what she'd thought they were. "I'm sorry if I've upset you," she apologized. "I haven't been sleeping well. I'd never intentionally hurt you."

"I know," Tillie admitted, still nettled by what had seemed to be Jess's holier-than-thou preachings. "Look, I'd better go if I'm going. I want to get down to the registrar's office and get started on the applications."

"I'm glad you've decided to change over." Jess smiled with effort. "I know you'll do well."

"Maybe," Tillie said, as she was going out, "you should get a prescription for sleeping pills or something. You're starting to look a little..." She couldn't find a word to describe how Jess looked. "Why not take a nap this afternoon?" she said, realizing Jess really did seem very frail. She derived the oddest feeling of superiority because of it. "I'll wake you when I get back, if you like. It won't take all day to enroll."

"I might," Jess said.

"Okay. See you later."

Jess looked around the spacious living room, abstractedly admiring the way the pale winter sun caught the curve of a small crystal vase on the table by the window. She'd have liked to go out to the kitchen and try some new, complicated recipe, but what was the point? She seemed trapped into inactivity by the presences of Mrs. Ferguson and Mrs. Polaski and the daily cleaning lady. She needed something to do. What, though? She'd been so young when the family had had staff. She couldn't seem to remember what her mother had done during the days, before she'd become bedridden. She opened the cigarette box on the coffee table, took out one of Sanford's Player's and lit it, sitting with her arms crossed under her breasts, absently smoking, watching the smoke collect in the sunlight from the windows, trying to think of how to fill the remainder of this day, and all the days. If she didn't find some way to divert herself, she'd most likely go mad.

"I've got to go to Ottawa on business," Sanford told her. They were sitting in the master bedroom on the third Sunday of their marriage.

"I see. For how long?"

"A week, ten days at most." *Ask me to bring you along* he thought. He'd gladly take her, do anything, if she'd just ask.

She lit a cigarette, trying to conceal the sudden tremor in her hands, thinking of the week or ten days she'd somehow have to fill, for the first time in her life frightened of time and its potential emptiness.

He waited for her to say something and when she didn't, he said, "I'll leave the hotel number, in case you need to reach me."

"Thank you." Very precisely, she tapped her cigarette against the lip of the ashtray. Smoking seemed her only interest lately, and she was becoming very good at it, up to almost a pack a day. The smoke managed to put a pleasantly fuzzy edge to everything, not as well fuzzed as the before-dinner drinks

Sanford mixed, but good enough.

"Is everything all right, Jess?" he asked, giving her a large opening, hoping she'd take it.

"Fine. Everything is fine." She wanted to hit him just as hard as she could.

"Do you use anything?" he asked, hoping to shock her off guard. "A diaphragm, douche, something of that nature?"

She couldn't respond for a moment, nervously wetting her lips. How could he so randomly interject these intimate questions into the heart of casual conversations? "A diaphragm," she answered, a fluttering in her throat, her hands palsied.

"Does it work?" he asked interestedly, as if investigating the properties of some new wonder drug.

"Not always."

"What does that mean?"

"Twice, it didn't."

"What did you do then?"

She looked down at her lap, then at the ashtray, taking her time putting out her cigarette. His asking brought it all back: the small heavily curtained room, the examining table, her hands clinging to the sides of the table. And the pain, the searing, monstrous pain. "Abortions," she whispered, close to hating him.

"What was it like?"

"Painful," she said, her desire to strike him growing. "Awful."

"Awful?"

"*Please!*" Her voice cracked.

"I've never known a woman who'd had it done. Some who threatened it, but no one who's actually experienced it. Twice," he added.

"Are you trying to remind me of what I am . . . was?"

"I don't have to do that. I'm sure you do it well enough yourself."

"Then what *are* you trying to do?" she demanded.

"I am trying," he said patiently, "to get you to talk to me about the things that matter to you."

"Why *that*, of all things?"

"Because it was important, and we've never discussed the things that are important to either one of us."

"You've told me nothing," she said flatly.

"Nor have you." He took out his cigarettes and offered her

one. She refused and he lit his own. "What if I told you I was going to spend the week with another woman?" he asked.

Her entire body turned cold. "Then I would hope you have a very pleasant time," she said icily. "You made the terms quite clear to me from the outset."

"I'll be alone, as it happens." He stood up directly in front of her, glad to have provoked her into a real reaction. "I'll call you."

His questions and the things he said took her body through temperatures from stiflingly hot to sub-zero. She couldn't look at him.

He said good night, ". . . and sleep well, Jess," and went off to the guest room. The omission of a good-night kiss puzzled her. It was the first time he'd failed to give it. She found a cigarette and returned to her chair to sit looking out the window at the frozen, denuded trees.

The telephone rang, rousing her from the only sound sleep she'd had in weeks. She felt about on the bedside table in the dark and lifted the receiver. An operator said, "Go ahead, sir."

"It isn't a game or any sort of contest, Jess," he said without preamble. "Nothing like that."

She pushed the pillows up behind her, instantly awake, holding the receiver to her ear with both hands, listening to the ghostlike, whispery long-distance noises on the line.

"What is it then?" she asked, able to speak to him because of his distance.

"I don't honestly know what to call it," he said, his voice very rich and clear. "All I know is that it has to be done."

"But *why?*" she begged, tears collecting.

He sighed. "I suppose to get you back into the world of the living."

"I'm not dead!" she protested.

"What do you want, Jess?"

"Me? I want nothing. I'm not . . ."

"Nothing at all?"

"I don't know what you want me to say."

"I want you to tell me how you feel, what you want. It isn't too complicated."

"You need someone to exercise your power on!"

"No. I don't feel that way about you."

"I . . . You . . ." She couldn't think or speak.

"It's late and I've had a long day. I just wanted to hear your voice. I like the way you sound on the telephone. I'll talk to you again tomorrow. Good night, Jess. Sleep well."

He hung up and she was left with the buzzing receiver welded damply to her ear. After a moment, she replaced it, then lowered her head into her hands, sobbing.

This time she was awake, waiting, an unlooked-at book facedown on her lap, and when the telephone rang, she lifted the receiver before the first ring had finished and heard the operator say, "You're through, sir."

"Were you waiting?" he asked, a pleased note in his voice.

"You said you'd call."

"What are you wearing?" he asked.

"Wearing? A nightgown."

"What's it like?"

"It's just a white nightgown."

"I want to be able to picture you. Are you in bed?"

"I . . . yes."

"With your hair down and a white nightgown. It sounds a very pretty picture. What sort of nightgown?"

"I . . ."

"Is everything all right?" he asked, not waiting for her to answer.

"Fine! Everything is *fine*!"

"You have a wonderful voice on the telephone, very throaty and soft. I can just see you."

"*Sanford! Why are you doing this?*"

"Do you know," he went on unperturbed, "that the people I care about call me Sandy?"

She said nothing.

"I've got to be up early. It's been another long day. I'll call you again tomorrow evening."

"This is obscene!" she cried. "*Obscene!*"

"What nonsense!" he chided her. "A telephone call from your husband?"

When she said nothing further, he said his ritual good night and sleep well, and hung up. She slammed down the receiver and lit a cigarette.

She let it ring four times before picking up. And after he'd said hello, she very firmly and coldly said, "You are *not* my husband!"

"You haven't allowed me to be."

"I . . . ? I've never stopped you . . . never . . ."

"You've never given me any indication whatsoever you were either willing or interested."

"But you're supposed to . . ."

"Do you want me, Jess?" His voice was golden as syrup, oozing thickly over her.

"How long is this going to go on?" she asked, quivering.

"I've never disliked anything more than these calls," he said truthfully. "But at least this way you'll talk to me."

"You never try to talk to me when you're here."

"You know that isn't true."

"I can't . . . Please, will you . . ." The tears made the breath catch in her throat. "*Please!*" she cried on a thin, desperate note.

"Are you crying, Jess? It's the most human thing you've done in all the months I've known you," he said softly. "Go back to sleep now. I'll talk to you tomorrow."

She allowed the receiver to slide away out of her hand.

She was dressed, sitting in the armchair by the windows, smoking, when the telephone rang. She got up leadenly and walked across the room to sit down on the side of the bed, resting her forehead on her hand as she answered.

"Do you hate me?" he asked.

Surprised, drained, she answered, "No, but I should. You're trying to drive me mad and I don't know why."

"No," he said, sounding hurt. "I'm not trying to do anything of the sort."

"I don't care," she sighed.

"I'll be back tomorrow night."

She jerked upright. "When?"

"Not later than nine. Don't wait dinner for me."

"No, all right. I won't."

"How's Tillie?"

"She's fine. She's going up to Collingwood skiing with Press and his parents tomorrow afternoon, for the weekend." She'd be there alone when he returned. What would happen? It had been more than five months since anyone had touched her. Would he? He had to. She couldn't fill the emptiness with cigarette smoke or before-dinner drinks or heavy meals she couldn't finish.

"Is she enjoying the Art College?"

"It seems so."

"Good. Are you wearing the white nightgown?"

"I'm not going to answer that, Sanford."

"Good night then, Jess. Sleep well."

She put the phone down and went into the dressing room to get ready for bed.

Tillie left for school carrying her weekend bag as well as her large, black portfolio. Jess watched her go off thinking, *We don't kiss anymore, or hug, or even talk the way we used to.* They were as distant as strangers, living politely formal lives in this big house.

She closed the door and returned to the dining room for a second cup of coffee. Looking down the length of the table at Sanford's empty chair, she was gripped by something very like dread. Not later than nine, he'd said. It was now only eight-thirty in the morning. It would be more than twelve hours before he came through the front door. She carried her cup up to the bedroom, feeling angrier than she'd known herself capable of being, so angry the blood rushed in her ears and her every gesture was short and sharp. She wanted to attack him, to vent her outrage at his refusal to approach her and his lack of susceptibility to her appeal. He seemed determined to go past the temptation of her sexuality and get into her feelings.

She wanted to confront him naked, and deprive him of his resistance so that she might firmly place him in the cold climate of her contempt for all men. But he seemed to know that and steadfastly deflected her at every turn. She wanted him, but was incapable of openly offering herself to anyone. He had to make the first move, and he simply would not. He would never touch her, she slowly understood, unless she made it clear that not only was she willing, but also that she wouldn't afterward hold him in contempt because he'd proved himself subject to her appeal. He wanted her to *love* him. This realization so flattened her that she had to sit down. Looking out the window sightlessly, she felt bereft, unable to imagine going on this way for month after month, for years. Love me, love me, love me. Her brain was heavy with images of her naked self moistly writhing in anticipation of his caresses, with pictures of Sanford without his clothes; darkened-room embraces, and his mouth descending on her throat, her breasts, between her thighs, his hands at last laying claim to her. She could see herself in the act of receiving him into her body, could hear her own anguished cry of pleasure and release.

She swallowed, her throat too dry, then took a sip of the now-cold coffee. With a fresh cigarette, she sat with her eyes closed, waiting.

◇ Twelve ◇

"*Why* do we have to wait two years?" Tillie asked, exasperated, looking around the huge lodge living room. "What difference is it going to make if we get married now?"

"A whole lot," he said, tired of going over and over this with her. "In two years, I'll be able to start some real work as a broker and there'll be money coming in for us to live on."

"You're not going to be working for nothing, are you?"

"Course not."

"Then that argument just isn't any good."

"Look, Tillie, I want to wait for a while. Okay? I can give you reasons until the cows come home but I'm still going to want to wait no matter how many times you insist on asking. I'm just not ready for a wife and all the . . . the responsibilities."

Tillie thought about the house on Brunswick that Jess would've given her if she hadn't been in such a big hurry to say no. But Jess had promised her down-payment money if and when.

"If all you're worried about is the money, you can forget it," she said. "Jess promised me a house for a wedding present." She'd ask Jess about it as soon as she got home. That money could make all the difference, get her what she wanted.

"I am *not* going to sponge off your sister," he said. "And not off my folks, either. That's not the way I happen to do things."

"It isn't sponging. It's a gift."

"Call it whatever you like, but I'm not taking on a wife and a house and kids until I can pay for them. And that's not going to be for at least two more years."

"And if I say I *won't* wait?"

His face turned very dark red. "Don't threaten me, Tillie," he warned.

"I'm not threatening you," she lied, suddenly quite thrilled at the prospect of going back out into the world without the burden of Press's affections. But she wasn't ready yet to give up on him. "I'm just asking what you'll do if I tell you I won't wait that long."

"Frankly," he said, sick to death of the whole never-ending argument, "maybe I don't feel like rehashing this every weekend for the next two years."

"What's that supposed to mean?"

"Just what I said. My idea of fun isn't arguing with my fiancée about when we're going to get married. We're engaged. I've given you the ring. If that's not enough for you, then maybe we just ought to forget the whole thing."

This wasn't the way it was supposed to go, she thought, getting to her feet. He was supposed to beg her to stay with him and promise anything to get her to do that, not offer to call it all off.

"Well, if that's all I mean to you," she said, pulling the ring from her finger, "then you're right. Let's just forget it!" She threw down the ring and ran to her room to start frantically tossing things into her bag, gripped by an excitement so acute it was almost sexual. She expected him to come knocking apologetically at the door any moment and slowed down with the packing after a few minutes to give him time. When it didn't happen, the excitement evolved into a small fear and she said aloud, "To hell with him!" and marched over to the closet to drag her coat off the hanger and shove her arms into it, then yank on her boots. Pulling her hat down firmly over her ears, she slung her shoulder bag over her arm, picked up the weekend case and her portfolio, and got the door open. He was still sitting on the floor by the fireplace where she'd left him. At the sound of the bedroom door opening, he looked over. He was holding her ring with the fingers of both hands, turning it slowly.

"What're you doing?" he asked, looking as if he were in a state of shock.

"I'm going home. And *you* can go to *hell*!"

She stomped through the lodge's living room to the front door, flung it open, and was assailed by a blast of freezing wind that stopped her breath for a moment. Then she lowered her head and went out, intending to walk the couple of miles to the main road where she'd flag down the bus to the city. She could hear him shouting, "Wait! You can't!" but ignored him and trudged on through the snow.

As she went, the suitcase heavier than it had seemed before and the portfolio the most awkward thing she'd ever had to carry, she wondered if she shouldn't have stayed and given him the silent treatment until morning. Stopping to look at her watch, she saw it was just past six and tried to remember what time the last bus went through, worried by the possibility that she might have missed it. Well, if she had, she'd just hitchhike. There was no way on earth she was going to stay in that lodge with that idiot. Not for an entire evening without even his parents to talk to—they were out for dinner with friends.

All they ever did was argue. What possible difference could it make when they got married? It was the stupidest, most unreasonable position anyone had ever taken.

It was very dark and she was grateful for the high snowbanks either side of the road that lent enough reflected light for her to see where she was going. She paused to rest at the end of a plowed-out driveway, looking up and down the road to see if anything was coming as she clapped her mittened hands together to warm them. It was so cold it hurt to breathe. She removed her scarf and wrapped it around her face so that only her eyes were uncovered, and tugged her knitted hat all the way down to her eyebrows. That felt better. She picked up her things and set off again. She guessed she wasn't more than half a mile from the bus stop.

Her head lowered, trying to avoid the wind, she suddenly saw an image of Press smiling and felt an advance pang of loneliness. She'd miss him. And she hated the idea of having to start all over, hoping to find someone more willing to take care of her. It depressed her to think of spending weekends alone, with only girl friends for company. He really was cute,

Press, except for being so damned stubborn and stupid when it came to this one issue. Why couldn't he just give in?

She felt like crying, and was so involved in inspecting her new aloneness that she failed to hear the car coming up behind her. She jumped, jolted, when the horn sounded, and scurried as far over to the side of the road as possible, waiting for the car to go past. When it didn't, she turned to see Press sitting behind the wheel of the red Ford looking like someone at a funeral. Abruptly, she turned and continued walking.

He rolled down his window, poked his head out, and said, "You've already missed the last bus. Unless you plan to walk sixty miles back to the city, you might as well get in."

She ignored him.

"Okay! Go ahead and pretend I'm not here! I'll just stick behind you to make sure you get home all right. I'm not going to be held responsible if something happens to you. Some gang of soldiers on leave roll up and see you walking alone and decide you're just what they've been looking for. I'm not having that on my head."

She kept on ignoring him.

His voice was closer to her when he spoke again. "You know something, Tillie? I'm really crazy about you. I actually love you. Which is probably the dumbest goddamned thing I've ever done in my life: getting hooked on a girl who only cares about getting her own way, no matter what. You think I'm such a goon, such a dummy. Reward poor Press, the sucker, he's been a good boy, so let him cop a feel. Big goddamned deal! All you care about is getting that stinking ring on your finger just as fast as you can, getting me hog-tied but good and then, *then*, you'll give me the big ultimate reward and let me lay you. As if that's all you think's important to me."

She was tempted to turn around, but didn't.

"You're the biggest pain in the ass I've ever known!" he shouted. "When you stop pushing and relax—which isn't all that bloody often, either—you're a lot of fun. And when you stop promoting all that romantic bullshit, you're a pretty bright girl. Why don't you just relax and let us enjoy being together without always pounding at me to marry you right away?"

"That is *not* the only thing I'm interested in!"

"The *hell* it *isn't*!"

"Oh, go *away*!" she flung back over her shoulder.

He stopped the car, jumped out and ran up, grabbed her by the shoulder, and pulled her to a stop. "Get in the goddamned car and stop all this shit, or so help me God, Tillie, I'll wallop you! You want to go home in the morning, that's jake with me. But there's no way I'm letting you do it tonight, so get your damned ass in that car *right now!*"

Taking her roughly by the arm, he pushed her back up the road to the car, shoved her in, flung her suitcase and portfolio over into the back and, fuming, got in behind the wheel, slammed the door, and put the car in reverse.

"Don't think you can get away with pushing me around!" she snapped.

"Shut up! I don't want to be with you right now any more than you want to be with me. But I won't be responsible for something happening to you because you're so mule-headed you won't wait twelve hours for a bus."

"Go to hell!"

"Go fuck yourself!"

She went silent, transfixed by this new view of him, secretly pleased to discover he wasn't so stupid or so malleable as she'd thought. It made him more of a challenge than ever.

When they arrived back at the lodge, he left her to get her own things from the car and went on ahead to open the front door, standing waiting while she made her way up the path.

"You hungry?" he asked brusquely.

"No, thank you."

"Fine! I'll eat by my goddamned self!" He stalked off to the kitchen, where he began banging pots and pans, opening and then slamming shut the pantry door.

Defeated—he'd won this round hands down—she carried her things back to the bedroom, hung up her coat and hat, kicked off her boots, and began unpacking. She'd probably managed to spoil everything for good now by saying and doing all the worst possible things. Next time, she promised herself, she'd be smarter about how she handled him, if there was a next time.

Oh, but there was bound to be. Because she was still here with him and they had all night. She sat down on the side of the bed trying to decide the best way to handle the situation.

Jess had dozed off in the chair. She awoke with a start when Polly Ferguson tapped at the door, opened it at Jess's, "Yes?"

and said, "There's a gentleman downstairs asking to see you, Mrs. Woodrich."

"A gentleman?" she repeated groggily.

"That's right. He said to tell you it's an old friend."

That sounded too chillingly as if it might be one of her former clients. Overwrought, she thanked Polly and sent her off to tell the gentleman she'd be right down. Then she went to the bathroom to tidy her hair and check her makeup before going out and slowly down the stairs. Why was she so frightened? She pictured Cotton's bulk spreading over the edges of one of the living-room chairs, and told herself that was ridiculous. He wouldn't dare come here.

The man turned.

"René!" Her relief was so enormous it left her weak as she embraced him, welcoming the comforting, familiar circle of his arms for a moment.

"I got your letter," he said almost shyly, looking around. "Me, I'm real happy for you."

"Come sit down with me," she invited. "Would you like something to drink, or some coffee? Have you eaten?"

"Nothing, eh? I know you're busy but I wanted to see you, talk with you a little and the phone it isn't listed, so I just come by. It's okay, I just come by?"

"It's perfectly all right. I'm so glad you did."

They sat at opposite ends of the sofa and he looked at her very respectfully, she thought, as if she'd altered almost beyond recognition. She reached for the cigarette box and offered it to him. He took a cigarette, then watched with interest as she lit hers before holding the lighter out to him.

"You're smokin' these days, eh?"

"A new habit," she said wryly, wondering what had happened to their old ease together. It seemed to have vanished.

He took a slow, deep breath, trying to absorb the changes in her. She looked so much older, and all tired out. The bones in her face seemed to show more than he remembered. And her hands, he noticed, they shook. "Okay," he said, "I tell you how come I'm here. See, I got me this good chance for startin' a truckin' company. Me, I got the two trucks now, and a chance for two more. With four trucks on the road, a year or two, I get maybe two more. I keep going and soon, I got me sixteen, twenty. Lots of consignments now with the war, so there's plenty business waiting."

"It sounds very good."

"Me, I think so too." He smiled, revealing his strong white teeth, losing his line of thought in the face of her sobriety and unusual distance, those trembling hands. "You don't look so much like you. You been sick, Jess?"

She looked at him for a long time, examining his features carefully, wishing she could climb into the cab of his truck and drive off with him, away from the morass she'd allowed her life to become. But even as she thought it, a picture of Sanford took shape in her mind, making her ache with yearning, causing her shoulders to curve inward slightly. She wanted to say, "I need him, René, in a way I've never needed anyone"; to say that she felt like a cripple, someone stunted, unable to offer even the smallest part of herself, and each day she spent here with this man seemed to further magnify her many flaws.

She thought of the evenings she and René had spent at that little Italian restaurant on Dundas and felt the same sense of loss she'd known at leaving Flora. Was life nothing more, she wondered, than a lengthy process of leaving people behind, moving on more and more disencumbered until one arrived, finally, at the end of the line utterly stripped? But no, she reasoned, there had to be more, had to be.

He looked at her dark, deep-set eyes and felt a growing anger at whoever or whatever was responsible for turning her so old and uncertain. If she needed help, why didn't she tell him? But no, he thought. She wouldn't tell him. They'd have to talk some about that.

"Insomnia," she said finally, and meeting his blank look, explained, "I don't sleep very well."

"Oh. It's too bad. Maybe too much on the mind."

"Maybe."

"Okay," he went on. "So, here's the thing: I gotta find somebody with the money. It's all legal and everything," he qualified. "I got the papers done up by the lawyer. To get the trucks, see, I got to get the money. And some extra to keep going until the consignments they're comin' in good."

"Are you asking me to lend you money, René?"

"I was hoping you maybe have a little put by."

"How much?"

"Twenty-five thousand I need," he said, looking cowed by his own boldness in asking for such a large sum.

"And in return," she asked far more calmly than she felt, "what would I be entitled to?"

"I make you the partner, half of everything."

"And you've already had papers drawn up? Were you so sure I'd agree?"

"Hey, Jess! Me, I'm not sure of nothing, eh? But you an' me, we're old friends. And when I hear how you marry up with this man, sell the old place, and come on to live here, I say to myself, René, maybe she's got a little money now and she help out."

If it had been anyone else, it would have sounded like a threat. But René, she knew, would never seek to harm her.

"I don't have twenty-five thousand dollars," she said.

"How much you got?"

"I could let you have . . . Just a moment. Let me think." She had twenty-two thousand in the bank. Ten of that was her profit from the sale of the house on Brunswick, ten was the marriage settlement, and the rest, savings. She'd promised at least ten to Tillie for a down payment on a house. But if they weren't going to be married for another two years, she'd easily be able to replace whatever she loaned René out of her monthly thousand from Sanford.

She was, she knew, taking a lot of time and creating uncertainty in René, but she couldn't seem to think as clearly as she'd have liked. There was no question she'd give him the money. He was a decent, honest man who'd worked himself half to death to repay her. He wasn't going in over his head, either. He knew about the trucking business. Of course she'd give him the money, if for no other reason than to again thank him for, years before, stopping in the middle of the night to pick up two tired and frightened girls at the roadside.

"I can give you twenty thousand," she said, at last. "It's almost everything I have."

He closed his eyes tightly for a moment, then opened them, saying, "You won't be sorry. I promise this. Five years, maybe ten, you get back every penny. More. You know René tells the truth, eh?"

"I know that," she said softly, with a smile, reassured by how very much she still liked him. He was so uncomplicated, truthful, and direct; a relief after Sanford. Sanford. He'd be coming back. . . .

"I got the papers right here." He opened a large manila envelope. "We put the date, how much, and then we put our names. And a witness."

"I'll have Polly witness it. Are you quite sure you wouldn't like something to drink?"

"How come?" he asked. "How come you do this for me and don't ask all the questions?"

"As you said, we're friends, René. I'd like to think you might one day do the same for me."

"Hey!" He grinned. "It's the truth. Me, I got the money, I give it to you."

Polly Ferguson signed on the carefully folded contract that revealed only Jess's and René's signatures, the date, and the line where she was to sign. She raised curious eyes, met Jess's approving nod, and bent to put her name to the document, thinking again what a hard woman Jess was to get to know. Yet she was an undemanding person, someone plainly accustomed to having staff. Sensitive to the gentleness and quiet fear in Jess, Polly liked her. If Jess wanted this document witnessed, for whatever reason, Polly had enough instinctive faith in her to do it. "Will you have tea, Mrs. Woodrich?" she asked, returning the pen to the coffee table.

"I think not, thank you."

She went out and Jess lit another cigarette, sitting turned toward René with her legs crossed, her skirt smoothed down carefully over her knees.

"If you'll give me the name of your bank," she said, "I'll arrange for my bank to transfer the money to you first thing Monday morning."

He wrote it down for her, then shifted uncomfortably and opened the large envelope again to withdraw a smaller one which he held onto, looking pained, saying, "I wanna give you this, eh?"

"What is it?" she asked, sitting up straighter, stubbing out the cigarette she'd just lit.

"I hear from a friend that Cotton has them and thinks to make some trouble. He shows them to me, says he thinks to sell them, so I break his nose. There ain't no more. I took 'em all. Even you don't give me the loan, I come to give you these so you know René's a good friend always." He paused, glancing down at the second envelope, then looked at her, softly asking, "How come you don't tell me you got trouble, eh, Jess?"

"Trouble?" My God! she thought. What's going on?

Maybe he was wrong, he decided, studying her worried expression.

"Okay," he said. "But you remember. Me, I look after my friends." He handed her the envelope, not sure what else to say, and got to his feet, extending his hand to her. "You won't be sorry, Jess," he promised, enclosing her slender hand in his huge one.

"You can't stay?" she asked.

"I gotta truckload waiting."

"I wish you could stay longer," she said. "It's so good to see you." The envelope was bulky in her hand, demanding her attention. *Sell them? Make trouble? Them?* Her heart was thudding heavily.

"I keep in touch, let you know. And you write to me, eh?"

"Always." She smiled with difficulty, her mind on the envelope.

"You got trouble, you call René," he said again, wishing he were less clumsy, that he knew the words and gestures that would brighten her features, ease her.

She nodded and he placed his hand on her hair, kissed her forehead, straightened, and then left.

After the sound of his truck's engine had died away, she returned to the sofa, feeling endangered. What she'd feared since that day she'd seen Cotton in the restaurant had happened, and sooner than she'd thought. He'd infiltrated her new life, and she was no longer safe. Holding her breath, she opened the envelope.

Photographs slithered out onto her lap. At first, she was unable to make sense of them. Then they suddenly came sharply into focus and she was looking at herself seven years earlier, in performance with five men. Her hands trembled as she went through the prints one by one, realizing there'd been a sixth man, one who'd hidden somewhere and taken these revolting pictures. They were all animals, she thought, including herself. Disgusting animals.

Cotton had had these. René had found out, and had broken the man's nose to get them. She tipped the envelope into her lap and a dozen or so strips of negatives slipped out. Cotton in the restaurant. Cotton holding her down. Cotton watching happily as his friends pushed themselves into her. Had he been planning all along to blackmail Sanford? God! What had she ever done to inspire such hatred? A man now in his sixties, surely he'd settle into some sort of quiet old age and leave people alone?

How could she have done that? she asked herself, looking closely at each photograph, forced to admit yet again what she'd been. Her insides roiled at the very clear memory of how she'd been tricked into it. And her face in the photographs showed no pleasure, but only an expression of shocked disbelief. She felt an overwhelming pity for that thin white creature captured in these acts of stunning ugliness. Poor little girl, she thought, feeling separated from that girl and yet integrally tied to her. Her feelings were such a potent mix of sympathy and repugnance she wanted both to cry and to vomit.

Would a broken nose put an end to it? *God, give him someone else to hate and let him leave me alone!*

She rose and carried the envelope and its contents over to the fireplace and dropped them in. Rigid with fear, she reached for one of the long fireplace matches, struck it, bent and held it to the paper at the bottom of the grate, then stood back as the paper and then the kindling caught and blazed. The negatives seemed to curl and melt; prints twisted, blackened, and disappeared. Yet even with the ashes of the evidence cooling right in front of her, she couldn't stop seeing and feeling the threat of the pictures and of the man who'd had them. She might never really feel safe as long as Cotton lived. But there was René, and as long as he was alive, some measure of safety existed for her.

René! He'd seen. "Oh, God!" she whispered, shamed anew. He'd seen and he knew exactly what she was. But he still cared. He still called her "friend." In her mind, she again saw him hesitate before giving her the envelope.

She looked into the fireplace and watched the flames, tucking her hands into her armpits to try to warm them. Burning the pictures could never destroy the images. They'd live as long as she did. They were all there in her mind, every last one of them. But that was then, she told herself. It isn't now. It isn't now!

She wet her lips and continued to stand, gazing into the fire.

*   *   *

Press had long since finished eating. He had a good fire going and was sitting on the floor studying, occasionally poking at the logs with a piece of kindling.

Tillie, clad in a flannel nightgown, woolen robe, and furry slippers, came silently out to sit down beside him, waiting for him to put down his textbook and take off his horn-rimmed reading glasses.

"I'm sorry," she said in a small voice. "I guess I really was wrong to keep nagging at you. We'll get married when you want to." She waited, and when he didn't say anything, she asked, "Could I have my ring back, do you think?"

It worked beautifully, just as she'd hoped. His face lost its carved-from-stone impenetrable glare and he smiled, tossing aside the textbook to ruffle her hair, saying, "You dope! Don't pull any more dumb stunts like that!"

"I won't," she said meekly. "I know it was stupid."

He had to say a few more things just to get his own back and she let him, accepting it all in a head-bowed show of humility. Then they started kissing and she didn't dare protest when he put his hand up under her nightgown to stroke her breasts. Nor did she stop him when his hand moved down and gently opened her thighs. The feeling surprised her. It was really quite exciting. But she couldn't escape the idea of how awful it would be if his parents unexpectedly arrived home. So, after a few minutes, she guided his hand back to the safer territory of her breasts and, a few minutes after that, yawned and said, "I think we'd better stop now. Your parents'll be back any time and I've really got to go to bed."

"You still going home in the morning?" he asked, unable to resist the ripe swell of her buttocks.

"No." She smiled. "I thought I'd stay. If you want me to."

"You'd better go to bed then, if you're going. Unless you want to get yourself raped."

She giggled and kissed him good night, then jumped up and went to her bedroom, highly pleased with her performance and its results.

◇ Thirteen ◇

Nine o'clock. Nine-thirty. Ten. Ten-thirty. It was another game, or part of the same old one. She got up, turned out the downstairs lights, left on the outside ones and the one in the foyer, then went to get ready for bed.

In the bath, she considered the possibility of an accident. Since his regular chauffeur had gone into the army, Sanford had been using temporaries, unable to find a suitable permanent replacement. The new man had been with him less than two weeks. There could have been some trouble with the car, or a crash. God! What if he were injured, or killed. . . . He'd said no later than nine and it was almost eleven. If not a mishap with the car, what? A last-minute meeting? That was possible.

The suspense of not knowing was worse than the anticipation of his return. She climbed from the tub, pulled the stopper, wrapped herself in a towel and studied her reflection in the mirror. She'd wanted to believe she could carry this through, but she couldn't. Turning from the mirror, she reached for the talc. As the tub finished draining, she could hear the sound of running water from the bathroom in the guest suite. He was home, using the shower. He had probably come in while she was bathing.

There was a rapid rattling knock in her chest, ears, and throat, and she was unable to move. She felt a wave of heat travel from her scalp down through her body, subsiding in the region of her knees. Then another wave, this one cold, enabled her to move. She got on her nightgown and robe, and haphazardly pulled the brush through her hair. In setting down the brush, she sent the water glass smashing into the sink. The sound of shattering glass was so loud she winced, grabbing a handful of tissues to soak them under the faucet before running them around the inside of the basin to pick up any stray shards. She wadded the lump of tissues and glass and dropped it into the wastebasket. She was positive he had to have heard the noise she'd made.

Listening closely, she heard the water go off. He was out of the shower. She visualized him toweling himself dry. What did he do? she wondered. Did he splash on some of his favorite cologne? Did he wear pajamas or sleep without? Even his most minor action was of interest simply because she knew nothing about his habits.

The cigarette burned down, singeing her fingers. She stubbed it out and lit another. Her leg was jerking up and down. Fear made her head feel as if it were clamped inside a large vise. She remembered being a little girl, perhaps five or six, waking up in the middle of the night in the summer house at Narragansett. In the darkness, she'd stared and stared, trying to see if it really was a person sitting in the chair over in the corner, or just the chair with her clothes piled on it. Her brain had told her, it's just the chair, silly. But something else inside her argued that it was a ghost waiting there to pounce on her. If she kept staring at it, watching very closely, it would stay a chair. But if she took her eyes off it just for one second, it would be a ghost. She had lain awake until dawn, then, feeling safe in the gray light, turned on her side and went to sleep. She felt now very much as she had then: If she failed to watch and listen carefully, the ghost—a collection of many small terrors—would pounce.

She recrossed her legs and folded her arms across her chest. She was perspiring heavily. The room was too hot. She put down the cigarette, raised the shade, and tugged at the window. It wouldn't budge. The fresh coat of paint had sealed it shut. Even wetter now, she drew down the shade, sat again and retrieved her cigarette. Why was she just sitting there? Why didn't she go to bed? Because he was coming. Surely he'd come tonight.

Two cigarettes later, she cleaned the ashtray with a tissue and got up to go down and make herself a drink. It might help her get to sleep, or wash down an effective number of sleeping pills; pills Sanford's Dr. Roland had been so willing to prescribe. So very sympathetic, Dr. Roland. *Sorry you've been having difficulty. These ought to help.*

She took a relieved breath at the sight of the dark, deserted landing and went quickly, quietly down the stairs, making her way through the living room in the dark to put on the light near the liquor cabinet. No ice. She went through the dining room and pushed into the kitchen, opening the refrigerator door for a tray of ice cubes. With a handful of ice, she was reaching for a glass when he said, "You're still up. I thought you'd gone to bed." His voice caused her to jump, the ice rapidly melting in her hand.

"I thought I'd have a drink," she said, her voice hoarser, deeper than usual. Her hand felt anesthetized as she forced it to open and drop the ice into a short glass. She was so tired she didn't think she could take any more of this mad games-playing. He'd worn her down to where she felt flimsy, breakable.

"I'll join you," he said, coming across the room.

His hand extended in front of her for a glass. His wrist was bare, strong, and solid-looking where it emerged from the sleeve of his robe. His cologne was overpowering. She could sense the residue of moisture on his hair and skin, could almost feel and taste it.

"We had a blowout," he said, "and the damned spare was flat. You waited." It wasn't a question, but a statement. She put down the bottle she'd picked up, a tremor taking possession of her entire body. Gripping the extended service tray of the liquor cabinet with both hands, she cried, *"You know I waited!"* then closed her eyes against the violence of further cries seeking to escape her, but unable to suppress them. "You *know* I did!" Her voice was as shattered as the tumbler in the basin. "You knew, just as you knew I'd wait for you to telephone every night! What do you want?"

He finished pouring his drink and went on to make one for her, calmly saying, "I'd far rather know what *you* want, Jess." The tendons in her throat were tautly prominent, and her hands were like white claws clinging to the edge of the bar. For a few seconds he was very afraid he'd gone too far, pushed her too hard. Perhaps what he was asking was beyond her. Had he the right to play God—no matter on how minor a scale—with someone else's thoughts and feelings? But it wasn't God-playing, he told himself. It was more like a healing process he was trying to effect. Nevertheless, he couldn't help wondering if he had the right to do any of what he'd done. You couldn't compel someone to care for you. Ah, but she did care! She did! Her response when he'd kissed her that afternoon had been so strong. "Tell me what you want, Jess," he repeated.

"Nothing!" she insisted, her chest heaving in a futile attempt to hold back tears. "I WANT NOTHING!"

"If that's the case, why are you so furious with me? Why are you screaming and crying?"

"I am not crying!"

"Why don't you?" he suggested benignly.

"I do not need to . . ." God! Why was this happening? She covered her face with her hand, sobbing, one arm wrapped tightly around her middle to ease the miserable ache there. More than anything else, she wanted to run away, to lie down in darkness and cry it out. But she couldn't seem to move and had to remain fully within his view, unable to stop sobbing.

He felt horribly cruel standing there, watching as she came to pieces, feeling sorry for her. If only she'd bend. It wasn't necessary to break. If she'd just give the least little bit and allow herself to feel, it wouldn't be nearly so painful or de-moralizing as she imagined. And then there'd be some secure ground for the two of them to build on.

She uncovered her face, letting her arms fall heavily to her sides as she directed her eyes to his, whispering, "All you have to do is say you love me and I'll do whatever you want."

He shook his head slowly, lifting the glass, about to explain when she screamed, "YOU DON'T HAVE TO MEAN IT! YOU JUST HAVE TO SAY IT!" Her eyes wide, her face was an anguished mask as she took flight, hurtling past him so quickly she was out of the room and halfway up the stairs before he had time to set down his drink and go after her.

In silence, he raced up the stairs and into the master bed-room. Her head start allowed her a split second to decide, then she ran into the bathroom, slamming and locking the door. She darted into the shower stall, pulled the door closed and crouched on the floor in the blackness praying he'd go away, leave her alone, go away. If he did, the pills were there in the medicine cabinet. After he went, she could creep out and take them, then lie down on the floor and go to sleep forever. If he'd just stop forcing her to see she could never make good the dream because she was a whore who no longer had feelings. *No more, please!* she silently begged, wanting it all to stop now.

Something slid against the door, the handle turned, and light flooded into the room. She cringed farther into the corner of the stall. He pulled open the door and lifted her, his hands under her arms bringing her to her feet as she shook her head frenziedly back and forth, her hair whipping his face, pleading, "Leave me, please leave me, *please?*"

But it was too late. He had possession of her arms and therefore of her treacherous body, and already her strength was seeping away, her tossing head losing its momentum. The pills were far beyond her reach. He had her.

"Tell me what you want, Jess," he asked softly, releasing one of her arms in order to shift the hair back from her face, then raised her chin, trying to get her to look at him. "Tell me. That's all I need. Don't you understand?"

He was so close, his naked body large and powerful under the robe. She met his eyes. There was nothing cruel there, only caring and concern. He couldn't care for her, could he? She didn't deserve it, but she wanted so badly to have him care.

She was, he thought, like a terrified animal caught in a snare, her body shuddering under his hands.

"Listen for a minute," he said gently, holding her chin firmly so she couldn't look away. "Listen! I want to tell you a little story. Will you listen?"

Her eyes, still round and glossy with fear, stared at him unblinking.

"I finished grade eight," he said. "And when I was thirty-eight years old, I went back to school and got my diploma. I was so proud of that damned piece of paper." He smiled. "It felt like a much bigger achievement than making a lot of money. Heady stuff. So I started going to the U. of T. five nights a week, every night for months, years. And I got a B.A. The pride was euphoria, better than liquor. So I kept going and, when I was forty-seven, I finally got an M.A. The funny thing, though, was that, by then, the pride had somehow turned into something a bit too much like vanity. I didn't feel comfortable with it. So, I had the diplomas framed and hung on the wall of my office, and stopped all that.

"Then, one night I saw you at the Royal Alex and turned proud again, vain, too; thinking a woman like you..." He shook his head slowly. "You were more alive, more of a challenge than making a million or getting an M.A. in economic science. Dangerous, pride and vanity. But I did it, I got you. And maybe winning you was a kind of contest. But not a game, Jess. What I've wanted from the start was for you to believe you had the right to say what you wanted, to admit to wanting something, never mind what. So I've been trying to get you to see that. That's all. That's the whole thing. You want me to leave you alone now?"

She'd been crying steadily and, by the time he'd finished, was sobbing again, shuddering distressingly. She tried to speak but could only get one fragmented word out at a time.

"I'm ... frightened ... of ... you."

"Why?"

"I ... don't ... know ... why."

"No," he disagreed. "You told me you weren't afraid of me and I believe that. It's *you*, Jess, only yourself you're afraid of. What frightens *me*," he said, relaxing his grip on her, "is how far you'd go, that you'd let yourself snap altogether before bending even the slightest bit."

She began shaking her head again and he firmed his grip on her chin to stop her.

"What are you trying to say?" he asked sadly, sympathetically. "For five nights in a row you've been trying to get it out."

"I can't!"

"What can't you?"

"Can't tell you what I want."

"Close your eyes and tell me. Just close your eyes." His thumb pressed lightly against one eyelid, then the other. His touch made her wonder why she was fighting when she only wanted him to go on touching her. "Tell me," he coaxed. "I'm trying to *help* you, Jess."

"Please!" she whispered, trembling. "Please! You've got to!"

"What?"

She had no idea what she was asking him to do. Here she was begging him, but for what? Things were very mixed up

in her mind. She tried to separate her thoughts and understood,
all at once, that there was no disgrace to giving in. *Just give
in!* she told herself. Yes! But it was impossible for her to
articulate her desires. If she didn't use words, she'd have to
find some other way to show him she couldn't live any longer
with the suspense or the waiting and wanting. She'd never had
to be the one, though. The men had always started it, and she'd
gone wherever they'd directed. Sanford was obliging her to
initiate this and thereby assume complete responsibility for her
actions.

The scent of his cologne, his hands, his body right there,
so close. *I need you,* she thought. And what was the point of
fighting? None. No point at all. She made her arms move—
heavy, heavy, impossible weights—and wound them around
his neck, bringing his mouth down to hers. Shocks of pleasure
went brilliant white, then black, inside her head as his tongue
moved over her lips and into her mouth very slowly, the pressure gradually increasing until she was boneless, her body
totally supported by her arms around his neck. His mouth was
so soft and the kiss so deeply stirring. She wanted it never to
end—hanging suspended from his lips—dependent on his substance now to keep her alive.

Finally, she pushed herself away, looking dazed, and stood
swaying slightly for a moment before hooking her arm around
his neck to have him kiss her again, hard wild, as her hand
slid past his robe and closed around him, almost falling at the
pleasure in this proof of his desire.

He whispered something she didn't hear, and eased her
away to pull her arms out of the sleeves of the dressing gown.
He grasped the hem of her nightgown with both hands and in
one sweeping gesture dragged it off over her head, then took
her by the hand and led her almost at a run back into the
bedroom, where he let go of her only long enough to yank off
the bedclothes. Then turning, he set her down on the bed and
threw off his robe before lowering himself upon her.

She could feel his heart pounding as he took control of the
tempo and slowed it all down, down, down. His weight and
the feel of him was exquisite and she experienced a moment
of pure happiness. He held her face between his hands and his
eyes penetrated everything she'd managed to keep intact since
the moment Jamieson Land had first caressed her, breaking
past the reserve that had protected her during the previous seven

years. She suffered his searching eyes until he closed the distance and kissed her again, then rested his cheeks against hers, whispering, "I've never in my life wanted a woman the way I've wanted you. You're so beautiful, *so* beautiful. Just, for God's sake, don't despise me for wanting you."

"No," she whispered, unable now to imagine ever hating or fearing him.

Again he examined her eyes and saw, with enormous relief, that she wouldn't hate him. It freed them both. He eased to one side so that he might take the weight of her breasts into his hands, his thumbs sinking into the softness of her flattened nipples, watching as they shrank and grew hard, then dropped his head to replace his thumbs with his mouth. He was more aware of her silence and shallow breathing than he'd have been of any other woman's murmured encouragement. His hands glided appreciatively down her sides, over her hips, and along her outer thighs. Her skin was slippery with talc, faintly perfumed; the scent and feel of her elated him. How incredible, he thought, that they were at last here together. He wished it were somehow possible for him to contain her, to absorb her completely.

She was awed by the way he touched her. No one had ever touched her in quite this way, so lovingly. She turned and lay on top of him, frantically kissing his mouth as she opened her legs either side of him, arching to guide him into her. The feeling stunned her; it was as if this was the first time. She dragged in a deep breath, her eyes startled as her arm went under his head and she pushed down and back to bring him all the way in, then rested for a moment, accustoming herself to his presence. His eyes widened slightly as he seemed to expand inside her and, at this close range, his face seemed utterly perfect to her. She returned her mouth to his and began moving fluidly, her hips rolling from side to side to heighten the pressure of his body against hers. It overtook her quickly—a circular continued thrusting, sweet delirium. His hands took charge, holding her fast as he pushed higher, harder. She buried her face in his neck, her mouth open to taste the smooth curve where his neck met his shoulder. Eyes tightly closed, she let it take her, let it throw her against him with its explosive force, rattling her bones and hurling her senses into chaos. She was convulsed, her arm rigid aound his neck as his increased motions propelled her into a second, and then a third grinding spasm, all very quickly. Then she lay deadened up on him, listening to his jagged breathing, feeling his hands tenderly stroking up and down the length of her spine.

After a time, he asked, "What did you do with it?"

"With what?"

"The diaphragm."

"I threw it away."

"Good." He smiled. "Good."

He went silent for a time, continuing to caress her, reveling in the softness of her skin and the narrow length of her body over his. Then he asked carefully, "Do you feel like a whore, Jess?"

"No."

"How do you feel?"

"Not like a whore."

Another silence. He was content with her answer. They shared a cigarette and she lay comfortably still while he studied her, his hand lazily stroking its way over her. Then he put out the cigarette and sat up, holding her down with his hand on her belly. She lay watching him, open as she'd never been and therefore defenseless. He urged her thighs apart and touched her. She jumped involuntarily. He touched her again. Her body jolted and her breast seemed to swell into his hand. She bent her arm over her eyes and extended her legs. He shifted down, draped her legs over his shoulders and touched her with his tongue, then his fingers. She opened further and made a sound low in her throat. He closed his mouth on her and she began contracting, her thighs going tight against his head.

She wound her fingers into his still-damp hair and tried not to make any sound at all, but couldn't control her groans of pleasure—dark, primal sounds—or the need to whisper, "God, yes!" It was the first time she'd acknowledged any man's reality or her own intense reactions, and she moaned as it took her more violently than before; she labored, giving birth to caring.

When it was ended, she surrounded him with her arms and legs, clasping him to her, poised to accept his body stabbing into hers. Kissing the taste of herself off his wet, cool mouth, she cried without knowing why, then at last held him as close and hard as she could, whispering, "I don't hate you, I'd never hate you. I care so much."

He had imagined how she might be, but wasn't prepared for the completeness of her response to his slightest touch. Her heat, her willingness, her absolute abandon inspired him beyond capacities he'd known he had. Finally, both of them exhausted, she lay motionless inside his arms, their legs tangled; all of her wonderfully eased. She cared so much, he might become her personal religion.

"I love you, Jess," he said. "It wasn't planned, it just happened."

She closed her eyes, trying to absorb this.

"Jess?"

She opened her eyes.

"It really is all right." He smiled.

"I can't . . . say what you want to hear."

"It doesn't matter."

"But I don't *feel* anything."

He laughed softly, hugging her. "That's not true, is it?"

She started to smile, admitting, "No, it isn't true." It felt like happiness, even love.

The next evening, as she walked through the front door, it was Tillie's intention to ask Jess about the down-payment money. She stopped in the living room doorway, disrupting the conversation Jess and Sanford had been having. As their heads turned toward her, Tillie was overcome by confusion, jealousy, and anger; all of it descending on her in the moment she saw Jess's face.

Instead of doing any of what she'd intended—asking about the money, having something to eat—she said, "Hi! I'm back. I'm going straight up to bed, 'Night," and made her way up the stairs feeling as if all the bones in her body had just sustained multiple hairline fractures.

Jess with her hair down, wearing something soft and old, not one of her usual daytime dresses. Her face transformed, and young again. Jess happy.

Tillie felt sick with jealousy, as if there were a huge hole in her chest that was rapidly filling with all the disappointments of her life, along with a raging envy of what was happening in Jess's. It was so *unfair!* Nothing was working out right for her. Press wouldn't marry her until the two years were up unless she let him do "it" to her and make her pregnant. Then, he'd have to marry her. The idea of it was revolting; still she knew she'd have to resort to fairly desperate measures if she was going to get him to do what she wanted.

But Jess.

Why should Jess be so suddenly happy? With another old man, too. Not that she'd been happy with Jamieson Land, she granted reluctantly. But here she was with another man more than twenty-five years older, sitting with him on the sofa, his arm extended across her shoulders, their two hands joined in Jess's lap. Both of them turning, Jess's face aglow with happiness.

She shouldn't feel this way, she told herself, yet was unable to fight it off. Depressed and feeling cheated, she wished they were back at the beginning, back to when Father died, back to the way they'd both been then. She wished she were still twelve years old and in full possession of Jess's undivided love and attention. Jess *had* loved her. She'd never doubted that. And she'd always been able to get Jess to do what she'd wanted. But all that was over now. She couldn't get anyone to do a damned thing.

Notes of laughter as she'd come through the front door. Two people sitting on the sofa. Jess turning with a smile on her face.

The echoes now of Jess's so-rare laughter were like repeated slaps in the face. It felt almost evil of her, she thought, to react the way she was, but she couldn't help it. Jess the tramp, the whore who didn't have the right to anything, was happy. Tillie wanted to fly back downstairs and hit her.

◇ Fourteen ◇

Seeing Jess happy made Tillie more determined than ever to get all she wanted. There were certain specifics—the house in Rosedale, money, mobility—but, essentially, there was just a feeling she had about the way she wanted things to be, a large nameless feeling that filled her with grating anxiety and a wild desperation. She splashed and slashed away at paintings, allowing some measure of the anxiety to transmit itself through her eyes and hands, but she had little more control of her work than she seemed to have of her life. The paintings were exercises performed almost without thought or conscious effort. The desperation forced her fingers to grip the brush, or pencil, or charcoal stick and apply the lurid colors of her need to disjointed compositions in an effort that, for a brief time, quelled some of the turmoil. But the final images failed to satisfy her in any but the most transitory fashion. These dabblings seemed only to be further evidence of her inability to make things evolve as she wished.

Hard in the grip of wanting and needing, her head filled with ceaselessly shifting pictures, she went about more than ever wanting to make everyone—Press, Sanford, Jess—finally pay attention, realize their omissions, and begin to provide her with what she needed.

Press seemed to be taking her and their relationship for granted. The question of waiting two years having been answered to his satisfaction, he'd now pulled into control and was prepared to wait it out.

She thought he was far too complacent. She wanted to jolt him, see him catapulted out of behavior she considered staid. Why couldn't they just do whatever they wanted without having guidelines that had to be followed?

"You're just plain impatient," he told her repeatedly. "You've got to learn to wait, Till. You can't rush things."

Well, she could, she thought, and went out to walk along the frozen streets, battling the lacerating wind, to bring herself to the last, and biggest, decision. In her present state of mind she hated this narrow-minded, provincial city with its empty Sundays and early closings, its rigorously maintained standards, and its reflections of a distant war. The city hall had a tall red thermometer to keep track of the latest war-bond drive, Sunnybrook Farm had been taken over for a hospital. There were victory gardens and blackouts and ARP wardens, quonset huts, and grandmothers going to shift work wearing bandannas. The Inglis plant was producing Bren guns, and De Havilland was turning out trainers and Ansons, Mosquito Bombers. There was rationing: books of stamps for sugar and other staples. Appliances had all but disappeared from the stores. The old horse-drawn fleets of milk and bread wagons that were to have been done away with continued their routes, clattering and clanking, up and down the streets. There were salvage drives for everything from coathangers to wrought-iron fencing. And every time you picked up a paper or a magazine, everything "bad"—from dirt to lost time—was denounced as a "silent saboteur" or a "secret fifth columnist." On the ten-o'clock nightly news Lorne Greene gave the latest war information in plummy, solemn tones that made the war seem more like some grotesque ongoing theatrical venture than something that actually involved bloodshed and the loss of lives.

What the hell, she wondered, was she doing here?

She crossed St. Clair and went down Spadina Road toward Casa Loma, Sir Henry Pellatt's monument to himself, complete with gold bathtubs. It had cost two million dollars, way back in 1914, to put up the place with its stables and greenhouses and bronze doors that had cost ten thousand dollars each. She remembered Jess taking her downtown back in March of '39, the two of them standing in the crowd watching the military funeral pageant for Pellatt move in slow time through the wretchedly cold streets. She hadn't even known then why Jess had made her be there.

Maybe it was just the weather she hated, the unrelentingly cold, gray days going on for so long. Spring seemed to last only a week or two before the sudden, energy-sapping heat of summer in July and August; two solid months of stifling, airless days. Then there'd be autumn, but by the end of October, winter would be back, with blizzards and immobilized traffic and abandoned streetcars standing frozen to the tracks, snow piled high on their red-painted roofs; people battling the wind on their way to work or home.

She crossed Davenport and walked down to Dupont, deciding for no special reason to go down Brunswick. She looked at the houses with their silly little patches of garden; two- and three-story brick houses lined up like a crowd of overcoated soldiers standing bleak-faced and ready for inspection on a parade ground. She wanted to run away, go someplace where her dreams, her *feeling* might have some better chance to come to fruition. How could anything possibly flourish in such a cold, ugly place? She'd die a nothing, a nobody, in this city.

She walked, the only person outdoors who seemed to be without a destination. Everyone else, head bowed against the wind, arms wrapped around a precious parcel of food, was hurrying to get home and into the warmth. Two women passed her, their lowered heads turned toward each other, babbling away in Lithuanian or Ukrainian or something. They had wide, ruddy faces with high, arching cheekbones, and Tillie found it amazing that they could make themselves understood with their strange-sounding unseparate words.

At the corner of Brunswick and Bloor a man approached her, trying to ask her something in another incomprehensible language. "You know . . . where is . . . ?" He held up a scrap of paper with printing on it, the sevens slashed through midway down their stems. She shook her head and pushed past him, then looked back feeling a stab of sympathy for the tall, thin, bewildered-looking man in his long leather overcoat. But to hell with him! she thought.

This lousy city. The cold, like a drill, bore into her ears

and eyes, eating the skin off her face. Her knees and calves
were frozen in the gap between the hem of her coat and the
tops of her boots. She jammed her hands deep into her coat
pockets. If she could just live in one of those wonderful houses
in Rosedale, with the mullioned windows and multiple fire-
places, set regally back from the street, overshadowed by towering oaks and maples. Her home would have a gracious entry
and a bricked front path lit by one of those globed street lamps
that glowed gently upon the street, the path, and the distinguished guests arriving at her front door.

   This defeating city. It only looked good on summer afternoons, or at night, with all the lights on. With the never-ending
war, the city looked like hell. She turned at the corner of Bay
and Bloor, thinking she'd better head home before it got dark,
then stopped, tired of walking, fed up with everything. She
stood looking in the window of a shoe store, seeing not the
display of spectator pumps or Joan Crawford ankle-strappers,
but an image of her own naked self. She made herself look
closely at this image, speculating on its possibilities. Press
wanted her, wanted to take off his clothes and lie down on top
of her, put himself inside her. It was disgusting, absurd! But
if she let him do it, if she made it seem unplanned, if she let
him . . .

   She blinked, turned away from the window, saw she was
free to cross and went running, sliding in the slush, across the
road to the streetcar stop to join the queue. Standing on the
crowded car, hanging on—one more swaying body packed
rump to rump as the car clanged and jolted its way along Bloor,
wet wool stinking in the heat of all the too-close bodies—she
made her decision. Her body went hotter still with embarrassment, and her brain was heated, too, with conviction. She
really had to smile at the remarkable thought that she could
take off her clothes and get Press to do whatever she wanted.
It was so easy! And if she viewed the act strictly as a means
toward a definite end, she felt quite self-assured. He'd damned
well do what she wanted. Already the words and gestures were
coming to her in sequence, and she knew how it would have
to be played.

   Jess was so preoccupied with her perplexing status as Sanford's wife that she was only distantly aware of Tillie. She felt
most certain of Sanford when they were in bed together. The

rest of the time, she fretted silently about what to do or say when they were in the company of others, and about what those others might think of her. Her worries were in no way reduced by the sporadic appearance of small articles, in the guise of social gossip, that appeared in *Flash*, that dreadful smut-gathering rag. The worst of the articles stopped a month or so after they were married, but every so often, there'd be something else, as if someone was intentionally planting these items solely for the purpose of upsetting her. After all, she and Sanford were stale news.

She told herself it was silly to think the way she did, but since the afternoon René had brought her the photographs, she'd felt invaded in some continuing, nonspecific way. And what was worse than the articles themselves was the fact that it invariably seemed to be Tillie who found and presented them to her.

Finally Jess got angry. "Why are you *reading* that paper?" she asked hotly, going on without allowing Tillie time to answer. "If you *have* to read it, for some reason I can't begin to comprehend, please stop coming to me with whatever you manage to find. I don't understand you . . . reading that trash."

"It's interesting." Tillie shrugged, mildly gratified at getting a rise out of Jess.

There was a streak of something low in Tillie, Jess thought, watching her go off with the newspaper. Low and a little cruel and quite frightening. At once she felt guilty, and told herself Tillie was just young, rather naive, and unaware of the implications of her actions.

Jess was so busy analyzing everything Sanford said, she could rarely relax. Even her response to him in bed sometimes worried her. She wondered if she was too uninhibited, too abandoned. She seemed to have lost her perspectives entirely. Was this natural? Was that questionable? Does a wife do this, feel that?

There were moments when something Sanford said or did filled her with a red-hot mix of confusion and mortification. She put her mouth to him in bed one night and he gasped, whispering, "Christ! The way you are!" She sat up, covering her mouth with her hand, and stared at him, positive the way she was was tainted and perverse.

"Jess," he chided, stroking her arm. "I love the way you

are. You don't have to measure and weigh everything I say. Stop it," he said softly. "It's just a habit you've got."

"I'm a fool," she said, shrinking inside.

"No, you've got a *habit*. You want to go on punishing yourself. You're not a fool," he said, drawing her against him. "I love your mouth, what you do. I can't censor my thoughts, the things I say in the middle of something so exciting." At this close range she saw emotion descend over his eyes like a clear film. "Your mouth," he whispered, his eyes liquid with desire, his hand on the back of her neck bringing her mouth hard against his.

She wanted to unwind and get on with her life but she didn't quite know how to accomplish it. Sometimes she felt completely in control of herself. Other times, she was at the mercy of arbitrary and admittedly irrational fears. What did he actually expect of her? As months passed she began very, very slowly to trust herself, and him.

Feeling a little more secure, she ventured outdoors for long walks around the city, rediscovering her fondness for it. She'd see mothers and children, and down deep inside she went soft with new wanting. Sanford's child growing inside her would make everything real beyond questioning. A child would turn them into a family, something she needed.

She took the streetcar down to the lakeshore and got off, heading toward Sunnyside, feeling an exceptional sense of well-being as she walked, her eyes on the rickety-looking roller coaster ahead with its peeling white paint. The amusements would open in June and kids would come down with their paper bags full of lunch and their nickels and dimes saved up for the rides. Tillie now refused to come here, and Jess couldn't understand why when she'd loved it so only a few years earlier.

It was a big city, yet it felt familiar to her, far more than New York ever had. It was as if her recognition of the streets and stores and monuments gave her, in turn, an identity she'd previously failed to have. It was a feeling that had been absent from her life since early childhood, when she'd done cartwheels on the lawn of the Narragansett house and had straightened to see her mother and father sitting on the porch glider, smiling over at her. She'd known then who she was, and that she was loved; she'd been part of those two smiling people, and secure.

There was an open refreshment stand near the park and, smelling the pungent scent of malt vinegar, she stopped to buy a cone of chips, liberally dousing them with vinegar before adding salt. She walked on, enjoying the tart, puckery taste. This simple act also seemed familiar and therefore comforting.

She gazed out at the lake with a rackety excitement in her chest. She belonged here. She had a home and someone who loved her, someone whose existence made her life worthwhile. Why couldn't she stop fretting? Her throat closed suddenly, her eyes fixed on the unclear horizon. She could stop, she realized. All she had to do was give up doubting.

She blinked and looked down. The vinegar had seeped through the bottom of the paper, staining her gloves. She dropped the cone into a refuse bin, then sat on a nearby bench and managed to get a cigarette lit. Holding her arm wrapped around herself for additional warmth, she smoked, trying to piece together a resolution.

If someone said he loved you, and demonstrated it consistently, then surely you had to believe it was real. He *wanted* to say he loved her; it wasn't involuntary. *Sanford Woodrich loves me,* she thought, and was suddenly warm. The muscles in her chest seemed to relax all at once, and breathing was easier. Disposing of the cigarette, she jumped up and hurried back toward the streetcar stop, anxious to see him, touch him. They were going to be all right. Because she loved him.

Press's parents went off to visit friends for an evening of bridge, leaving the house to Press and Tillie, and Tillie decided this was the moment she'd been waiting for. However, it wasn't something she could just baldly propose. Shall we go upstairs to your room, Press, and take off our clothes? No. It had to be subtle. Perhaps, she'd allow things to run as usual, and then simply allow them to run on.

She kept wanting to laugh because it was so easy. When he got to the point of heavy breathing and heavy kisses, she didn't try to stop his hands from pushing up under her sweater to unfasten her brassiere and lay claim to her breasts. From moment to moment, she found herself forgetting her plan. His kisses and stroking hands diverted her pleasurably, making her feel small and perfect, as if her construction was utterly right to both their minds. It wasn't in the least unpleasant to lie crowded beside him on the living-room sofa, accepting all he had to offer; effortless, passive pleasure. She had no particular desire to touch him, nor any wish to make him stop; curiosity had overtaken her and she lay back to examine the sensations being generated by his increasingly heated explorations.

He, too, kept forgetting himself, remotely wondering why she wasn't chanting her usual "don'ts" and "stops" and "pleases." After months of grimly self-satisfied desire, he couldn't hold back, though his common sense warned him that something wasn't right.

She wanted to suggest that they move somewhere safer and less public, but thought that if she spoke it might spoil his mood and she didn't want to risk losing this opportunity. So, after what seemed like hours, with her mouth and chin rubbed raw from his prolonged kisses and her breasts irritated from the continued pressure of his grating caresses, she felt both his hands reaching up under her skirt and knew it was going to happen now. For a moment she wanted to say, "No, I really didn't mean this to happen," but her pants came down and his fingers began playing against her.

He felt somehow shattered at having access to her pale round breasts and crinkled nipples that tempted him to put his tongue to them to taste their shape and texture. Spread beneath him with her sweater pushed high up her chest and her skirt bunched around her middle, exposing soft, white thighs, her near-naked body was too much for him to resist.

Fear and curiosity did active battle inside her as he wedged himself between her thighs. Fear won out as she felt him butting against her. Impossible, she thought. It just wasn't possible for him to put himself inside her; there wasn't room. She couldn't. His pushing seemed an outrageous assault she began to resist. But it was too late. Her eyes and mouth gaping open, her throat closed around words of protest, she could feel something giving way inside her. He pushed, harder and faster, until suddenly he was a dead, unmoving weight on her, and she wondered if it was over; she was afraid to ask and reveal herself not only ignorant, but perhaps a failure as a woman. But was this what it was? she wondered. *This?* In shock and disenchantment, she began to cry, having altogether forgotten her reason for doing this.

At seeing her tears, he whispered guiltily, "I'm sorry. I couldn't stop. Are you all right, Till?"

He went on anxiously apologizing as he withdrew from her and the empty awfulness she felt inside then made her cry harder. She couldn't stand to look at him and shut her eyes.

She wanted to close her mind to the seeping wetness and the
hurt between her thighs as she drew her legs tightly together,
pushing her skirt down to cover herself.

Her tears flowed faster; her sobs were noisy and childlike.
Watching, longing to touch her breasts again, he was overcome
by a renewed influx of caring for her. Quickly rearranging his
clothes, he knelt on the floor and awkwardly straightened her
bra and sweater before taking hold of her hand, earnestly saying, "I'm really sorry, Till. Did I hurt you?"

She shook her head back and forth, rising slowly from the
depths of her brief-lived misery, realizing she'd succeeded in
gaining the upper hand. He was patting and crooning, trying
to soothe her, and she allowed him to go on, relishing a small
sense of accomplishment. It wasn't, however, the towering,
giddy feeling of power she'd anticipated. Her brain was assailed
over and over by the stark reality of what they'd just done, or,
more accurately, she thought, what he'd just done to her. She
ventured to look at him—his face was creased with consternation—and for one distinct moment was filled with loathing
for him. Only a moment. Then it passed and she said, as
rehearsed, "We shouldn't have done it. What if I get pregnant?"
The thought of pregnancy was now endowed with horrific
overtones. To think of having done something so nasty and
then to find herself further punished with a pregnancy would
be almost as if he'd planted some foul growth in her that would
overtake and, ultimately, destroy her. She felt such disgust for
both of them that she wanted to scream.

He looked properly aghast at the idea and couldn't speak
for several seconds, mechanically continuing to smooth and
pat her as his thoughts traveled through layers of cause and
effect, guilt versus gratification, to arrive finally at the logical
conclusion that if she did become pregnant, he'd have to assume
full responsibility.

"Don't worry about it," he said. "Whatever happens, I'll
look after you." He wanted all at once to ask if she'd enjoyed
it, to know if she was capable, even if only for half an hour,
of forgetting herself in order to savor being part of someone
else. But her tears and distress kept the question safely inside
his head. He went on comforting her until at last she stopped
crying and sat up, saying, "I'd better go to the bathroom."

She went out and he remained on his haunches, staring at
the stain her departure had revealed on the sofa, a glutinous,

pink-tinged smear on the pale gray brocade. He got out his handkerchief and tried to clean it up but a discoloration remained. He bent down to sniff at it, to find out if there was any smell. He breathed in deeply, smelling only the faintly dusty scent of the sofa itself. Perhaps it would dry up and disappear, he thought, debating the use of soap and water. If his mother saw it, she'd have a fit, and never mind how the stain got there. It could have been something perfectly innocent. Except that it wasn't. Frantically, he turned the pillow over, then stepped back to study the effect. She'd never notice. At least he hoped to God she wouldn't.

Feeling sticky and uncomfortable, he fixed himself a watery scotch and went to stand by the fireplace, staring into its empty depths, wishing fervently he'd never met Tillie and fallen in love with her. She was so blondly, misleadingly pretty. And telling himself how young she was didn't diminish his growing unease at his involvement with her. It really wasn't necessary, after the fact, to ask if she'd enjoyed it. She hadn't, and he knew it. Next time, he thought, optimistically, once she got used to it. Then, Screw it! he thought, depressed. If she didn't get pregnant, they wouldn't do it again, that was for damned sure. And once they were both sure she wasn't pregnant . . . maybe they'd ease off and stop seeing each other so much. . . . He'd start going out with other girls again. If she wasn't pregnant, a little time apart . . .

Edward and his wife were coming for dinner. Jess nervously wished they weren't. But Edward was her husband's older brother, after all. . . . Still, she didn't like him. She fastened on her garter belt, then sorted through her stockings, trying to match up a pair. She wondered again if Edward knew about her past. He so reminded her of Cotton. Two men both overweight, both after money, both in the habit of looking at her in a way that made her feel not only naked but dirty.

"What did Edward do before he came to work with you?" she asked Sanford.

"He moved around." Folding back his cuffs, he picked up a gold cufflink and pushed it home.

"Doing what?"

"He farmed for a time. Then a while back he moved June and the kids here, and worked at the station for some years."

"Union Station, you mean?"

"Uhm. Give me a hand with this, will you, Jess? I can never get the damned things fastened with my left hand."

She finished doing up the garters to one stocking and then fit the cufflink through his right sleeve. He rewarded her with a quick kiss on the lips. She smiled back, taking several seconds to study his face, liking very much what she saw, then reached for her other stocking. As she was checking to see her seams were straight, she asked, "What did he do at the station?"

"Baggage master. Why do you ask?" He stood in front of her, threading his belt through the loops in his trousers, knowing Jess wasn't given to asking idle questions. "You don't like him, do you?"

"You're the only man I've known who doesn't wear suspenders," she said, watching him finish with the belt, staring as if mesmerized. "I've never liked men in suspenders. I don't know why. I don't think Edward likes me."

"And that matters to you?"

"He is your brother."

Remaining in front of her, he leaned his arm on top of his chest of drawers and watched her continue dressing. "His being my brother doesn't mean the two of you have to like each other."

"How do *you* feel about him?"

"He's my brother. Not the world's brightest man, or the worst. He works reasonably hard. He's good to his wife and children."

"But how do you *feel* about him?" she asked, wondering if brothers felt differently toward each other than sisters did.

"Truthfully, if choices were involved, I doubt I'd have chosen him for my brother. But since he is, we tolerate each other."

"Oh?"

"I've given him a job at more money than he ever dreamed of earning. It's a handout of sorts and we both know it. He likes the prestige that comes with being vice-president of the Riverwood Stores and tries to fight his resentment at having his kid brother for a boss. I let him do as much as I feel he can handle, and try to put up with his self-importance and his fondness for prestige. We put up with each other, the same way you tolerate Tillie."

She thought about that, stepping into the wheat-colored, long-sleeved dress they'd shopped for together, swiveling automatically to have him do up the zipper. He lifted her hair, then brushed his lips against the back of her neck. Reluctant to end the moment, she reached blindly over her shoulder to touch his face. "I don't like him," she said quietly.

"There's no law that says you have to."

She turned and put her arms around him. "I wish you could protect me," she said, "or that I'd never been what I was before I met you. I wish you and I had started together one day and that was the beginning."

"What're you trying to say?" he asked, resting his chin on the top of her head.

"I don't know."

"Are you afraid of Edward?"

"I'm afriad of *men*."

"That's all over now, Jess."

"I know," she admitted, annoyed with herself. "I didn't mean to say any of that." She leaned away to smile at him. "I started out... I meant to talk about having a baby."

"We will." He squeezed her, then glanced at his watch. "We'd better get a move on."

"You go ahead. I'll finish here and be right down."

He turned back from the doorway. "Jess?"

She looked over.

"Nobody else really matters. It's just you and me."

She nodded. "I know you get impatient with me, and I'm sorry."

"It's *all right*," he said with a smile, collecting his package of Player's from the dresser top before leaving.

She was trying so hard she felt exhausted, but she wanted him never to feel sorry he'd chosen her.

June and Sanford went ahead into the dining room. Edward hung back to put his arm around Jess's waist. She wanted to shove him away.

"What're you doing with yourself these days, eh?" he asked, his fingers creeping up over her ribs.

"Finishing the last of the decorating on the house and staff quarters." A strained smile forced her lips upward.

"Skinny." He grinned at her, his fingers crawling up against the side of her breast. "Ought to eat more, Jessie."

She found him so despicable it turned her breathing shallow. "If you'll excuse me," she said, moving away, "I'll just have a word with Mrs. Polaski in the kitchen."

On her way through the dining room, her eyes met fleetingly with Sanford's as she passed the table, then she pushed through into the kitchen and came to a halt at the counter. Her hands gripping the metal-trimmed edge, she looked at her white knuckles and breathed deeply, feeling ill. Edward hates both of us, she thought. Not just me, but Sanford, too.

"You okay?" Olga asked, her hand settling warmly on Jess's arm.

She shook her head, swallowing, thinking about ambiguous remarks and pudgy fingers digging into her ribs before sidling along toward her breast. "I'll be all right in a moment."

Olga went to the sink, ran a glass of cold water, and gave it to Jess. "Here, you drink this."

Dutifully, she drank the water, then stood staring into space, blankly saying, "Thank you, Olga." She was paying close attention to her body, to its reaction to the water. Her stomach, like a cupped hand, closed around the water, becoming a fist. "Thank you," she said again and straightened her shoulders before returning to the dining room.

Sanford's eyes were questioning. It's nothing, her eyes assured him. He smiled and she wanted to reach out to him and explain that there were men who made her skin crawl and his brother was one of them. He reminded her of someone who'd once given her to four other men and called it a "party," had given her to them so they could pull her open like a party favor with treats inside.

Once just wasn't going to be enough, Tillie thought. She'd have to do this with Press a few more times to make sure it really worked. She emerged from the bathroom geared up to do it again, already past her shock and dismay, telling herself it was nothing. She could do it a hundred times, a thousand.

Arranging her face into loving lines, she went over to where Press was standing to take a sip from his glass, then melted against his side. He looked so sober and stern gazing into the fireplace. She reached up to kiss his cheek, surprising him.

"You're all right?" he asked.

"Fine." She smiled. "Are *you*?"

"Me? I'm fine, sure."

"What time is it?"

Puzzled by her capacity for dazzling mood swings, he looked at his watch. It felt as if it should have been at least four in the morning, but it was only nine-fifteen.

"What time d'you suppose your parents'll get back?" she asked, secure at his side, her arm around his waist.

"Not before eleven anyway. Why?"

"Let's go up to your room," she suggested.

"What?"

"Well," she said, flagging somewhat at having to explain herself. "It wasn't so good, was it? I mean... all crowded together on the sofa. You *know*. Come on, Press! Let's go up to your room."

She'd liked it! he thought, astonished. Leaving his drink on the mantel, he took her by the hand and the two of them ran laughing up the stairs. At the top, he had to ask, "You're sure?"

"We've done it once," she replied brightly, "we might as well *really* do it."

By ten-thirty, they'd done it two more times and she had a stomachache, a bruise on her breast, and a blazing sense of satisfaction that enabled her to kiss him lingeringly before they got up, got dressed, and he saw her home. At the front door, she kissed him a final time, then went inside leaving a dazed Press on the doorstep. Upstairs, she soaked in a hot tub for half an hour, distantly wondering if the hot water would kill off the baby-making seeds, but too tired to care.

Jess couldn't eat. The cauliflower au gratin smelled foul. June's Arpège smelled worse. The sounds of Edward's noisy eating made her stomach contract. She held down the sickness through the meal, and the coffee after in the living room, and the brandies everyone drank but her. At last, they were clustered in the foyer saying good night.

She didn't mind June, finding her a pleasant woman, and embraced her gladly. But while Sanford was kissing June good night, Edward took advantage of the sisterly little hug that Jess offered to push his tongue into her ear. Repelled, she uttered a strangled, "Good night," knowing her eyes were round with disgust, and ran up to her bathroom where she hung over the sink retching until her eyes were streaming.

She cleared the sink, drank a glass of water, then looked at herself in the mirror. She was ashen, her eyes sunken. Her stomach, though, was starting to settle. She brushed her teeth, drank a second glass of water, then opened the door to see

Sanford sitting in the dark in one of the armchairs by the window, smoking a cigarette.

"What's wrong, Jess?" he asked quietly, his figure shadowed.

"I felt ill. Perhaps I'm coming down with some sort of 'flu."

"That's all?"

"Yes," she lied. "I'm . . . I think I'll take a shower."

She undressed in the dark, very aware of him. Wrapping herself in the emerald-green satin dressing gown that Sanford insisted was one of the best-looking things she owned, she shivered. Her stomach ached, her throat and mouth were sour despite the toothpaste and the water she'd had. She returned to the bathroom, blinking against the glare of light as she pinned up her hair. His silence was disturbing. Had he seen Edward? Did he think perhaps she'd encouraged him?

She stepped under the shower and stood for a moment. Her breasts hurt. She looked down at herself, thinking, *It's happening!* and was both frightened and euphoric. It couldn't be anything else. . . . the smells, and throwing up. Her breasts, were they bigger or was she just imagining it? She finished quickly and turned off the water, calling out to Sanford as she picked up a towel.

Alerted by the tremor in her voice, he got up and walked over to the doorway, to ask, "What is it?" pleased by the sight of her, slimly nude, clutching the towel.

"I don't know." Her words and thoughts tumbled haphazardly. "But I think . . . The cauliflower smelled so vile. . . . and June's perfume, too. All day I've felt so tired, nauseated. And just now"—she pointed to the shower stall—"when I was . . . I'm sore. My breasts are swollen. I think it . . . I don't know what else it could be."

"You're pregnant," he said it for her, beginning to smile.

"Are you pleased?"

"Not in the least." He grinned. "Are *you* pleased?"

"Not at all." She gave him a wide smile and he seemed to leap through the air to surround her, gathering her up into giddy, escalating emotion.

Tillie made herself smile upon hearing the news and opened her arms to embrace Jess, but was sick with envy at Jess's having managed to do—probably without even trying—what

her own hateful and sordid performances with Press had failed
to accomplish. She'd just have to keep on with it, she decided,
making appropriate noises for Jess's benefit. Then, for several
moments, she was genuinely glad because Jess was so touchingly happy. She closed her eyes, holding Jess in her arms,
wishing with all her heart she'd never had to grow up. She
might have lived in paradise, a child forever. Instead, in a few
days, when her period was over, she'd have to lie down under
Press and do it all again, and again. Until she got herself well
and truly pregnant. Then she'd have Press and all the wishes
fulfilled that would come with him.

THREE

Toronto

1946–1947

◇ Fifteen ◇

Justin was demanding to be picked up—pulling at her skirt, his face screwed up ready for tears—and Jess absently patted him on the head, looking at the contents of the registered envelope from Thibeault Trucking that Polly Ferguson had brought in to her moments before. They seemed to be some sort of stock certificates.

"Mummy up! *Up*!" He was at the point where he'd kick and scream and roll around on the floor drumming his heels on the carpet to get her attention.

"All right, Justin. Just a moment, darling."

The covering note from René simply read, "Like I promised," in a thick, broad scrawl.

She'd call Press, she decided. He'd be able to decipher this for her. Putting the envelope on top of the chest of drawers where Justin couldn't get at it, she looked down at him, wishing he didn't always start demanding her attention when she was least prepared to give it. It was as if he had inner sensors that told him, Get her to pick you up now; she's reading something, or she's tired; she's got a great big belly and it's hard for her to pick you up, so make her do it now.

She took him by the hand and walked over to the armchair

211

by the window, settling him as best she could on her lap, then checked her wristwatch. Another half hour and Polly would put him down for his nap. Then she'd be free to call Press at the office and ask him to explain the contents of the envelope.

Contented now that he'd managed to secure her attention, Justin smiled and began his usual inspection of her hair and nose, eyes and ears. He poked and pushed his small fingers everywhere, convincing himself, perhaps, that she was real and not some big stuffed robot. She didn't mind and smiled as he climbed about on her lap making himself comfortable. At just over two, he looked so much like her it often made her want to laugh in delighted surprise; at the same time she experienced such a clutching at her heart that it countered the laughter and robbed her of it. He had wild black hair in tangled curls, and round brown eyes, a nose that would grow out of its babyish snub into something more closely approximating hers. There were hints of Sanford in his chin and high, wide forehead, and in his size. He was a good deal taller and broader than Tillie's Owen. Of course, Owen was almost four months younger, and having been supposedly premature, not quite so robust as his cousin. Compared to Owen, Justin looked and acted a lot older.

Just as the sight of Justin delighted her, his existence amazed her. That she could hold and touch him, that he was alive and had a curiosity that kept him poking at her was almost more than she could believe. It felt like happiness. Yet that was so difficult to accept. Happiness was something that might have trapdoors she might inadvertently fall through, to become hopelessly lost. She couldn't help wondering if it wasn't a question of paying for the privilege of recognizing happy moments as one went along, because even though she was more and more accustomed to her life and to being loved, and to her role as a wife and the mother of this inquisitive little boy, there was invariably some incident that had her paying with pain for what she had.

She thought again—wondering if she'd ever be sufficiently confident to forget it—of the afternoon she'd gone downtown shopping after her monthly visit to the obstetrician. Six months pregnant with Justin, and daring to indulge in a fine sense of well-being, she'd gone to the tobacco department at Simpson's to buy Sanford a gift. The salesman had been helping her select a Dunhill lighter and they'd been involved in the question of engraving when all at once there'd been a third presence at the counter and the hotly unpleasant reek of whiskey breath in her face. A slurred voice she'd failed to recognize had said, "Hiya, Jessie! How's tricks, kid?" And prepared for the worst, she'd turned, at once recognizing the red-headed, pale-skinned man she'd serviced twice before refusing further appointments with him. He'd been the one, she'd remembered with darting fear, who'd insisted at their first meeting on putting on her underwear. She'd been so sickened she'd carried it home in her handbag and thrown it out in the trash. On the second occasion, he had, without warning, begun beating her about the breasts and belly with a wooden-backed hairbrush. In terror, she'd gathered up her clothes and locked herself into the bathroom until he left. Now, there he was beside her at the counter, breathing foully in her face, his eyes loose and unfocused as a result of a long lunchtime spent drinking. Not knowing what to say or do, she'd looked at him a moment longer, then had slowly turned away as he'd begun, in a loud voice, saying, "I love you, Jessie baby. Isn't that the way it goes? You wanna spend a little time, eh?"

Mortified, she'd gazed down at the counter, acutely aware of the salesman closely following this exchange. She'd forced herself to think, *I belong to someone who loves me. You're not important. You don't exist. I won't allow you to shame me.*

"Will that be cash, madame, or a charge?" the salesman had asked, causing her to look up and see sympathy and encouragement in his eyes. His expression had said, "Don't allow this drunk to do this to you! Fight back!"

Strengthened by this unexpected ally, she'd found her voice to say, "Cash."

"Gift-wrapped, madame?"

"Yes, I think so. Please."

Beside her, her onetime client had launched into a tirade that she tried not to hear. At last, giving up, he'd exclaimed, "Oh, fuck you!" and pushed her with the flat of his hand before lurching away.

"Are you all right?" the salesman had asked. And she'd mutely marveled at his kindness.

"I'm all right," she'd said as she'd opened her bag to pay.

After placing the lighter in a box, he'd said, "The giftwrapping department..."

"I won't bother after all," she'd said, accepting the box and slipping it into her bag. Their eyes still holding, she'd thanked him. And with a congratulatory smile, he'd said, "Thank *you*, madame."

She thought often now both of that unusually kind man, and of Flora; two strangers who'd cared.

Justin was playing with her hand, examining her rings. She trailed her fingers over his hair, considering the contrast between Owen and Justin. The differences between the two boys fascinated her, as did Tillie's obsessive behavior with Owen. She rushed him to the pediatrician if he coughed or sneezed or spit up or did anything that didn't seem quite right to her. If he cried too long or didn't cry at all, she was on the telephone to Dr. Alan Brown's office, asking for an appointment, or to talk to the doctor.

"You'd think that man was God," Tillie complained regularly. "It's just about that hard to get him on the phone."

"He's very busy," Jess said just as regularly, bored and irked by Tillie so that she had to work at being patient with her. "There are children who probably need his time a little more than Owen does." She strove to keep any note of sarcasm out of her voice because she was very fond of Owen. She had found that she liked children. Their hurts and needs seemed far realer and more readily understandable to her than those of most adults. She could deal with them effortlessly, and with sympathy, because so often she felt as defenseless and subject to the whims of adults.

Jess had put it together about Press and Tillie well before they'd announced they were getting married. Press had gone about looking very drawn and tight-mouthed, and Tillie, although slightly green at the nostrils, had visibly shone with satisfaction. The convenient tale of Owen's prematurity was simply further proof of just how Tillie had managed to break Press down.

Tillie was just short of amazing, Jess thought, in her refusal to accept anything less than everything she wanted. Not that it had all worked out to plan. For one thing, there'd been the matter of the down-payment money; a dreadful moment when Jess had had to admit she didn't have the ten thousand she'd promised but would give Tillie the thirty-six she did have, and pay her the remaining sixty-four hundred over the next three years.

"Get it from Sanford!" Tillie had insisted.

"I will not!"

"Why not? He's got tons. You know he'll give you anything."

It had been shocking and even a little frightening to see the anger and something more Jess hadn't wanted to believe was actually jealousy flashing at her from Tillie's gray eyes.

"*Sanford* didn't promise you the money. *I* did. I've told you you'll have it. If you'll stop for a second and think, Tillie, you're two years ahead of time asking. I thought the two of you were going to wait."

"Well, we're not and we need the money."

"Surely Press's parents will give you some."

"He won't ask them," she'd said bitterly. "The two of *you* ought to be married. Neither one of you'll do a damned thing for anyone if it means asking."

Jess had chosen to ignore that. After all, Tillie was pregnant and distraught, plainly not herself. She'd gone off with the thirty-six hundred. Not to the house she'd dreamed of in Rosedale, but to a small place Press bought in Agincourt. "Out in the goddamned back of beyond!" Tillie had raged. "Surrounded on all sides by mailmen and policemen and factory workers."

"There's nothing wrong with that. And it's a lovely house," Jess had argued, on seeing the place. A solidly built brick bungalow about ten years old, it was situated at the foot of a dead-end street on almost a third of an acre, which was a sizable piece of property in view of the surrounding, much smaller lots. The house was sunny and nicely laid out, with a large L-shaped living/dining room, a spacious eat-in kitchen, two good-sized bedrooms, a fully-tiled bathroom, and a bone-dry cellar.

"It's a crap can!" Tillie had whined. "I'll be damned if I'll spend my life stuck way the hell out here without even a stinking car because Press needs it to drive downtown every day."

So, feeling sorry for her and a little guilty, too, at having as much as she did, Jess used part of the settlement money she'd received from Sanford at Justin's birth to buy Tillie a new Volkswagen. Although she never said so, Jess knew Tillie was as disappointed with the car as she was with the house. If she was going to have a car, Jess suspected, Tillie wanted something impressive, like Sanford's new black Cadillac limousine. Nothing seemed good enough, nothing made Tillie happy, because reality, as it evolved, in no way approximated her dreams. The only thing in her life that made her happy was

Owen. Yet even he failed to live up. As months passed, he evidenced his lack of perfection. He was colicky. He vomited. He got diarrhea. He cried. His teeth were late coming in and so was his hair. She loved him to the point of suffocation but deplored his failings. He refused to eat, rejecting everything but zwieback coated liberally with peanut butter.

"But peanut butter's loaded with protein," Jess had tried to reassure her. "He'll eat what he needs. Don't worry so much about it. He's not going to starve. If he's hungry, he'll eat."

"How the hell do you know so much about it anyway?" Tillie had demanded, annoyed by what she saw as Jess's know-it-all complacency.

"You seem to forget I raised you from the time you were five years old," Jess had snapped back, starting to lose her temper.

It had shut Tillie up. But only for a short time.

Tillie couldn't seem to become pregnant again, no matter how hard she tried. She went to work on it as soon as the obstetrician told her it was all right to try; gritting her teeth, she bore it while Press pumped away, huffing and puffing. But nothing happened.

"Stop trying so hard," Jess had consoled her gently, nearly out of patience. "The minute you stop thinking about it, you'll get pregnant."

Poor Tillie, Jess thought now, laughing as Justin pressed his nose against hers, staring wide-eyed into her eyes at too-close range.

"Time for your nap," she said, struggling out of the chair with him. The baby inside her kicked furiously, protesting Justin's weight. She carried Justin out to the landing, and called to Polly, who came hurrying up the stairs, saying, "I was just on my way. Nap time, eh?" She smiled, holding out her arms and he went willingly. He adored her, and Olga, too. Jess was grateful for his independence and his willingness to go with Polly or Olga, especially now with only four or five weeks before the new baby was due.

She went for the envelope and carried it downstairs to the den, where she dialed Press's office number.

"Sounds like stock certificates, all right," he said. "But I'd have to see them to be sure. Are you going to be downtown at all today?"

"I could come down if you think I should," she said, looking out the window. Warm for September. It would be good to get out, see Press and, perhaps look around Eaton's or Simpson's for a while, then meet Sanford at the office and come home with him.

"How about lunch?" Press suggested. "I'll be happy to look at your shares or whatever over lunch."

They agreed to meet at twelve-thirty and Jess hung up, then got on the intercom to ask Robert, the chauffeur, to have the car ready for twelve.

Robert was one of the best things Sanford had done for all of them. He'd hired him through the Veterans' Administration. A double amputee, he was able to do more with his prostheses than most men could or would have been interested in doing. He kept the car in perfect running order, looked after the grounds and flower beds in summer, shoveled out the paths and driveway in winter, and ran the daily cleaning woman back and forth, as well as taking Polly or Olga on their errands. He lived in the attic apartment Sanford had had done over after the War, and seemed not to mind at all being on call at all hours for anything that might arise in the house.

Up at six every morning, he was ready and waiting, fully uniformed, cap in hand, at the passenger door of the gleaming car when Sanford emerged at eight to go to the office. By nine, he was back at the house and changing into his work clothes. He vied with Polly over which of them would take Justin for his daily walks and, come the afternoon, Justin could usually be found trailing after Robert as he pruned the bushes, or polished the car, or helped Olga unload the groceries. In the eighteen months he'd been with them, he'd managed to make himself indispensable. Polly and Olga doted on him, encouraging him to come to the kitchen for coffee and a sample of the latest batch of cookies, or cake, or pie. He was an improbable combination of father and son, someone young enough at twenty-six to display filial respect for the two women, as well as for Jess and Sanford, yet someone with such serenity and strength that none of them had any compunction about calling on him for help.

For his part, having grown up an orphan in Cabbagetown, in a series of foster homes, the job was more than he'd ever hoped for. He'd been in the depths of a terrible depression upon being shipped home armless from the elbows down, knowing his career as a mechanic was over. So this job, complete with accommodations and a decent salary, was like an answered prayer.

Olga was just the woman he'd have chosen for a mother—warm and round, usually flushed from the heat of the kitchen, she was forever smiling as she offered him more cake, more coffee, another sandwich. And Polly always had time to explain things to him, like a kindly schoolteacher.

The only disagreeable aspect of the job came when he either had to go out to Agincourt to pick up Mrs. Ames, or to take her home. He couldn't make himself like her and resented the way she ordered people around as if it were her place and not her sister's. He disliked the fussbudget way she treated her little boy, and how she talked to Mrs. Woodrich, who was quiet and polite while her sister was made of sharp edges and brittle shiny bits. Something about Tillie made his teeth ache. It had to do with how she climbed into the back of the car as if, by rights, the car and the house—all of it—should have been hers. She'd never bother to tell him where they were going, forcing him every time to ask, "Home, madame?" so that she crossly snapped, "Of course!" as if saying, "Where the hell else would we be going, you fucking idiot?"

The little boy was cute, though nowhere near as cute as Justin. Justin had real personality and character, but Owen was just another kid; sweet but ordinary. Although to see *her* fussing over him, a person might get put off.

"This is very interesting," Press said, examining the certificates. "Apparently, you own fifty percent of the shares in this Thibeault Trucking outfit. How did you manage that?"

"Some money I loaned to a friend a few years ago."

"Well, it looks as if your friend's coming through with the goods. If you like, I can run a check and find out the value of the shares. The company's not public, though."

"I don't understand any of that, Press. Just tell me what you think I should do with them."

"If you want to hold on to them, nothing. But they ought to be put in a safe place. And you really should be doing something with whatever money you've got sitting around in savings accounts. Why not put it to work for you?"

"I get interest on the money."

He smiled. The longer he knew Jess, the better he liked her. In a way, one of the rewards of being married to Tillie was getting to know her sister. Being with Jess was so pleasant, especially compared to the strain it was most of the time now being with Tillie.

"You'd get a lot more *interest*," he said, "if you'd let me start investing for you."

"It's awfully risky, isn't it?"

"Look," he said. "We'll keep it small and safe. Give me a couple of thousand and I'll start a small portfolio, nothing risky in it. All good solid steady-yield stocks. And I'll keep these for you, too,"—he patted the certificates—"in a safe place."

She returned his smile, thinking again that Tillie was lucky to have married someone as intrinsically good-natured as Press. He was a kind, gentle man. "Two thousand?" she asked.

"That's keeping it small, all right," he said with a laugh. "But fine to start with."

She wrote out a check and gave it to him, saying, "I'll give you a bit more from time to time. Surprise me in ten years with a fortune."

"I might just do that."

"How is Tillie?"

"Oh," he sighed, losing much of his verve. "You know. Tillie's Tillie. I don't know what's come over her the last couple of years. Ever since we got married, really. When we first met . . . I go to church alone. She's not interested. Sometimes, I can't help feeling all that avid interest back then in going with my parents and me every Sunday was just part . . . All she does is complain, to be truthful. She hates the house and the neighbors and wants us to move back into the city, has her heart set on one of those Victorian monsters in Rosedale. I'm spending half my life explaining to her why we can't afford to do that."

"Perhaps if she got pregnant again."

"To tell you the God's honest truth, Jess, I don't think it'd make a bit of difference. I just wish I knew what'd happened to turn her around so completely. I mean, sure she was a little petulant and overeager at times, but we had fun. I swear, overnight she changed. I could almost tell you the exact day. It was about a month after you and Sandy got married."

"Anyway," he went on, brightening, "we're not here to talk about Tillie. How's Justin? And Sandy?"

For some reason, she couldn't bring herself to call Sanford

by his nickname. She quite liked hearing others call him that, but the name simply wouldn't come out of her mouth. "We're all fine," she answered. "I'm getting a little tired of waiting for this one to be born. I'm sure it's a girl. She likes to poke at me inside the way Justin does outside. Between the two of them,"—she laughed—"I feel like a large pincushion."

She was so undemanding, Press thought, and couldn't help wishing Tillie were more like her, that she had some of Jess's calm and sensible acceptance of the way things were, instead of always wanting something else newer, better, and more expensive. He was beginning to wish he'd given Tillie the money for an abortion and never let himself be guilt-trapped into marriage. Of course, he'd never have been able to live with himself had he done that, but he did think about it now and again. The only good part of their marriage was Owen, and the early mornings when he made breakfast—quietly, in order not to wake Tillie, who liked to sleep late—then ate standing up while overseeing Owen in the high chair. He couldn't see why Tillie complained that Owen was fussy about his food. The kid ate his breakfasts like a pint-sized truckdriver, shoveling it in with both hands, and never mind the spoon. Usually, he helped himself to some of Press's meal, too; one small hand delicately poised over Press's plate while a pair of round blue eyes looked up questioningly, and his mouth curved into a mostly toothless, ear-to-ear grin. Press would look down to see Owen had a sausage, or a piece of toast, or a strip of bacon, and was gumming away on it just as fast and hard as he could, laughing at the same time. Jesus, his laughter! How he loved that kid! Tillie's planned accident. Oh, he knew. Tillie didn't have the kind of *sang-froid* to carry it off; she'd been far too pleased at getting herself pregnant, and it'd showed.

Making love to her now, no matter how inventively, was no pleasure. She didn't want him. She wanted another child. She had herself all greased up and ready to go every night like a channel swimmer. It was depressing. He knew she didn't like any of it. She made an effort to pretend, but she simply didn't have the experience to fake it. So she just opened her legs, suffered it through and, afterward, patted him on the back the way she used to pat Owen after a feeding.

To his chagrin, he more and more often found himself day-dreaming about a soft woman, a wanting woman capable of becoming moist with arousal, without the need for large-sized jars of Vaseline kept on the bedside table.

His secretary, he thought, showed more interest in him than Tillie did. Nelda brought his coffee first thing in the morning with a smile. She quietly reminded him of appointments and said, "Good morning," and, "Have a nice lunch," and, "Hope you have a good evening," all with a smile. She brought afternoon coffee in without having to be asked. And once, she'd sponged a spot off his tie, looking up at him in a way that made him feel like a schoolboy, yet also very much a grown man.

She was polite to clients without being officious, and kind of pretty, too, with reddish brown hair and nice skin and laughy brown eyes; not as pretty as Tillie, but different. Nelda looked soft, which was odd because she was a lot thinner and taller and more angular than Tillie. But everything about her seemed that way: her hair, her breasts under her blouses and sweaters, and her behind as she walked away. From time to time, he'd look up in the middle of dictation, to admire the breadth of her shoulders and the length of her legs. And sometimes, he daydreamed—dangerously—about being single again and taking up with Nelda, talking with her, holding her hand and laughing with her; peaceful.

Why the hell couldn't Tillie back down, relax a bit, and let herself soften? If she would, then he wouldn't feel guilty for daydreaming about a woman who was.

He took Jess's arm as they climbed the stairs from the restaurant to street level and said hello to Robert who was waiting with the car.

"It was great to see you," Press said, kissing her cheek.

"Thank you for lunch," she said, looking into his eyes in a way that made him want to look away from the sympathy there, from the knowledge they shared of his unhappiness. "It's always good to see you," she said, then smiled.

"Good day, Mr. Ames," Robert said, assisting Jess into the car.

Press returned the greeting, then looked back at Jess as Robert went around to the driver's side. When the car smoothly pulled away, he felt sad. Jess's envelope was in his hand, her check in his breast pocket. Watching as the car merged into the stream of traffic, he imagined her arriving home. He could see her laughing as Justin came running to meet her, could see her welcoming Sandy later with a smile and a kiss. The images were diametrically opposed to his own homecomings. Tillie was usually down in the cellar pretending to be at work on some painting or other—he'd gone down late at night a couple of times to look, but had only found discarded fragments of drawings in the wastebasket—shouting up to ask would he change Owen, she couldn't stop what she was doing, and would he mind putting that tuna casserole on the counter in the oven at 350 and setting the timer for forty minutes. Owen would usually be sitting dejectedly in his playpen, surrounded by toys, with a sopping diaper, and a food-smeared coverall on to protect the ludicrously expensive playsuits Tillie dressed him in, so bundled up in protective layers he could hardly move. How could she love Owen as much as she claimed, he wondered, and yet leave him alone so much of the time? What would happen if Owen managed to climb out of the playpen and started investigating around the house? There were drawers full of sharp knives, bottles of ammonia and bleach and heaven only knew what else in the kitchen. There were razor blades and iodine and 222 tablets in the bathroom. Dozens of dangerous things Owen might get into while Tillie was downstairs bemoaning her failure to complete her degree at O.C.A.

He got home that evening to find her upstairs for a change, and in a new dress, with dinner already in the oven and the table set. Free from the playpen, Owen tottered across the living room to arrive at his father's legs, chortling, waving his hands to be picked up. It felt so right that he was doubly guilty for his disloyal thoughts at lunch. Tillie was only twenty-one. She needed time to grow into the marriage.

During dinner, he mentioned he'd had lunch with Jess and watched, galvanized, as her face transformed itself into a suspicious, resentful mask.

"What for?" she asked, her knife and fork held suspended in midair.

"Business. I'm starting a small portfolio for her."

"I suppose she arrived dressed to a fare-thee-well with a very chic maternity frock, in the limousine with Robert in uniform, tipping his hat and bowing and scraping."

"What's the matter with you?" he asked quietly, regretting he'd mentioned Jess.

"Nothing!" she said sullenly, trying to regain control of herself. "Nothing. Where did you have lunch?"

"Never mind where. And, please, before you start in on why I don't take *you* out for lunch, it was *business* and on the firm. Okay?"

She sniffed peevishly, and began eating again. "I suppose she's investing thirty or forty thousand of her pocket money."

"*What* is the *matter* with you?" he asked, getting angry. "It's none of your business how much she's investing. It's her money. She always speaks so well of you," he said, shaking his head. "She bought you the car, she's given Owen just about everything he's got, and all you ever do is make snide, bitchy remarks about her."

"Some car," she scoffed.

"It beats hell out of walking," he reminded her. "And it didn't cost you one cent. Did you even say thank you, Tillie?"

"Of course I did."

"I damned well hope so. You take an awful lot for granted, you know."

"I do not. Look, let's not argue, okay? I'm sorry. It's just that..."

"What?"

"She gets to do whatever she wants and I'm stuck here with the baby and can't do *anything*." She hadn't planned it, but she began crying. Jess could go downtown for expensive lunches and didn't have to worry about a thing because there were servants to look after Justin, and her shoes could always look brand goddamned new because she never had to set foot on a streetcar or bus. Feeling trapped and frightened, she asked, "Couldn't we *please* find a place closer to downtown? I can't even go for a walk here. There aren't any sidewalks, or trees. Please, Press? I hate it here. I don't care if we have to live in an apartment. Anything would be better than this. *Please*?"

It *was* awfully far, he admitted to himself. And maybe an apartment would be easier all around. He'd have less driving time mornings and evenings, and even possibly less nagging to put up with.

"All right." He gave in. "Why don't you look around and see what you can find?"

"Oh, *thank* you!" She jumped up to put her arms around his neck. "You won't be sorry, I promise."

Later that night, with Owen safely in his crib, all fresh and pink and smelling sweetly of baby powder, she actually seemed to want Press to make love to her. But after, on reconsideration, he decided it hadn't been any more real or affectionate than any of the other times when they grappled in the bedroom.

Against his will, his daydreams of Nelda proliferated. His eyes remained on her for longer periods of times as she approached him and as she walked away. She looked so *soft*.

◊ Sixteen ◊

Tillie found an apartment in a building nearing completion on Jameson Avenue just north of Lakeshore Boulevard. Without consulting Press, she went ahead and put down the required deposit of first and last month's rent, signed a two-year lease, then hurried home to list the Agincourt house with a local real-estate broker. She was positive Press would be highly pleased by her initiative and good taste, but planned to tell him only when every last detail had been taken care of.

When he asked how her search was coming, she made vague noises about still looking, and, in the meantime, was on the telephone first thing every morning chasing after the brokers to show the house. She was desperate to get rid of the place so they could move into that gorgeous new building. The apartment had every element of romance Tillie had ever wished for: a large corner living room with wall-to-wall windows offering a breathtaking panoramic view of the lake, a balcony on the waterfront side where, she imagined, they'd sit on warm evenings and have cocktails as they watched the sunset. There was a cleverly designed kitchen with every built-in conceivable, including a pull-out ironing board and more storage space than she could possibly use. The master suite had a lake view, too, and huge walk-in closets, and room enough to accommodate two double beds side by side with space left over. The second, smaller bedroom, being on the inside, had no window. But it was large and also had ample walk-in closet space. A second bathroom was off the foyer, and a short way down the outside hall was a laundry room.

She couldn't wait to decorate the place, to stand at the living room window in the evening with a snifter of brandy and good music playing on the hi-fi set she planned to buy, listening while she looked out at the lights of the city. She just knew everything would be wonderful once they were living there.

Finally, one of the brokers brought a young couple to look at the house. They loved it. After a quick huddle outside in the car, the broker came back to make Tillie an offer and she accepted it. Everyone shook hands, delighted.

When Press got in that evening, Tillie announced, "I've sold the house and found us an apartment downtown."

He felt his breath stop in apprehension and had to inhale slowly before asking what sort of arrangements she'd made. "How," he asked, "have you managed to sell the house?"

"Oh, I listed it a few weeks ago. The broker came today with a couple. They made me an offer and I accepted it."

"What kind of offer?"

"Sixteen thousand," she said proudly.

"I'm going to kill you," he said, deadly quiet.

"What? Why?"

"I'll bet they were just tickled pink to have you accept sixteen thousand," he said, wanting a drink badly but not daring to move. Anything might trigger him and he'd end up with his hands around her throat. "I paid more than that for this house two years ago."

"I . . . Well, how was *I* to know?"

"I paid seventeen five for this house and you accepted an offer of sixteen. I'm going to kill you. God help me, I know I will. You've gone too far this time."

"How was I to *know*?" she insisted. "You never *tell* me anything, never talk to me about money."

"Give me the broker's number! Give it to me!"

"All right. Take it easy." She went to the cork bulletin board by the telephone in the kitchen to get the broker's card.

He snatched it from her, lifted the receiver, paused, then

ordered her to go give Owen his bath and put him to bed.

Frightened now, she went to get Owen from the playpen and readied him for his bath, listening to Press on the telephone with the broker.

"I'm sorry," he was saying. "No. You'll just have to call it off. My wife is *not* legally able to sign a binder, not without me. The house is in *both* our names and I did not consent. I realize it's an inconvenience, but this is the first I knew of it. You can go back to your people and tell them I'll accept twenty-one five for the house. If they can't make it, they're off the hook. Otherwise, give them their check back first thing in the morning with my apologies. Yes, I understand that. No, I'm quite willing to have you keep the listing. But the asking price is twenty-four five and I won't accept less than twenty-one. I realize that. Yes, I know and I'll gladly sign a new listing sheet. I'll give you my office number. But any offer you get has to come to *me*, *not* my wife. That's right, yes. I really am sorry for the trouble. Well, you're most understanding. Thank you. Yes. Thank you."

Tillie came in dusting baby powder off her hands, saying, "Are you coming to say good night to Owen?"

Without a word, he pushed past her and went down the hall to Owen's room, smiling automatically at the sight of him clad in a bright yellow sleeper suit, standing hanging on to the rail of the crib. Defying Tillie's rule about never taking him from the crib once he'd been put down for the night, Press scooped him up and carried him to the rocker by the window, where he held the boy close against his chest. He rocked him gently, whispering endearments, and Owen settled happily, going to sleep almost at once. Press sat, holding him, feeling that the only true sanity in his life was his time with Owen. He stroked the boy's impossibly silken hair—a legacy from his mother—and breathed in the wholesome baby scent of him. After a time, he got up with a sigh and returned the sleeping child to the crib, carefully covering him.

Feeling he had himself in somewhat better control, he returned to the kitchen to fix a strong Scotch on the rocks—fully aware of Tillie nervously awaiting some kind of explosion—and said, "You might as well tell me the rest of it. What's this about an apartment?"

She started to describe the place, going on about the view

and the size of the rooms, but he cut her off saying, "I'm sure it's bloody fantastic. Just tell me how much. And what have you signed?"

"It's only four twenty-five a month," she said brightly, thinking he'd probably strike her—he looked as if he would. "And a two-year lease. I've got our copy in my bag." She moved to get her handbag, but he stopped her.

"Never mind. I don't want to see it. You made a deposit?"

"Well, yes, I did."

"How much?"

"Eight hundred and fifty dollars."

He closed his eyes for a moment, his hand so tight around the glass he thought it might shatter, and leaned heavily against the counter. "Where'd you get the money?" he asked, looking like a haggard old man.

"I wrote a check, then transferred the money from the savings account to cover it."

"Which means," he went on in that same leaden manner, "you've all but wiped us out."

"No, I haven't. There's still almost a thousand left."

"Did you ever once in your entire life stop to consult anyone when you made your unbelievable decisions?" he said. "Did it ever *occur* to you, just once, when you were downtown at Holt Renfrew buying a dress exactly like one you happened to see Jess wear, that you're *not* Jess but Tillie and I'm *not* Sandy but me and that possibly, just possibly, I couldn't *afford* to lay out a hundred dollars for a dress? Did you ever once stop to think that what you were doing might not be *reasonable*? Or about, for example, whether or not we could *afford* four hundred and twenty-five dollars a month for rent? Rent! Not even mortgage payments against a place we own, something with equity."

"But we'll have the money once we sell this house."

"I don't know what to do about you," he said. "This is something I can't get us out of with a telephone call unless I'm willing to forfeit almost a thousand dollars. Which I am *not* prepared to do. Don't you understand one goddamned thing?" His voice became louder. "We *can't afford* that kind of money!"

"The heat's included," she offered.

He laughed, a dark, dead sound. "That's swell! How about

the telephone and the Hydro bill? I'll bet none of that's included, huh?"

"Jess still owes me twenty-three hundred dollars."

"Oh, Jesus!" His face turned scarlet. "The woman's given
you a car, practically *furnished* this whole damned house, not
to mention almost every piece of clothing Owen wears, and
you've still got the *balls* to go after her for twenty-three hundred
dollars she *supposedly* owes you?"

"Well, she *does* owe it to me!"

"Nobody owes you shit, Tillie! But you'd sure as hell like
to think so! Jesus! She's been better to us than my own stinking
parents and you've got the steaming effrontery to stand here
talking about money Jess still *owes* you! You'd bleed her dry
if you got a chance. And poor Jess, she loves you, so she'd
let you do it. You're *disgusting!*"

"Poor Jess," she sneered, getting angry too. "*Poor Jess* gets
more from that *old man* in a month than you make in a year!"

"Don't go on with that," he warned, "or so help me God,
I really will hit you!"

Abruptly, she went quiet. He looked capable of doing it.
"All right," she said thinly after a moment. "What'll we do?"

He didn't hear her. He was thinking about Nelda. Soft Nelda
who went out on her lunch hour to shop for a nice, warm
cardigan for her mother, "Because she feels the cold so terribly." Nelda went home to London every Saturday to visit her
mother, no matter what the weather. If the roads were bad, she
took the train. When he stayed in for lunch, she offered to
share her sandwiches with him. She wasn't trying to make
points with him, he didn't think, or to be anything but what
she was. She put in overtime without having to be asked. And
she'd blushed so beautifully when the company rewarded her
with a surprise bonus of a hundred dollars. He couldn't imagine
that Nelda would ever commit herself or anyone else to the
kind of disastrous arrangements Tillie had so blithely endorsed.
Nelda lived, he knew, in a two-and-a-half-room apartment on
the ground floor of a house on Hazelton, with shutterettes
stained a golden brown enclosing the front bay window. Nelda.
He'd sat outside that house one evening in his car, knowing
she was in there, probably making her dinner, feeling thawed
and comforted simply by the knowledge of her proximity.

"I *said*," Tillie repeated, "*what* will we *do*?"

He tuned back in to take a long look at her, thinking, *I don't love you anymore*. It was gone. He'd loved her so much and it was dead. She'd killed it with her demands and her lack of caring and consideration. The only good thing she'd ever done was to give him Owen. If he were to leave her and go after someone he thought he could love who might possibly love him in return, he'd lose his child. And he wouldn't give him up; he loved and needed Owen.

"We'll sell this house," he said, his voice cracking, wanting to cry. "And move into the apartment."

Like a child's, her face lit up and she made a move to embrace him, but he held up his hand like a crossing guard. He put down his drink and went past her to lock himself into the bathroom where he sagged against the wall, covered his face with his hands, and wept as he hadn't done since boyhood. He felt as if she'd jumped up and down on him in her high-heeled shoes until she'd crushed all his organs, puncturing them so that slow leaking blood was seeping into all his vital cavities. Death by interior drowning.

In the end, they got twenty-one thousand for the house and a thirty-day closing, which allowed them to move into the apartment on the first of December. And Tillie, unaware of anything but her enchantment with the new place, put it down to his continuing moodiness when Press glumly observed, "There's nowhere for Owen to play."

"There's the balcony," she said, without thinking.

"The balcony!" He could only gape at her. "You'd let a *two-year-old* play on a balcony *nine* stories up?"

"I'll make sure he can't get near the edge," she said airily. "You worry too much, Press."

"I worry too much. At least at the house he could play outside. Here, I've got to sit every day wondering if while you're busy picking out curtain material maybe Owen hasn't fallen off the fucking balcony!"

"He is *not* going to *fall* off the *balcony*! You're getting to be an old woman. I happen to look after him, in case you didn't know."

"There isn't even a window in his bedroom."

"If there was," she countered, "you'd probably be worrying about that."

She held up two samples of wallpaper, asking, "Which do

you think'll look better in the dining alcove?" When he failed to answer, she turned to see he'd left. Putting down the samples, she went to the hallway to see Press getting Owen into his snowsuit.

"What're you doing?" she asked.

"What does it *look* like I'm doing? I'm getting Owen ready to go out. Right, Owen?"

"Right, Daddy!" Owen chirped, beaming. "Going walk!"

"It's freezing outside," she protested.

"Fresh air's good for people, Tillie. Little boys need to run and play in the snow. They can't spend all day every day in a room without windows, or out on some balcony. C'mon, Owen." He smiled down at the boy. "Say good-bye to Mummy."

"'Bye, Mummy."

"Wait a minute." Agitated, Tillie dashed into Owen's room to snatch up a scarf and wind it twice around the neck of the snowsuit. "I don't want him catching cold."

"Strangle him instead," Press muttered, pulling on his gloves, then his galoshes. Opening the apartment door, he took Owen's hand and led him down the hall saying, "You can push the button, son. Do you know which number we want?"

"One!" Owen piped.

"Good boy!"

Tillie watched until they got into the elevator, then returned inside to her wallpaper samples, thinking Press was still angry about the house and the move, but once he got used to it all, he'd calm down and be himself again. Hadn't he admitted that the view was spectacular?

He rang the doorbell. What in hell was he doing? he wondered. Was he crazy? He shouldn't have been doing this.

She came to the door looking surprised, but pleased.

"Press!"

"Hi! We've been out and . . . I thought we'd stop by, see if you were . . . home."

"Well, come in." She swung open the door and he directed Owen inside to a room with highly polished wood floors, a fireplace with shelves either side, and the bay window with the shutterettes. There were plants on the floor, and a Scandinavian wall hanging over the fireplace, a teak table down near the windows with a chess game set up on it, and two chairs. Against the inside wall sat a teak sofa with spare, clean lines and black cushions. The air smelled of polish and wood smoke and her perfume.

"What's your name?" she asked, leaning over Owen to unwind the scarf from around his neck.

"Owen!" he stated proudly.

"Owen," she repeated, starting to unzip his snowsuit, then looked up at Press.

"You don't mind, do you?" he said. "I mean . . ."

"I don't mind," she said quietly. "Would you like some coffee?"

"That'd be great." He risked a smile. She returned it, then got Owen quickly out of his snowsuit. Rising, she took his hand and, still looking at Press, said, "Come with me, Owen. We'll make some coffee." They went through the middle room—the bedroom, Press saw—to the tiny kitchen at the rear. She kept looking back at Press as if he'd given her a splendid gift.

Just before Christmas, Jess came for lunch with Tillie, bringing Justin and Todd, the new baby. She sent Justin off to play with Owen in his room, then shrugged off her coat and sat down on the sofa to unwrap Todd from his many layers of blankets. Picking him up, she smiled and said, "It's just beautiful, Tillie. Show me everything."

Tillie was staring at the coat lying so casually on the sofa. "Is that new?" she asked. "It's fabulous. What is it, mink?"

"Try it on if you like. Go ahead."

It was still warm from Jess, and Tillie wrapped the coat around her feeling a little disoriented as she ran her hands over the spiky fur. "It's not soft," she said. "I thought it would be."

"I know. I always thought so, too. But it isn't."

"But it *looks* so soft." Tillie studied her reflection in the mirror on the back of the bedroom door. The coat was not only warm but scented with Jess's perfume. The combination made her feel a quick revulsion for the coat. She took it off and returned it to the sofa, saying, "Let me show you the wallpaper I've picked out for the dining alcove."

Later, while the boys sat at one end of the new dining table—carefully covered with plastic mats to protect it from their sticky fingers—Tillie brought out coffee and sandwiches. Jess accepted a cup of coffee, saying, "I'll get Todd fed. Then he'll sleep and I'll be able to relax and enjoy the lunch."

She opened her dress, unhooked the front of her nursing brassiere, and fitted the infant to her nipple before sitting back with a sigh.

"I don't know how you can stand it," Tillie said, riveted to the sight of Jess's breast and the baby's smooth, almost hairless head. "I hated nursing Owen, quit after three days."

"Oh, I like it." Jess looked down at the baby. "I can't imagine not doing it." The pleasure was so intense it was difficult to keep her mind on the conversation. She reached for her cup. "Good coffee," she said. Tillie failed to hear. She was still gazing fixedly at Todd. "You'll have another one before you know it, Till," Jess said.

Tillie blinked and looked up. "Oh," she said. "I know." But she doubted it. There was no way Press would allow them to live here with two children, which meant either they'd have to wait out the lease, or—she smiled to herself at the thought—she'd have to go through Press's cache of contraceptives and puncture each of them with a pin. It was something to think about. "Isn't it marvelous!" she exclaimed, smiling suddenly, as she craned around to look at the room. "I just adore it here."

Jess politely admired the apartment, far more interested in Tillie's renewed staring at her breast.

"Is something wrong?" she asked, shifting Todd to the other breast. "You seem a little . . . distracted."

"Not really." Except for her breasts, Jess was as thin as she'd been before her pregnancy. Tillie, two years later, was still trying to work off the pudge around her middle. "I've been thinking I'd like to go back to college and finish my certificate."

"That sounds like a fine idea." Jess lifted half the brassiere over to cover herself, starting to feel self-conscious. "Why don't you?"

"We've put every penny from the house into the bank and Press won't spend any of it. His salary is going on the apartment."

"I still owe you a little over two thousand. If you like, I'll let you have it now and you could use it for your tuition."

"Would you?" Press couldn't argue with this, she thought. She hadn't asked; Jess had offered.

"Of course. I'll give you a check before we go. Justin! Drink your own milk, not Owen's."

"That's so great!" Tillie's face turned to sunshine. "I'll be able to register for the January term and have enough to pay a sitter, too."

Jess smiled at her, then returned her attention to the baby, laying him across her knees while she got her clothes done up, then, with a diaper over her shoulder, she held Todd, lightly rubbing his back until he burped. She laughed softly and put him down beside her on the sofa where he fussed and chewed on his fists for a few minutes before going to sleep.

Tillie followed all this, feeling hate building for her sister for coming here in her mink coat, in her chauffeur-driven limousine, with her two so-perfect children, giving out money and exuding wealth and contentment, playing Lady Bountiful while pretending to like the place. Tillie's pleasure in the apartment was suddenly destroyed by the thought of Jess's house on Gleneden Road, with the servants' quarters and the servants, and the three cars, and the swimming pool planned for the summer. This place was a dump compared to that house, and all her carefully chosen furniture only so much junk from the Crippled Civilians contrasted to Sanford's Chippendale chairs and thick Persian carpets. Why should Jess have all that, she wondered, when she had to fight Press for every single thing she wanted? Jess didn't even *care* about what she had. She'd tossed off the coat like some old rag, hadn't even bothered to hang it up. She never had known how to take care of valuable things. Like that time she'd left a small child to look after a suitcase instead of doing it herself. Then she'd blamed Tillie when it was stolen.

Jess ate half a sandwich. Tillie ate two whole ones and felt even more antipathy toward Jess for being able to resist food while she made a pig of herself. She hated to throw away what Owen was always leaving on his plate, so she'd eat it, and now she couldn't get rid of the extra twelve pounds she was carrying around. It showed, too. Because she wasn't five foot seven like Jess, but only five three, and she had a middle like a forty-year-old woman with five kids.

Who the hell was Jess anyway, to come praising the apartment and the egg salad, patting Owen on the head and giving him Auntie Jess kisses, playing it up for all she was worth? She had nothing, and Jess came and made it feel like less than nothing. She wanted to say, "Leave my kid alone, and leave my life alone! Don't come here with your two-hundred-dollar dresses, and your eighty-dollar handbags, and your Italian leather boots, and your diamond goddamned earrings. I don't need your charity, don't need you making me look bad. You don't *deserve* any of it. All those years doing the things you must've done with all those men! It's positively sickening! And you've got the nerve to come here with your two precious babies and the brand-new mink your rich old husband gave you for kissing his ass and doing God-knows-what-else."

Her feelings were so violently hate-filled, they shocked her. She had to look closely at Jess and make herself see the sister who'd always taken care of her, and had done what she had in order to provide a home and an education for her younger sister. Jess had been someone who almost never smiled and who'd laughed so seldom that when she did, it had been startling. Jess had a right to be happy.

On impulse, she put her hand on Jess's arm, saying, "Thank you for wanting to help. I really do appreciate it."

"You've done a lovely job on this place," Jess said, not wanting to be thanked. "The view at night must be fabulous." It was exhausting her to make this effort to support the weight of Tillie's new dreams, as well as to ignore her envy.

"Oh, it is!" Tillie enthused, liking the apartment again. "You and Sandy will have to come for dinner one night soon and see for yourselves."

"We'd love to."

Much as she didn't want it to, Jess's "we," and her smile, even her enthusiasm irked Tillie.

Jess could see her sister moving back and forth between her feelings and felt stifled. Invariably, Tillie's covetousness sapped Jess's energy. She wished to God she'd had the sense to leave the mink at home so she wouldn't have had to feel embarrassed by Tillie's longing glances at it.

Why do I allow you to upset me? she wondered, seeing Tillie's eyes again straying back to the coat. She even managed to make Jess feel uncomfortable about loving her children. If Tillie hadn't been her sister, she thought, she wouldn't have put up with her for ten minutes.

When Jess began getting ready to go, Justin announced, "I want to stay 'n' play some more with Owen."

"You'll see Owen in a few days, darling. He'll be coming on Friday, remember? For Christmas."

"Oh!" Justin nodded thoughtfully, then scooted back into Owen's room, shouting, "Hey, Owen! You're comin' on Fri-

day. I forgot. 'Bye!" He dashed back to grab his snowsuit from
Jess, saying, "Do it myself!" and sat down on the floor to push
his feet through the elasticized bottoms of the leggings, then
struggled into the arms. Getting to his feet, his face screwed
up with concentration, he tugged at the zipper until he got it
up. Jess stood and watched, making no effort to help.

Tillie watched, too, rankled. Owen couldn't even put on his
socks, and here was Justin getting on his own snowsuit with
Jess saying, "Here's your hat and don't forget your galoshes,"
smiling while she waited for him to finish. She seemed all
patience and fond indulgence, leaning across her armload of
new baby to kiss Tillie and thank her for the lunch. "We'll see
you Friday. Come early and we'll let the kids attack the tree."
She went off down the corridor with Justin running ahead to
punch the call button for the elevator. Then she turned to wave.
The doors slid open and Justin darted in. Jess, a blur of dark
mink, moved in after him. The elevator doors closed and the
corridor was empty and silent.

Behind Tillie, Owen was howling, wanting Jussie to stay
and play some more. Her eyes remained on the deserted corridor, seeing Jess, feeling and smelling her.

She closed the door and shouted at Owen to be quiet.

◇ Seventeen ◇

The incident with the snowsuit prompted Tillie to go out and buy an identical one for Owen, thinking perhaps that having an outfit the same as his cousin's might induce Owen to become a little more independent and take some interest in dressing himself. But Owen clutched the snowsuit to his chest, hugging it the way he did his favorite soft toys, then let it fall to the floor and wandered away, sucking on his fingers, looking for something else. Tillie snatched up the suit, screaming at him. "I paid *sixty* dollars for this goddamned suit and you're going to put it on!" She chased after him to thrust the suit at him. Looking at her fearfully, wanting badly to return his fingers to his mouth, he stood holding the suit, completely confused.

"Put it on!" she yelled, her foot tapping impatiently, her hands clenched into fists. "Go *on*! Put it on! You're a big boy! You can put on your own clothes."

He sat down on the floor and turned the snowsuit this way and that, his pale, usually smooth forehead creased with concentration, and finally tried to push his feet through the arm-holes.

"You're an *idiot*!" she shrieked, grabbing the suit away from him, starting him crying. He sat on the floor with his fingers

237

jammed into his mouth, eyes and nose streaming, sobbing loudly, his eyes fearfully following her every move. She felt like ripping the thing to bits. Instead she tossed it at the wall and grabbed Owen, intent on slinging him into his crib. But his body in her arms, his weight and heat and tears overcame her. "Mummy isn't mad at you," she apologized, very ashamed of herself, trying to calm him. "I didn't mean to yell at you, honey. You're the brightest, best little boy in the world, the smartest and handsomest, the very, very best. How about some zwieback? Would you like that?"

His tears stopping, he gazed at her with huge reproachful blue eyes.

"Come on, Owen. We'll get you some zwieback and peanut butter."

Perked up by this reward, he settled happily into the playpen with several little cloth books and his favorite teddy bear and munched away on the hard toast, making peanut butter designs on the pages of one of the books while Tillie retrieved the snowsuit and went to hang it away. He might not be able to put it on by himself, but he'd wear the damned thing until he outgrew it.

Christmas with Jess and Sandy only depressed Tillie. Their tree filled one entire corner of the living room. It was rigged with strings of popcorn and cranberries and all-red decorations and underneath were dozens of presents. Sandy was all cashmere and sporty elegance, Jess all silk and sleek. Having to be there to witness firsthand further examples of Sandy's largesse was like having stones pushed down her throat. There were toys and clothes for all the children. The boys fought each other to sit on a lifelike lion standing three feet high that had been imported from F.A.O. Schwarz in New York. Wild-eyed and greedy in the face of all these new and exceptional things to play with, the boys were like crazed little animals. After a quiet word from Jess, Justin calmed down and magnanimously offered to share everything with Owen. It was a relief when Mrs. Ferguson finally took the two of them off to the den to play there.

The relief only lasted a short time because Sanford, dressed in a rented costume and beard, went on playing Santa, tossing boxes over to a happy-for-a-change Press, and to her and Jess and the staff. There was even a gift for the absent daily cleaning woman. The opulence of the gifts made hers and Press's of-

ferings look paltry and unimaginative and she sank even deeper
into her depression.

During the lull just before dinner, Tillie happened to look
over and see Jess and Sanford in the hallway. Believing themselves unobserved, Sanford ran his hand down Jess's arm and
over her breast before pressing a kiss on her lips. Jess drew
away after a moment, smiling, and whispered something in-
audible. The small episode revolted Tillie. Real people, she
told herself, didn't act that way. But was that it? No, it was
the gut-destroying desperation of wanting all this for herself,
wanting more, always; to be Jess going off on trips to Banff
and Bermuda, to receive expensive gifts and be cosseted as Jess
was.

The roast duck and candied yams, the stuffing and roast
potatoes and petit pois lodged in her throat; more stones. Feeling ill, she admitted to herself that she wanted to *be* Jess and
have this house and a husband like Sandy and children like
Justin and Todd, as well as a loyal and adoring staff. She
wanted it so much she was unable to look at Press or Owen
during the meal. And when she finally did look at Press, she
was surprised to be able to see him—somehow more clearly
than she had in years—as a handsome young man with fine,
regular features and a lovely smile. He was no one to be
ashamed of, nor was Owen. They'd go on to have another child
and Press would keep rising in the business and one day take
over from his father. He'd start making a decent salary and
some hefty commissions and they *would* have the house in
Rosedale, maybe a housekeeper too. It was just so hard to wait.
It might be ten years before they'd have any of it. *And I want
it now*, she thought, as Olga removed her plate and set a dessert
dish down in front of her.

The depression hung on. She decided the only way to get
out of it would be to go to the College, get herself registered,
then go out and buy her supplies. She'd always enjoyed debating over camel-hair versus sable brushes, Reeves' watercolors or Winsor & Newton, 4B or 5B pencils. She'd buy felt
sticks and watercolor mixing pans and sanding blocks and feath-
ery-edged sheets of first-quality watercolor stock, and thick
tubes of oils in chromium yellow, magenta, pure black, and
blinding white.

The idea that she'd be getting back to work in only another

couple of weeks gave her a lift. But what about Owen? Maybe Polly or Olga wouldn't mind babysitting him for a couple of hours while she got everything done. She considered telephoning Jess but decided to take her chances and just stop by the house. Someone was bound to be there and Jess wouldn't mind her leaving Owen for a while.

Polly came to the door. "Mrs. Woodrich is out with Justin. They've gone to the doctor's for Justin's checkup."

"Oh, hell!" Tillie said as planned. "I was hoping to leave Owen for a couple of hours while I run down to O.C.A. and get registered, then pick up some supplies."

"That's all right." Polly smiled down at Owen. "He'll be just fine here. You go along and don't worry about a thing. Has he had lunch? Would you like something to eat, dear heart?" she asked, helping him out of his snowsuit.

"Well, if you're sure it's no problem," Tillie said, barely able to conceal both her relief and her prickling irritation at Polly's calling Owen "dear heart." She looked down at the top of the woman's head, noticing broad streaks of gray overtaking her brown hair, which was smoothly fixed in an old-maidish bun. Her face powder and rouge seemed to sit on top of her skin like a mask. "I'll just go on," Tillie said. "The sooner I get it all done, the sooner I'll be able to get back."

"Don't you rush," Polly said, smoothing Owen's hair. "Take your time."

"Okay. Kiss Mummy good-bye, Owen." She dropped down to receive a wet, little-boy kiss.

"Where's Jussie?" Owen was asking Polly as Tillie let herself out the front door and crunched her way down the sanded, snow-packed walk to the driveway where she'd left the VW. Freedom. Two or three hours of it. She got in, stepped on the clutch, turned the key, threw the shift into first, and took off.

Robert was in the kitchen having lunch. "I left them off at the doctor's office," he was saying. "Mrs. Woodrich said they'd probably go shopping and then come home later with Mr. Woodrich, or they might go out to dinner. But they'll call to let us know."

Owen climbed up on one of the chairs and picked up the salt shaker.

Olga came over to pat him on the head, asking, "You hungry, eh?"

"Hungry!" he verified, banging the shaker on the oilcloth-covered table.

"Okay, we feed you." Olga grinned and went for a plate. "You like *piroges*?" she chuckled.

"Pee-row-hees!" Owen mimicked her.

They all laughed.

"Where's Jussie?" he asked again.

"Out with Mama," Olga answered, setting two *piroges* on a plate, then cutting them into small pieces before tucking a napkin into the neckline of his sweater. "Eat. It's good, eh?"

He managed to spear a piece on his fork, popped it into his mouth, chewed with a quizzical look on his face, then announced, "Good, eh?" He speared another piece, nodding happily to himself when they all laughed again.

"You finish your lunch," Robert said, "and then we'll go outside and make a snowman."

He usually took Justin out after lunch. But since Justin wasn't there, he'd take Owen. The kid sure looked as if he could use a little fresh air. Such a pale color, but a cute son of a gun. He smiled at the boy.

"Make a snowman," Owen chortled. "We make a snowman."

"Finish your lunch first." Robert helped direct his fork down into the food. "Eat up and drink all your milk, then we'll go out and play. Where'd she go anyway?" he asked Polly.

"She said she was going over to the Art College to sign up."

"Oh. Did Mrs. Woodrich know she was coming?"

"I don't think so."

"Figures," he said. They exchanged a look.

"Careful, dear heart." Polly picked a lump of food from Owen's lap. "You're spilling."

Robert didn't see anything. There was the sense of someone or something rushing up behind him, then a terrible crashing pain in his head, a sick spinning as snow-covered earth and clouded sky overturned, then nothing. When he came to, he wanted to touch his head but his prostheses were gone. They and his shirt and jacket were lying over by the garage. Shivering, he staggered to his feet—a trickle of blood running down into his eye—thinking Owen must have gone back indoors. He stood staring at footprints in the fresh snow and turned to follow them down the driveway. He reeled along, following until they disappeared at the curb, where there was a set of fresh tire marks. It didn't make sense. And his head hurt horribly. He needed Polly or Olga to come out and pick up his arms. He went to kick at the back door. Olga glanced over from the stove, started to smile, then stopped and flew to open the door, exclaiming, "My God! What's happened to you? And what's this, blood?"

He felt confused and humiliated at having to ask her to go get his things. "They're over by the garage," he said, hanging his head.

She motioned him down onto a chair, then fetched a blanket from the den and threw it around him before going to the sink to soak a dish towel in cold water. She pressed the cold cloth to his head, then went outside for his clothes and the prostheses. Once his arms were fastened on, she asked again, "What *happened*, eh?"

"I don't know," he said stupidly, the pain in his head fogging his thoughts. "It felt like something dropped on my head." Suddenly remembering, he asked, "Where's the kid? Did he come back in?"

"He didn't come in. He isn't outside?"

"He *must've* come in!"

"I'd of seen him! I been here the whole time."

He put his head down on the table, trying to sort things out. Seized by nausea, he jumped up and ran into the half-bathroom next to the pantry to vomit, then put his mouth under the faucet and drank some water, every move of his head excruciatingly painful. Finally, he came back to the kitchen, again trying to think. Something fell on his head. He woke up and the kid was gone, his arms and clothes gone, too, thrown over by the garage. "He *must've* come in!" he repeated urgently. "Or else he's still outside playing and I just didn't see him." Before Olga could argue, he was up and out the door. Through the window, she watched him dart here and there around the property, looking behind bushes and in back of the garage. Polly came up behind her, asking, "What's he doing?" and Olga started, saying, "You give me such a scare!"

"But what's he *doing*?" Polly asked again.

"Looking for the little boy."

"Owen?"

"Yuh. I'm scared. He says to me something fell on his head, and when he wakes up, he don't got his arms and he comes kicking at the door here, thinkin' the little boy must've come in, but he didn't come in I told him."

"You're *sure*?" Polly asked, dry-mouthed.

"I'm tellin' you! He *didn't* come *in*! I'd of seen him, eh?"

Robert came in in tears, saying, "He isn't *there*! You're positive he isn't in here?"

"Polly's gone to look. But he's not here, I'm tellin' you."

He began to cry harder. "Then somebody *took* him!" he wailed, sick with fear. "Hit me over the head, took my arms so I couldn't fight back, and took him. But *why*?"

"Took who?" Polly asked, returning. "He's not in the house. I've looked everywhere, including the linen closet." She stopped, absorbing what Robert had said as well as the terror-stricken look of him and his blood-soaked hair. "You don't mean to say you think someone's *taken* little Owen?"

Robert nodded somberly, the motion heightening his nausea.

"I'll call the police!" Polly moved to the wall 'phone. "You're absolutely sure he's not outside?"

Robert had his head down on the table and murmured, "He's not out there. I looked. Oh, sweet Jesus, somebody took him."

Polly had the receiver in her hand when car doors slammed in the front driveway. She put the receiver down, saying, "Maybe . . ." and hurried to open the front door. Jess was paying a taxi driver while Justin came running up the walk. The taxi drove off and Jess followed after Justin, studying the peculiar expression on Polly's face.

"Hang up your snowsuit in the pantry, Justin," Jess told him, giving him a gentle push. Once he was out of earshot, she asked, "What is it, Polly? You look ill."

"Mrs. Ames came over and asked if she could leave Owen while she went to register at the College."

"Yes?"

"He was outside with Robert, you see. Then . . ."

The telephone rang. Jess said, "Wait a minute, let me just get this." She stepped into the living room and picked up the receiver to hear a neutered, muffled male voice say, "We got your kid. It'll cost you a hundred thousand to get him back. Get the money together. We'll let you know where to bring it. And don't call the cops, if you want the kid back alive." A click, then buzzing. She wet her lips and put down the receiver, staring at Polly.

"Who was that?" Polly asked, forgetting herself.

Jess held up her hand to silence her, trying to think. Tillie had come with Owen and left him here. Robert had taken him outside to play and someone had kidnapped Owen believing him to be Justin. "Is Robert all right?" she asked, digging her fingernails into the palms of her hands, thinking this couldn't be real. It simply could not be real.

"He's got a pretty nasty cut on his head. Who was that on the 'phone?"

"They said they had *my* kid. They want a hundred thousand dollars. I've got to call Sanford. Then we've got to find Tillie, and get a doctor for Robert. Oh, my God!" she said softly, feeling it hit her. "Tillie! Press! I can't *think*! I must talk to Robert." She ran down the hall to the kitchen, where Robert was at the table with his head cradled in his hands. Olga was holding an ice pack to the top of his head. And Justin, still in his snowsuit, stood gazing open-mouthed at the two of them.

Jess went over to help him out of his snowsuit, saying, "Go upstairs and see if Todd's awake, will you, darling? Be very quiet now. If he's awake, come down and tell Polly and she'll go up with you to get him. You're to go and help her change him. All right?"

"What's the matter with Robert?"

"He hurt his head. Off you go. And remember, don't wake him. But if he's up, come and tell Polly."

"Okay," he said, his eyes still on Robert as he went sideways out of the kitchen.

"Robert, are you all right?" Jess asked, touching his shoulder.

"I guess I'm okay," he said, sitting up with effort. His eyes refused to focus.

Seeing his greatly dilated pupils, Jess said to Olga, "Call the doctor right now!"

"Somebody took Owen!" he cried, sick and hurting.

"Can you tell me what happened?" she asked.

"That's just it! I don't *know*! We were out there making a snowman and the next thing I knew I thought I heard a sound and then something fell on my head with an almighty crash and when I woke up the boy wasn't there. And they'd . . . my arms . . . threw them over by the garage. Well, then I thought he must've come back inside, but he isn't . . . wasn't . . . I'm *sorry*, Mrs. Woodrich! I wouldn't've let anything happen to him."

"I know that, Robert," she said softly.

Don't call the cops if you want the kid back alive.

It was something you heard on "The Shadow" or "Inner Sanctum," not on the telephone in your own home.

"I'm going to call Sanford," she said, her stomach knotted, hands trembling, jaw aching from clenching her teeth. *If you want the kid back alive*.

"I'm calling the police," Sanford told her. "Then I'll be home. Don't move, Jess! Is Robert all right?"

"I don't think so. His pupils are very dilated. Olga's called the doctor."

"I'll take care of everything. Keep Todd and Justin where you can see them! I'll get home as fast as I can."

She hung up, then turned to look at Robert and Olga.

"He's calling the police. Robert, why don't you go into the den and lie down?"

Holding the ice bag to his head, he got up, saying, "If it's all the same to you, Mrs. Woodrich, I'll go on up and lie down in my room."

"Of course."

He took several steps, then turned back. "I'm sorry," he said again. "I'd rather die than have anything happen . . ."

"It's all right, Robert. We all know that."

"You don't think they'll hurt him, do you?"

She couldn't begin to answer that. "Go ahead and lie down," she said. "Olga will help you." Olga took his arm and they set off up the back stairs.

Tillie!

She went upstairs, choked with relief to find Polly chatting with the two boys as if everything were normal. *My sons*, Jess thought, putting her arms around Justin, hugging him hard before plastering on a smile and getting to her feet, with forced calm saying, "I'll just take Todd and feed him. Will you stay with Justin, please?"

"Oh, certainly."

She carried Todd out into the hall. Someone had kidnapped Owen believing he was Justin. If she hadn't taken Justin for his checkup, *it would have been him*. But it was Owen. Oh God, Tillie! She went back to the doorway of the nursery, to ask, "What time did Tillie come by?"

"Around about one."

"Thank you."

She got Todd started at her breast, then looked at her watch. Almost three-thirty. Tillie would be coming soon. If she arrived to find Owen gone . . . Holding Todd with one hand, she picked up the receiver with the other hand and set it down while she dialed. After misdialing twice, she finally got it right, and lifted the receiver to her ear.

"Press, something's happened. I think you'd better come here at once."

"What's the matter?" he asked, instantly panicked.

"I can't talk about it over the telephone. Just, please, come right now!"

"Jesus!" he exclaimed, causing Nelda in the outer office to turn and look in at him. "Okay!"

Jess said, "I'm terribly sorry, Press," then hung up, leaving him on the other end of the line believing someone, either Tillie or Owen, was dead. Appalled at himself, he thought, *If someone's dead, please God, make it Tillie and not Owen. Please, not Owen!*

◊ Eighteen ◊

She wandered through Eaton's College Street, enjoying a few more minutes of freedom before returning to collect Owen. It was getting late, almost four. Just another minute or two to look at the art books and see if she couldn't find a present to buy herself for starting back to school.

She stared at the dust cover of a large coffee-table book, unable to look away. The face on the cover seemed so familiar. Moving closer, she stood directly in front of the display, looking down, her eyes going from the photograph to the title. Jamieson Land. She picked up the book feeling suddenly shaky, turning it over to see that, according to the caption, Flora Ogilvie had taken the cover portrait of the famed photographer and had also compiled the contents, the best of the works of the late Land. *Late?* He was dead?

Setting down her handbag, she held the book on the flat of her right hand and opened the cover with her left. Text. She'd read that later. An excitement was building, a pulsing sense of expectation as she quickly flipped through the pages, glimpsed something and slowly turned back, her heartbeat accelerating as she found the page, took a quivery breath, and looked at Jess. She didn't know how to react. Jess was nude,

to all intents and purposes, in a frilly robe that merely served
to frame her body, covering only part of her arms and shoulders.
She looked very young, her face fuller and rounder, her expression almost defiant. Her features seemed somehow too young
compared to her body and the pose. She still wasn't sure how
to react and lifted the page to see if there was anything more.

Another shot of Jess: standing in a room near a window,
half-turned toward the camera, her dress lowered to her waist.
The light from the window cast deep shadows on her face and
body, highlighting one breast. Tillie turned to the next page,
startled by the sudden softness of the setting, and the filtered
light. This, too, was Jess. Alone by the edge of Echo Lake,
profiled nude, looking down at the water, her hair pinned up
but a few loose curls escaping down her long neck. For a
moment, the artist in Tillie stood entranced by this other artist's
view of the model, finding her very beautiful with her long,
slender limbs and graceful neck, her starkly white skin and rich
black hair. She admired the gentle strength of Jess's face in
repose. Her thick lashes cast a shadow along her cheek. And
the definition and lift of one perfect breast took Tillie's breath
away. Reluctantly, she turned the page, promising herself another look at this photograph before putting the book down.

She turned the page and there it was. If she closed her eyes,
she could remember how she'd insisted that she wouldn't do
it, and Jess had talked about things people sometimes had to
do whether they wanted to or not. She looked at her twelve-
year-old self peeking over her shoulder. Her body was as innocent and unformed as a baby's beside Jess, who was concentrating on pinning up Tillie's hair. This shot, too, was painfully beautiful: sunpoints shimmering on the water, everything
captured in its starkest clarity. Each rock and blade of grass,
every leaf illumined by the filtration of morning sun. Jess's
expression contained only tenderness.

On the next page was another shot of Jess. Fully clothed,
she looked like a schoolgirl, sitting on the front steps of the
Vermont house with her arms wrapped around her knees, her
head turned to one side, as if caught up in a daydream. Her
long feet were bare and her hair was a cascading tangle framing
her always too-white face. Her eyelids were lowered slightly,
cementing the aspect of pleasure.

That was it. The last. She turned ahead to confirm that the

book went on to other subjects. Any number of street scenes and rather too formal, highly stylized portraits of twenties, thirties, and forties "names." She looked at the price. Pre-Christmas at $29.95, after Christmas, $34.95. She walked over to a salesclerk and paid the full after-Christmas price.

"Has this been selling well?" she asked the girl.

"Oh, very well. Surprising at the price. But it's a first edition and I guess that makes a difference. They say in a couple of years it'll be worth double. Nice pictures, aren't they?"

"Mmmm," Tillie agreed distantly, thinking. It wasn't just anyone who'd been photographed by the old man. The damned book was crawling with celebrities: Thornton Wilder, after the 1927 opening of *The Bridge of San Luis Rey*; Richard Rodgers and Lorenz Hart, also 1927, after the opening of their big hit musical, *A Connecticut Yankee*; Thomas Wolfe in 1929 upon publication of his first novel, *Look Homeward Angel*; Pearl Buck in 1938 winning the Nobel Prize; Orson Welles after the panic created by his radio play *Invasion from Mars*; Robert L. Riggs, winner of the U.S. Lawn Tennis men's singles in 1939 and 1941; jockey Edward Arcaro and the horse Whirlaway after winning the 1941 Belmont Stakes. Lots of people, all sorts, most of them important. And her and Jess, too. She tucked the book down the side of the shopping bag next to her art supplies, looked at her watch and hurried out of the store. It was twenty past four.

Nelda asked, "What's wrong, Press?"

"I don't know." He was pulling on his coat in a frenzy.

She put her hand on his arm and he paused to look at her.

"Come to me if you need somewhere to go."

Suddenly, he knew why he liked her and was so drawn to her: She reminded him of Jess.

She left the art supplies in the car, but carried the book in with her, thinking she'd show it to Jess. She was puzzled by the number of cars parked haphazardly around the drive. Press's car, too. What was Press doing here? There was an ambulance, with its motor running. There must have been an accident. She went up the front steps and rang the bell. Polly opened the door at once, regarded Tillie with an odd, sympathetic expression, saying, "Everyone's been waiting for you, dear. Come in."

"Waiting for me?" She put the book and her bag down on the table in the foyer and walked over to the living-room doorway to see Press on the sofa with Jess beside him, patting his hand. Sanford was standing watching the two of them, with a distressed look on his face. Two other men were perched on the edges of armchairs. Hearing a noise behind her, she turned to see a pair of uniformed attendants carrying Robert down the stairs on a stretcher, and another man, apparently a doctor, supervising. They carried Robert out and the door closed. The ambulance drove off. No siren. The doctor moved past Tillie into the living room. Then they all saw her at once. Press jumped up and came over, silently putting his arms around her. Beyond him, Tillie watched Jess rise and move to Sanford's side. The men in the chairs turned inquisitively, their pencils poised over the notebooks on their knees.

"What's going on?" she asked, extricating herself from Press's too-tight embrace, directing her question at Jess. "What's happening? What's wrong with Robert?"

"He has a concussion," Jess answered. "They're taking him to the hospital for a few days, for observation. Tillie, come sit down with me."

"What's going *on*?" Tillie asked again. The situation had the feeling of a disaster and she'd gone tense, every muscle in her body tight.

Jess came toward her, softly saying, "Come sit down with me and we'll explain."

Reluctantly, she allowed Jess to lead her to the sofa, but refused to let Jess hold her hand. Turning, she gave her a sharp, "What are you doing?" look, to which Jess responded with that same peculiar look of sympathy Polly had displayed at the door.

"We're wasting valuable time here," one of the men in the armchairs said with gruff impatience. "Time's the only thing we've got going for us right now. We can't afford to waste it."

"What?" She glanced over at him, then turned back to Jess.

"There's been a kidnapping," Jess said, trying once more to take hold of Tillie's hand, and succeeding. "It's . . . it was a mistake. They meant to take Justin, but they took Owen, thinking *he* was Justin."

"What? Who took Owen? What're you *talking* about?" Panic surged into her bloodstream, along her nerve endings.

"We need to know what he was wearing." It was the second man who spoke.

"Wearing? A snowsuit. Like Justin's. Blue overalls. A swea... Why do you need to know what he was wearing? Where is he?" She got up thinking she'd run up to the nursery and see for herself that the children were still there—Owen playing with Justin, and Todd asleep in the crib. That's the way it would be.

"A snowsuit like Justin's?" Jess asked. "*Exactly* like his?"

"That's right. I thought if he had a suit like Justin's he'd take more of an interest in dressing himself. So I bought him one."

"That's why!" Jess whispered. "My God! *That's* why!"

"That's why what? What the *hell* is going *on*?"

"Whoever they were," Jess said more audibly, "they'd obviously been watching... our routines... They knew Robert took Justin out to play every day after lunch. Justin wasn't here today, though. He was with me. For his checkup. But Owen was here. In an identical snowsuit. So they thought he was Justin, and they took him." How could she be sitting here, she wondered, rationally explaining all this, when someone had wanted to steal her child? But they hadn't. They'd taken Tillie's baby. Poor you, she thought. This is...

"*Who* took him?" Tillie demanded. "*How?*"

"They struck Robert from behind and they took Owen," Jess explained again.

"*Owen?*" Tillie lamented. "They've *taken* him? But *why*?" This was ridiculous, the logical part of her brain declared. She'd just run up to the nursery and get Owen, put him in his snowsuit and take him home. It was time for his supper.

"Tillie, please sit down," Press said.

"No!" She jerked around. He looked absolutely dreadful. Did that mean all this was real?

"What else was he wearing, Mrs. Ames?" the second, more quiet-spoken man asked.

"What else? A white sweater. With blue stripes. Shoes, socks, galoshes. Why do you need to know what he was *wearing*?"

"To help us locate him," the first man interjected, still sounding impatient. "To find out if anyone in the neighborhood saw anything."

"*I want Owen!*" she said loudly. If she was loud enough,

she'd shout some sense into all these fools. "I want him *right now*! It's his suppertime. And he hasn't had his nap today."

"*Tillie, sit down!*" Press ordered, placing his hand on her shoulder to force her down.

She sat. The sofa should have been hard. It wasn't, and the softness was a further shock.

"They want a hundred thousand dollars," Press told her.

"*Pay it!*"

"We're going to," Sanford said calmly. "We're waiting for them to call again and tell us where to deliver the money. You're not to worry, Tillie. We're going to get him back."

"You're going to pay it," she said, unable to breathe properly. A hundred thousand dollars? All that money for a two-year-old.

There was a moment of silence. And then it hit her like a fist driving into her stomach at a hundred miles an hour: Owen wasn't there. Someone had taken him and it was going to cost a hundred thousand dollars to get him back. PAY IT! The words screamed inside her head. PAY WHATEVER THEY WANT! I WANT MY BABY BACK! She doubled over, her forehead coming to rest on her knees, fighting down the sudden faintness that made her face cold and the back of her neck prickly. Her mouth filled with foul-tasting fluid so that she had to keep swallowing. Her stomach ached. The words of the others were distorted by the rushing noise inside her head. She couldn't move or see or hear or speak; she could only keep swallowing over and over, until they took her to one of the guest rooms and the doctor gave her an injection that sent her spiraling mercifully into blackness.

The police examined the footprints as well as the tire tracks left by the kidnap vehicle, and actually took fingerprints off Robert's arms. Detectives discreetly interviewed householders nearby, asking if they or their staffs had seen anything, amassing whatever information they could very quickly and quietly. At Sanford's insistence—unnecessary because they'd have kept media silence in any case—nothing was allowed to leak to the press while Sanford arranged with his broker for seventy thousand dollars and Press spoke to his father, who promised the balance. Within two hours, the money had been collected. They were waiting for a telephone call to tell them what to do.

Jess went up to look in on the boys and to nurse Todd while supervising Justin's bath. She changed the baby while Polly got Justin out of the tub and into his pajamas, and with Todd settled in his crib, Jess sat down to read Justin his bedtime story. Before beginning, she quietly asked Polly if she'd spend the night in the room with the boys. She was terrified the kidnappers would discover their error and somehow return, this time to take the right child, or both. Polly said, "Of course, dear," and Jess got on with the story while Polly went to get her night things.

Jess read, astonished to think her voice could sound so usual, that she could smile and then kiss and cuddle Justin as if nothing had happened and Owen wasn't out there somewhere in the hands of people who'd meant to take Justin. She waited anxiously for Polly to come back so she could go check on Tillie, worried by the way Tillie had taken the news: like a series of rapid physical blows that had silently felled her. She'd just folded over and not moved again until the doctor had suggested they take her upstairs and sedate her.

Polly came back, bringing with her a rush of cold air and the scent of winter, her face reddened by the cold. "I'll be here now," she told Jess. "I won't leave them. If there's anything I have to do, I'll get Olga to come stay with the boys."

Jess kissed Justin a final time and got up. Her legs felt thin, so thin they might break under her weight as she walked unsteadily to the guest room to look in at a deeply sleeping Tillie, drugged into peacefulness. She stood for several minutes beside the bed, watching Tillie sleep, thinking Tillie was a lot of things—some good and some bad—but whatever she was, she didn't deserve this. They were both grown women with children, Jess thought, finding it hard, for a moment, to accept the reality of that. How had so many years managed to get by them so fast?

She tiptoed out and went into the bathroom to wash her hands and, as an afterthought, fixed her hair and freshened her makeup. She felt she had to do these things, as if everyday acts might lessen the horror.

Downstairs, she found Olga in the middle of providing everyone with sandwiches and coffee, casting sorrowful eyes upon Jess as she indicated Jess's coffee and plate, then excused herself.

The telephone rang. They all looked up.

"You answer it, Mr. Woodrich," the second, evidently more senior, detective instructed. "I'll get on the extension in the kitchen. Let it ring twice more, then count to five and I'll pick up when you do." The man ran out and Sanford walked over to the phone. There followed two more loud, long rings that set Press visibly trembling. Jess instinctively put her hand on his arm. Then Sanford picked up the telephone, said hello, and listened for what seemed like hours, saying nothing. The German-made four-hundred-day clock on the mantel went on whirling, whirling soundlessly. Sanford said, "I have the money," and listened again. Then, he heard something that made him close his eyes and caused the pulse in his temple to throb. After a moment, he opened his eyes, said, "I understand," and put down the receiver.

"What did they say?" Press asked frantically, his fingers like ice as he removed Jess's hand from his arm.

"Owen's all right. They put him on and told him to say hello. We're going to pay them tonight."

"Tonight," Press repeated.

"I'll take care of it," Sanford said reassuringly, gripping Press's upper arm. "Try not to get yourself worked up. *Try!*"

The second detective returned from the kitchen to join Sanford and the other detective in a conference on the logistics. He was to drive alone at 4 A.M. to Kew Beach where he'd leave a paper shopping bag containing the money on a specific bench. Then he'd drive directly to the ball park on the lakeshore where he'd find Owen behind the first ticket booth, the one facing Bathurst Street.

"Okay," the first detective said. "Do it all exactly the way they told you. Mac, get on the phone and order surveillance of that booth. With luck, we'll pick them up when they drop the kid. Now, Mr. Woodrich, we'll have unmarked cars in the area. You'll be completely covered even though you might not see us. Just drop the money, get back in your car and head for the ball park. We'll be waiting for them to make the pickup from the bench. They're amateurs," he said, turning to include Jess and Prescott on the sofa. "They've made so many mistakes there's no way we won't get them. You'll have your boy back by morning," he said to Press, smiling for the first time.

"But shouldn't I be the one . . . ?" Press started to ask, then stopped. The kidnappers didn't know they had the wrong child.

Jesus! Don't let them hurt him! Please don't let them hurt my son.

The doctor had left a sedative for Press, should he need it. He did, but wouldn't take it. "I'll go up and lie down with Tillie for a while," he said.

"It'll be hours," Jess said. "Try to sleep."

"Sleep," he said, as if the word was completely new to him, and walked woodenly out of the room. He wished he had someone to hold on to, someone who understood how he felt.

After he'd gone, Jess asked, "You don't think they'll harm Owen, do you?"

Both detectives started to speak. The first gave way to the second, so that Jess decided they were equals, neither one superior to the other. For some reason, it seemed important to know their relative levels of seniority. Ludicrous things were suddenly very significant.

"It's impossible to predict what they'll do," the one named Mac told her. "They said on the phone that if the police were brought in, they'd kill the boy. Unless they've got a line into headquarters, there's no way they can possibly know we're already in it. The odds're all in our favor. But there's always the possibility they'll panic. They're kids, from the sound of it, and in way deeper than maybe they thought they'd be. It might've started out as a prank and turned into something a whole lot bigger. There can't be more than three of them, we figure. And we're bound to pick up at least two: the one waiting for the money, and the one delivering the boy to the ball park. They haven't thought this through at all carefully. There are holes miles wide. My hope is they won't harm the child. I can't give you any more than that. Now, if you'll excuse me, I've got some phoning to do. Is there somewhere more private than the kitchen?"

Jess showed him into the den while Sanford again went over the details with the first man. Returning, she sat on the sofa and lit a cigarette, poured herself a fresh coffee and warmed her hands on the cup for a moment before taking a swallow. Only the detectives had eaten any sandwiches; the rest sat, starting to curl at the edges. She went out to the kitchen where Olga was sitting at the table, a cup of tea in front of her, her head in her hands, staring fixedly at the tea.

"Why don't you go to bed, Olga?" Jess suggested. "We'll

let you know when we've got Owen back."

Olga shook her head. "Couldn't sleep right now. And I don't want to stay by myself over there. Nothin' feels right. I'll just sit here, drink my tea, wait."

"Why don't you stay in Robert's room?" Jess offered. "That way, you won't have to be alone."

"Maybe in a while. You think he's gonna be okay Robert?"

"I'm sure he'll be fine."

"Nobody blames him, eh?"

"Of course not. It wasn't his fault."

"That's right," she said earnestly. "It wasn't his fault. What kinda people steal a little boy, go hitting people over the head?"

"I know," Jess said quietly. "If you want to, please use Robert's room. All right?"

Olga nodded several times and Jess went back to the living room.

After completing his calls, the detective named Mac beckoned the other man into the den. Sanford took advantage of the lull to sit down on the sofa beside Jess, easing her over against him. For a moment, all she could do was stare at the shopping bag full of money on the coffee table.

"Charlie brought it from downtown," Sanford said.

Responding to his body warmth, she turned to rest her head on his shoulder.

"I want to ask you something, Jess."

"What?"

"Why didn't you come to the office this afternoon as planned?"

She had to stop and think. The afternoon seemed like years ago.

"Oh," she said, remembering. "I thought I wasn't due yet. But while we were waiting for the doctor, I started my period. I didn't have anything with me and it went right through my dress. I couldn't stand the idea of stopping somewhere to pick up some Tampax, then spending the rest of the afternoon and evening with my coat on, so I decided to come home and change. I thought I'd have Robert bring us down again. God! If I'd been able to get a taxi sooner, it might have been Justin. But when I called, they said it would be forty-five minutes, so we went back to the waiting room where Justin could play with the toys." She lifted her hand to grasp his. "Sandy, I'm so frightened. I don't think I can live here anymore. All I can think of is that they'll come back for Justin, and maybe Todd."

"That's *not* going to happen," he said emphatically. "And we're not going to be frightened into changing the way we live."

"But anyone could walk up the driveway..."

"I'll have the property fenced in and get an electronically controlled gate across the drive, with another intercom. No one will come in unannounced."

"That's changing our lives!"

"No, it isn't. It's simply exercising some sensible precautions. I don't want the boys growing up scared and I don't want *us* living scared."

"I don't know what to think."

"I'll take care of it," he promised. "Don't dwell on the what-if's. You'll only upset yourself more."

"I can't help it! It was supposed to be Justin! They wanted to take *our child* away!"

"What is it you're not telling me?" he asked very quietly.

"Nothing...I..."

"Why not tell me?"

"There's nothing...I mean...just thoughts and I'm not sure they mean anything. It's just...I was safe being what I was, Sandy. All the boundaries had been marked out and I was careful to stay inside them. I *knew* we'd get hurt. I knew it!"

"It's because of me, Jess, because I am who I am. Not you," he argued.

"You're wrong. Please don't make light of what I'm trying to say."

He smoothed the hair back from her face, then kissed the corner of her mouth. "It's *me*," he said. "I'm a businessman and a rich one. They're after the money, not to put you in your place."

"This is insane!" she cried. "We're arguing about which one of us is responsible for the fact that they wanted to take Justin. It's crazy. Owen's missing and we're arguing, as if we could solve anything that way."

"We'll deal with this," he said, "and we won't blame anyone but the responsible parties."

"All right," she sighed, thinking he was wrong. She *knew* he was wrong.

At three-twenty, Sanford left carrying the shopping bag of money. A new plainclothes detective came to stay in the house.

Jess went to the kitchen, saw that Olga had taken herself off to bed somewhere, and made a fresh pot of coffee. She brought out the sandwiches for the new man, then sat down with yet another cup of coffee and a cigarette, to wait it out.

◇ Nineteen ◇

When it got to be six A.M. and Sanford and the detectives still hadn't returned, Jess knew something had gone wrong. Something going wrong incorporated too many possibilities, and each one filled her with dread. She felt more and more victimized simply by the open length of their driveway, the easy accessibility of the house, and the probability that the radio and newspaper people would get wind of what had happened and begin to arrive, asking questions and demanding answers and interviews. She had to do something about the driveway; it made her feel too defenseless.

Convinced there was only one person who could keep the driveway closed, she got up and walked past the dozing detective to the den to put in a call to Trois Rivières trying to imagine what René's wife might think if she picked up the receiver to hear a strange woman's voice asking for her husband at this time of the morning. Fortunately, René himself answered and in response to her apologies, said, "Hey! Everybody here's already up."

Briefly, then, she told him what had happened.

"This is terrible," he said. "I'm happy it's not your boy,

259

but terrible for the little one. Jesus, but this is bad!"

"I'm sorry to bother you with this, but you're the only one I knew to call. I don't think Sanford's going to be able to handle this. At least, not right now. We've been up all night. And press people are bound to start coming around. It'll only upset Tillie more. And me, too," she admitted.

"You let me think on it, eh? You leave it with me, I think on it. Don't you worry."

"I'm very grateful..."

"Hey! I'm proud you call me like a friend. You don't worry. I take care of it."

"René," she said hesitantly, "there's something else. I have this *feeling*. I'm probably wrong, but I can't help..." She trailed off, not sure what she'd wanted to tell him, yet gratified to hear him say, "I find out. You go rest, and don't worry."

Somewhat eased, she returned to the living room believing he'd do something.

It was miserably cold. The roads were sheer ice, and the slick streetcar tracks on Queen Street didn't help matters as Sanford headed toward the ball park. He drove along thinking random thoughts, feeling strengthened by the silly fact that, after all this time, Jess had called him Sandy. He lit a cigarette, keeping his eyes on the deserted street, going again over the matter of Jess's feelings.

They showed in any number of ways, and especially with the boys. And when the two of them were alone together and he said, "I love you, Jess," she softened, her gestures and caresses becoming even gentler, telling him physically what she couldn't put into words. It sometimes seemed to him like a lengthy archaeological search, digging out fragments of information about her past, as well as her thoughts and reactions, then piecing the fragments together to make one complete corner of a picture.

Tonight, she'd leaned against him and called him Sandy. It was almost like hearing her say, "I love you," and he couldn't help feeling they were getting closer to a time when she'd no longer feel the need to withhold anything. He got impatient from time to time. It was only natural, he supposed, because he continued to expect her to move toward him more quickly than she did. Being truthful, he had to admit that complete capitulation on her part would not only have been suspect, but also unrewarding. She was a permanent challenge to him.

Where are those unmarked cars? he wondered, scanning the street.

He looked at the speedometer. Twenty miles an hour. He eased his foot down slightly, and the car veered to the right. He lifted his foot back. The unreality, the seeming theatricality of all this was starting to bear down on him. Was he actually out alone on the predawn streets on his way to pick up his kidnapped nephew? It felt like a dream. *Bring the police into this and we'll kill the kid.* Would they murder a child not yet two years old? He thought of Justin and shuddered. No wonder Jess was scared. He was scared, too. There was a cold area deep in his belly. Like not-quite-congealed gelatin, it shivered and trembled, making bile rise into his throat. He swallowed and took such a hard drag on the cigarette that it stung his lips.

What unmarked cars? There wasn't a damned thing moving on the streets. Did those detectives really know what they were doing? Christ! He hoped so.

For the first time in years, he thought about Bess. Boring, ever accommodating Bess with that inevitable hint of a whine to her voice, coming to him for everything from what to order from the butcher to when to have the floors polished. No challenge, no mystery, just day-after-day predictability that galled and irritated. But if she hadn't died, he'd have stuck it out with her. Because that was the way things were done then. An occasional woman on the side that had left him feeling guilty and uncomfortable.

Was that one of the cars? Someone seemed to be sitting in that parked car, but he couldn't be sure. He was sweating and reached to turn off the heater, leaving the defrosters on, then rolled the window down a few inches and threw out his cigarette. He turned left down Spadina, going into a skid at the intersection of the streetcar tracks. Going with the skid, he took his foot off the accelerator and gently pumped the brakes until the car slowly righted itself. A damned good thing there was no traffic, he thought. He'd have hit something on that wild turn.

He glanced at the factories as he went past, the familiar-sounding names of garment manufacturers that seemed to have been there for as long as he could remember. Lu-Bob Belts.

Da-Ron Manufacturing. He lit another cigarette as he turned right onto Lakeshore.

Not a car in sight. He was alone in this damned thing. Or else they were so good at being inconspicuous . . . There was the ball park. His heart beating too fast, he pulled up at an angle so that his headlights were shining on the area in the rear of the booth, revealing a small blue figure sitting against the back wall. He experienced a sizzling shock of alarm and outrage. How could they leave a baby alone out here with the temperature well below zero? And why was Owen simply sitting there?

His heart was beating so irregularly it hurt as he jumped out of the car and lumbered through the banks of snow toward the small, still figure at the rear of the booth. Something preceded him, registering in his brain: No small child was capable of sitting so perfectly still. Didn't Justin fidget and wriggle and bounce up and down ceaselessly? Small boys couldn't sit still. He bent down with his arms extended, wanting to believe Owen's lolling head meant he'd simply fallen asleep. But gently tilting his head up, he was presented with an almost blue face and closed eyes. He touched the soft, pallid baby face, noticing the delicate vein-tracings in Owen's eyelids and the thick length of his lashes. Cold. Was he sleeping? Sanford ran awkwardly with him back to the car and turned on the interior light to look more closely at the boy. The only sound was a thin noise that escaped from Sanford's throat as he fiercely clutched the child to his chest and threw back his head, his throat working and eyes blinking rapidly against the tears. He'd get them and see them dead for doing this!

The old lady didn't understand what they wanted, and just stood holding her robe around her gazing at them in terror.

"Where *is* he?" the younger one demanded.

"He's not here." She turned to look up the stairs. "There was a phone call about an hour ago. He got dressed, went running out like a crazy man. I'm always warning him, 'Stosh, you'll give youself a heart attack.' A big man running around like that. What d'you want him for? What's he done, eh?"

"Where'd he go?"

"I don't know," she said slowly.

"Okay, lady. Sorry to bother you. You go on back to bed now."

"What's he done?" she asked after them, but they were already running down the front walk, jumping into a truck and driving away.

They jimmied the front door.

"We better make it fast, in case they got some kinda alarm system."

They hurried through the factory toward the office at the rear where a light was on.

He was opening a wall safe hidden behind a big old photograph and jumped away, the safe door swinging open, as they stepped into the office, one of them reaching to lock the door.

"Whatcha doin', fat man?" the first one asked him.

"What *is* this?" he barked, red-faced and frightened. "If you've come to hold us up, there's nothing here, so forget it."

"Whatcha gettin' so worked up about, eh? You're actin' all kinda guilty and nervous, fat man."

"What do you want? How did you get in here?"

"We got a question to ask you. It's about this little kid that's missing."

Cotton's eyes rounded and his mouth fell open. How had they found out? He'd been so careful. No one could've known, unless those three idiots had screwed up. Shit! He shouldn't have trusted them to keep their mouths shut.

One turned and said to the other, "Looks like we found the guilty party, eh?"

"Looks that way, for true."

"What d'you think you're doing?" he cried, taking a step backward. "You keep away from me." Moving with surprising agility for someone so big, he darted to his desk, yanked open the top drawer and fumbled with a gun that fell to the floor. He dropped to one knee with a grunt, trying to grab it up.

Gracefully, the first one bent and retrieved the gun, then held it admiringly in his hand. The second one moved around behind Cotton and wrapped his arm around the fat man's throat, softly saying, "Just sit yourself down here in this chair. Nice and easy now, sit yourself down. That's right. Now, Claude here's gonna put the gun in your hand. Right, Claude? That's right. And you're gonna hold the gun nice 'n' steady. Good! That's *very good*, fat man." He smiled, his hand enclosing Cotton's with the gun. "Now, see, we're gonna do this." He

264 *Charlotte Vale Allen*

forced Cotton's hand up so that the gun was pushing toward his mouth. "Don't you fight now, fat man. Just do what you're told. We're gonna put this here gun in your mouth, so open up like a good boy."

Cotton was sobbing, his eyes huge and his body writhing as the one with his hands on Cotton's shoulders kept him down in the chair and the other slowly thrust the gun into his mouth and kept it there. Cotton gagged.

"Hurry up!" the second one whispered.

"Okay! Oh, yeah, I almost forgot. I gotta message for you. From an old friend, eh? René said to tell you this is for Jess."

Cotton's eyes bulged as the meaning penetrated. Liquid terror spread a dark stain on his trousers. The second man pressed Cotton's finger against the trigger. Down, down. Until the explosion. The two men leaped out of the way but were spattered nevertheless with bits of tissue, blood.

"Let's go!"

They raced through the empty building, taking the time to close the front door, then jumped into the truck and, without lights, drove from the lot, turning the lights on only when they were well away from the factory. They could hear the whine of a siren in the distance.

"Maybe they had a silent alarm," the first one said.

"Stop over there to that phone box, eh?"

"Right."

The first one pulled the truck over to the curb. The second one climbed down and closed himself into the phone booth.

"Boss? We got him! Yeah, sure. No, we kept our gloves on. Did just like you said. He didn't say nothin', but he done it. You could tell from his eyes. What? No, he had him a gun, eh? Yeah. But we didn't touch nothin'. Yeah, okay. No, we're on our way right now. Okay. Yeah."

René put down the receiver and sat staring at his hands, thinking, *I should of done it a long long time ago. Jesus God forgive me, I just killed a man. But he shouldn't of done those things to her.*

He closed his eyes and held his fingertips to his lips, reciting Hail Mary's, apologizing to God, trying to explain how it was to love a woman you couldn't have, but to want nothing bad to happen to her, to love her and know she could never forgive him if she knew.

*   *   *

Press awakened with a jolt and in the darkness tried to place himself. Where was he? Becoming aware of Tillie's weight beside him on the bed, he remembered and sat up slowly, rubbing his face with his hands. He went into the bathroom and turned on the light, then looked at Tillie in the spill of light from the bathroom. She lay deep in a drugged sleep. He glanced at his watch. A quarter to seven. With a quickening inside, he thought Sandy must be back by now with Owen. He splashed water on his face, drank some, then felt for his pocket comb and fixed his hair. After straightening his tie and smoothing some of the creases in his jacket, he turned out the light and went as noiselessly as possible out of the room, carefully closing the door behind him.

As he was coming down the stairs, the telephone rang and he heard sudden movements in the living room and then Jess's voice answering. She seemed to listen for a long time and still was when Press came into the room. She held the receiver with both hands, her head bowed and her eyes closed. The detective went past Press and down the hall to the den to pick up on the extension. Something was wrong. On impulse, Press dashed down to the kitchen and snatched up the extension there, to hear a voice he didn't know saying, ". . . the mother needn't come. But we'll want the father, to make the identification. And later this morning, you and the mother for a look at the lineup, see if you or she knows or recognizes any of them. Okay?"

"I'm on the line, Don," the detective said from the den. "You want to go back over the first part of that for me?"

"May I hang up now?" Jess asked, sounding unlike herself.

The voice belonging to Don said, "Okay, Mrs. Woodrich," and there was the sound of the receiver being replaced. "You still there, Wally?" Don asked.

"Yeah, I'm here. Read me back that first part, eh, I missed it."

"Sure. We got one when he went to pick up the money. He fell apart in no time flat, told us everything. We sent out a couple of cars and nailed the other two. We've got the three of them in being questioned now. Making statements, brother! They can't spill it fast enough."

"What about the kid?" Wally asked.

Press went rigid.

"The two said it was an accident. They didn't mean anything to happen, but the kid started screaming and crying and the one guy panicked, clapped his hand over the kid's face to shut him up and when he took his hand away, he said, the kid was dead."

Press screamed and dropped the receiver, slamming his hands against his ears as if to prevent himself from hearing what he already had. His whole body vibrating, he pressed the palms of his hands into his ears, crying, "*NOOOOO*!" Jess came running in to throw herself against him, holding him until his hands fell to his sides and he was whispering, "No, no, no."

"Press, you've got to go downtown and identify Owen."

He shook his head violently, moving away from her. She reached out—with surprising strength, he thought—and took hold of his arm.

"Press! I'm so sorry. But you've *got* to do it. Unless you want Tillie to be the one."

That reached him. Whatever he felt about her, he couldn't do that to Tillie.

"Down where?" he asked, everything paining.

"The detective will take you. Come with me, Press." She took hold of his hand, coaxing him to go with her, and led him to the den where the detective nodded soberly and thanked her, then indicated she could go. The door closed. The detective's voice began. She backed away, colliding with Olga and Polly, both of them in housecoats and slippers, their faces starkly white.

"What's happened?" Polly asked, her arm around Olga's shoulders as if to protect the older, larger woman.

"Owen's dead," she said bluntly. Their faces crumpled and ran with tears. Jess watched, wondering, What's the matter with me? appalled by her inability to react. She felt dazed and deadened. *Owen's dead*, she repeated silently, and then it struck her—above the eyes and in the pit of her stomach and in her thighs. She covered her face with her hand. The two women disengaged to comfort her.

The den door opened and Press and the detective, Wally, came out.

"Two patrolmen will be posted outside the house," Wally told the women. "They're on their way over now. Mr. Ames and I are going downtown." Tactfully, he omitted mentioning

the morgue. "Someone will be calling later on in the morning
for you to come down with your sister, to take a look at a
lineup."

"All right," Jess agreed, looking at Press. His face was
completely devoid of color, his eyes blank and empty. He
looked destroyed, Jess thought. He turned and went down the
hall with the detective, stopping to put on his coat but forgetting
his hat and overshoes. The two of them went out and the front
door closed quietly.

Sanford was there, waiting. He looked exhausted, his face
covered with gray stubble, his tie pulled loose and the top
button of his shirt open. Press was captivated by this view of
him. He'd never seen Sanford anything but impeccably
groomed, closely shaven and smelling pleasantly of cologne.
Now he smelled faintly sweaty and his eyes looked gritty. He
was smoking a cigarette and fell in beside Press as the group
of men continued along the corridor, down some stairs and
along another corridor, coming to a halt in front of an unmarked
door.

One of the detectives opened the door and they were in the
morgue. The air was gelid, heavy with formaldehyde. The
walls were paneled with oversized filing-cabinet-type drawers.
A white-coated attendant came toward them carrying a clipboard, and led the way down the wall to take hold of the handle
of one of the drawers, pulling it slowly forward to reveal
Owen's naked blue body, which took up only a fifth of the
huge slab. There was a tag looped over one tiny toe and at his
feet lay the bundle of clothing.

With a cry, Press snatched Owen from the slab, rocking
him locked against his chest, moving frenziedly about the room
as if searching for some previously unnoticed door he might
go through with his son, to return on the far side with a live,
laughing Owen.

Sanford watched, thinking, It would have been me. This
is how it would have been for me. Press staggered drunkenly
around the chilly room with his son's body in his arms, sobbing,
looking anxiously, hopelessly at the faces of the men as if for
confirmation of something. Sanford couldn't bear it and put
his arms around the man, embracing him tightly to stop his
dreadful floundering, holding the man with the baby caught
between them, while Press's head dropped heavily onto San-

ford's shoulder and he wept brokenly. His reluctant hands finally released the small corpse and while Sanford kept hold of Press, the attendant returned Owen to the drawer in the wall, then made several notes on his clipboard.

There were no words, Sanford thought despairingly, and no point groping for things to say that couldn't possibly have meaning or consolation here in this place, at this time. Feeling greatly aged, he got Press out into the corridor where they stood for some time, silently smoking, until the detectives came to take them to view the lineup. Both men looked at the faces of a group of disheveled young men, all of them appearing relentlessly criminal under the white blaze of the overhead lights.

"Recognize any of them?" the detective named Mac asked.

Press shook his head dully.

Sanford said, "No."

Mac said, "Okay, that's it." The lights went off and the young men filed away. "You two can go on home now. We'll be in touch later today. You need a ride?"

"I have my car," Sanford said, and took Press's arm to direct him out into the blaze of morning. Sun glinted like daggers off the ice and snow, making both men's eyes water as they shrank inside their clothes against the cold, hurrying across the parking lot.

The car warmed up fast and Sanford turned on the blowers, then offered Press another cigarette. They drove along, smoking, the visors down to protect their eyes from the sun. Then Press, his voice unexpectedly steady now, said, "I think this is going to send Tillie right off the deep end. I think it's going to be the end of us, too. We don't have enough to hold us together without Owen." He said Owen's name and had to stop, swallowing hard against the constriction in his throat. Then, doggedly, he went on. "I loved her so much and it went so damned fast. I still can't believe how fast. It just . . . *went*. But that doesn't matter," he said. "I know she loved him. I think," he said, trying to reason it through, "the only people she's ever really loved have been Jess and Owen. She'd argue it, because for some reason she doesn't *want* to love Jess. Oh, Jesus, I don't know." He sighed shudderingly. "I don't even know what I'm trying to say. But at least she won't have to go down to that *place*, see him there . . . that way."

Sanford listened, driving cautiously through the early morning downtown traffic.

"I'm going to say a kind of funny thing," Press said. "I don't know why. I guess it's just the way I feel right now." He was silent for several seconds, staring out the window. Then he rubbed his eyes with his fists. "I'm glad it wasn't you," he said at last. "It was supposed to be you and Jess, but it turned out to be me and Tillie. There's a kind of insane irony to all this that actually makes sense to me. But I'm glad it wasn't you, Sandy. In a way," he said, measuring every word, "I guess I always had a feeling Owen wasn't going to get a chance to grow up. There was too much stacked against it."

He went quiet then, and Sanford tried to think of something to say. He'd never felt closer to any man than he had all these hours to Press. But Press's last remarks separated them, and he couldn't seem to find anything to say that would return them to that closeness. Perhaps, he thought, this kind of kinship was something that couldn't be prolonged. Yet while it lasted, Sanford treasured the closeness. "If you like," he said, "I'll tell Tillie for you."

Press turned, studying the older man.

"You've done more for me in the last twenty-four hours than my own father's done in my whole life. You haven't made me feel . . . ashamed, I guess. Without ever intending to, my dad would've made me feel I wasn't being 'manly.' He'd have done it one way or another and I'd have felt like a fool . . . for crying . . . I don't know."

It reminded Sanford of a night, years ago, with Jess. He felt then as he did now, when confronted with the self-doubt of people he loved. "You're not a fool, Press. I've never put much faith in men who think the 'manly' way to handle things is with a lot of bullshit blustering and phony shows of strength. I feel responsible for what's happened. My name and money, my life cost you Owen. I'm going to have to think about that— a lot—for the rest of my life. Don't say anything, because it's the truth and we both know it. I think we should drop it now. We're not going to get anywhere trying to analyze what's happened. But you're not a fool. I'd have done exactly what you did."

◇ Twenty ◇

Jess was upstairs in her bedroom nursing Todd when Tillie came in just after seven. She made her way over in a drug-dazed state and sat down in the other armchair, gazing at Todd for several long moments before lifting her head to look at Jess.

"He's dead, isn't he," she said flatly.

"Let me just take Todd back to the nursery, then we'll talk." The baby was already half asleep and she burped him as she carried him down the hall to turn him over to Polly.

Fastening her clothes—they felt thick and filthy as if she'd been wearing them for months—she went back to see that Tillie hadn't moved and was sitting gazing out the window. Jess sat down and automatically lit a cigarette, her mouth foul from the dozens she'd smoked throughout the night.

Without turning from the window, Tillie said, "I dreamed about him just before I woke up. I dreamed he was dead and made myself wake up because I didn't want it to be real. But I knew it was. It's the truth, isn't it?"

"It was an accident. They didn't mean to harm him."

Tillie emitted a harsh ugly bark of laughter. "An accident," she scoffed, her face as empty as a deserted warehouse. "They

270

took him and he's dead, but it was an accident. You know what else I dreamed?" She turned to look at Jess. "I dreamed I couldn't have any more. I'm never going to have another baby. And the one I had is dead. This is real and Owen's dead but I can't seem to stop believing this is just a dream."

"I know," Jess said low, anguished.

"This is only more of the dream," she went on. "The two of us are here, quietly talking about my dead baby, but I'm going to wake up soon. This is how dreams feel. You know? All slow and out of whack. I can probably fly, too. I usually can in my dreams. I do a lot of it. Mostly back to Branksome Hall. I fly around the classroom with the girls and the teacher pointing up at me, all excited and amazed. The ceiling's very high, with rafters and beams—not the way it really was. There's a window way down at the end of the room that's open, a tiny little one, just big enough for me to fly through. I'm free and I go over the trees, around the city. Sometimes, when I see people on the streets, I come down low to let them see me. It's dangerous though because I have to run along the ground for a good way to get back up again, and sometimes I can't. Then I get scared. Because if I don't have enough room to run in, I can't get up. If I can't get up, they'll catch me and that'll be the end. I'll never be able to fly anymore.

"Why doesn't any of it ever come out the way I want? I'm forever thinking if I just do this and then that, it'll fit together and everything'll be the way I want. But I go ahead and it never fits at all. There's always a piece sticking out here and one sticking out over there." She paused and took a slow breath. "Why'd they have to kill him? We gave them the money, did what they wanted. Why'd they have to *kill* him?"

"I don't know. They didn't mean to, Tillie."

"I don't care if they *meant* to. They *did*."

As they approached the house, Sanford couldn't believe what he was seeing and said, "What the hell is that?"

Press looked up and answered, "I don't know. A truck?"

Two huge tractor-trailors were parked back to back, blocking off the driveway and access to the house. In the road, half a dozen cars were parked every which way, and the occupants were shouting and waving their hands at two uniformed policemen and several leather-jacketed broad-chested men who shook their heads to quiet them. The shouters and wavers were carrying cameras and heavy-looking tape recorders.

Sanford put the car in neutral as one of the leather-jacketed men came over. "What's going on?" he asked. "Why have you blocked the driveway?"

"Who're you?" the man asked, not unpleasantly.

"Woodrich. I live here. Why have you got those trucks parked that way?"

"Your missus she called René. He sent us. I'm real sorry, sir. We move the trucks, let you in."

"But what are you *doing* here?"

"Keepin' them out." He indicated the press and radio people. "Keepin' everybody out 'cept for the ones belong here. Just you wait, I'll get the boys to let you through."

Fuddled, Sanford closed the window while the man stood with his hand on the hood of the car, looking proud and protective both of the car and its occupants.

Two men climbed into the cabs of the trucks, whose engines had been left idling. As Sanford put the car into gear, the crowd of people suddenly started running toward them. The truckers and the two policemen cut them off and Sanford continued on up the drive to the house, then looked into the rearview mirror to see the trucks once more closing the gap.

Who on earth had Jess called?

Polly said, "Breakfast's on the sideboard in the dining room, sir."

"Thank you, Polly." Sanford gave her his coat and turned to watch Press struggle out of his.

"I want you to know we're all deeply sorry, Mr. Ames," Polly said.

Press nodded, unable to speak.

"Come in and eat something, Press," Sanford said. "We both need to. Is my wife up, Polly?"

"Yes, sir. They're both upstairs in the bedroom."

"Tell them we're back, would you? We might as well wait in here for them." He propelled Press gently into the living room.

Polly knocked at the door to say, "The gentlemen have returned, Mrs. Woodrich," then she went back to the kitchen where the baby was asleep in a basket on the counter and Justin was perched atop two telephone books at the table, eating his breakfast. Neither Olga nor Polly would allow the children out of their sight for an instant. Owen's death had turned them into vigilant guards.

Jess said, "We'll go down and have some breakfast. You've got to eat."

Tillie stood up, a ticking starting inside her, and without a word, walked to the door. She could feel it inside, like the clock part of a bomb, with the second hand ticking its way toward the explosion. The dynamite was in there, too. She could feel it wedged in her chest, right behind her breasts. When the blast came, it would take her with it. *Good*, she thought. *Good*.

She went down the stairs, the ticking becoming louder. The low sounds of Press and Sandy's voices came to her from the living room. Glasses were being set down on hard surfaces. She was going faster, faster, the dream rushing forward, the ticking louder and louder. She ran into the living room and stopped dead at the sight of Press. All of it was getting faster and louder. Hearing footsteps, she whirled around to see Jess coming in behind her. Press. Sandy. Jess. She heard the sudden high notes of Justin's laughter. Tick. Tick. Jess stopped beside her, her eyes going suddenly wide as Tillie began to scream.

"You never deserved any of the things you got, none of them! It was supposed to be *your* baby, not *mine*! But that's always the way, *you* getting things you don't deserve and nothing ever turning out right for *me*, nothing, *not ever*! A tramp, a slut, fucking anybody who'd pay you! You don't deserve any of what you've got! Me! I'm the one! Did you know what she was?" she shrilled at Sanford. "Did you know your precious wife, mother of your wonderful little babies was a common *whore*? *Tell him, Jess! Go on! Does he know? Does he?*"

Press put out his hand, saying, "Tillie! You don't know what you're saying..."

She smacked his hand away. "I KNOW! I know all right! Fucking her way from one end of this goddamned city to the other! I know *all about it*! And what does she *get*? Oh, *God*! It kills me, *kills* me! She gets it *all*! Another old man, a rich one this time, and this *house*, and *mink coats* and *servants* to wipe her *ass* if she needs it!"

Jess tried to hold herself together, telling herself she understood why Tillie was doing this, but it didn't lessen the impact. Her hand swung out and she struck Tillie as hard as she could across the face.

Tillie went instantly silent, her eyes for several seconds remaining large and crazed, then she began to shake, crying, "You *hit* me! Jess, I'm sorry. I love you. I didn't mean it. I love you and I made you hit me. All my life you never . . . all the things I said and did . . . you never hit me!" She threw herself into her sister's arms, sobbing. "I knew you did it for me, Jess. I always knew that. I'm sorry, I'm sorry. I can't be with you. I love you and all the time when I see you I feel as if I hate you. I've got to get out of here, got to, I can't be with you." She pushed herself away and ran from the room. Press ran out after her.

"I always knew she knew," Jess said to herself.

"I've got to get out of here!" Tillie raved, breathlessly dragging on her coat and snatching up her bag. *"I can't stay, can't stay!"*

"Wait! I'll come with you!"

She threw open the front door. "You *can't* come with me!" She took a breath and held her hand out. "You can't come, Press. I'm sorry, but you can't."

Her hand slid away out of his grasp and she ran again. She fell on the front walk, awkwardly picked herself up and jumped into the car, started it with a roar, then drove across the snow-covered lawn and down the driveway. As if by magic, the two trucks parted to let her through and she was gone. The trucks pulled together again. Press closed the door and returned to the living room. There was a low buzzing in his ears as he looked at Jess standing woodenly inside the circle of Sandy's arms. "She didn't mean all that," he said lamely.

"Yes, she did," Jess said, turning to reveal surprisingly calm features. "She only told the truth, Press. Sanford's known from the first. And now," she sighed, "you know too. If you'll excuse me, I'm going to go up and lie down." She paused to touch his cheek with her fingertips, saying, "I'm sorry," before continuing on her way.

She undressed and climbed under the shower, sighing beneath the soothing heat of the water. She let it beat down on her, looking at the floor of the stall, thinking about Tillie. She was gone and might never come back. *I stunted her,* she thought. With the best possible intentions, she'd kept Tillie small and in need of protection. Tillie had never had to lift a finger to help herself because Jess had promised their father she'd take care of her. And she had. She'd taken such good care of Tillie that she'd grown up without values. She felt sick with regret, but there was no guilt. I did the best I could, she thought. I tried.

When Sanford came in, she was lying on top of the bed, dressed in a pair of black slacks and a black sweater. Her face, hands, and feet looked shockingly white. He sat down on the bed and took hold of her hand, asking, "Are you all right, Jess?"

"You look so tired. How did he die?"

"Asphyxiation. The kid apparently didn't mean to do it. They told you that when they called?"

She nodded.

"I want to believe that," he said, smoothing her hand. "I'm sorry about Tillie."

"So am I."

"I'll clean up, then come lie down with you," he said, standing up.

He closed himself into the bathroom as the bedroom door burst open and Justin came running in to jump on the bed and knee-walk over to his mother.

"You sleepin'?" he asked, jiggling her breast with his hand.

"I'm not sleeping." She smiled, stilling his hand. "What are *you* doing?"

"Makin' cookies. I stamp 'em out."

"Are you having fun?"

"Nah! Owen comin' to play today?"

It ate the smile off her face like acid. She drew him over beside her, saying, "Owen's not going to be coming to play, Justin."

"Tomorrow?"

"Not ever again," she said very quietly. "Owen's dead, darling."

Justin blinked. "Day after then?" he asked.

"Never again. Owen isn't here anymore. He's dead, Justin."

"What's 'dead'?"

"You know how you breathe and eat and play and do all the things you do?"

"Sure." He smiled.

"Well, Owen's stopped breathing."

"How?"

"His heart stopped beating. You don't understand, do you?"

"Sure I do." He smiled more widely. "Owen's dead and not breathing."

"That's right."

"Okay," he said.

"Kiss?"

He offered his cookie-crumbed mouth to hers, then wriggled backward off the bed.

"C'n he come next week, then?" he asked.

"Not next week," she said, giving up. "You run along back to Polly now."

"Okay." He scampered out and slammed the door.

She covered her eyes with her hand.

Sanford came out of the bathroom with a towel wrapped around his waist. He locked the door, then drew the curtains before sitting down on the side of the bed. "Jess?"

She wiped her eyes with both hands and looked at him.

"There's something I want to tell you."

"What?" she asked, tensing.

"The three boys," he said, "it wasn't their idea alone."

"Oh, my God!" She sat up, staring at him.

"They admitted everything as soon as they were picked up."

"Cotton," she whispered, shivering.

He nodded and started to say more but she got off the bed and ran to the door, then to the window. Stopping at last in the middle of the room, she cried, "WHY? I never . . . Owen's dead and it's because of *me*!"

"Come here, Jess."

"I *loved* that little boy. I loved him and he's dead because of my life! I can't stand it!"

"Jess, come here," he said again.

The pain was consuming. She had to grope her way past it in order to be able to see him standing there, to force into her brain the knowledge that she wasn't alone. Sanford loved her. She huddled against him, shivering, her teeth chattering.

"He's dead, Jess."

"I know that, I *know*!"

"Not Owen. This man Cotton."

"He's *dead*?"

"Suicide. He put a gun in his mouth. Now, listen," he said, realizing she was close to hysteria. "You're not responsible for some insane man's attempt to capitalize on other people's misfortunes. Do you hear me? You're *not* responsible!"

"But it'll come out. There'll be a trial. It'll be in all the newspapers."

"Certainly, there'll be a trial. But no one could possibly blame you for Owen's death."

"Tillie will, when she knows."

"You're wrong. Tillie loved that boy. She might be jealous as hell of you, but she knows you'd never wish her harm."

"You believe that? Do you actually believe that?"

"She's not going to be thinking about anyone but herself, and Owen. She may hold you responsible for other things, but not this. If anything, she'll probably find some way to blame herself, because she brought Owen here and left him when she could just as easily have taken him with her. You need to sleep, Jess. You're completely exhausted."

Like a plaster statue, she stood while he undressed her. Once in bed, she closed her eyes, asking, "Tell me about it."

"It was frightening," he said, his body warming her. In a low, tired voice, he described what had happened after he'd left the house. He could feel her shivering finally stop as she slowly began to relax. "By the way," he asked at the end, "who did you call?"

"René, an old friend."

"I'd like to meet him sometime, and thank him. I feel a hell of a lot easier knowing those men are out there."

Maybe it would end now, she thought, her tears subsiding as her eyes closed heavily.

"Sleep, Jess," he whispered. "It's all over now."

FOUR

Interlude
Tillie

◇ Twenty-One ◇

Press agreed to stay on at his parents' house for a few more days to give Tillie the time she said she needed to herself.

After the funeral, she returned alone to the apartment and went to the window in the living room to stand for a long time looking out at the gray, choppy waters of the lake and the shoreline clotted wth a jagged rim of yellowish ice. She didn't know what to do; she couldn't bear to risk seeing one of Owen's toys lying under a chair, or the open doorway to his room.

Her insides seething, her hands trembling, she thought, I've got to get out of here.

Then, losing her slight grip on that idea, she thought of her sister, a tall, elegant figure in black, her face unnaturally pale behind a net veil. Tillie thought Jess had looked far more like a grieving, bereft mother than she herself had. Jess's grief was bewildering, even awesome. Throughout the proceedings, Tillie had been more aware of Jess than of what was happening. She'd watched, captivated, as Jess had taken hold of Sanford's hand and still had hold of it when the two of them climbed into the limousine to have Robert drive them home.

As had happened when she'd examined the Land photographs, Tillie was impressed by Jess's beauty. Not her features, taken separately, but the beautiful total of Jess. Everyone had looked at her repeatedly throughout the service, perhaps sensing this same quality that Tillie could not now define. Staring out the window, she thought if she could only define it, she mightn't go on feeling she hated her sister.

Press had looked old and ill, as if he were suffering from some prolonged, but inevitably terminal disease. For the first time, she'd actually felt herself caring about him, and wished she could comfort him. But she couldn't.

From a distance, she knew she loved her sister. But, up close, she hated her. She didn't love Press. And what would she do with all the love she still had for the little boy she shouldn't have left behind? *Kiss Mummy good-bye.* She'd gone out after something she'd called freedom, but had to admit now had been escape.

She'd been wanting to escape for a long time. Just how long, she wasn't certain. It didn't matter. All of her twitched with the need to take flight, to get away and try to find something or someplace else, to fit some of the pieces of her self and her life back together.

Watching the slow progress on the horizon of what looked like a large tanker making its way across the lake, she remembered the Jamieson Land book. She'd left it on the table in the foyer at Jess's house. All at once, she wanted that book. Something in it would give her the clue she needed to the direction she should take. She wanted the book, but couldn't risk going back to the house for fear of encountering Jess. She'd have to go out and buy another copy. But no, wait. She held her hand over her mouth, trying to get it to come clear. *I'm just a forty-year-old fat lady.* That had been just about ten years ago. Flora was only fifty years old. And very much alive. *Come on down here. I'll show you what I'm trying to do.* A hand caressing her hair, loud appreciative laughter. *Some head you got on those shoulders.*

She ran to the telephone to call the book department at Eaton's College Street to get the name of the publisher of the Land book, then called New York information and obtained the publisher's number. She was about to call them, but had to stop and think what she was doing. If she was someone, say, from a Canadian publishing company . . . yes . . . interested in discussing the book with Miss Ogilvie . . . yes. Which company? Macmillan's came to mind. Why not?

She picked up the receiver and got the operator to place a

station-to-station call. With the publishing house switchboard on the line, she said, "Good afternoon, this is Matilda Greaves of Macmillan Company of Canada, calling from Toronto. I'd like to speak to someone who could put me in touch with one of your authors." Easy. She was asked to please hold, then someone else came on the line. This someone else told her that she couldn't give out Miss Ogilvie's number but would certainly give her the number of Miss Ogilvie's agent.

Tillie called the agent, gave the same story and got the number. She stood shaking, drenched with perspiration. She had no idea what she was doing. The woman probably wouldn't even remember her. What on earth could she say?

She had the operator place another station call. It rang. She waited. It rang again. Then a very deep voice, sounding neither especially male nor female, said, "Hello?" Nervously wetting her lips, Tillie asked, "Could I speak to Flora Ogilvie?"

"Who's calling?" the voice asked brusquely.

"Well, it's hard to explain," she began. Then, annoyed with herself, she gave her name.

"Who?"

"Tillie Greaves."

"Wait a minute," the voice said. There was the unmistakable sound of a cigarette being lit. Several moments passed. Then the voice said, "Jess's sister, Tillie?"

Excited, she said, "Yes, that's right! Is that you? Is that Flora?"

"Tillie Greaves," Flora repeated, dragging over an ashtray. "I'll be damned."

"Listen," Tillie said urgently. "Are you going to be there? I mean, are you going to be around for a while? I'd really like to see you, talk to you."

"Where're you calling from?"

"Toronto."

"*Toronto*? Is that where you two flew off to?"

"Yes. But listen, could I come see you?"

"Sure. Why not?"

"When?"

"You're calling me from Toronto and you're asking *me* when?" Flora laughed. "When you get here, call me. We'll get together."

Tillie looked at her watch. If she went straight to the airport, she'd be able to catch the late afternoon Trans Canada flight to New York. "Will it be all right if I come tonight?"

"Sure," Flora said, and laughed again. "In some kind of rush, huh?"

"Oh, *thank* you!"

Tillie's words and manner of speaking brought her back completely to Flora, so that all at once she had a very clear image of a pretty, fair-haired child lying beside her on the grass. "You know the address?" she asked.

"I've got it. I'll be there by nine at the latest."

She flew through the apartment to pack, taking only what she wanted right then. A second suitcase was filled with items she planned to leave in a locker at Malton. The first bag was mainly clothes, but down the sides she crammed her art supplies. Finally, with masking tape she sealed the edges of her portfolio, thinking she'd leave it in the locker too. The packing done, she called for a taxi, then called Press.

"I'm going away," she told him. "I don't know for how long. You can go ahead and get rid of this place, do whatever you want. I'm taking my things with me."

"Where are you going?"

"New York."

"For how long?"

"I don't know."

"Tillie, d'you have *any* idea what you're doing?"

"Of course I do!"

"All right," he said, played out.

"Good-bye, Press."

"Take care of yourself." He hung up.

He put down the receiver and went into the living room to draw his father away from the crowd who'd come back to the house after the funeral. "I need to get some fresh air," Press told him.

His father said, "I understand. Will you be back for dinner?"

"I probably won't be back at all, so don't wait for me."

Reluctant to further upset him, his father simply nodded and Press went to put on his hat and boots, then get his suitcase from the closet where he'd put it that morning. Outside, he paused for a moment, watching the snow fall in thick, fat flakes. There were already several inches on the ground and he stared at a set of tire marks going off down the street and

disappearing around the corner. He wished they weren't there—
they destroyed the still, white perfection of the snow. Snow-
flakes caught in his eyelashes and he blinked several times,
then brushed them away with the back of his hand before
slinging the bag into the trunk of the car and walking around
to slide in behind the wheel. At once he lost momentum. He
could go back to the apartment. Tillie wouldn't be there. But
he didn't want to have to see her things or Owen's, didn't want
to have to sit there and think about how the move into that
apartment had somehow precipitated all that followed.

Nelda.

She had come to the funeral. But then all the office staff
had. It might not mean anything.

"Come to me if you need somewhere to go."

He started the car.

She invited him in, saying, "I hoped you'd come."

She put his suitcase down inside the door, then took him
by the hand to the bedroom where she began undoing the
buttons of his topcoat. After a few seconds he looked down
and put his hands over hers. When he'd finished undressing,
she dropped her robe and drew him down on the bed, whispering, "It's all right, it's all right."

All the way to New York, Tillie tried to get things straight
in her head. First: Flora. She kept trying to think what she
wanted to ask her, what the woman could possibly have to say
that would make any difference. Second . . . She couldn't remember what came next. She kept moving back and forth
between what she might ask Flora, and sudden, too painful
visions of Owen running chunky-legged through her head,
across the rooms of her mind, running toward her, never arriving.

She took a taxi into Manhattan from the airport and sat
looking out the window at the slushy streets. Most of what she
saw seemed familiar, but larger, darker and more forbidding
than she remembered. She'd hoped to feel a positive surge of
recognition that might revive fond feelings for the city, but all
she felt was a kind of dull confirmation: This was the place,
all right. So what?

As they were about to turn into Thirty-ninth Street, she
remembered she'd said she'd call, and asked the driver to stop

outside a bar on the corner. Carrying her suitcase, she went inside to the pay phone at the rear.

"Will it be all right if I come up and see you now?" she asked.

"Don't tell me you're already here!"

"I'm calling from the place at the corner."

"Well, hell, come on then!"

She walked down the street, scanning the house numbers, stopping in front of a cream-colored, three-story house with black shutters and black iron grillwork shielding the basement and ground-floor windows, which were lit behind the curtains. She climbed the steps and rang the bell. The front door made a clicking sound and opened. Pushing through the door, she realized that what she'd assumed was an apartment building was a private home.

A slim, fairly tall, fiery-haired woman in high heels appeared at the far end of the hall and came toward her. Tillie was positive she'd made a mistake and was more convinced of it as the woman came closer. Not more than a hundred and five pounds at most. If this was Flora Ogilvie at fifty, Tillie must have known some other Flora Ogilvie ten years before. This woman had the slender body of someone perhaps twenty-five, and the startling good looks of a model. Perfect skin, large green eyes, and that fiery hair, short and curling about her face. Her mouth, Tillie thought, was . . . sensual, beautiful. She was entranced by the shape of Flora's mouth. When she stopped about three feet away, Tillie was able to see the fine lines around her eyes and a definite softness to her throat that gave away her age. She stood looking at Tillie with her head to one side, a hand on her hip, taking a hard drag on her cigarette.

You haven't changed, Flora thought, aware of a definite sexual energy being generated by the girl's long, slow, appraising look at her. Perhaps, Flora thought on, she shouldn't have invited her here. She felt she'd unwittingly made a serious tactical error in a game she hadn't known existed until that moment, and took her time before smiling and saying, "I'd've known you."

"I wouldn't have known *you*," Tillie said. Not sure if she should set down her bag, she kept hold of it.

Flora laughed loudly, then advanced to give her a surprisingly warm hug. "Come on, put that thing down. You hungry?

Had dinner yet?" She looked like a waif, Flora thought, a lost child in a railway station.

Was she hungry? When had she eaten? She couldn't remember. When she'd dressed that morning, she'd thought it odd that her black dress hung on her. Only belatedly did it occur to her that she'd lost a lot of weight very quickly.

"I haven't eaten," she said, setting down the bag while Flora closed and locked the front door, then showed her into the living room. It was a large, high-ceilinged room that extended from the front to the rear of the house, perhaps thirty-five feet long by twenty feet wide, with a fireplace in the middle of the far wall and two dark-printed sofas either side, laden with primary-colored pillows. A pair of deep, oversized armchairs and a big round table were set before the front windows, and large blowups hung on the walls. A fire was going in the grate. Tillie gazed at the fire a moment, thinking the room seemed more familiar than the woman. It was the sort of comfortable place the fat Flora would have had. Looking up from the fire, she saw a silver-framed photograph of Jamieson Land at the far end of the mantel. It was the same as the one on the dust cover.

"Sit down," Flora said, waving at the sofa opposite as she dropped down and picked up a glass that had been sitting on the large, square coffee table positioned between the two sofas. "How about something to drink?"

"No, thank you." Tillie sat down, wondering why she was here with this woman she didn't recognize. Her eyes were drawn again to Flora's mouth, as she thought that only the voice and the color of the woman's hair were even vaguely familiar. And if this was the fat Flora, what had happened to all those pounds and pounds of flesh?

"You haven't changed much," Flora observed. "Given five minutes in a roomful of people, I'd've been able to pick you out. You look a little under the weather." Why the hell did this kid scare her? she wondered, aware that the air had changed since Tillie had come in. It had become charged, filled with static.

"I'm all right," Tillie said, watching Flora take a long swallow of her drink.

"Bring me up to date," she said with a sudden smile. "How's Jess? What's she up to these days?"

"When did you get so thin?" Tillie asked bluntly.

Flora laughed again, her hair shimmering with reflected firelight. "You asked me the same thing in reverse, years ago. You really *haven't* changed."

"Oh, but I have though," Tillie said urgently. "I've changed so . . ."

"I've got some stuff cooking," she said, draining her glass. "Give me a couple of minutes and then we'll eat." She went to the doorway, then turned back. "Did you get yourself a hotel room?"

"I haven't had a chance. I just arrived and . . ."

"You'll stay here." She turned and walked out to the kitchen, instantly regretting the invitation. But this damned house was so big and she hated being alone at night when the silence seemed to yawn at her like the mouth of some dream monster.

Tillie sat, confused. She'd come expecting a big fat lady and, instead, there was this thin, pretty woman who sounded and acted the same, but was utterly different. In many ways she was as mystified by the changes in Flora as she'd been seeing the ones take place in Jess. Except that with this woman she didn't feel as undermined and desperate as she did with Jess. She felt . . . better. Yes. And why hadn't she remembered Flora's remarkable mouth?

She got up and found her way to the kitchen to see Flora lift something out of the oven and put the hot dish down on the stove top before turning to smile. "You really are hungry, huh?"

"I guess I am. Flora, what happened to Jamieson Land?"

"What d'you mean *what happened*?"

"After we left . . . and how he died. What did he think? You know, when we ran away."

Flora retrieved her cigarette from the ashtray and leaned against the counter, looking thoughtfully at Tillie. "He got over it," she said. "The whole thing was your idea, wasn't it?" She wondered if Tillie would admit it.

Tillie nodded.

"I figured that," she said. "It wasn't Jess's style. She didn't like hurting people. She still that way?"

Tillie nodded again.

Lowering her guard, Flora said, "The funny thing about loving is that once you've done it, you keep on wanting it. Jess was Jamie's first time. And he got into the habit. It *is* a kind of habit. Anyway, I was there so I took over his habit for him.

It wasn't exactly what he'd had in mind, but it worked out pretty well for both of us. I dropped thirty pounds the first year. By the end of three years, I was where I am now. Never gained back a pound, because I had what I wanted. That takes some doing, you know: knowing what you want. But I'd wanted him for years. It took Jess to make it happen for me and Jamie. He never loved me the way he did Jess, but he was good to me. And sexually he was very good to me. She did him more good than either of them knew, got him unlocked and moving. Right into me. You looked shocked. Are you shocked?"

"No."

"You're bothered about something. What?" She damned well *was* shocked, Flora thought. A prudish little girl who gave an old woman a long, smoldering once-over. What the hell *was* that?

"Nothing," Tillie said.

"Sweetheart, nobody comes flying hundreds of miles, after God knows how many—ten, eleven?—years to see somebody she once knew for a couple of months, without a pretty big reason. You want something," she said, grasping this truth a little fearfully, "something you think I can give you."

Again Tillie nodded and it made Flora even more afraid. Maybe she should have discouraged her from coming here. Then, looking at Tillie, she told herself she was being stupid. A forlorn kid, what the hell could she do to anyone?

"You got married, huh?" She tilted her head at Tillie's wedding ring, for a moment heartened by the sight of it.

Tillie looked down at her hand, then back at Flora. "Yes, I did."

"No good, huh?" The slight reassurance evaporated.

"Nothing's any good," Tillie said, her voice heavy. She was going to start crying. "Nothing."

Flora's eyes remained on her for another moment, then she stubbed out her cigarette saying, "Might as well talk while we eat. No point in letting the stuff go cold."

Tillie sat down at the table and Flora put a plateful of food in front of her. Tillie watched Flora's every move, unable to stop staring at her. She was so incredibly altered, so unexpectedly attractive. She kept trying to see the fat Flora surrounding the perimeters of this thin, whiskey-voiced woman, but they weren't there.

Flora started to eat, then aware of the waves of misery

emanating from Tillie, told herself she was being a jackass to feel scared of this unhappy little girl and reached to cover Tillie's hand with her own, saying, "Get it off your chest, why don't you?"

"Did you like it?" Tillie asked, her thoughts popping from her mouth like bread from a toaster. "Sex, I mean. Did you?"

Taken aback by the directness of the question and its personal implications, Flora wondered first if there was something about herself that had prompted Tillie to dispense with manners and go delving into such private matters, and second, if Tillie wasn't in fact, hoping to be asked to talk about her own sexuality. Deciding on the latter, Flora responded, "You don't, I take it?"

"I hate it!" Tillie spat out, confirming Flora's suspicion. "It was only for the baby, and wanting another one."

"You've got a baby, huh?"

That finished her. Owen scampered off down a hallway in her mind, and she broke.

Flora said, "Oh, boy, lady! You're in some big kind of trouble, aren't you?"

Tillie felt her head bobbing like a moron's, while her mouth opened and words came tumbling out—like piece after piece of fresh-made toast, she thought. "They meant to kidnap Jess's little boy, but I was jealous because Justin could put on his own snowsuit and Owen couldn't, so I bought Owen a suit just like his. But he couldn't figure out how to put it on and I *screamed* at him! God! I shouldn't have. How could I have screamed at him that way? He was so little, not even two years old and I stood there shouting at him because he couldn't do the things Justin could. They took my baby by mistake and they . . . they *killed* him! Sandy and Press's father paid all the money, but he was already dead. They told me he was blue. I couldn't go to see him, I knew I'd die if I did." She stopped suddenly and looked down. Flora still had hold of her hand. She looked up to see Flora's eyes were wide with concern.

"Go on," she said. "Finish."

Tillie gulped, then opened her mouth. *Toast*, she thought. *Bread-words.* "Jess was a whore. I knew it and I let her because I wanted new clothes and Branksome Hall and she gave me whatever I wanted, so I let her. Always wanting things, but I *knew*, oh, I knew how she got them, and how she hated it but she did it and wouldn't let them come near our house or even phone up when I was home. But I knew it all right. She was a fool, I thought, a fool, doing all that, but I wasn't going to stop her. Why should I? *I* didn't make her do any of it. She was grown up and if that was the way she wanted to do it, okay, she could do it. Why should I say anything? And Press, he really loved me. I didn't even *like* him very much after a while, but that was the way it was supposed to be, so we did it, I did it and got Owen. I *loved* him. My baby, and I loved him so much, and they *murdered* him, held a hand over his face until he stopped breathing. *Why?* I need someone to tell me why, someone to help me not to hate her, she's my sister. I don't know what to *do!*"

There was a long silence and then Flora pulled at her hand to get her to move, saying, "Come on! We're not going to get any eating done, so *come on!*"

Tillie allowed herself to be moved back to the living room where she sat beside Flora on the sofa. Then Flora did something that made Tillie flinch and feel frightened, made her stomach give an excited little jump. Flora put her hand on Tillie's face and then kissed her on the cheek, her cool hand stroking Tillie's face. She was so close that Tillie could see flecks of black in the green of her eyes and silver strands here and there in her hair; she was so close, Tillie thought she shouldn't have come here. She felt scared but not scared, as if this was what she'd wanted but hadn't expected to happen.

Flora still had hold of her hand and suddenly tugged on it, saying, "You came here for the impossible and I'm giving you what I can, so don't be such a damned coward, and accept what I'm giving."

"I'm *scared*," Tillie wailed.

"Everybody's scared," Flora said with unruffled, philosophical calm. "The whole damned *world's* scared. Don't you know that? We're all scared people will think we're peculiar, or out of step, or foolish; we're scared of the dark, scared of ourselves, scared of other people. And you're not so much scared of me as you are of what you might find out about yourself. Jesus Christ! You're a *mess!*" She smiled to soften it, refusing to let this girl make her feel self-conscious about performing spontaneously. A kiss on the cheek, a pat on the hand, and this kid was acting as though they were overt, sexual gestures. Jesus! "How the hell old're you now, anyway?" she asked.

"Twenty-two."

"I could be your mother, for chrissake!" Flora kept smiling.

"My mother died when I was little."

"That's right, I forgot. And sisters never are like mothers, not even the best of them."

"What does that mean?"

"Your sister's your *sister*, kid. Not your mother. And you can't spend your whole life blaming her for everything that goes wrong, because it wasn't her choice to have the responsibility. She took you on because she had to, and she stuck with it. So she wound up turning tricks to look after you and, because that offends you, you condemn the hell out of her. Well, let me tell you something, kiddo! Your sister was one hell of a girl. And you know why? Because she did what she had to and didn't bitch about it. And while I'm at it, let me tell you something else: I can practically guarantee you she probably didn't get any more sex than the average newlywed. Big goddamned deal, huh?"

"You *liked* her! Why?"

"There was nothing *not* to like. Yeah, well, maybe I felt like killing her a few times, watching her sit down to a meal and eat like a field hand while she stayed skinny as a stick and there I was like a beached whale living on goddamned carrot sticks and celery, hungry all the time. That bothered me. But that didn't have anything to do with Jess. It had to do with *me*. Now, wait a minute." She put her hand to her forehead, aligning her thoughts. "I remember. You asked how Jamie died. It's not very exciting or dramatic. Thirteen months ago, he went to sleep one night and didn't wake up in the morning. That's it. Now, listen to me. You're whacked out, your eyes aren't even in focus. I'm going to take you upstairs and put you to bed. I've got to go out in the morning, but I'll be back around noon. And when I get back, we're going to talk a whole lot."

"But . . ."

"No, you *listen*! You came here looking for a box of understanding you could wrap up with ribbons and take home with you, all neat and presentable, so you could go back all shipshape and ready for whatever. That doesn't get done in half an hour of hysterics over somebody's kitchen table while the food's getting cold on the plates." A voice in her head suddenly told her she shouldn't be doing this. But hell! she thought. She couldn't throw somebody in this kind of a mess out on the street. And the house was empty.... So what the hell!

"You don't even *know* me," Tillie protested.

"I scare you, huh?"

"Yes."

"Because you came looking for the fat lady and she doesn't live here anymore, right?"

"That's right."

"Wrong! The fat lady still lives here. She never left. I'm still a goddamned human sponge. I'm sorry as hell your baby died. Now come on and we'll get you to bed."

Obediently, Tillie stood up and went with her.

Mentally shaking her head, Flora thought, Maybe I'm a bit of a sucker, too. This kid's out for blood and it might wind up being mine.

◇ Twenty-Two ◇

Day and night for two solid weeks, Tillie talked and talked, until she felt purged. Flora listened, sometimes interrupting to argue or disagree, exhausted by Tillie's youth, self-absorption, and energy, but too sympathetic to stop her. It was obviously a cathartic exercise and, in a way, Flora was flattered that Tillie had chosen her as an audience.

Tillie talked, and occasionally Flora engaged her in an unpremeditated embrace that left Tillie flustered. She was unaccustomed to affectionate displays, and tried to put her discomfort down to that, and to Flora's being highly demonstrative. But there seemed more to it than simple affection, and the seed of a new feeling took root in Tillie.

Flora was also a very busy woman, out once or twice a day for three or four hours at a time, and occupied two full days a week upstairs in her top floor studio where Tillie was politely discouraged from going. Models and an odd assortment of people came in, went up, then left a few hours later. After these sessions, Flora came down carrying her high heels, a cigarette bobbing in the corner of her mouth, looking blinded and drained. She went directly to the kitchen to pour herself half a tumbler of neat whiskey, which she then sipped at steadily for the next half hour, while she sat collapsed on the sofa, her feet propped on the coffee table, smoking, and strictly unavailable for conversation. During that time she seemed entirely unaware of Tillie. Then she snapped back into herself and got up to make dinner.

There were constant telephone calls and an answering service Flora allowed to intercept her calls most of the time. "Can't be bothered answering," she said. "Just more people wanting something."

The remark made Tillie feel guilty, as intended. Flora was obviously not predisposed toward taking on people who wanted things. Did that mean, Tillie wondered, she was no longer predisposed toward Tillie, and perhaps even wanted her to leave? She hoped not, because she'd already decided she didn't want to. There was a lot about Flora and the house she liked.

"Why did you invite me to stay?" she asked finally, confronting Flora in the kitchen while she was making a very good-smelling spaghetti sauce.

"Good question," Flora answered, stirring the sauce. "Damned good question. I don't know why."

"You don't *know* why?"

"Oh, hell! I guess, for one thing, because it's flattering. Having somebody in need call you up and come flying hundreds of miles because there are questions maybe I'm the only one can answer. That's not bad for the ego, you know."

"But what you said . . . about the 'phone calls and people just wanting something."

Right effect, wrong result, Flora thought wearily, putting down the wooden spoon and reaching for her cigarette in the ashtray on the counter. "You've got more questions than Carter has pills, you know that? I'm not the *Encyclopaedia Britannica*, kid. I don't happen to have all the answers." She studied the earnest expression on Tillie's pretty face, wishing Tillie knew how to relax and stop pressing so hard. "Did you ever *love* anybody, kid?" she asked.

"I've *told* you . . ." She shut up at Flora's look of impatience, then said, "Not that way, no."

"And you hated sex. Did you ever consider the possibility that you hated it because you were with a man you didn't really want?"

"But I *did* want him."

"That's possession. I'm talking about *desire*, about *wanting*."

"No. I mean, I didn't think of that." The direction the conversation was headed was making her very jittery.

"Ever try anybody else?"

Feeling her face take fire, she answered, "No."

"Well, maybe you should. You might find out you like it after all. Was there *anything* about it you liked?"

"No."

"You're not telling the truth."

"I can't *talk* about it."

"You're *dying* to talk about it!"

"All right. The kissing, I suppose. Some of it."

"Did he ever try anything besides going straight at it?"

"I don't know what you mean."

Flora looked at her hard, shaken by the mix of innocence and determination she found in Tillie's eyes.

"What're you going to do when you go back, Tillie?"

"I don't know. I haven't thought about it."

"You'd better start thinking about it, because you've got to go back eventually." Sooner than that, Flora thought. This was starting to feel dangerous.

"No, I don't."

"Yes, you *do*. You can't just walk away and leave everything hanging in midair." Oh, but of course she could. And with a sinking sensation inside her, Flora thought, *I'm already trapped*. This girl wasn't going to leave until she was good and ready, and had taken everything she'd come for.

"Why do you talk so tough?" Tillie challenged. "You always do. But you're not. You're soft. Look at you! You're softer than I am . . . I . . ."

"You're getting what I *look like* mixed up with what I am," Flora said, trying to stay calm. "That's a big mistake to make about anyone."

"No," Tillie argued, gaining strength. "I'm not wrong. I was too little to make sense of it ten years ago, but I'm not now. Maybe I'm saying it wrong, but I'm right and I know it."

"Let's eat this stuff," Flora said, crushing out her cigarette. She slid her hands into red oven mitts and carried the spaghetti pot over to the sink. Feeling genuinely endangered now, she tried to tell herself she had nothing to fear from this kid. But her interior voice said, *Run for your life! You're in over your head but you're too stupid to know it.*

"Flora, I..." Tillie had to stop, not knowing what she wanted to say.

"Yeah, I know," Flora said enigmatically, responding to what Tillie was only beginning to discover, but what she herself had recognized the first night Tillie spent in the house.

That put an end to the conversation, because Tillie had been moving on instinct, feeling her way toward something that promised to be richly rewarding, but Flora was already there, saying she knew. What does she know? Tillie wondered as they ate in silence and then Flora announced she was going out for the evening.

"You didn't tell me..." Tillie pouted.

"I'll probably be pretty late," Flora said quickly, "so you go ahead to bed whenever." She dumped the dishes in the sink and hurried off to change, failing for the first time since Tillie's arrival to touch or embrace her in some fashion—afraid of touching Tillie at all. Tillie's remarks had put her in a state of chilled dread. No matter how she chided herself and tried to convince herself she was being ridiculous, she couldn't shake the fear. Not with Tillie saying, "You're soft," while her eyes moved up and down Flora's body just as boldly as any man's. She got out of the house as fast as she could, trying to think of some way to extricate herself and get Tillie out without unduly hurting the girl, before the girl unduly hurt her.

For the remainder of the evening Tillie wandered around the house, finally deciding to go up to the third floor and sneak a look at Flora's studio. She expected the door to be locked and when it wasn't, she felt almost wicked at going inside. But her curiosity overcame her and she turned on the light, then walked into the center of the large room to stand looking at the photographs on the walls. They were the sort of pictures Jamieson Land used to do, but stronger and more graphic than his. There was a layout she recognized from one of last year's issues of *Vogue*, featuring a stunningly beautiful blonde with black eyes in a series of peignoirs. It surprised Tillie that Flora had done it. Then in complete surprise, her heart giving a leap, she saw a blowup of the shot of Jess in the nightgown. It was clear from its curling edges and discoloration that it had been on the wall for years. Flora really had liked Jess; here was the proof of it.

Seeing Jess brought all the events of the too recent past crowding back on her. She left the studio, being careful to turn

off the light and shut the door before going downstairs. On
impulse, she walked past her own room toward Flora's. She'd
never been beyond the doorway, although Flora rarely closed
the door and even slept with it open, claiming she couldn't
sleep in a "sealed room." Now, curiosity propelled her forward
once again and she turned on the light to look at the white
curtains on the window and the drawn shades underneath, the
large, neatly made-up bed, with its polished mahogany headboard. The dressing-table top was covered with a variety of
cosmetic bottles, a box of Elizabeth Arden face powder, French
perfume, and a gold necklace dropped hurriedly so that it lay
partially caught in the bristles of a hairbrush; strands of red
hair coiled around the delicate links.

What was she doing in here? she wondered, extending her
hand to lift the bottle of perfume, removing the stopper and
bending her head to breathe in the fragrance. Flora. In a small
crystal bottle. She took another deep, satisfying breath, then
stoppered the bottle and put it back on the table. The fragrance
seemed to spread so that she carried it with her back to her
bedroom, where she undressed in a haze before going into the
bathroom, leaving the door open as she filled the tub.

She got in, reached for the soap, then stopped, looking at
herself to see that her bulges were gone. She examined her
breasts, belly, and thighs, then began soaping herself, deriving
an odd and decided pleasure from the act; eyes closed, she
contemplated the sensations. Picturing Flora, she felt a darting
flare of excitement. Soft her hair and her hand, her mouth,
Flora's exquisite mouth. The excitement turning to heat, she
thought, *I want someone to have me. I want you.*

She heard the front door slam and sat bolt upright in the
tub, gaping at the wide-open door. Flora was home and coming
up the stairs. She couldn't move, positive Flora was going to
come through the bathroom door, terrified of that, yet willing
it to happen. *See me, find me pretty, admire me, touch me.
Please keep going, go right past the door. Don't . . .*

"I'm back," Flora announced on her way down the hall.
"Taking a bath, huh?"

"Yes."

"Okay. Good night." Her high heels clicked away down the
corridor.

Feeling leaden and a little dizzy from the rapid loss of that
banking pleasure, she rinsed off and quickly got herself dried.

Emerging from the bathroom, she turned to see Flora standing in her dressing gown in front of the mirror, brushing her hair.

Out of the corner of her eye, Flora saw Tillie stop, and told herself to keep on with what she was doing and not react. Don't do this to me, she pleaded silently. I'm too alone here, too lonely and vulnerable to deal with you, and you've guessed that.

What am I doing? Tillie wondered, traveling down the hall toward Flora in the light from the dressing table. Flora turned and her eyes stayed on Tillie's until she was standing directly in front of her. Then Flora put down the hairbrush. She wet her lips, casting about for something to say. Tillie moved closer.

Finding it hard to speak at all, Flora said, "I'm old, Tillie." Her voice was deeper than ever, with a vibrato of fear shivering on the edges of her words. "I'm old as the hills, and it's all coming apart, going downhill a whole lot faster than I ever thought it would. Don't do this, huh?" She put out her hand to raise Tillie's chin, knowing then that nothing she said could stop her. The tenacious intensity etched into Tillie's features told her that. "I've done it all," she whispered, in a last attempt to save herself. "If you condemn Jess, you've got to condemn me, too. Because I did it too, but for free, for the feeling. And a lot of times, for love." Wrong, all the wrong things to say; she was simply stoking the girl's fire.

Her heart hammering, deaf to whatever Flora was saying, she tugged at Flora's robe and got it open. Small pretty breasts, a slim waist, a slightly rounded belly. She didn't look old, Tillie thought, and touched her hand to Flora's belly. The skin was very very soft; it seemed to want to absorb her hand. Wonderful.

"Do you want to touch me?" Tillie asked dreamily.

Flora was speechless. Tillie came closer still. Flora's perfume, that fragrance from the little crystal bottle was warm in her nostrils as her arms closed around the naked flesh so she could feel Flora's breasts pressing against her own. Oh, perfect. Dizzy, wanting, blind, she kissed Flora's shoulder, looking up in surprise at Flora's weak, agonized cry. She touched the woman's spine, and Flora shivered. She put her mouth to Flora's, eager for the ripe warmth of that exquisite mouth, but Flora leaned away, resisting, whispering, "Please stop this!"

Tillie simply stared at her, her hand independently gliding

over the hard curve of Flora's hip.

"Please stop!" Flora could feel the thick pressure building inside her and watched, desolated, as Tillie began to remove her nightgown. "*Please!*"

"I can't," Tillie said simply. The nightgown fell around her ankles as her hand closed greedily over Flora's breast.

Trembling, her insides gone berserk, Flora thought, Don't! It's been so long, my God. So long without touching, being touched, don't do this. Making me wet, another moment, it'll be too late. I won't be able to stop you. She felt crucified as Tillie's hands rose and fell over her, then one sure hand deftly insinuated itself between her thighs.

Perfect, perfect, Tillie thought, drugged with satisfaction. A woman, another woman, how can I . . . I was right. You are soft. I knew you would be, I knew. . . . She felt an overwhelming sense of victory as Flora suddenly surrendered. She kept one hand on Flora's breast while her other probed adeptly, astounding her with a knowledge she hadn't known she had. The slick heat of this other woman's body thrilled her and she brought her open mouth down on Flora's in sudden hunger. Flora shut her eyes at last, and responded, her lips parting.

After a moment or two, Tillie drew away slightly to look at Flora's now heavy-lidded eyes and wet lips; she felt the delicate weight of Flora's breast against her hand and was overcome by a sense of power, and extraordinary pleasure, too. She had never wanted anything more than she wanted all of this. She touched her fingers to the hardened bud of this woman's nipple and thought, *Yes!* Oh, yes, and threw herself headlong into what she believed was the safety of this encounter, and in giving up to it, was totally unprepared for Flora's all at once assuming control and saying as if uttering a curse, "You *want* this! All right, then! We'll damned well *do* this!"

Frightened now—it had gone out of her control so quickly—Tillie whispered, "Oh, no, please don't do that to me!" and tried to shift away. But Flora shook her head. "You want to play with matches, sweetheart, then you'd better learn how they burn." Flora knew that in this area she was superior, infinitely more experienced than Tillie. And sadly angry, but aroused, she went ahead.

Her eyes closed, her thighs taut with resistance, Tillie went quiet, too involved to actively fight back. After only a few seconds, her tension evaporated. Startled by the silken glide of Flora's hair across her thighs, and the shock of Flora's initial caress, she felt her hands curl into fists as her body instinctively lifted open. The sensations were so beyond anything she'd ever experienced or imagined, she could only gasp at the violent response that began beating like a drum in her groin. The heat of her own reactions was almost as astonishing as what Flora was doing to her. Flora's stroking hands and mouth and tongue thrust her into a state of pure need and complete submission, her stomach muscles going tight, tighter, the drum beating harder. The wild interior thrumming was going out of control; she couldn't contain it, couldn't prevent any of this from happening. A tiny portion of her awareness stood in reserved dismay, appalled, but the rest of her was lost to total dependence on Flora's mouth. She gave up and it took her: a feeling that forced her completely into herself while at the same time dragged her right out. She went gasping, quaking directly into the heart of it, and something that had been with her all her life left her: she could never again condemn any woman for acts performed out of a need she now fully understood. It was this. *This*.

Afterward, she turned upon Flora in renewed power and comprehension, in a frenzy of pleasure, overwhelming the woman with her avidity. She found Flora the ideal person upon whom to vent all her years of frustrations, and exhausted her with newly acquired expertise. At last, Flora pushed herself away, looking bruised and bewildered, and got up to put on her robe, her movements slow and almost hesitant. Retrieving Tillie's nightgown from the floor, she walked over to the bed, summoning the last of her strength and self-respect to say, "Go on to bed. Better still, get on a plane tomorrow and go home, get going on your life."

Childishly, Tillie shook her head.

"One night with me doesn't turn you into a lesbian," Flora said. "It doesn't make me one either. You needed to do this to get where you wanted to be. Okay, you're there. Now you can go home."

Tillie climbed off the bed holding her nightgown, still shaking her head—no longer childlike—saying, "But Flora, you don't understand." With eyes like ripe cornflowers at midday, she said, "I love you," and put her arms around Flora to hold her with such strength and youthful conviction that Flora could only sigh and look longingly at her cigarettes on the dressing table, wanting nothing more than to be left alone so she could take a bath, smoke a cigarette, then go to sleep and forget she'd ever opened the door to this girl.

"You don't believe me," Tillie persisted, stroking Flora's throat, sliding her hand down over her breast. "I love you, I love you."

Don't use love on me, Flora thought, with despair, responding when she thought she hadn't any responses left. It was too strong a weapon, too big; she couldn't fight it. Trembling with fatigue, satiation, and returning desire, she asked hoarsely, "D'you have any idea what you're doing?" Feeling lost, she asked, "Any idea at all?"

"I don't care. It doesn't matter. I love you. You smell so good, feel so good and what you did, that was so wonderful. I want to do it for you just once more, just once more."

FIVE

Toronto

1953

◊ Twenty-Three ◊

Jess knew the moment Sanford walked into the room that evening that something was terribly wrong. She'd never seen him display such controlled anger, and even fear. Her knowing was at once compounded by the absentminded kiss he gave her before pouring himself a full glass of rye, then tossing half of it down in one swallow.

"What's wrong?" she asked, as he dropped down on the sofa loosening his tie, then his collar.

"Edward's gone."

"Gone?"

"He'd been planning it for years, apparently. The house is empty, the cars are gone, and so are Edward, June, and the kids."

"Planning what?"

"I've got an audit coming up in two weeks and he knew it. What I can't understand is why. It wasn't as if he'd been badly treated. But once I found it, all I had to do was go back through the books and there it was, regular as clockwork, dating back to just before you and I got married."

"Sanford," she said quietly, "please explain this to me."

What she saw when he turned frightened her. Until that

moment she'd given little consideration to his twenty-seven years' seniority. But now she had the sudden distressing insight that in the not too distant future she would find herself alone, and had to force herself to listen closely to every word he spoke.

"It's the sort of thing that happens to other people," he said, his eyes leaving her to fix on an indefinite point in space. "You never think it's going to happen to you." He looked down at his glass, then said, "He's taken June and the four kids, and almost a quarter of a million dollars from the payroll account."

"Oh, my God! What does that *mean*?"

"Unless I can replace it, number one, I won't be able to meet the next payroll. Number two, the audit's bound to show up the shortage, and number three,"—he took another long swallow of his drink—"number three, I'll be sitting on the fine edge of bankruptcy. Because even throwing in all my personal assets, I'll still be shy almost a hundred thousand and I can't possibly raise that kind of money with any hope of paying it off on a short-term basis."

"What about your private accounts?"

"I can put together about a hundred and fifty thousand. Everything else is either tied up for expansion, or in trust funds for you and the boys." He shook his head disbelievingly. "Month after month, for years," he said. "He wasn't as stupid as I thought. And he covered himself beautifully. We weren't close, but I never dreamed he hated me."

"What will you do?" she asked, her throat dry. "And what happened to all . . . ?"

"I've been turning most of my income back to the company for years, Jess, in order to keep expanding; taking just enough to maintain our way of life. The rest went to set up Todd's trust five-odd years ago. The hundred and fifty I'm talking about is all the cash I've got. I don't honestly know what I'll do. If I start going after second mortgages on the properties, I'll just be taking on additional debts I'll have a hard time covering. But it looks as if that's my only option. That, and mortgages on the properties I own outright. There's no other conceivable way I can put that kind of money together in time. I've been racking my brains all afternoon, trying to find some area of cash I might have missed."

"And what about Edward?" Another Cotton, she thought.

Perhaps the man never dies, or they're an entirely separate race. When one dies, another springs up.

"I don't know," he sighed. "Nothing, I guess. What's the point of doing anything? We'll probably never find him. Unless I get the R.C.M.P.'s after him. Which would be another big, beautiful scandal the papers would have a field day with. He'd make bloody sure the money was squirreled away where I couldn't get my hands on it anyway. I just don't know."

She moved closer to him and, enervated, he put his arm around her shoulders.

"I feel as if I'm getting too damned old for all this, Jess. Maybe I should just mortgage everything, cover myself, then sell out. I'd realize enough to retire on with plenty left to take care of you and the boys."

"You can't do that!" she argued, more alarmed by his attitude than anything else. "You *know* you can't! The business means everything to you. You'd be lost without it. What would you do?"

He gave her a thin smile. "Play a lot of golf, maybe fool around with city politics, spend more time with you and the boys."

"You'd hate that!"

He sat away from her and reached for his glass. "You're right. I'd be at 999 Queen, or in Whitby inside a month."

He quickly finished the drink, then got up to make another while she tried to think. She'd have to save her news; this would be the worst possible time to tell him. There had to be something she could do to help, she thought, looking at her rings. She had René's stock certificates. They had to be worth at least the twenty thousand she'd initially given him. And there was the few thousand she'd been giving to Press each year, all this time. That was another twenty-five or thirty thousand. It was almost nothing, she thought glumly, brought down hard. Why didn't she know more about these things? She should have taken more of an interest, but he'd never really involved her, hadn't ever discussed any but the most minor of his business affairs with her, and she'd felt it would have been intrusive of her to question him. She'd always relied on his being in control.

"Have you thought about this house?" she asked. "We could mortgage it. It has to be worth more than we paid, and I could easily make the mortgage payments out of the trust income. If only we could get the money out of trust. That would take care of most of what you need."

"Absolutely, no!" he said hotly, returning to sit beside her with another full glass of rye, setting it down untasted on the coffee table as he turned a reddened face to her. "Those trusts are for you and the boys after I'm gone. Under no circumstances are they to be touched!"

Cowed by his adamance, she said, "What about mortgaging the house then? I'm sure we could get fifty or sixty thousand."

"I don't like the idea of invading trusts and putting liens against the roof over our heads. Jesus, Jess! Don't you hear what I'm *saying*?"

"I'm trying to help," she said softly. "A mortgage doesn't mean anything, Sandy. Everyone has them."

"I know that. I know." The flush of color had gone, leaving him pale. "I'd forgotten about the house. Let me think about it. It might not be such a bad idea," he conceded. "Let *me* worry about this. I shouldn't even have told you."

"Of course you should! What happens to you is important to me. Maybe I don't know very much about business, but I'm not stupid and I might be able to help. I want to! Don't close me out! You've never done it before." She took hold of his hand, in a lower voice saying, "I'd sell everything if it would help."

"I know you would, Jess. I'm sorry for barking at you that way. I'm not thinking clearly." He patted her on the knee. "I'm going to take a quick shower. Where are the boys?"

"Out with Robert, picking up their skates."

"You don't think Todd's a little young for hockey?"

"He doesn't think so. You know how he is. He has to do whatever Justin does, and if Justin's going to play hockey, he has to play, too."

"He'll probably be good," he said, his tone a sober match to hers, as if they were still discussing the other, more important issue. "When he goes after something, Todd's out for it all. I'd hate to get in his way when he's twenty-five."

"He's like you. He likes to build things and see them grow."

"I still don't believe it," he said. "Month after month, for years, stealing . . . my own damned brother." He got up, saying, "I'll be half an hour," and was touching his cheeks and chin as he went out.

He'd shave, she knew. He wouldn't appear for dinner, or get into bed with her with stubble on his face. Just as she wouldn't make love with him until she'd bathed. We're people of such habits, she thought. I know why I bathe, why Sandy shaves. I was a whore, and he was a poor boy who saw his father go down with slumped shoulders and three days' growth of beard on his face.

Habits, the routines of a family. All of it felt threatened now by what Edward had done. She wanted to find the man and kill him. She picked up Sanford's glass and poured the rye back into the decanter. Then, without thinking, she used the same glass to hold a little dry vermouth over ice. She sat with her drink, debating when to call Press. Now, she decided, too agitated and upset to wait until morning. She could still hear Sanford's voice, exclaiming, "*Jesus, Jess!*" in exasperation and anger—with her.

She went to the den, spoke to Nelda briefly, and asked about the children, then Press came on and they made an appointment to meet in the morning at his office. That done, she returned to the living room where she sat sipping the vermouth. It occurred to her, not for the first time, that Press had remained more involved with her and Sandy than Tillie had. And it was good to see him so happy. Nelda was affectionate and honest, sensible with their two little girls. A quietly self-possessed woman, she had a simplicity and directness that made it impossible not to like her.

Her thoughts came back to Edward and the money and, again, she deplored her failure to involve herself more in the business. But how could she have done that? She hadn't expected it and she hadn't volunteered, and that struck her now as wrong. All these years when she'd tended to the children and supervised the running of the house and the planning of meals, she could have been learning about things that would have been valuable now. But it wasn't too late, and she'd do what she could. She couldn't believe Sandy actually wanted her to just put this out of her mind and not give it a second thought.

"You've got about forty-five thousand in holdings," Press told her. "That's a rough figure, clear, after commissions and what-have-you." He smiled at her surprise. "I've been taking good care of your money, Jess. I promised I would."

"I had no idea it would be quite this much," she said, silently swearing she'd never again allow herself to drift along assuming someone else was taking care of everything. It seemed all at once ridiculous that she should contribute so little, while her husband shouldered all the real burdens. Not that looking after two small boys was easy. But she was capable of more. "It's quite a bit," she said, "but not enough. I need more."

He raised his eyebrows, but didn't ask why, and she was grateful. "Well," he said consideringly, "there's always your holdings in Thibeault Trucking. They're worth upwards of two hundred thousand."

"Are you *serious*? How can they possibly be worth that much?"

"It's fairly simple. About four years ago, the company went public and made a stock offering. Accordingly, I converted your holdings. Since then, the stocks have doubled twice and split once."

"Sell it! I need the money."

"Hold on a minute, Jess! Before you start talking about selling, let me explain a thing or two. The current market value of this stock is contingent upon a hell of a lot of factors, none of which are relevant to this conversation. What *is* relevant is that if you dump a big load of stock back on the market, you're going to start a run and hurt this company badly. You've got a large block of shares and therefore a responsibility not to do something as potentially dangerous to the company as simply dumping your stock, taking your profit and then sitting back while the remaining stock plummets. Which, I assure you, is exactly what'll happen. Other stockholders see a big block being dumped, they decide something's gone wrong and they want out fast before they lose too many percentage points and wind up out of pocket."

"What'll I do then?"

"You've got other options. We could do it this way: Cash in your other stocks, and for the rest, go to the bank with your Thibeault holdings as collateral and take a note on however much more you need. They won't refuse you the money with this kind of collateral. How much do you need?"

"A hundred thousand. But Press, if I do what you're suggesting, I'll have to repay the bank and I don't know when or how I'll be able to."

"I see. Do you want to play it big?"

"I don't understand."

"Go to the bank tomorrow and borrow against the full amount of your collateral, the maximum. Leave all your holdings as they are. Turn back fifty thousand of what you borrow to me and let me combine it with your present holdings. It'll give me a good amount to work with and I'll run it back up for you. And then some."

"What if you can't?"

"Trust me. When we're talking this kind of money, I can turn it around and double it in almost no time flat."

"You're *sure*?"

"I'm a good broker, a scrupulous and damned careful one. I know the board and what's coming up. Turn back that amount to me by the end of this week, and in six months, you'll have what you need to repay the note and some extra. If I can't do what I'm saying, I'll cover your bank note out of my personal holdings from Dad's estate."

"I couldn't let you do that. It's a generous offer . . . I don't know, Press. It all seems so risky."

"If you need big money in the hurry you obviously do, this is the only way to get it and cover yourself at the same time."

"But if we lose what you invest . . ." She'd be the one to bankrupt Sandy, not Edward. "All right," she agreed. "Tell me what I have to do."

Everything happened almost too quickly to make complete sense. Two days after her visit to Press, she was leaving the Toronto Dominion Bank with a cashier's check made out to Sanford for a hundred thousand dollars, and another for fifty thousand made out to Bloomfield and Ames, Press's company. Feeling almost frenzied, she dropped the check off at Press's office, then went home to wait for Sanford, nervous about his reaction, but determined to be involved.

She fingered her rings, turning them around and around. It felt as if she'd done something dangerous that could have unpredictable repercussions. But never mind that, she told herself. All that was important was Sanford's being able to replace the money. In six months, she'd worry about the bank note. In six months . . .

They went through the nightly ritual of the boys' baths and bedtime stories, each preoccupied. She was trying to think of the best way to give Sandy the money. He was regretting having told her, yet not nearly so much as he might have. Oddly enough, her grasp of the problem and her sympathy took some of the pressure off him. And he hadn't considered the house; he'd completely overlooked it in his frantic figuring.

She noticed that although he made an effort to romp with the boys, he didn't seem quite himself, not even when he announced, "That's it! Time, gentlemen!"

Giggling, the boys climbed into their beds. She watched Sandy bend over each boy in turn, again experiencing a stab of fear. Gazing at his broad back, and listening to his exchanges with the boys, she told herself she was being morbid. So he'd snapped at her. It would have been unnatural if he hadn't displayed some reaction to what had happened.

"Jess? Come on. We're all waiting for you."

She smiled, but he didn't return it as she'd expected. His expression was odd, as if she weren't entirely familiar to him and he wasn't sure he recognized her. The look on his face in those few seconds bothered her more than anything else so far. She wished she had the time to think slowly and carefully about all this. Instead, the boys were waiting and she sat down on Todd's bed, entranced as always at how different her children looked scrubbed and ready for sleep. Their faces were pure and round, perfect and vulnerable. The sight of them created a pressure against her lungs, and she kissed each boy lingeringly, then turned on the night-light and closed the door.

"You looked upset in there," he said as they were going down the stairs. "You're not still worrying about that Edward business, I hope."

"I thought *you* looked upset," she said.

"Well, naturally, I am."

"You looked at me as if you'd never seen me before."

He smiled and put his arm around her waist. "I'm always wondering if I've ever really seen you. Do you ever feel that way? I look at Justin and Todd and see something about them I've never noticed before, like the shape of Justin's nose, or Todd's chin. You remember last month when I took Justin downtown with me? We were going down in the elevator and I looked over at him—he was watching the floor indicator— and I was fascinated by his face."

She knew what he meant, but didn't believe it was what he'd been thinking when he'd looked at her upstairs. "I haven't had a letter from Tillie in months," she said, deciding not to pursue the other matter.

"Is that what's upsetting you?"

"No."

"Did she say anything in her last letter about taking a trip? Maybe she's gone off for a holiday. Drink?"

"No, thank you. I don't think she's off on a holiday. She was teaching art nights, and still living with the mysterious 'X.' One of these days, I'm going to go down there to that place on Thirty-ninth Street and find out who this 'X' is. The whole thing sounds funny."

"She's probably involved with some married man and doesn't want anyone to know."

"This doesn't sound like a married man. And anyway, they live together."

"Then his wife won't give him a divorce."

He was willing, she could see, to stay well away from the Edward issue, and it bothered her. "Have you decided about the mortgage?" she asked.

"I'm taking care of things," he said evasively. "I'll make sure you and the boys are provided for if anything should happen to me."

"*Nothing's* going to happen to you!" she exploded. "Will you please stop trying to keep me out of this!"

"Old men like me are dropping off on golf courses and in steam rooms every day of the week," he said lightly.

"That is *not* funny, and I am *not* going to let you put me off!"

Seriously, he said, "Just be aware of the probabilities, Jess, because no one lives forever. Maybe at thirty-five, you don't think so, but it's a fact and you've got to be prepared. I am."

"Will you *stop* that! I want to know what you're planning to do about the money."

"I've *told* you I'm taking care of it."

"What involves you involves me," she said firmly, "and you don't seem to want me in it for some reason."

"Look, I'm doing my job, looking after you and the boys. As long as I am, there's no reason for you to get worked up about how I'm doing it."

"Christ! What's the *matter* with you? You're treating me like...I don't know what. Why can't we talk about this?"

"Why won't you trust me to set things right?"

"I *trust* you! We're not talking about that. We're talking about my wanting to be part of everything, not just what happens inside this house."

"What's the matter with *you*?" he demanded. "Since when do you question my actions?"

"Is that how you see it? I'm questioning your actions? My God, Sandy! This isn't you. You don't talk this way."

"Since when do you give me the third degree on business matters?"

"Since you walked through that door last night and told me about Edward."

"Well that was my mistake," he said, furious.

"Mine," she said, equally furious, "is obviously caring about your mistakes!"

There was a second or two of silence during which they stood glaring at each other. Then he started to say something, but she held up her hand. "We're just going to keep saying the same things," she said. "I'm going up to take a bath."

She was getting undressed when he came in and sat down on the end of the bed, his drink poised on his knee.

"I'm sorry," he said quietly. "I don't know what the hell's come over me."

She opened her handbag, took out the envelope, and walked over to him. Drawing a deep breath, she held out the envelope.

"What's this?" he asked.

"Give me your glass while you open it."

He stared at her for a moment, then tore open the flap and sat staring at the check.

"Where did you get this, Jess?" he asked finally.

"I'm not sure I want to tell you. It's mine, and I want you to have it. I love you enough to want to help. So let me."

"God damn it!" he exclaimed, getting to his feet. "I'm not letting some woman save my ass!"

"*Some woman*? I'm your *wife*, not *some woman*! Stop marching around and talk to me. You're making me feel as if I've done something criminal."

"You don't *do* things without consulting me first!" he yelled.

"Sandy," she said quietly, "do you hear what you're saying? Do you hear how you're talking to me? Why are you doing this?"

"Half of me wants to tear this up and say I'll be damned if I'll let my wife bail me out!"

"What about the other half?"

"The other half," he said, his tone and volume diminishing, "can't get over how much you've changed."

"And that's why you're shouting at me?"

"I don't know why the hell I'm shouting. I *feel* like shouting, all right?"

"I see," she lied. "In that case, I'll take my bath. Because *I* don't feel like having you shout at me."

While she was pinning up her hair, he came to the doorway to stand watching. Her belly had softened, rounded out from the two pregnancies, and her breasts were beginning to sag slightly. But she was still beautiful, he thought, and reached out to take hold of her arm, pulling her over to him.

Was it punishment? she wondered. Or was it an apology? It seemed a little of both. He kissed her hard, then bent her forward, fastened his hands to her thighs and made quick, frantic love to her. She wasn't ready and didn't think she'd react but was surprised by the force and immediacy of her response. She heard him make a sound and realized he was going to finish, so quickly, when the motions caught her and she clutched the rim of the counter, her eyes tightly closed, overwhelmed.

After, he stroked her breasts, catching his breath.

Returning to herself, she said, "Will you check on the boys while I finish in here?"

He continued caressing her for another moment or two, then said, "I'll shower in the guest room," and went off.

While he was gone, she bathed, then got into her nightgown.

He came in and lay down beside her, his arms folded under his head.

"Are the boys all right?" she asked.

"They're fine."

"You checked the windows?"

"Everything's locked, Jess."

"Good. Thank you. Are we going to be able to talk?"

"I took a mortgage on the house," he said, "then saw my insurance man and made arrangements to have a term rider added, to cover the mortgage." His eyes on the ceiling, he said, "Maybe I've been wrong not including you. But that's

the way I've always understood it was done. Don't blame me
for that."

"I don't. I understand."

"I'm not sure *I* really do, but you've made your point. You
deserve to be involved if that's what you want. Let's just say
I'm going to have to shift a lot of my thinking."

"So am I. It doesn't feel right to just go along letting everything ride on your shoulders."

"I'd like to know where you got it, though, Jess."

She explained about René and the stock, and about Press
and the investments, and he listened to all of it, then said,
"At my age, a man's pretty well set in his ways. It isn't easy
to shift gears and start a new program."

"Nothing's easy," she agreed. "Nothing's *ever* been easy.
I don't want to push my way in where I don't belong, Sandy.
But we should be able to share the responsibilities."

"Come here." She moved closer to him. "Thank you," he
whispered against her hair, his hand seeking her breast.

"I'm pregnant again. The timing feels all wrong."

He didn't say anything for several seconds and again she
thought he looked old. His hair had turned a silvery white, and
there were deep creases around his eyes and mouth.

"The timing's fine," he said at last. Then he kissed her.
"I shouldn't have come at you that way," he said, his hand
traveling over her belly.

"It doesn't matter," she said truthfully, lifting her nightgown
as his hand slid down.

◇ Twenty-Four ◇

"It's been almost six months since I've heard from Tillie, and I'm worried," Jess said. "I'd like to go to New York."

"What do you hope to accomplish by that?" he asked sharply.

"I want to satisfy myself that she's all right."

"You're going to fly all that way just to see that your twenty-eight-year-old sister is looking after herself properly? Think about that for a minute, Jess."

"She's my sister. I can't help worrying about her any more than I can about you and the boys. I'm sorry if it seems silly to you, but I want to go. I thought I'd leave Thursday morning and come home Saturday, in time for dinner that evening at the Bockens." Why were they arguing? she wondered. They'd done more of it in the last six months than they had in their entire marriage. He seemed so easily angered these days, so . . .

"I'm not going to stop you," he said in a softer tone of voice. "I'm only trying to make you see that your responsibility to Tillie ended a long time ago. Sooner or later, we all have to let everyone go. That's a fact of life."

"I know all about the facts of life. What if she's ill?"

"She's always been healthy as a horse. I think the truth is you're curious about this 'X.'"

"Of course, I am. Aren't you?"

He smiled and kissed her. It confused her. Lately, he'd become completely unpredictable and capable, from one moment to the next, of about-faces that kept her constantly on edge. "Go on," he said. "Do some shopping while you're there. You might as well take advantage of being there."

Taking her time to find the appropriate words, she said, "The last few months have felt like some kind of game where the rules are never posted. I can never be sure you won't change the rules and I'll fail at something important because you didn't bother to tell me."

He looked hurt. "You think I'm playing some kind of *game*?"

"I don't know," she said nervously, wishing she'd kept silent. "Are you . . . Have you stopped loving me?"

He stared at her. "Is that how you feel?" he asked.

"When we argue this way . . . I shouldn't have started this."

"It's damned important! Don't start this and run, Jess! Let's talk about it. As you've pointed out so often to me, we're supposed to be able to talk to each other about the things that bother us. How could you just sit on your feelings this way for so long?"

"Maybe I'm tired of 'sitting' on my feelings."

He clapped his hands together loudly. She jumped, not sure what he meant by the gesture.

"Well, congratulations!" he exclaimed. "I never thought I'd see the day."

"What does that mean?" she asked. The baby chose that moment to start kicking, and automatically she put her hand against the side of her belly.

"It means: good for you. I love you the way you are. I *love* you. How could you doubt that?"

She wanted to hit him, to cry, to hold him. He looked so *tired*, and his color seemed to be visibly, alarmingly fading as he let his head fall back against the sofa. The baby was kicking wildly inside her as if the flaring of its parents' tempers had triggered it into a tantrum of its own. She leaned forward into his arms, closing her eyes. "I love you and we've argued so much lately. Please let's stop it now." The baby's kicking stopped and it settled heavily.

"I know I've been touchy, and I'm sorry." He reached to stroke her hair, feeling so weary it was an effort simply to move his hand.

"I understand," she lied, anxious to put the exchange behind them.

"I really am sorry, Jess. You go on down to New York on Thursday and find out about Tillie. I didn't intend us to argue about it."

"This will be the first time I've gone away without you."

"You managed for years before I ever came along."

"That doesn't mean I liked it. I used to dream about someone taking care of me. But I told myself there was no chance. Then you came along and I thought, 'All right, I'll let myself be taken care of.' And I did it all these years. But lately I've wanted to be responsible for myself. That business with Edward made me see it's wrong to expect anyone else to do it all for me."

He studied her for a moment, silently approving of her blue, light wool dress and the neat, thick coil of her hair.

"Don't you know how appealing that is?" he asked. "Now, don't get angry with me for saying this. It's the truth and I really have to say it. Bess was like your sister Tillie. In a lot of ways, they were very alike. Dependent, in constant need of attention and care. I've come to see I don't have the time or the energy or the disposition to look after some dishrag of a woman who can't do a damned thing for herself. Go to New York. Stay until Saturday. And then come home."

There was a long silence. She held his hand, trying to ignore the visible effects of time on his face and manner, but unable. Despite the fine cut of his suit, he appeared somehow less well-turned-out than usual. And the whiteness of his shirt pointed up his pallor.

Externally, superficially, nothing had changed. He was dressed as immaculately as ever, right down to the silk paisley handkerchief tucked into his breast pocket, and the gold cuff-links she'd given him for Christmas the year before. But it was all slightly off. For a few seconds, she considered discussing it, then abandoned the idea. They'd argue about it, as they seemed to do about everything lately.

She got out of the taxi in front of the house at 56 East Thirty-ninth Street and stood looking at the cream-colored building with its scrolled grillwork on the windows of the lower stories, apprehensive about what she might discover inside. It was cool for a May afternoon and, shivering in her light dress, she thought she should have worn her coat after all. She went up the front steps to ring the bell and was startled when a deep, disembodied voice asked, "Who is it?"

She looked around for somewhere to speak but couldn't see any sort of intercom.

"Just go ahead and talk," the voice said. "I can hear you just fine."

"I'm looking for Tillie. Tillie Ames, or Greaves."

There was a slight pause, then the voice asked, "Who're you?"

"An old friend of hers. Do I have the right address? I think I do."

"Come on in," the voice said. And the front door clicked ajar.

Jess pushed open the door and hesitantly stepped inside. The sound of footsteps on carpet came from the room to the right, and a slim, red-headed woman in a very good-looking, grass-green dress appeared in the doorway. For a few seconds, Jess could do no more than stare at her admiringly, noticing the fine, porcelain quality of her skin and the tired-looking darker areas around her eyes. *I know you*, she thought, her heart beating more quickly. There was something very familiar about the wide, green eyes and the mobility of the mouth, the glossy look of the red hair.

"Jess," the woman said and smiled beautifully. "I'll be damned!"

"Flora?" Her voice emerged high with sudden emotion.

"I'll be damned!" Flora said again, and came into the foyer to embrace her.

"Flora. My God, Flora." She began to cry and held the woman close to her, overcome. "Flora!" She laughed, drawing away to look at her, thinking she'd been right: Flora had always been beautiful. Then as her thinking started to shift gears doubtfully, Flora said, "Come in! Come in! I'll make some coffee."

Jess put her hand on her arm to stop her, afraid to hear the answer. "You're X?"

"Afraid so. Come on, sweetheart, let's sit down and we'll talk. You want some coffee?"

"I'd love some. Let me come with you. I'm just stunned; so happy to see you."

"Stunned that I'm the mystery person, huh?"

"That. And the way you look."

"Oh, sweetheart," Flora laughed. "I look like hell! I'm still nursing last night's hangover."

"No, no. Do you remember how angry I used to get with you when you ran yourself down? Do you remember? You were *beautiful*, Flora. I used to sit and stare at you, trying to imagine how you'd be without all that . . ."

"Fat," Flora said it for her. "F.A.T."

"Without it," Jess went on. "And I knew you'd look exactly the way you do. I'm *so* happy to see you. I just can't tell you."

"You always were a nice kid," she said, getting a can of coffee from the cupboard. She filled the percolator with water, tossed in some coffee, jammed the lid on and sat it down on the burner. Then she lit a cigarette and leaned against the counter.

"Tillie's gone, sweetheart," she said.

"Gone?"

"Gone," she confirmed. "Took off almost a year ago with some guy from Texas or Montana or wherever."

"To Texas?"

"Nope. I think he had a boat somewhere on the Gulf of Mexico. Florida, I think it was."

"I don't understand," Jess said. "Her letters . . . she made it sound . . ."

"That's right."

"You and Tillie?"

"Hey!" she said suddenly. "What'm I doing, keeping you standing here? Sit down, sweetheart." She pulled a chair out from the table and urged Jess down into it. "When's the baby coming, huh?"

"The beginning of September. Flora, I'm sorry to be so stupid, but I simply don't understand any of this. You weren't . . . I mean, you were in love with Jamieson."

"Stayed with him right to the end," she said. "We got along just fine together."

"But how did . . . you and Tillie . . . ?" she asked, noticing that the large kitchen looked in need of a good cleaning, repainting. What little she'd so far seen of the house struck her as dusty and somehow too dark to contain a presence as bright as this woman's. The apparent disarray told of someone either too busy or too demoralized to make any effort at restoring order.

"I was kind of at loose ends at that point," Flora explained, tapping her cigarette against the ashtray. "This damned mausoleum of a house, and I'd just spent months on that book of Jamie's work. To make it short, the timing was right and it happened."

"But . . . you're not . . . And Tillie's gone off with a man. This is all so confusing."

"She's a lovely kid, your sister. No sarcasm. She's lovely, got a lot of nice qualities. She's sensitive, and pretty thoughtful. She's flattering—which doesn't hurt anybody's ego—and she's talented. But Tillie's got a big problem, Jess. She can't seem to make it on her own. She has to have somebody she thinks she's in control of who's really in control of her. You follow that?"

"No. I'm sorry. I don't."

"Okay, I'll be blunt. A couple of years from now, Tillie's going to see someone—male or female, it doesn't matter which—she thinks is more worthy of her love, is more interesting and more of a challenge, might offer her more of what she wants than this guy from Texas or wherever. So, she'll leave him and take off with the new someone. And then, a couple or three years after that, there'll be another someone. And then another. Until one day, she's going to find herself out of someones. Because her looks'll be gone and maybe she'll be running to fat, 'cause she loves her food, Tillie does. And then the chances are pretty damned good that if you're still around, still willing to look after her, little sister Tillie—at age fifty, or so—is going to hotfoot it home so you can look after her. Now, you got it?"

"Sandy was right," Jess said quietly.

"Your husband?"

"Sanford, that's right. He said fairly much what you're saying, but I had to come here to find it out for myself. I expected a man. How did she . . . I mean, were you in touch all those years? How did she come to be here?"

"She found the book on Jamie I'd put together, called my agent and got my address, and came flying right on down."

"It's boiling over," Jess said. Flora turned down the flame under the percolator. "Did she tell you she was leaving?" she asked as Flora returned to the table with two cups of coffee.

"Oh, sure," she smiled. "Came rushing in one afternoon all lit up like a Christmas tree to say she was leaving right away. An hour later, she was gone, bag and baggage. She never did want anyone to know about us, you know. Every time she wrote to you, I'd tell her to send you my love. She just gave me one of those looks. That was the too-bad part of it, I always thought. I'd've enjoyed seeing you, being in touch, you know?"

Jess reached for the cigarette pack on the kitchen counter. She'd been very strict with herself about not smoking, but she needed one now. She lit it and Flora pushed the ashtray over into the middle of the table.

"That shakes you up, huh?" Flora said. Jess nodded, trying to think. "Tell you the truth, it kind of shook me up a little, too. I'd been wanting her to go for a long, long time, hoping she'd get up the gumption to do it under her own steam so I wouldn't have a scene with her about it. But I've got to admit, I wasn't prepared for any of that."

"I don't *like* it," Jess said. "I don't like it one bit. I don't mean about the two of you. I'm the last person on earth who has the right to question anything like that. But running off. I don't like that at all."

"As I said,"—Flora smiled—"I wasn't too thrilled myself. But what the hell? I wasn't surprised. And to tell you the truth, I was glad. She's a very hard lady to say no to."

"I know that."

"I hear you've got two swell little boys, huh? And quite a husband."

"I'm very lucky," Jess said.

"Hey! *They're* very lucky, too. You were always a good kid."

"Oh, Flora, I was a tramp."

"So? Most every woman feels like a whore some time or another. Are you one now?"

"No, of course not."

"So what does it matter what you *were*, once upon a time?"

"You sound so much like Sanford."

"Good! Then he's a sensible man!"

"I couldn't hate him, you know," Jess said, rediscovering that old luxurious feeling of having a woman to talk to. "I tried with everything I had to hate him, but he wouldn't let me."

"Why'd you want to hate him?" Flora got up. "You want cream or sugar?"

"No, thank you. I hated all of them. Sandy wouldn't *allow* me to hate him."

"So you fell in love with him. Smart fella."

"What about you?" Jess asked.

"What about me?"

"What do you . . . I mean, is there someone?"

"Sweetheart, this is it. The house, the cameras, and me. You're looking at the entire package."

Again, she said. "I really don't like what she did. It grates. And she hasn't written. That's why I came down."

"Oh, she'll get in touch eventually. Sooner or later, you'll hear from her. Tillie likes to keep all the bases covered."

"You don't like her."

"Not much," Flora admitted. "I loved her. But I sure as hell didn't like her much."

"Isn't it awfully lonely here, on your own?" Jess looked over at the sinkful of dishes.

"Oh, sometimes," she lied. "I manage."

"Flora, come to Canada!" she said impulsively. Seeing Flora's eyes widen, she hurried on. "If there's nothing here for you, there's a lot in Toronto. Things are changing now, loosening up, opening to a little fresh air and new ideas. My boys need someone like you to be Auntie to them. And *I* need you. Get rid of this big old place, pack your things and come! At least there you'll have friends and things to see and do."

"Sweetheart, you don't . . ."

"No! I *mean it*! Something's happening," she said, finally daring to put it into words. "Something's wrong with Sanford. And I'm so frightened. I've been seeing it . . . He's everything to me, except for the boys. Maybe I'm just as bad as Tillie in my own way, but I'd never abuse your friendship or try to take advantage of you. I don't think I can face this without someone to talk to. For years after Tillie and I ran away I thought about you. You were the one I missed, not Jamieson. You were the only woman friend I had. And I'd like somehow to try to make it up to you . . . for Tillie. It isn't charity or anything like that, but I'd gladly help you find a place to live and get settled and welcome you into my family."

"That's quite an offer," Flora said, touched. "But I can't make up my mind on the spur of the moment. What's wrong with your fella anyway?"

"I don't know," she said, the panic surfacing. "I've been noticing for months but wouldn't let myself even think about it, let alone admit to seeing. I can *feel* it, and I'm so frightened. If anything happens to him . . ."

"If anything does," Flora said, with feeling, "you'll pick up the pieces and keep on playing. I know how it goes."

"I can't *think* about it! I shouldn't have said anything."

"Putting it into words doesn't make it any more or less real, sweetheart. It's better to admit it and deal with it than close your eyes and pretend it's going to go away."

"You're right. It's just that it's been a difficult time these past few months. And now the baby. I need a friend," she said, not in the least fearful of stating the truth. Taking hold of Flora's hand, she asked, "Don't you sometimes feel you simply have to have someone to really talk to?"

"I do," Flora admitted.

"I have no friends," Jess said. "Sandy never had any real friends either until the kidnapping. Not *real* friends, people he could confide in. And then, when all that happened and he was there to see Press going through it, for the first time in his life he found a closeness with another man, an understanding. They could talk the way neither of them had ever been able with other men. It's always been difficult for me to talk openly about myself. You were the only one I could be truthful with. And coming here today, finding you, it's made me so happy. I know it's absurd of me to show up and start asking you to uproot your whole life because of a whim of mine. But it's more than that, Flora. I'm not suggesting it to compensate because I'm ashamed of Tillie's behavior. I'm saying this because I *am* able to talk to you. And it feels so good."

The following Monday morning, the telephone rang. Tired from two late nights out in a row, Jess decided to let one of the others in the house pick it up. Polly knocked at the bedroom door to say, "It's long distance for you, Mrs. Woodrich."

Getting up, she reached for the receiver.

"Sweetheart!" Flora laughed. "You really any good at finding houses?"

"Flora! Are you going to do it?"

"Well, I'll tell you. After you left, I sat down here with my afternoon glass of whiskey, to have my daily think session and I went over all that business about friends, and I thought to myself, 'You know, she's got a big point there.' So, I got my address book and started going through it. And you know something?"

"What?"

"Half the damned people in the book were dead. And the other half were spongers. So, I've decided to give Canada a chance. Listen, Jess," she said seriously, "you gave me a hell of a shot in the arm. I owe you one. Actually, come to think of it, I owe you two. I had a few good years with Jamie, thanks to you. Maybe I've got a few more coming up there. I like the idea of having a friend as much as you do. And I'm not too proud to admit I've been lonely as sin here."

Unable to stop herself, Jess began to cry.

"What's the matter?" Flora asked, unnerved.

"Come as soon as you can," Jess choked out. "I'm sorry I'm crying. Don't be upset. I'm just a little on edge."

"Jess?"

"Yes?"

"Don't worry, huh? I'll be there."

◊ Twenty-Five ◊

For weeks she kept asking him to go for a checkup, but he refused.

"I had that exam a few months back, Jess, when I added the term coverage to my life policy. And I was perfectly fine. Just accept it: I'm getting old and slowing down. I'm sixty-two and there's nothing more to it than that."

She couldn't push it for fear of starting an argument. So, for another few weeks, she let it slide.

All the feelings were right. She was gliding steadily forward, experiencing that interior flutter that meant she was getting very close, she'd come in another few moments, when suddenly everything changed and he was apologizing, looking distraught, saying, "I'm sorry. I'm sorry, Jess. I guess I'm more tired than I thought tonight."

His embarrassment and this admission, combined with what had just happened, all struck her as so ominous, she was unable to move for several seconds. Then she lifted herself off him, and sat on her heels taking hold of both his hands, trying to calm down sufficiently to talk to him.

"If you won't go for a checkup," she said, "I'm going to

make an appointment and take you there myself. *Please!* Do
it to humor me if you have to have a reason. I'm very pregnant
and oversensitive these days. Put it down to that and make an
appointment to pacify me."

Unexpectedly, he agreed. "All right. I'll call Roland and
make a date. To tell you the truth, I do feel kind of sluggish."

His agreeing so readily cemented her fear. She knew right
then that he was going to die; she knew it and had no idea what
to do or say next. He was constantly tired, had lost weight,
and had been sleeping badly for months—almost since the
beginning of her pregnancy seven months earlier.

"I'll come with you," she said after a time, unable to let
go of his hands.

Another shock: He said, "All right, Jess. Come with me."

It was all too scarily out of character. Softly, she asked,
"Sandy, do you know something you're not telling me?"

"I don't know a damned thing." He summoned up a smile.
"Whatever there is, we might as well find it out together. I
probably need liver pills or some damned silly thing like that."

She made herself return his smile, hoping the fear didn't
show on her face.

"Come on," he said. "Let's get some sleep."

She spent the entire night listening to the sound of his
breathing for any possible deviation in the regularity or the
rhythm. She fell asleep finally near dawn. When she awakened
just after ten, she came straight up into the fear and sat gazing
into space, steeling herself for what she knew was coming.

The following Thursday morning, Robert drove them to Dr.
Roland's office. She sat in the waiting room, chain-smoking,
until Roland summoned her in to repeat what he'd already told
Sanford.

"I want him in the hospital, for tests."

"When? What kind of tests?"

"Right now."

She felt so dizzy she had to sit down. "What is it?" she
asked, reaching for Sandy's hand. "Do you know?"

"It could be any one of a number of things. We'll have a
better idea once we've seen the test results. It could be the
liver or the gall bladder. Several possibilities."

"Sandy?" She looked up at him, wanting his reactions.

"I guess I'm going into the hospital," he said.

"All right." She stood up.

She sent Robert home to pack the things Sanford would need, then sat in the hospital waiting room while Sanford and Dr. Roland filled out the admittance forms. It was irrational, she told herself, but she was afraid to leave the hospital. If she did, she might not see him again. So, when they eventually got up to his room, she excused herself to go down the hall to the nurse's station and call Roland at his office.

"I want to stay here with Sandy," she said. "Could you arrange it?"

"Jess, you're free to spend as much time as you like there."

"No. I want to *stay* here. During the day, I've got the boys to see to, but the rest of the time I intend to be here with him."

"I'll make the necessary arrangements."

She returned to the room, stricken by the sight of Sanford in a hospital gown, already in the bed. Before she had a chance to speak, a nurse came in to take half a dozen tubes of blood from his arm, then slapped an adhesive strip across the inside of his elbow and went on her way. Jess moved to the side of the bed, asking, "How do you feel?"

"Fine, but I don't know what in hell I'm doing here."

Aside from looking tired, she didn't think he really appeared ill. Was her mind playing tricks? she wondered. Until this moment, she'd thought he looked very ill.

"I'm going home with Robert. I'll pick up whatever I need and come right back."

"Jess, that's ridiculous! You need your rest. You can't sit here all night."

"I'm not going to sit here. They're bringing me a bed. Please don't argue about this. I need to be here, Sandy."

"You always look so beautiful when you're pregnant," he said with a sudden smile. "I'd like to lock that door and make love to you right now."

She was able to laugh and say, "I'd like a raincheck and I'll take you up on that later tonight." She bent over to kiss him with a heightened awareness of the shape and feel of his lips. *Don't leave me!* she thought. "I love you," she whispered. "I have to be here."

As she was leaving with Robert, Sanford called her back.

"What is it?" she asked, breathless. Was there pain? Please, no pain!

"Whatever it is, Jess, neither of us can change it. So, for

God's sake, don't worry yourself sick over it. Okay?"

"How can I *help* but worry?"

"No. It doesn't solve anything. It's not the way to go about this. Go on home and have dinner with the boys. Then, when you're ready, come back. But, please, don't make this more than it is. Now, give me another kiss and go on."

She kissed him again, trying not to touch him with her icy hands. Then she said, "I'll try," and left him.

In the back of the car, she closed the partition between her and Robert, then let some of the fear run out of her eyes and mouth as she wept. Regaining control, she decided she'd tell the boys the truth. If she tried prettying it up or being evasive, she'd simply be creating additional problems.

So, at dinner, when they asked—as she'd known they would—she took a deep breath and told them. "Your father's in the hospital. I don't know how long he's going to be there or what's wrong with him. But when *I* know, you have my word that *you'll* know. All right?"

They accepted that. Without further questions just then. But when she was kissing them good night, Todd asked, "Can we go see him?"

Justin chimed in, "Yeah, Mom, can we?"

"I'll take you to see him," she promised, then kissed them good night, went down the hall to her bedroom and called Flora.

"Looks like you were right, huh?" she said. "I'm sorry, sweetheart. But he could be right, too, you know. He could just come out with a couple of prescriptions."

Unsteadily but with conviction, she said, "Flora, he's never going to leave that hospital. Don't say anything or try to persuade me otherwise. Just believe me. When I kissed him good-bye this afternoon, there was that same smell on his breath there was on my father's before he died."

"What can I do? Tell me and I'll do it."

"When I know, I'll tell you."

The nurse on duty explained, "Dr. Roland insisted that you have a bed and not a cot because of your being pregnant. We've moved your husband into what would normally be a semi-private, so you can have the other bed. It's just down the hall there. If you need anything, ring. The door locks," she added understandingly.

"The children," Jess began, stopped, and had to start again.

"The children would like to come see their father."

"How old are they?"

"Six and eight."

"Children under fourteen aren't allowed up here."

"Will you . . . never mind." She'd ask Dr. Roland to arrange it.

"I'm glad you did this," Sanford admitted. "I never sleep properly when you're not with me. I usually wake up in the middle of the night feeling around in the bed for you."

"You'll only have to put out your hand," she said, sitting on the edge of his bed in her nightgown. "I'll be right here."

He took hold of her hand now, saying, "I'm kind of scared, Jess."

"I know. I'm terrified."

"I just want to get the damned thing over with," he said, sounding resigned.

"He said it'll only take a few days."

He let go of her hand and touched her breasts, then her belly, asking, "How's it going?"

"It's going to be a girl, you know."

"You said that last time. Some girl Todd turned out to be."

"Well, this time it will be. Could I turn in my raincheck now?" She felt bold and foolish, desperate and needy, asking him to reassure her when she thought it should have been the reverse.

That look of embarrassment overtook him again and he averted his eyes. "I can't, Jess."

She shifted and slid her hand under the bedclothes onto his chest, finding all this close to impossible to believe, knowing now with a devastating sense of finality, that they were never again going to make love. It was over. "Could I lie down with you for a little while?" she asked quietly.

He moved over to make room for her. She lay on her side trying to cope with the near agony she felt. "Tell me how it feels," she whispered after a moment, finding his hand.

"Numb," he whispered back. "From my chest to my knees."

She laid her head against his chest. "Pain?"

"No, not really."

"As long as there's no pain."

"I want you as much as always, but I can't."

"It doesn't matter."

"It matters."

"Oh, God, Sandy, it really doesn't. Being with you is all I've ever wanted. Even before I got to know you, when you were just a strange man asking me out on dates, I wanted to be with you. I sat by the telephone waiting and hoping you'd call me again. I loved you the first time you held my hand."

When he failed to say anything, not trusting himself to speak, she made a deliberate effort to cheer both of them, saying, "You drove me crazy with those 'phone calls every night, and never touching me."

He wiped his face with the back of his hand and suddenly grinned. "Drove myself crazy while I was at it."

"And those two weeks we spent in Bermuda when we never left the hotel room, not even once. Remember?"

"They probably thought I was having a good go at my secretary while my wife was visiting relatives." He chuckled, weaving his fingers through her hair. "Jess, about the money."

She leaned on her elbow. "What about it?"

"You still own half the stock in Thibeault Trucking?"

"I suppose I do."

"Your friend René must be quite a guy. That's one of the hottest stocks going right now."

"I don't know about those things. But René...he was a good friend."

Knowing what she meant, he asked, "What about the note?"

"Press repaid it for me last month. He doesn't want to stop what he calls 'my run,' so he only sold enough to cover the note and the interest. He says he'll quit when we're well ahead."

He was quiet then and she let the minutes pass until she had to ask, "What's the matter?"

"Nothing. Sorry. I was just thinking about something."

"What?"

"You're a smart, gutsy woman, Jess. I've just been making up my mind to leave you in charge of the business."

"I don't know anything about running a business!"

"You know enough. And Charlie Bocken will keep you on the right track. So will Press. With those two behind you, you could keep things going until the boys're old enough to take over. I like the idea, Jess. I want you to do it for me."

"You're talking as if it's going to be tomorrow."

"Whenever. Do it for me?"

"Sandy," she said slowly, "don't you think it might harm the company to have the wife of the president take over when she just happens to be a former call girl?"

"Ah, Jess,"—he smiled—"you've been here a long time, but you still haven't figured out the way things work. This is Canada, my love, not New York. This is a country that was started by two groups of people who believed, and still do, that subjection's normal. The French with the Church, and the good old United Empire Loyalists who got the hell out of the States because those nasty Yanks were revolting against their beloved king.

"We Canadians," he went on, warming to the subject, "have a passion for order and wouldn't dream of rejecting authority. Once you've got it, you're above scandal. I'm a rich man, Jess, and well-known. The very fact that you're my wife eliminates you from any possibility of *talk*, let alone anything worse." He smiled widely, enjoying himself. Then the smile dimmed and he was serious again. "No one'll challenge you, Jess. Aside from everything else, people in this city have purposely short memories. It's one of the things I've always loved about my life here."

"I'm going to have three children to look after," she protested. "How am I supposed to run all those stores, too?"

"You'll do it."

"I'm not going to be allowed to say no, am I?"

"Of course you are, if you honestly don't think you can handle it. I'll set it up so Press and Charlie run the company until the boys are of age. Then, if none of the children are interested, you'll be able to go ahead and sell the whole damned thing, take the money and run."

"Let me think about it. I don't even know what you're actually asking me to do."

"I'll give you a week to decide. Fair enough?"

They were talking of his death as a certainty, she realized, and nearly lost control. But if he was already accepting this, she thought, then she had to, as well. "I'll give you my answer on Thursday."

Again, he reached inside the nightgown to shape her breasts and belly with his hand. "What makes you think this one's going to be a girl?"

"Because I insist." She laughed softly, then, remembering where they were, was sobered and put her arms around him as best she could, holding him hard, whispering, "I love you. All these years I should have been telling you. I love you."

"I've always known that, Jess. You don't have anything to make up for."

"Inside of me, I do. I'll tell you all day every day forever."

On Friday, there were X rays and more blood tests.

Over the weekend, the first of the tests were being reviewed in the lab and Jess was given permission to bring the boys in for fifteen minutes on Sunday afternoon. They climbed up on the bed and spent their allotted time arguing about hockey. Then they kissed their father good-bye and went home with Robert.

On Monday, Roland came in to say they'd scheduled Sanford for exploratory surgery on Tuesday afternoon. The most he could tell them was, "There seems to be some kind of tumor."

On Tuesday night, while Sanford was still in the recovery room, Roland came to tell Jess, "It's cancer, I'm afraid. Everywhere. We simply closed him back up again."

"How long has he got?" she asked, clinging to the arms of her chair.

"At the very outside, two weeks."

"*Two weeks*? That's *all*?"

"I'm deeply sorry," he said. "Do you want a whiff of something?"

"No, no." She waved her hand in the air, then lifted her head. "Two weeks," she repeated. "But it might be sooner?"

"Give or take a day or two. It's just about over."

"Is he going to suffer? Will there be pain?"

"Not any more than he's had. He's been walking around with it inside him for a long time, Jess. Maybe years. Who knows?"

"But it *can't* be. He was examined about six months ago, a little less. I can't remember. It doesn't matter. For insurance. They said he was fine. Fine."

"It's entirely possible they missed it, or equally possible that's when it started. At least he won't go through months wasting away."

"No," she agreed dully. "Better not to go through months."

"They'll be bringing him back in about an hour."

"Yes," she said, unable to understand how she and this doctor could be holding a rational conversation while she was disintegrating inside, and Sandy was dying. "Thank you," she added mechanically.

"Would you like me to tell him?"

"Of course!" she said abruptly, shocked to think he wouldn't. "Of course you must tell him."

"Sometimes, it's not always wise."

"No! You have to tell him. If you don't, I will. It's his *right* to know."

"I'll tell him, Jess."

He moved to go.

Only two weeks?

"Dr. Roland?" she called after him. He reappeared in the doorway. "Could you arrange permission for the boys to come again next week?"

"I'll take care of it."

"Thank you."

She got up and lit a cigarette, then began pacing back and forth, her hands shaking wildly, trying to absorb the fact that it was all going to be over far sooner than she'd ever imagined. He was going to die. She wrote the words in her mind and made herself look at them, considering what Sandy had said. He was right: They couldn't change it. But God, she *wanted* to change it. Two weeks. He wouldn't live to see the baby. It would be born after he was dead.

She had to accept this. But how? *All the rest of my life without you. I don't think I can.*

She lit a fresh cigarette from the one she was finishing, closed the door and continued to pace, fishing in her pocket for a handkerchief, throwing her head back to look at the ceiling. Tears, where did they come from? She had to get them all out of her system now, not inflict them on him. But it was so unfair, so unfair.

In the morning, when he'd come past the aftereffects of the anesthetic, they talked about it. Jess announced, "I'm not leaving again after today. I'm going home this afternoon to tell the boys, and then I'll be back. To stay. It's important that I be with you now. The boys will be all right."

"So this is how it ends," he said thickly, looking at his hands. "It isn't exactly what I had in mind."

"No," she whispered. "I know."

"Jess, you don't want to hang around and watch this."

"There's no way on this earth I'm not going to be here. If we've got two weeks, I want every minute of two weeks. *Every minute!*"

He sat up and put his arms around her.

She crumbled. More tears. "I don't want to *lose* you! Sandy, I'm sorry, I didn't mean to do this. I swore I wouldn't *do* this!"

"I don't want to be dying," he said, then pressed her to him, hiding his face against her shoulder.

Later, he said, "I guess I'd better get Charlie down here and take care of some last details. Will you do it for me, Jess, take over running the company?"

"Yes," she promised, unable to imagine what it would entail, but not caring. If it was what he wanted, she had to consent.

"Good. I hoped you would. It means a great deal to me."

"I know. I'll do whatever you want. Anything."

◊ Twenty-Six ◊

When the boys came home from school, Jess sat them down in the living room. Both boys were alert to this departure from routine. "Your father's going to die," she told them gently. "He's very ill and the doctors can't make him better. He's not going to come home from the hospital."

"What's he got?" Justin asked a little belligerently, disbelieving. Todd's face crumpled and he began to cry.

"He has cancer," she said, easing Todd over against her. "And it's all right to cry if you feel like it. I've been crying myself."

Justin struggled, not wanting to give in and be a baby like Todd. *"When's* he going to die?" he asked. His eyebrows drew together and made him look angry.

"Within the next two weeks." Cry, Justin! React, and let it start being real to you. You can't argue this away.

"How do you *know* it's going to be two weeks?"

"Doctor Roland said that's when he and the other doctors thought it would be." Todd was crying steadily, his face hot and very wet against her chest. She tightened her arm around him, insisting, Give in, Justin! You're too much like me. You

337

hate to give in without a battle. But not this time. This time, you must give in."

"How does *he* know?"

"He knows, Justin." She extended her arm to him, and he broke, hiding his face against her.

Polly came down the hall, looked in, then turned and went back to the kitchen to rejoin Olga at the table. Robert was standing by the counter looking grim. "How're they taking it?" he asked.

Polly shook her head, unable to reply.

The baby began kicking fiercely, protesting the pressure of the boys' bodies. Jess ignored it and continued holding them as close to her as she could.

That Sunday afternoon, Polly brought the boys down to the hospital. Jess was there and took them into the small waiting room near the elevators.

"Shall I stay here?" Polly asked.

"I thought you might like to see him," Jess said. Olga had come up with Robert that morning to see Sanford. The entire week had seen an almost nonstop flow of visitors, so much so that Jess finally had to call Charlie Bocken and ask him to tell people not to come. The visitors were sapping Sanford's energy.

"I would. Thank you." Polly left them.

Jess turned to look at her sons in their new fall suits, with their hair carefully combed, and their faces unnaturally clean and pale. She reached out to take hold of each boy's hand, saying, "He's still your father and there's nothing to be afraid of. You can stay with him as long as you like and no one will disturb you. Don't be afraid to talk to him, ask him whatever questions you like and tell him whatever you want. All right?" Both boys nodded, their hands damp in hers. "You understand this is the last time you'll be seeing him?" They nodded again. "It's all right to cry," she told them as she'd done every day since the beginning. "You've never had to hide anything from me or your father and you don't have to start now. We know how unhappy you are about this. And you know how unhappy I am. I'll be here when you're finished, to say good-bye. Then Polly and Robert will take you home."

Todd's face was screwed up and he scratched his forehead with his free hand.

"What is it, Todd?"

"Where's he going to after he's dead?"

"You're so dumb!" Justin snapped at him. "He's going to get buried. He's not *going* anywhere."

"Don't be unkind, Justin," Jess said. "He's younger than you are. It's harder for him to understand. Instead of yelling at him, why don't you try to help him understand?"

"Dead people," Justin said more patiently, "don't *go* anywhere, Todd. They stop living and get buried. Mom told you about that and how we'll have the funeral and everything."

"But how can he just stop *living*?" Todd asked, exasperated.

Jess was about to answer but Justin was already explaining. "When your heart stops beating, you're not alive anymore. Oh, for Pete's sake! I'll tell you about it later, okay?"

"Okay," Todd said doubtfully, then leaned close to Jess to whisper, "What I want to know is what happens to the *person* part of him? You know? The way he is and the things he thinks about. That's what I don't understand."

She hugged him, whispering, "Neither do I, Todd. I don't know the answer."

Polly returned and Jess got up to take the boys to see their father. They went in on their own and she stood outside in the hallway for a moment, hearing the boys saying, "Hi, Dad," and the exhausted-sounding effort Sanford made greeting them, then she turned and went back to the waiting room to sit with Polly.

Polly wondered if it was simply a stunningly good face Jess was putting on all this, or if she'd actually been able to absorb it. She seemed to be dealing with it admirably as far as the two boys were concerned and Polly respected her for being so truthful and open with them. But still, she couldn't help wondering how Jess was actually taking it.

"Are you really all right?" she asked at last.

Jess took several seconds to focus on the woman, then gave her a faint smile and said, "No."

"I didn't think so," Polly said.

"I keep telling myself I've got the rest of my life for grieving. I ask myself why I keep crying now, sneaking down here every few hours to cry, wanting to pound my fists on the walls. I get it all pushed down and under control again, so I can go back to him and try to be strong. God, I *hate* this! My life feels as if it's ending down the hall. I keep having to remind myself I've got two children to look after and another one coming. I'm just doing the best I can. You knew what I was, Polly. You knew," she said, losing her train of thought for a moment. "But none of you judged me."

"It's not my place to judge you," Polly said quietly.

She opened her mouth, tried to swallow the clot of tears, but failed. "I can't let him go," she cried helplessly, "I can't!" She covered her eyes with her hand, then swallowed hard. "The boys have been quite a while. I'd better just go see that everything's all right."

She arrived outside the doorway in time to hear Sanford saying, "... I want you both to remember that. Okay? What's important is doing what you know is right. And when you do the right thing, then you never have to worry about whether or not you're being a 'man.' Understand?"

Justin said, "Okay, Dad."

Todd said, "But how do you *know* when you're right?"

She moved away down the hall, not wanting to intrude upon these final moments, and returned a little bit later to see the boys kissing him good-bye. No tears. They moved to her side, then Todd ran back to Sanford, reaching up for another kiss. She could feel Justin straining and released his hand so he, too, could go back for a last embrace.

"I'll just see the boys off and be back," she told Sanford.

He nodded and she escorted the boys back to Polly. At the elevator, she kissed them good-bye, seeing the struggle on both their faces. Polly got them into the elevator and as the doors started to close, Todd's face gave way. Both children were crying audibly as the elevator bore them down and away. She stood with her hand raised to press the call button, then let her hand drop and walked woodenly back to the room.

By the following Tuesday, it was plain he was failing. Roland increased the medication order, and Jess sat in the chair beside the bed, holding Sanford's hand, talking with him as he drifted, the periods of unconsciousness becoming longer and longer. When he was awake, he was as lucid as ever, and she had moments of blind hope that finally gave way to acceptance.

"You've never told me much about your parents," he said. "Just dribs and drabs. What was your mother like? Do you look like her?"

Resting her cheek against the back of his hand, she smiled, saying "Tillie looks like Mother. I'm built more like her, though. Except in the breast. She was very tiny, fragile, tall, like me, but so delicate. I used to sit with her while she bathed. I think now it was because she was afraid of being alone, in case she felt faint and couldn't get out of the tub. But I loved those times. We talked and I'd sit looking at her, idolizing her, wanting to be just like her when I grew up."

"And are you just like her?"

"Not in the least. I'm much more like my father. But you know who is like her, in a funny way? Flora. She used to be enormously fat. I've told you that. And I used to sit and look at her, just the way I did with my mother. And we talked the same way, too. It's never occurred to me that it's because she reminds me of Mother. Oh, not the way she talks or any of that. But underneath. There's such gentleness and caring, and the same kind of fragility. She's almost the same age Mother would be now. How funny to think of that."

"I saw the photographs, you know, Jess."

"What photographs?" She was so worn out from lack of sleep it was difficult for her to keep up with the sudden turns of his thoughts.

"The Jamieson Land book."

"What book? You've lost me."

"You don't know?"

"Flora mentioned something about a book. I've never seen it, though."

"But I thought it was yours. It's in the bookcase."

"In our bookcase? I wonder how it got there."

"There are a number of photographs of you in it," he said. "And one with Tillie."

"Really? Which bookcase? I'll have to have a look when I..."

"When you go home," he finished for her. "On the window side of the fireplace, third or fourth shelf down from the top. He must've loved you one hell of a lot, the old buzzard. They're exquisite pictures."

"The only person I can think of who'd have brought that book into the house is Tillie. What I don't understand is how it got..." She didn't bother to finish. He'd gone off again.

She got up and went into the bathroom, to have a cigarette and use the toilet. She dropped the partially smoked cigarette into the toilet as a strong cramp gripped her so that she had to hang on to the edge of the sink until it passed. Then she flushed the toilet and moved to the door as she felt a familiar giving sensation inside and warm liquid gushed down her thighs. She stood paralyzed, thinking, *Not now! It's too soon! It can't be coming now!* She dried herself with one of the towels, then returned to her seat, once more taking hold of Sanford's hand. It would just have to wait.

Two hours later, the contractions were coming between ten and twelve minutes apart, gradually getting closer. *I will* not *leave here*, she promised his sleeping figure.

He stayed out almost an hour, then was awake only a few minutes. She stood for a while to ease herself, holding the rail at the foot of the bed as she clenched her teeth and shuddered her way through another, stronger contraction; studying his face throughout. He awakened again and smiled at her, talking very slowly, with difficulty.

"You must be tired, Jess. Why don't you lie down for a while?"

"I'm not tired." She sat and reached for his hand. She leaned over to kiss him and could taste death on his lips. It had a rancid flavor, a fetid odor. "Sandy, are you awake?" she whispered.

His eyelids fluttered.

"I love you, Sandy."

". . . you, too."

He slid away, his hand once more loose in hers. She stroked his forehead, then braced herself against the side of the bed for the duration of another contraction. When it was done, she continued stroking his face, watching closely and listening intently as his breathing slowed, became less and less, holding her own breath to hear better. And then it stopped. His last exhalation was the longest, slowest, most audible.

Like Todd, she was all at once overpowered by a desperate need to know where he was going, and to try to stop him. How was it possible for the person inside the body to simply go this way? Tears ran unheeded down her cheeks as she sat staring at him, still clutching his hand, trying to make herself understand. Then she rang for the nurse, her hand stiffly opening to let him go.

When the nurse came, she straightened and said, "He's dead." Her voice crazed with cracks, she asked, "Would you do something for me? Would you put your arms around me for a moment?" and closed her eyes gratefully as the young nurse, without hesitation, enfolded her in her arms. After a moment, Jess stepped away, asking, "Do you think you could call my obstetrician and ask him to come down here? I'll give you his number. And could someone please take me to your maternity floor? I'm in labor." She took hold of the hand the nurse instinctively held out, feeling as if she were drowning in the wells of sympathy in the girl's eyes. "The contractions are about three minutes apart."

"Sit down here, dear," the nurse said, carefully easing Jess back down into the chair. "I'll get a wheelchair and ask the other nurse to put in a call for your obstetrician and for Dr. Roland. Will you be all right here on your own for a minute or two?"

Jess nodded, turning to look at Sandy, again taking hold of his hand. How was she to know if she'd be all right?

There was no time for the usual preparations. A nurse came into the delivery room thinking to shave Jess, but hurried out again, at Dr. Ennis's order, to prepare a spinal block.

"No!" Jess cried, her face crimson with exertion. "*Nothing!* I want to feel *all* of it!"

"But it's not necessary," he argued. "You had the block each time with the boys."

"Not this time!" she insisted, trying to go with the pain, wiping her eyes and nose on the sleeve of the hospital gown. "*Not this time!*"

The pain, it could be death, Sandy, like dying, but it's a birth and it's everywhere. I can't separate the pain of one from the pain of the other, I feel it all. God, without you how will I . . . without you. It's coming now, God, pushing. Sandy! *It's coming. I can feel it. Coming.*

"It's a girl, Jess. A bit on the small side, but a fine healthy little girl. Have a quick look, then we'll get her cleaned up and put her in an incubator for a while. Jess?"

She had to touch her just to be sure. Then she collapsed back, her eyes closing against her will. *I told you. Didn't I tell you it would be a girl.*

Flora brought the boys in the morning and took them to the nursery to see their new sister, then to see their mother. Downstairs, at the rear of the hospital, the funeral home attendants were loading Sanford's body into the hearse.

First thing in the morning, two days later, Jess telephoned Dr. Ennis.

"I wanted to tell you I'm going home today," she said.

"Jess, that's out of the question! You can't! You're not ready to get up yet."

"I'm leaving. My husband's funeral is today. When it's over, I'll go home to bed. When will I be able to take the baby home?"

"Not for at least another week. And what'll you do about nursing her, Jess?"

"I'll come and nurse her."

"This is impossible! You can't do that *and* rest."

"Then *what* do you *want* me to do?" she cried. "Are you trying to tell me I shouldn't attend my husband's funeral?"

He sighed, then said, "Use the breast pump and have Robert bring the milk down. But take it very, very easy, will you please?"

There were hundreds of people. Robert, Polly and Olga, Press, Nelda, and Flora managed to keep most of them away from Jess. But as they were leaving for the cemetery, someone touched Jess on the arm and she looked up through her veil to see René, in a dark blue suit, holding his hat in both hands.

"I come to see you're okay and say I'm sorry. Anything you need, you'll call me?"

Mutely, she embraced him.

Knowing at once this was someone special, Flora took his arm, in an undertone saying, "Come on with me. There'll be a few of us going back to the house later. You'll come, huh?"

He went with her.

She stood at the graveside with the boys, acutely aware of pain. The stitches hurt and her insides felt shredded. Her head was so filled with colliding, grief-stricken thoughts she heard nothing that was being said. As she watched the casket being lowered into the ground, she tried to imagine how she could possibly keep this promise. *I don't know how to do it*, she told the box slowly dropping down. She couldn't imagine the days beginning and ending without him, or how she was going to sleep alone in that bed. *You shouldn't have made me promise. If I fail . . .*

At a signal, she and the boys stepped forward to drop their flowers onto the casket, then stepped back. Their hands were so small inside hers.

I can't fail.

The rustling movements of the crowd alerted her to the end of the ceremony. The boys seemed hypnotized, unable to move.

I won't fail you.

She cleared her throat and looked at her sons. "It's time to go home now," she said, and led them over the grass toward the car.

SIX

Interlude

1953-1954

◇ Twenty-Seven ◇

The heat was dreadful. She felt all at once as if she'd lost what little strength she'd had. There was a low humming in her ears and a sudden coolness on her skin. She was moving, but like some improbable piece of human machinery, she could feel herself stopping; everything inside her was slowing down so that even her vision was affected. It took a long time for her to lift her head and see Flora just over there. Just over there. Miles.

She forced her mouth to open and found her voice as she touched each of the boys lightly on the back, telling them, "Go with Flora. Run ahead and go with her. I'll be right along." She was afraid to have anything happen in front of them. They were upset enough.

"What's the matter, sweetheart?" Flora's voice was very loud, knifelike against Jess's ears.

"Take the boys and go back to the house," she murmured, feeling it overtaking her faster.

"But what about you? We can't just leave you here."

"Please, take them. There are dozens of people. Someone will bring me back. Flora, *please*!"

Feeling the urgency emanating from her, Flora hurried the

boys into the back of the limousine, telling Robert, "Pull out! We'll take the boys home."

"What about Mom?" Justin asked, craning past Flora to see his mother standing a few feet away. She didn't look right, he thought. "Why isn't she coming? How come she's just standing there?"

"Go on, Robert," Flora said, keeping her voice low, turning to see that Jess still hadn't moved. "She'll be along in a few minutes. She's just staying to talk to a few people." Jesus Christ! she thought. It was frightening the way Jess looked.

The car was moving and both boys knelt on the back seat, looking out through the rear window at their mother. "Why isn't she coming *now*?" Todd asked.

"Aunt Flora just *told* you why!" Justin replied. "Don't you ever *listen*!" He spoke with more confidence than he had, because it scared him, too, to be leaving her.

She managed to lift her hand to wave, seeing the boys' small faces in the rear window, and held herself upright until the car turned down the drive and out of sight. Then her hand dropped heavily and she lowered her head, her eyes on the ground. The humming was louder now. She felt someone's presence and slowly raised her head to see René. She wanted to say something but was aware of a sudden sick giving sensation inside and an accompanying rush of wetness. Her head dropped as she felt the blood running down her legs.

René, too, looked down, saw, and put out his hand just as her head came up and she whispered, "My God! I'm bleeding." Then she seemed to spin, her head lolling to one side, and her body—as if comprised of separate, disconnected sections— bent at odd angles as she began to fall. He caught her and, frightened, looked around for someone to help.

Press and Nelda came running across the grass, Press exclaiming, "Somebody better call an ambulance!" But Nelda shook her head. "She's hemorrhaging. There's no time."

"We're going to the hospital!" René decided. "You come," he told Nelda, thinking she looked competent and cool-headed. "Come and drive my car."

"Yes, all right. Press, follow us in our car!"

"I'll get that motorcycle cop to lead us, otherwise, with all the traffic . . ." Press was saying as he ran off toward the long row of cars while Nelda ran alongside René, who was carrying Jess, toward René's rented car. She opened the back door and

René slipped in, arranging Jess on the seat with her head and shoulders on his lap. Nelda climbed in behind the wheel. "The seat's too far back!" she cried, turning the key René had left in the ignition.

"You push down at the side and the seat goes up."

She got the seat moved forward, put the car into gear and reversed, quickly planning the fastest route downtown to the hospital.

René removed Jess's hat and veil, scared by the whiteness of her face and her dead weight across his lap. Blood was running along the seams of the seat's upholstery, and his sleeve was black with it.

She opened her eyes, determining from the motion that they were in a car. She recognized René's hand on her arm. It took too much effort to move her eyes. She let them close again, listening to René's voice telling her everything would be all right, we'll get you to the hospital, you'll be all right. "I'm so cold," she whispered, her teeth chattering.

Hearing, Nelda turned on the car heater in spite of the already stifling heat of the day, then returned her attention to the path the motorcycle was cutting through the traffic.

René wrapped his arms around Jess, holding her closer to his chest, trying to warm her.

Turning her head slightly inward against him, she breathed slowly and steadily, inhaling René's scent of fresh-laundered linen, a faint trace of lemon, and underlying that, the warm flesh smell of the man himself. He had both her hands in his and was chafing them.

René stood in the corridor, smoking a cigarette, absently touching the drying sleeve of his jacket. It was caked stiff; flakes of dried blood wafted to the floor as he inadvertently knocked them loose. Press leaned against the wall beside the telephone, half-listening as Nelda told Flora where they were and what was happening. "We're waiting for Dr. Ennis to get here," she said, holding the receiver so tightly that both her ear and hand hurt. "Perhaps you should plan on staying overnight with the boys. We'll call the minute we know anything."

Press was looking at René, finally seeing this man about whom he'd been hearing for years. He'd created an image of him that had no basis in reality, an image shaped around what he knew of René's success, clothed in sedate suits, and molded, perhaps, by McGill or Laval, or even the U. of T. Now, Press felt embarrassed by his prior assumptions. René was a large, muscular man with huge, strong-looking hands; the overall impression he gave was of strength. He would, Press thought, have looked more comfortable in a plaid flannel shirt and work pants. At once, he felt guilty for attempting to classify the man in this fashion. René was well dressed in a hand-tailored suit and even his shoes were expensive and shiny from recent polishing. But still, he seemed the epitome of the self-made man and Press was both curious and puzzled. He wanted to ask René all sorts of questions about his success and how he'd managed to build his company into one of the biggest in the country. But the timing was all wrong, and for some reason Press felt very young compared to him. There was something about René that stated categorically that he'd never known the indulgences of childhood and youth, but had worked almost from the time he could walk. There was also something very familiar about him, as if they'd met several times before. It wasn't his physical appearance so much as the feeling he generated in Press, and it came to him with a jolt that René seemed so familiar because he put Press in mind of Sandy. He was younger and bigger, but had that same aura of confidence and caring Sandy had had; he was less polished and elegant, yet had a natural grace. He moved cleanly, without seeming to disturb the air or the people around him.

Press had to drag his attention back into line to look over at Nelda, who'd finished her call and was opening her bag for a Chiclet. It was a sure sign she was nervous. She kept gum in her bag for the girls but never chewed it unless she was concentrating particularly hard on something, or upset.

"Want one, Press?" She offered him the pack.

"No, thanks." Once again, he was brought to a standstill by the renewed realization that Nelda was no longer a fantasy but very much a part of him, the person who bewildered, elated, intrigued, confused, and loved him. This woman with her softness and intelligence combined control and spontaneity, and worked on a level he doubted he'd ever fully comprehend. She went forward on an instinct that was seldom misguided. She was always calm, so that he was able, through her, to dispense with his sometime illogical fear for their children.

"What time is it?" he asked, wanting instead to say, I love you.

"Just after four."

"What's taking so long?"

"Let's go sit down," she suggested, snapping closed her handbag and starting toward the waiting area. Press fell in beside her. "Why not come with us?" she asked René, sensing he wouldn't leave here until Jess did.

René followed them down the corridor, wondering who these people were. They'd been the first to come running, people he'd decided wouldn't lose their heads and start doing foolish things.

Nelda sank down into a cracked leather armchair, Press chose the sofa, and René stood by a small table strewn with tattered magazines, putting out his cigarette in an ashtray crowded with crumpled gum wrappers. Straightening, he said, "I'm René Thibeault. Me and Jess, we're old friends." He stepped over to extend his hand to Press, who got to his feet accepting René's huge hand.

"I'm Press Ames. And this is Nelda."

"Friends of Jess?" René asked, releasing Press's hand to shake Nelda's. He sat down on a wooden, straight-backed chair, at once reaching for his Export A's. He lit one before remembering to offer the pack around.

"No, thanks," Press said, then explained, "I was married to Tillie."

"Ah! Where is she, the little one?"

"I have no idea," he said, discomfited. "We haven't heard from her in a couple of years."

"So," René said quietly, "it was your baby, eh?"

"Yes."

"Terrible," he said. "Very sad. I'm real sorry."

"We have two girls," Nelda interjected with a smile, moving them quickly over the old wound.

"Hey! Nice to have little girls." René grinned at her. "How old?"

"Six and five."

"Me, I got three girls, five boys. Had two girls, one boy who died."

"How many children do you actually have?" she asked, liking this man.

"We had eleven. Eight left, now. All big. The little boy, he's fifteen. The oldest girl, she's older than you, thirty-six."

"Thirty-six! You must've married very young."

"Sixteen."

"And your wife?" Press asked.

"Marie, she's gone two years. She got sick with the kidneys, was sick a long time."

"That's too bad," Nelda said sympathetically, sitting back in her chair, chewing thoughtfully, steadily on the Chiclet. Then, with typical directness, she leaned forward again, saying, "Forgive me if it's rude, but how old *are* you?"

"Fifty-three soon."

"You don't look it," Press said, grateful that Nelda's openness was allowing him an opportunity to satisfy his curiosity.

"No," René said proudly. "I know." Losing much of his élan, he said, "I knew Jess when she was eighteen. We're good friends a long time. She'll be okay, you think?"

"I'm sure she'll be fine," Nelda said, not at all sure of that.

"Did you know Sandy?" Press asked, anxious to keep the conversation moving.

"I never knew him, but I heard about him. A good man. You don't know where she is, Tillie?"

"No." Press wondered if it bothered Nelda hearing them talk about Tillie. He glanced at her. She seemed interested in the conversation, as if they were discussing someone they'd known only socially. "She went off to live in New York after our boy . . . died. That was the last I saw of her. It's been seven years, at least."

"She used to send Christmas cards," Nelda said. "Beautiful ones. Little collage-type things she made herself. But she hasn't sent any the last two years. Really, the most beautiful cards. I had them framed." How funny to be talking about her this way, she thought. She no longer disliked even so much as the thought of Tillie. She and Press had managed, she thought, looking sidelong at her husband, to relegate Tillie to the past.

"Why do they take so long?" René said, grinding out his cigarette before going to look up and down the length of the corridor, returning to his chair after a time to light another cigarette. The three of them fell into a companionable silence, waiting.

She surfaced as they were undressing her in the examining room, looking slowly at the set faces of the two nurses and the doctor—was he a doctor? It was hard to tell—as they moved efficiently, doing this and that. One nurse with a pair of shears

cut straight up Jess's dress, slid the pieces out from beneath
her and dropped them to the floor. A second nurse suddenly
appeared above her, smiling. Touching Jess's face gently for
a moment, she said, "Your doctor's scrubbing up. He'll be
right in. Try to relax. Everything's going to be all right. Are
you in pain?"

She whispered, "Yes."

"Don't you worry. Hang on and we'll get you squared away
just as fast as we can."

The nurse was distracting her from the fact that all her
clothes were gone and she was naked on a cold table with a
sheet being draped over her. She whispered, "I'm cold,"
shocked by the warmth of the nurse's hand moving to enclose
hers.

"You sure are," she smiled, and turned to ask the other
nurse to get an extra sheet. She wrapped a blood-pressure cuff
around Jess's upper arm, saying, "You're cold because you've
lost a lot of blood. We'll put some of it back and you'll be just
as warm as can be."

She could feel herself starting to fade and willed herself to
go. In sleep there was no cold, no pain. She came back, her
descent aborted by the stern voice of Dr. Ennis.

"Didn't I warn you?" he said, coming into her viewing
range. "Take it easy, Jess," he said less sternly, taking her
hand, bothered by the emptied quality of her eyes as well as
the too-low blood-pressure reading the nurse had noted on the
chart. "We're going to get you cleaned up now and see what
seems to be the problem."

As Nelda was returning from calling home to check on the
girls, Dr. Ennis came down the corridor and she stopped to
wait for him. He looked fatigued, she thought. "How is she?"
she asked him. Press and René appeared from the waiting room
at the sound of her question.

"She'll be all right," he answered, accepting a cigarette
from the pack René held out. "Thanks." He glanced up at the
big man, idly wondering who he was. "We had to transfuse
her," he sighed, drawing hard on the cigarette. "She'd lost a
lot of blood. And her general condition's damned run down.
Anyway, she's on the last of the blood, and we've got her on
a glucose I.V. She'll be fine," he said again. "But she's not

going to be seeing anybody before tomorrow. So why don't you all go on home. Leave me a number and if there's any change, I'll let you know."

Press got out one of his cards and scribbled their home number on the back.

"Could I talk with you privately for a moment, Dr. Ennis?" Nelda asked. The two of them moved down the corridor, leaving Press and René alone together. "I'd like to know what happened," she said.

"Look, Nelda," he sighed again. "It's a pretty straight-forward case of too goddamned much. She shouldn't have tried getting up so soon after the delivery. That, and all those hours of labor while she was sitting with Sandy . . . It's called vaginal prolapse, and it's caused by a long, difficult labor. It isn't all that unusual and it certainly isn't critical. There are, if you can *imagine* it, half a dozen women a year who come into my office and ask to have that kind of reconstruction work done purely as cosmetic surgery." He made a face that clearly stated what he thought of those women, and then went on. "With plenty of bed rest for a couple of weeks here and a couple at home, she'll be just fine."

"I see," Nelda said. "Thank you."

"You and Press go on home," he told her, patting her shoulder. "You'll be able to see her tomorrow. How're the girls, anyway? Everything all right?"

"They're fine."

"The other fellow, is he a member of the family?"

"A close friend of hers. Let him be with her, will you? I've got a feeling his being around will be good for her."

"I'll take care of it. Now you two run along home, okay?"

René left his rental car in the hospital lot and walked back to the Royal York. As he walked, he thought about how, twenty years ago, he'd promised himself he'd one day have the money to have a room in a fine hotel like the Royal York. Now he had the money and he stayed here half a dozen times a year when he came to town on business, and he probably owed most of it to Jess because of that loan she'd made him when he was just starting out. He decided he'd wash, change his clothes, have a meal, and go to bed early. And tomorrow, after the meetings, he'd go back to the hospital. He'd stay here in town until she was well again. His hand on his stiffened, blood-caked sleeve, he was awed by what had happened, and more determined than ever to stay until he was satisfied she was all right again. Touching the sleeve of the ruined jacket, he thought, *You might have died. I might have lost you.*

When he went back to the hospital tomorrow, he'd go up to the nursery to see the new baby.

◇ Twenty-Eight ◇

One afternoon, after months of staring stupidly at columns of figures and tear sheets of ad copy, at salesmen and suppliers, at advertising people and Riverwood store managers, everything suddenly pulled together and began making sense. There was a quite beautiful logic to how it was all structured, and she was at last able to see it. Upon arriving at this comprehension of the rudiments, she became excited, challenged by the idea that there actually was a job here she might be able to do.

Charlie attended to everything pertaining in any way to the legalities: customer claims, in-store accidents, workmen's compensation problems, and insurance. Press saw to the banking and general purchasing, mediated staff disputes, oversaw the store managers as well as the office staff and, in between times, tried to see to the advertising. Both men were, admittedly, run ragged.

"What am I supposed to do?" she asked them. "There doesn't seem to be anything so far but a lot of letter-signing."

With a smile, Charlie deferred to Press, allowing him to speak first.

"There's so much for you to do, Jess, I almost don't know

where to begin. There's the question of our advertising which, everyone seems to agree, isn't to anyone's satisfaction. That's for openers. Then, there are all the company functions where you're expected to put in an appearance, and that means out of town, not just locally. The list is pretty long and I don't honestly think you're going to be able to handle everything on your own. But there sure as hell's a lot to be done. We need at least two more secretaries, and someone to deal with new Riverwood product development. On and on."

"Our advertising?" That intrigued her. "What's wrong with it?"

"Take another good long look at those tear sheets and tell *us* what's wrong with it!" Charlie said. "We need help in that department, that's for damned sure."

"We've got to get going on some kind of staff incentive plan," Press threw in. "I'm telling you, Jess, there's a plateload here. All you've got to do is grab a fork and dig in."

"But what needs doing first?" She was beginning to feel she'd jumped too fast, and into water far too deep. Charlie— usually warm and helpful—seemed so angry as he said, "All of it! I don't know how in hell Sandy ever managed to get all this done on his own, let alone do the job he did. The thing is," he softened his tone, and relaxed his sharp features some- what, "times are changing fast and our advertising, not to mention our stores, just aren't keeping up. The city's finally starting to come out of its hundred-year coma; it's getting to be more like a *city* instead of some provincial hitching post. We've got some damned sophisticated people living here since the war, you know. They're not the same old puritanical crew they were. Have you been to the suburbs lately? There's a building boom you wouldn't believe. No kidding!" He turned to include Press. "Took a drive last Sunday to Malton, the kids like to look at the planes, eh? Jesus! It used to be miles of bloody nothing—fields and a couple of farms out that way. Not any more, brother. Razed acres where they're throwing up bungalows just as fast as they can.

"And all that talk about dumping the old city hall and getting some plans on the board for a new one isn't just talk anymore. It's going to happen. Riverwood's starting to look old-fash- ioned. Here's Loblaw's putting up new markets, *huge* bloody places. We'd better start giving them competition or we're going to wind up in receivership. But opening duplicate Loblaw's stores isn't going to do it for us. We've got to offer something different, like an all-kosher section, maybe, in the new Bathurst and Lawrence store. I mean, do you *know* the size of the Jewish population north of Eglinton? It's like a suburb of Tel Aviv. And maybe an Italian section in the old Dundas and Ossington store. *Something!* We're not even *trying* to pull in any of that market, never mind the Lithuanian, or the Polish, or the Czech. We've got to start offering something special in the heavily ethnic areas, localize the stores to fit in with the neighborhoods."

"It's an idea, Jess," Press said mildly, as if to temper Charlie's swing to overzealousness. "There *are* big groups we could cater to profitably."

"Can't we just go ahead and do as Charlie's suggesting?" she asked.

"We're working on it." Charlie sounded tired now after his outburst. "We're trying to make a deal with the Shopsy's people and another with a small outfit to supply us with an Italian line. Pasta, tinned goods. We're *working* on it. We just can't work on *everything*, Jess. We're understaffed. I can't even *tell* you what we need. I'm up to my ears in my own stuff, never mind the rest of it. But the thing is, the days of Dad's cookies and basic white bread are over. Kids just don't take the old peanut butter and jelly to school anymore. It's salami on double rye with mustard. Or cold *frittata.* Or a hunk of summer sausage and a kaiser roll. Those Polish markets and Italian markets, the old neighborhood stores are doing just fine, while we're losing that business."

"But you say we're working on it," she said, bewildered.

"Yeah, we are. I guess I'm getting a little carried away," he apologized, and sat back smoothing the hair down over his bald patch. "I used to think I was bored with law," he smiled, "that the challenge was gone once I'd got my degree. Now, I'm beginning to think about the old law practice like a long vacation I once took."

"Let me start with these," she said, and appropriated the folder of tear sheets.

She returned to Sandy's office, now hers, with the folder and several pages of notes she'd taken during the meeting. Sitting down behind the large, polished desk, she spread out the ads and stared at them trying to see what was wrong. She couldn't tell, and realized she was going to have to get in someone who'd know. Her enthusiasm coming back, she got an outside line and called Flora, asking straight off, "How would you like a job?"

"Sweetheart, I've got more going than I can handle. What kind of job anyway?"

"Nothing full time," Jess said quickly, anxious to involve her in this. "I want someone to look at our ads, tell me what's wrong and how to fix them. You're the only one I know who'd be able to do that."

"I'll give 'em a look over to help you out, but I can't guarantee more than that."

"I've got an idea. Come to the house tonight, have dinner, and we'll talk. Are you free?"

"Sure. Seven?"

"Fine."

Next she got on to Nelda, inviting her to dinner as well. That arranged, she gathered the tear sheets and returned them to their folder before reaching for her note pad. She drew a line down the center of the next clean page and wrote "Flora" on one side, "Nelda" on the other, and across the lower third, her own name.

Then, referring to the notes, she began jotting down comments in the appropriate sections. When she'd finished and looked at her watch, it was after four. She pushed the chair back from the desk, lit a cigarette, and turned to look out the window at Bay Street below. The stock market had closed for the day and there were quite a number of people on the street, some heading south toward Union Station, others hurrying down the side streets to the parking lots. In another hour there'd be solid traffic down there, with cars backed up all the way to the lakeshore.

Sitting in Sandy's office, in Sandy's chair, her hand gripping the padded arm as if some residue of his warmth, his essence might still be contained within it, she looked at the pale yellow walls above the wood paneling, at the photographs of Sandy with store managers, and Sandy with old Riverton; at the watercolor of autumn trees Sandy had bought some thirty years before for twenty-five dollars at an amateur art exhibit; at the brass desk lamp and the leather armchair for visitors; at the small liquor cabinet in the corner and the Persian rug. Every item was of good quality, chosen with care.

She felt suddenly undone, in the midst of all these things,

by his absence. It was more real for a moment than anything else. Everything she'd done for months had simply been to fill time, and the only realities that had any definition were this job and the baby—the job, at the outset, because she'd given her word, and now because it had finally captured her interest; and Belinda because she was still so small and in need of so much. Caring for Belinda wasn't anything like caring for Justin and Todd had been. It wasn't just that she was a girl. It had to do with her birth coming when it had, and all that had followed. She felt guilty about Belinda and didn't know why. Every time she looked at her daughter's tiny, naked body and saw its femaleness, she was somehow defeated. Belinda was going to grow up to be a woman and know all sorts of uncertainties. She'd experience pain unlike anything Todd or Justin would ever know. She'd grow to take her female vulnerability out into the world and fall in love, be hurt perhaps, and nothing Jess could say to her or do for her would alter that. There were certain fundamental, inescapable experiences awaiting her, and unlike with Tillie, where a definite detachment had come to exist in time, that could never be the case with Belinda because she wasn't Jess's sister but her child. And it wasn't the same. Not at all.

Throughout her life so far Jess had gone along, dealing with events as they occurred but always with a minimum of freedom and mobility, simply because she was a woman. Now, having given Sandy her promise, she could see that more than just putting in hours was involved. He had, intentionally or not, given her an opportunity to excel and succeed in a way that mightn't ever have existed if he hadn't died. She could, if she tried, transcend her femaleness and achieve some small measure of distinction. She was in the odd position of having been freed from playing out her role of wife and mother if she chose, but she felt compelled to continue it and so was experiencing something she'd always before considered male: being a householder and a parent who daily went off to business and nightly returned home. She'd never fully understood or appreciated Sandy's equanimity until she was forced daily to set aside her business thinking in order to enter the house and, simultaneously, her role as mother. It wasn't easy.

She was light-headed from too many cigarettes, too much coffee, too many complications, and unsure if she really cared about rising above her hard-won status as a mother and head of the household. But there wasn't even a real choice involved. She'd given her word, so she'd go on with it.

But Belinda. God! So many threats, so many dangers. Insane men who raped small girls, boys to fall in love with, rejections to be suffered, sex. Why was she *thinking* of these things?

She felt too alone and unsupported to deal with the exhausting possibilities of Belinda's future. Yet it concerned her far more than that of the boys. They were boys, after all, and would grow into their positions as men. It was all so simple, so well-defined. But how could she possibly predict Belinda's future when her own contained problems and challenges she'd never dreamed of? Whenever she held the baby, touching and looking at her, something in her longed to have Belinda remain safely an infant forever, while something else in her wanted Belinda already full-grown and making her own decisions, well beyond the need for facing her mother with yet another problem, yet another painful aspect of her growth.

Where were the guidelines? What were the rules? Everything had changed; nothing remained as it had been, except her seemingly endless responsibilities. And now this job. She sighed, again facing the window. Well, damn it, she'd do it! She wasn't kidding anyone, certainly not herself, in making a pretense of literally running the company. But, as Press and Charlie had pointed out, she *could* make herself useful, even important. So, get to work, she told herself. Stop mourning, stop fretting and get on with it!

"I want to offer you a job, too. I probably sound crazy," Jess smiled at Nelda, then turned to include Flora. "But I said I'd do the damned job and I will. I just happen to need a lot of help. Right now, the most pressing area seems to be the advertising. But there's so much more I'm almost afraid to start thinking about it. I've got to have someone with some business experience to tell me what might work and what's simply ridiculous, to manage the office and take that weight off Press, to hire and fire the office staff and work closely with me. I'll pay you whatever you think you're worth, give you complete control of all the office hiring and firing." She looked from Nelda to Flora and back again at Nelda. "I need help," she said simply. "I was sitting in the office today, thinking about what I've taken on, deciding I'd take this seriously. I see it as an opportunity. All I know is that I need good people nearby to teach me, help me. Because all the enthusiasm in the world isn't going to do the job for me. I just don't know enough about business."

Flora finished looking through the tear sheets, announcing, "Christ! These stink!"

"Why?" Jess asked, leaning eagerly toward her, elbows on her knees, a cigarette in her right hand. "Why? Explain it to me."

"There's no composition, no interest, no focus, no *grabber*. Look, sweetheart, when you see a photograph that grabs you, you don't know why the hell it's good. It doesn't even *matter* to half the people in the world what makes it good. But it's the lighting and the way things are grouped to direct the eye where you want it to go. As far as this copy goes, *I* could write better stuff. For chrissake, *Todd* could! You think all this quiet, earnest crap catches anyone's attention? Forget it! You've got to hit 'em between the eyes, stop 'em before they turn the page. 'Cause they turn that page, you've lost 'em."

"Help me fix it then. I'll pay you whatever you want to work on the ads, make them attention-getting, attractive. And advise us on the stores, make *them* better-looking and more appealing."

"I don't know, sweetheart." She tapped her fingers on the folder in her lap. "I could do it better myself than I could explain to anyone else how to do it."

"Then *do* it! *Please!* I'll get you whatever you want and need. You can work your own hours, hire your staff. I think we need an advertising department, and someone to coordinate with the architect and the contractors, to improve the design of the stores."

"Let me think about it, huh?"

"Of course." Jess sat back, crossed her legs, and held the cigarette to her mouth. Why had she thought this would be easy? You didn't just go casually rearranging peoples' lives to suit your own needs. She knew absolutely nothing about business or how to get done what required doing. She was, she thought, going to have to learn all of it.

Nelda followed all this, gratified to see Jess showing such an interest in the business—in anything. She seemed to be coming back to life. Jess looked very much like a business-woman these days, Nelda thought. She'd gone from the sedate, very understated dresses she'd once worn to rather sporty, good-looking suits with more color and style to them. She was wearing a new suit this evening, of a deep burgundy wool, with a pale pink, long-sleeved silk shirt. The colors were good for her, helping to relieve the perenially too-white look of her skin.

"I'm not sure, Jess," Nelda said at last, doubtfully.

"I kinda like the idea of some women running things," Flora said with a big smile. "We've got a whole hospital downtown working like clockwork with nothing but women. Get the right combination going and women'll do the job just as well, maybe even better than any bunch of fellas."

"Does that mean you'll do it?" Jess asked her.

"Like I said, I'm gonna have to have some time to think it over."

"So am I," Nelda added. "There are the children, after all, and the house, shopping. A dozen different things."

Jess couldn't understand why they weren't displaying more enthusiasm. For a moment, she felt angry with them for not immediately leaping in to join her. Then, thinking it through, she realized she was thinking, if not behaving, erratically.

"I'm not asking either of you to put in nine-to-five days," she said, "but to pick the hours that suit you and work when it's convenient."

"And what about you, Jess?" Nelda asked.

"What about me?"

"Are you planning to continue being there nine to five every day?"

"I don't know. I think it's become a habit now. But truthfully I don't see what difference it makes how many hours are spent in the office. I seem to do my best thinking when I'm getting ready for bed, or when Robert's driving me somewhere. I believe what I'm proposing makes sense and you're the two people I know who could do the best job."

Nelda looked carefully at Jess for several long minutes while Jess went on explaining some of her other ideas to Flora. She admitted to herself that she'd been getting bored by staying home now that the girls were away at school during the day, and there was no question of the challenge in what Jess was offering. What concerned her was the feeling of near desperation Jess was transmitting. For a few moments she wondered if Jess wasn't going to wind up one of those dreadfully dedi-

cated women who threw themselves almost fanatically into an
endeavor and then found they'd lost their identity in the process. If that was a possibility, Nelda thought, then it might be
a very sensible idea for her to take this job in order to ensure
that that didn't happen to Jess. She cared too much about her
to let Jess lose herself entirely; it might be too much of a
temptation to jump headlong into the business and leave the
children to the servants. It could happen. Obviously, she still
wasn't thinking entirely clearly. *I've got to talk to Press*, she
decided. Getting up, she said, "I've got to go. Let me call you
tomorrow, Jess. I'll talk this over with Press and see how he
feels."

"I understand."

Jess walked with her to the door, then came back to sit
beside Flora, saying tiredly, "I suppose I didn't give it enough
thought. I hadn't even considered Nelda's girls or her household. It's probably a bad idea all the way down the line."

"Oh, I don't know about that." Flora helped herself to a
cigarette from the box on the coffee table, taking her time to
light it, considering Jess's proposal from a number of angles,
and thinking, too, about how Jess seemed to be rising and
falling in direct accord with whatever she and Nelda had to
say. "To tell you the truth," she said, keeping a close watch
on Jess's face, "I'm kind of interested."

"Really?"

There it was again, Flora thought, seeing Jess's expression
lighten, and her eyes widen with hope.

"I'll probably do it," Flora went on. "Maybe even work up
some of the layouts myself."

Jess took hold of her hand, for a moment staring into space.
"I've taken on too much," she admitted. "But just today, for
the first time, I thought perhaps I could do it after all."

"How's it going anyway, sweetheart?" She pulled gently
on Jess's hand to regain her attention.

"I don't know. I'm getting through the days. But it feels
as if . . ."

"As if what?"

She closed her eyes for a moment and, to her confusion and
chagrin, saw a very clear, detailed image of herself and René
making love. She felt a pang of guilt at the image, thinking
herself disloyal. How could she even *imagine* that?

"It feels not quite right," she said. "Empty."

"What about René?" Flora asked incisively.

"Oh, René," she sighed, shifting to face Flora, their hands still joined. "He's something to look forward to, the way family outings and trips used to be. But when he's here and we go out to dinner, or we're alone together, I just feel guilty, as if I'm cheating on Sandy. I know what you're going to say. I *know* I'm being absurd. But I still love him, Flora. I don't know how to stop, or even if I want to, let alone whether I'm able."

"René's a swell guy and he's nuts about you. If you asked him to move, he'd be here in a flash. Are you sure you're not selling yourself a bill of goods, using Sandy as an excuse for not getting involved?"

"What about you, Flora?"

"We're not talking about *me*, sweetheart. We're talking about *you*."

"There's nothing to talk about. All right, there is. But I don't feel like it. I'd rather discuss you, or anything else."

"There's no big rush on fifty-seven-year-old women these days, you know. My life isn't exactly a big, ongoing party."

"But what about that nice man you said you met? The one who had some sort of gallery?"

Flora smiled wistfully. "What'm I gonna do with a nice old man? He made *me* feel old. And I'm not ready to feel *that* old, not yet anyway. But you, you're what, thirty-six? You've got years, *years*. Why don't you give René the word, have him around at least when you need him?"

"I'm not *ready* to do anything like that. I may never be."

"Yeah, you will. Be honest with yourself. A little more time and you'll be ready. You're not the sort of woman who's good at living without a man."

"Neither are you."

"True. But I'm a hell of a lot better at it than you. You need the sex part of it more than I do. I *told* you." She smiled. "Nowadays, my fantasies have more energy than I do."

"You're lying," Jess said, finding the conversation turning depressing.

"So, all right. I'm lying. But only a little. And I'm not wrong, either, am I?"

"No," Jess said very quietly. "You're not wrong. But I feel so *shabby*, needing . . . thinking about . . . needing."

"There's no reason to feel that way. Shabby," she repeated,

with a little grimace. "That's a hell of a way to think about yourself. We've all got needs, sweetheart. As long as you feel it, do something about it."

"I can't! I don't *feel* ready. I don't care strongly enough about René to want him around more often. I almost can't bear having the children around me with their squabbling, their fights and demands. It's all I can do not to scream at them, or at the baby when she cries. It's a *relief* to get out of here every day and go to the office."

"Be careful about that," Flora warned. "You can't hide out in the job, Jess. They're your kids and they need you. You need *them*, for that matter. A job's only a job, you know. Don't you go making it more than it is. What you've got to do is get rid of some of that steam you've been building the last couple of months. That's why the kids're getting on your nerves. Months on end without anything's no good for someone like you."

"Are you giving me your permission to get into bed with René, Flora?"

"Don't do that, sweetheart," Flora said kindly. "We're all big grown-up ladies here, remember. All I'm trying to say is that you're coming a little loose at the edges and it's no sin to want to get everything all patched up. Go ahead and do your job, but don't think the need's going to quietly go away all by itself, because it won't. It'll probably get a whole lot worse."

"Part of me," Jess said, looking pained, "wants nothing more than to turn myself over to René and let everything happen. I've even started . . . daydreaming about it. But when I do, another part of me goes crazy."

"It stinks, doesn't it? Walking around like a robot. I know how it goes. The brain's in one place, the feeling, the body's in another. I guess you're gonna have to give yourself more time, after all."

"Some moments, I feel too young to be going through all this. And other times, I feel so old it hurts just to get out of bed in the morning. I tell myself I've got to forget and stop thinking about him all the time. But it's so *hard*. I walk into that office and every single morning I realize he's dead. It feels as if I've been hit in the face with a rock. I pass some man in Eaton's wearing Sandy's cologne, or see someone in a camel-hair coat like his and it hits me again. I miss him so much and it doesn't stop. I want it ended. I do, Flora. But what do I do about this feeling of expectation I have every time I see another man with something about him that reminds me of Sandy?"

"It'll end, sweetheart. I promise you. It gets a little less one week, and the next week it's a bit less than that. On and on until it's a whole lot less and you're able to get on with things. I know about it, Jess."

"My God! Flora, I'm sorry. I've got to stop being so self-pitying. You don't think I'm being stupid about the job, do you?" she asked, alarmed by the thought.

"Let's talk about it, see if I can't get you straightened out."

"You'll help?"

"Nelda will, too. She's just going home to get Press used to the idea of her working again."

"You think so?"

That look again. Flora said, "Count on it, sweetheart," then hugged her. "You may still be a little up in the air, but I think you've got some damn good ideas. And I'm interested." She stroked Jess's hair for a moment, then eased herself away, saying, "You're gonna be okay, sweetheart." They sat looking at each other and Jess said, "I love you, Flora."

Flora smiled and patted her on the hand. "Yeah, I know. I love you, too. Things'll work out."

In the next few weeks, so many ideas emerged as a result of their daily meetings that Jess knew she'd been right in enlisting Nelda and Flora. The photographs and ad copy Flora produced were an immediate, highly visible improvement. Nelda came up with a suggestion for nursery areas in the larger stores, and Jess had the idea of free coffee from opening until noon in all the stores. Suggestion boxes, a consumer complaint department—one thing after another. Flora decided the stores ought to go in for color in a big way. "Let's get rid of all that insipid pale green and white and go with sunshine yellow, or brilliant green, or a terrific warm orange. Who the hell wants to go shopping in an institution?"

Jess also thought of having all the weekly specials grouped in one area so the customers wouldn't have to go through, coupons in hand, looking for them. And Nelda, fully fired, said, "Let's hire girls to bag if they apply and they're strong enough to do the job. They'll probably be better at it than the boys. And while we're at it, how about some female managers?

Let's offer our employees a real honest-to-God training program with a chance at decent wages and room to rise in the company. If a cashier thinks there's a chance to work her way up to store manager, she's going to be the best damned cashier in town."

"We ought to go into this Riverwood-brand thing a little more," Flora said. "More than just tea and a few tins of stuff. Let's *really* go into it. For chrissake, A & P has all that Ann Page stuff or whatever the hell it's called, so why not us? And while we're on the subject, the packaging's a mess. Let's throw it out and start fresh. Might as well make our house brands look as good as the more expensive stuff."

Jess couldn't write fast enough to keep up with the flow, nor could she move fast enough in her travels back and forth between the women and Press and Charlie to implement the best of the suggestions. But at least she was finally contributing. And it did use up some of her energy, so that she was less irritated by the children and less anxiety-ridden. Yet she was no less alone. Being so wildly busy during the days only served to make the evenings and weekends seem emptier by comparison. In the back of her mind there was always Flora's voice warning her about hiding out in the job. She didn't think she was, but everything seemed so misshapen and distorted she was never entirely certain of her motives.

SEVEN

Toronto
1953-1960

◇ Twenty-Nine ◇

"You look real good," René said approvingly.

"I'm feeling very well."

"You like it, working?"

"It's finally starting to make sense to me," she said eagerly. "In a lot of ways, it's quite an opportunity. And now that Flora and I have got the advertising department going, and Nelda's taken over the office, I do seem to have a definite job. It's not just sitting looking at financial statements every day trying to figure out what I'm supposed to make of them. I'm involved in the advertising department, and of course there's the figurehead business, you know. Signing letters, putting in appearances here and there. What I mean to say is, I have some idea what I'm doing now."

"So, you'll stick with it, eh?" he asked, thinking how really well she looked.

She didn't hear him for a moment, that shocked realization overtaking her again as she studied him. Sandy had been dead for six months. Six months with too many empty spaces to fill everywhere. She was beginning to find herself going for hours not thinking of him, then she remembered and felt guilty. Now, looking at René, she was all at once aware of him as more than just an old friend. He was a man, an attractive one. She looked at his hands and her legs felt suddenly rubbery. At the same time, she felt confused and disloyal to Sandy at being here with this man.

"I'm sorry, René. What did you say?"

"I'm asking if you'll stick with it?"

"Oh, the business. I've put a proposal to Charlie and Press that I act as chairman of the board and Press take over as president, with Charlie as vice-president. That way, we'll have full-time legal and financial counsel. They've both agreed and Charlie's drawing up the papers. I . . ." She was finding herself unusually distracted. "What I mean is, if you make some-one . . . feel involved . . ." Her thoughts dwindled away as she examined his eyes, then his mouth, appalled by her thoughts and reactions.

She looked around the restaurant, finding the polished cop-per pots on the wall and the brick floor very familiar. She'd come here often with Sandy. There was a strong, not unpleasant aroma of garlic in the air, kept moving by the flow of people being led to tables by the slim, distinguished man in black she knew was the owner and not the maitre d' as most people supposed. The pots ran along the walls just below the roof, dozens of them. And beside her was the small fountain with its low brick wall.

I shouldn't be here with another man, she thought, then looked over at René, wondering why she thought that. René had, with the years, grown even more attractive than she'd remembered him being at thirty-five. Or had he been thirty-six? She couldn't recall. It didn't matter, she thought, going on to consider how close they'd been in so many ways recently. He'd stayed on in the city and had come to the hospital twice a day to hold her hand and talk. And later, when she'd been discharged, he'd come to the house each evening, to take the boys to the Gardens to a hockey game, or to the ball park. It had been René who'd brought Belinda home from the hospital, carrying the infant with such a look of pride he might have been her father.

His hair was turning gray, she saw now, but his teeth were just as startlingly white as ever. He'd taken to dressing well, too. His hands . . .

"You've done so much for us," she said. "I've never really thanked you."

"Hey! Don't thank me. You want to hear something good, something funny?" His wide grin coaxed her smile back.

"What?"

"I'm taking English lessons. What," he enunciated carefully, "do you think of that?"

"You are?" Her smile grew.

"I am. My second girl, Marie-Claire, she says I'm a peasant, talk like a peasant. An important businessman should know how to speak good English. So I have lessons. I don't sound no better, eh?"

"Some." She laughed. "But I'm accustomed to the way you sound, René."

"Not Marie-Claire. She calls me a peasant."

The idea of anyone thinking or saying that of him distressed her. "You're not a peasant, René," she said softly. "How someone speaks hasn't anything to do with the person he is."

He shook his head. "Nope. She's right, Marie-Claire. So, when I think of it, I make myself talk properly. And I'm keeping on with the lessons."

"Which one is Marie-Claire again?"

"The second one. She's thirty-four. Michelle, she's the oldest. She's thirty-seven."

"It gives me the oddest feeling knowing you have children older than I."

"Why is this?"

"I don't really know."

"I don't think of you like a daughter."

"How *do* you think of me?" she asked, curious to have, perhaps, a new image of herself.

"Me? I love you. I've always loved you."

His saying that made her feel the full weight of her need to touch someone, make contact.

"You're not eating," he noticed.

She looked down at her plate. "Everything's gone."

"Hey!" He touched her hand, looking hurt. "You're still young. You got two nice boys and the baby. Pretty soon, you'll meet some nice young man and have good times again."

"I do not," she said slowly, "want to know any nice, young men."

"So," he smiled encouragingly, "you meet some nice *old* man."

"*You're* a nice old man." She gave him a full smile, feeling despicably transparent, wondering if what she wanted didn't constitute *using*. She hated the thought of using anyone, especially René. She turned her hand over so that it lay palm upward beneath his, acutely aware of their every action, finding each word and gesture varnished with a thick layer of her too obvious need. "I feel *empty*," she said almost inaudibly, then wet her lips as she glanced again around the busy restaurant, embarrassed. Feeling his fingers slowly spread and interlock with hers, she turned back. He was gazing at their linked hands.

He could have had her years ago, she thought, when anyone who'd wanted her had had her. But he'd refused; he'd made it clear that wasn't what he'd wanted, wasn't the way he'd thought of her. Now, it was all these years later and she had to have someone hold her, someone who wouldn't make her feel as if she were sliding backward into that old ugliness. Someone had to touch her and make her feel alive again.

"Hey, Jess," he said in a quiet rumble, "what is it you're saying to me? I'm stupid sometimes. Maybe Marie-Claire she's right when she tells me I need English lessons. I'm not too good on the words."

"It's been so difficult," she said, her thoughts traveling off on a tangent. "In a lot of ways I hadn't anticipated, having to get up every morning and go to the office has been good for me. I haven't had time to think about Sandy too much. At night, though, and on the weekends, I'll go out to dinner with Nelda and Press, or with Flora, or you when you're here. And at some point in the evening, I suddenly can't swallow my food or whatever I happen to be drinking because it hits me again that he's dead and I'm alone. I feel so hollow, as if parts of me are missing. Did you feel this way when Marie died?"

The waiter approached the table and, seeing him, René asked her, "Some dessert, Jess?"

"I don't think so, thank you."

"Coffee," he told the waiter, then waited until the man left their table before returning his attention to Jess, saying again, "You really look so good. It's a pretty dress." He touched his free hand to her sleeve. "Silk?" he asked. She nodded. "Pretty," he repeated, his hand lingering for a moment longer on her arm before descending to cover their joined hands on the table. "I know how it feels," he said. "Me and Marie, we were kids together. We know each other all our lives and marry up when we're sixteen, start having the kids. I remember when I stopped for you and the little one and I said to you I have eleven children and how you looked at me. For a long time, I thought about how you looked when I told you this. And other people, how they think about us French. We all got ten kids, maybe fifteen, some of us we got twenty. That's the way we know it should be, eh? Because we're all good Catholics, so we have the kids. But when Marie died, I thought to myself maybe it's not so good bein' Catholic, because if we didn't have all the kids, Marie she wouldn't have died so young. And other things I think about," he continued, feeling the grabbing in his stomach, remembering Cotton. "I think about it a lot and what I think is maybe it's not so good for me, being Catholic. Not when they keep you on the rhythm so you got to go on having the kids, and the women they die at thirty-five, forty. My girl, Michelle, my oldest, she's some smart woman, works in Montreal teaching school and she tells me, 'Papa, I can't believe in something that tells me I can't have any life but having babies.' So she doesn't go to church anymore. And now, Marie-Claire, she's stopped too. They both go to this Unitarian church. Anyway, it makes me think, and I decided maybe I don't believe so much anymore myself, because I think the girls are right. They're good girls, good women."

"You've given up your religion?" It seemed to her a monumental thing for him to have done.

"I don't give up God," he said, pausing while the waiter set down their coffee, then silently moved away. "I give up having the priest tell me how to live," he continued, "when he never in his life had to see his woman die from having kids she didn't want. The priests telling us how to think, what's good to think and what's bad. Me, I know that for myself. So, when I go down to Montreal, sometimes I go with Michelle and Marie-Claire to this church. And it's not so bad." He pulled over his pack of Export A's and, keeping his left hand joined to hers, used his right to extract a cigarette and light it. "It's been a long time for me," he admitted. "After Marie died, I didn't want to be with any women. I *loved* her," he said emotionally. "Nothing's the same without her. I have the big new house and just me and the two boys home now. I go home and watch television, watch 'The Plouffe Family' sometimes. You ever see that?"

"Once or twice."

"Lots of people just like that. I know lots. They go on down to the hockey game Saturday night, get excited over the hockey. Hoping maybe for a big fight, blood. Drinking lots of beer and maybe Canadian Club when they got the money. And everybody I know has a brother, a sister's a priest or a nun. Me, too. It's a big honor, eh? I got two brothers priests, one sister a nun. But I sit home at night thinking it's not such a good way to live. We got the hockey and the beer, and we don't think too much of *les anglaises*. We don't like them much at all." He sighed. "It doesn't make sense to me anymore. None of it."

He stopped to lift his cup and take a drink of the coffee. She watched, seeing him with an entirely new perspective, as if he were someone she'd just met. She felt compelled to keep reexamining his features, trying to fix them in her mind—in a sense, forming first impressions. She liked the shape of his mouth and his dark complexion, and the contrast between the deep ruddy tone of his skin against the white of his shirt. She liked the strong warmth of his hand. "Go on, René," she said. "Tell me about your life, what you think."

What he wanted was to touch again the weightless pale blue crêpe de chine sleeve that floated from her arm when she held her cigarette to her mouth. Or her hair. He wondered how long it was, unable to judge because of the way she had it coiled against the nape of her neck. He wanted to measure the narrow circumference of her waist with his hands, to run his fingertips down the side of her long neck. He put out his cigarette, took another drink of the coffee and began talking.

"Me and the boys in the big house with the television set. I do the cooking, so we eat steak all the time. Nobody to . . . make a fuss, eh? We have a woman, she comes a couple of days every week. She cleans up, makes over the beds. She leaves us clean beds, clean towels for the bath. But there's nobody to buy the food, or do the cooking, or to sit with, talking. It feels empty, like you said, and quiet. So I work more and more. And my young boy he's already got himself a girl. A few more years, he'll marry and then I'll have the big house and the woman coming a couple of days every week and the television. So I work even more. And five or six times a year, I come down to Toronto to do some business and visit with you so it doesn't feel so empty." He stopped again, not knowing how to tell her he wanted her, not even sure if it was the right thing to say, or if he'd correctly understood her meaning. He didn't want to make a mistake, or do anything that would hurt their friendship. But, I love you, he thought. Just to touch her, hold her. For a long time he'd been thinking about how it would be to love her.

"René?" He lifted his head. "Let's leave," she said, allowing her hand to remain joined to his for a few more seconds before withdrawing it.

"Okay, sure."

Outside on the street, she pushed up her coat collar, holding it closed against her throat, trying to catch her breath in the stingingly cold air. There was always about this city, she thought, a feeling that wasn't at all similar to anywhere else she'd ever been. There was definite reassurance in the wretched cold of every winter, and in the sight of sturdy red brick houses built in anticipation of that cold; it was also in the lightness and unexpected splendor of the streets in spring. She wanted to be happy again, to feel alive again in this city of people, the majority of whom were, like her, foreigners.

He took her arm and, ducking their heads against the wind, they hurried down the street and around the corner to the lot where his car was parked. By the time she was inside the car her eyes were watering and her legs felt numb and frozen. She opened her bag for a tissue and dabbed at her eyes and nose, shivering as he started the car.

"You okay, Jess?" he asked, looking over.

"Fine. Just cold."

"You want to go somewhere, have a drink? We've got time."

She finished drying her eyes and stared straight ahead, holding the tissue crumpled in her gloved fist. *Make a decision!* her brain told her. She could say yes and they'd go somewhere, have another drink, sit and talk for an hour or two more before he drove her home and gave her a good-night kiss on the cheek. Or she could say no. She could say, Take me to your room and we'll lie down together, warm each other and try to fill some of the emptiness. But she was afraid, and thought of Dr. Ennis telling her it was perfectly all right, everything had mended. She had a reconstructed vagina like some secondhand car with a new engine. God! She was so afraid. But she didn't want to go home.

"Let's go back to the Royal York," she said, getting out a cigarette, needing something to give her courage, even if it was only the illusory comfort of a cigarette.

"Okay, sure."

They left the car for the doorman to park and went inside. René stopped just inside the foyer to say, "You want to go down to the bar?"

"No." Taking her courage in both hands, holding on to it tightly, she said, "Not the bar."

He understood and for several seconds couldn't move, trying to absorb the impact. Then he reached for her hand and they started up the half dozen or so stairs that led to the huge, elegant old two-story lobby with its mezzanine running above on three sides, and the marble columns and fine old carpets, the groupings of armchairs and sofas.

"I love this place," she said quietly, noticing a young couple holding hands, leaning over the mezzanine railing, looking down into the lobby. "It's like the living room of a giant." They looked at each other and she smiled, asking, "Don't you think so?"

His eyes took in the settees and brass standing ashtrays, the wood-paneled reception desk and the bell captain's station before he replied simply, "It's good."

She was very moved, deeply satisfied by his agreeing. But as they began walking toward the elevators, her feelings shifted again and she was once more afraid. She found she had to keep swallowing as they stood in the elevator, rising slowly.

He placed the Do Not Disturb sign on the outer handle, then locked the door. He felt scared, the way he'd been at sixteen, married to Marie but not knowing what to do, and frightened by how small she was and how soft, hurtable.

She stood by the desk looking at the room-service menu, taking a lot of time removing her gloves, placing them and her bag on the desk top. "I'm frightened, René," she said, as her eyes took in the Gideon Bible. She'd seen hundreds of these hotel-room Bibles and always wondered if anyone ever read them. Hundreds of rooms she'd entered for an hour or two, all of them somehow identical. She'd taken off her clothes and done things she wouldn't have believed herself capable of doing, letting herself be used in the most debasing ways in return for dollars. It had been more than ten years, yet the moment she'd entered this room, it all came back.

She stood looking at the rings on her finger. Still married to a dead man. And René had stopped believing. Where were they going? she wondered. Where would they arrive finally? Was it all a matter of just using up time, or was there some real purpose behind the never-ending changes?

"I'll take your coat," he said, coming up behind her.

She turned and he put his arms around her. Her eyes closing, she thought how fine a feeling it was to be held. She placed her arms around him, then opened her eyes and moved her head back to look at him. They'd known each other almost eighteen years, but had never kissed. Years ago, she'd thought of how it might be to put her mouth to his, to have someone who claimed to care for her put her down with his enormous gentle hands and heal all the small wounds. She thought it again now.

His lips parted slightly and her heart seemed to leap in anticipation. Holding motionless, she once more let her eyes close as his mouth grazed hers, then went away. Her hand delved into the pleasing softness of his abundant hair, signaling; a slight pressure of her fingertips and his mouth came back to hers. The hunger tremendous, she sighed, half-crying, opening her mouth to taste and know the smooth firmness of his lips. She felt suddenly warm, for the first time in months, and grew quickly warmer as the kiss ended and she watched with startled eyes as his hands unfastened her coat, opened it, and his arms slid around her inside the coat, bringing her even closer to him to kiss her again.

He felt anew the shock, the deeply pleasurable surprise of having a woman in his arms, the satisfaction of holding close so much frail substance. He'd always undergone a moment of disbelief upon taking Marie into his arms and it was the same now. He made himself gentle, aware of how easily, unthinkingly, he might bruise the delicate flesh or crush the air out of something so exquisitely gratifying as the body of a woman.

So this was how he was, she thought, aware of each small detail of what was happening. Gentle he was and slow. She was thankful because she was filled with uncertainty and fear; she didn't want to feel guilty.

"I'd like to use the bathroom," she said, her voice choked with desire and guilt. She left him and went into the bathroom, avoiding the sight of herself in the mirror. It might prove too dangerous to confront her image at this moment. Moving stiffly, as if fear had prematurely aged her limbs, she removed her dress, saw a hook on the back of the door and hung it

there. Then, feeling for the pins in her hair, she withdrew them
one by one, laying them down in a pile on the edge of the sink.
She shook her hair free, combing it with her fingers before
dropping her straps, pushing her slip down. Then she bent to
pull off her boots. The tiled floor was cold under her stockinged
feet as she reached behind to unfasten her brassiere. Undoing
the suspenders, she removed her garter belt and stockings, and
finally her underpants. An expensive pile of lace-trimmed underwear. Her hands went automatically to the faucets of the
sink.

She bathed, battling off treacherous memories and the jibing
inner voice chanting, Wash up like a good whore. Water trick-
led down her thighs, making her shiver. After drying with one
of the towels, she looked down at herself, placing her hand
over her no longer flat belly, risking touching one of her
breasts, smaller now after three babies, yet still heavy. It
couldn't be hidden. She was no longer young. Was desire just
vanity? she wondered. She didn't want to think about it. She
felt like a whore as she switched out the light and opened the
bathroom door. Standing naked in the doorway, she looked
over to see he was already undressed and in the bed. The light
on the desk cast a mellow light, one that wouldn't instantly
highlight flaws neither of them wanted to reveal. He sat up as
she approached the side of the bed and held his arms out to
her, finding her every bit as beautiful as he'd always imagined
her to be.

Weakened with misgivings, she stood with one hand on his
shoulder; his skin was new and different to a hand accustomed
to the feel of Sandy. Placing her other hand, already familiar
to this, in his hair, she examined the sensation of his cheek
resting against her breast. Then she went tight everywhere in
agreeable tension as his hand curved around her breast and his
mouth opened on her nipple, his other hand molded to her
spine.

As if knowing how deeply fearful she felt—or perhaps, she
thought, he was fearful himself—he went very slowly, bringing
her down on the bed beside him to whisper words of praise
over her breasts and throat, hips and belly and thighs. He
touched her lovingly, disconcertingly with his big dark hands
as his mouth came and went, back and forth, striking softly
against her lips, her shoulder, her breasts. It felt wonderful but

she couldn't relax sufficiently to do more than hold him and offer reluctant access.

Taking his hands down the sides of her body, he dipped his tongue into her navel, then across her belly, stopping to look up at her questioningly. She allowed her thighs to part, holding her breath as his hands caressed the length of her inner thighs, then went down under her, lifting her to his mouth. An involuntary groan escaped her as, faultlessly, he located the source of her pleasure and probed its depths.

Her reconstructed body had feelings, she discovered, trembling under the onslaught of painful reawakening. There was every sensation in the world and she liked the new feel of him and how he touched her, the way he was making love to her. Nothing was more direct or more achingly arousing than this.

She had to silently motion to stop him. They lay side by side in the lull, touching each other hesitantly, then she bent her leg over his hip, her hand guiding him. Breath held, she withdrew her hand; poised, ready as he moved forward into her.

He watched her features alter as he slowly brought himself into her. "It hurts," she whispered. Looking agonized, she murmured, "Give me a moment." It hurt and she was going to start crying. Why hadn't Dr. Ennis warned her? She shifted slightly to accommodate him, to better feel the pressure of his body, trying to adjust to his presence inside her, deeply dismayed by the absence of pleasure. "Oh, God!" She felt bereft. "It isn't the same. I don't know . . . Nothing feels the same. It's as if I don't know how . . ." Tears of futility overcame her at feeling only his body like some large blockage inside her.

"Hey! It's been a long time," he said with an understanding smile. "For you, and for me, too." Stroking her breast, his mouth touched against hers, then his fingers applied a slight pressure that made her twitch and gasp. "It's okay," he crooned. "We'll make it good."

"I was so . . ." She couldn't explain it, could only cry brokenly.

"It's no good the old way," he said undaunted, "we'll make it good a new way." With astonishing strength, holding her secure, he turned so that she lay above him. His hands played gracefully, appreciatively over her, sliding the length of her body before coming to rest on her face, catching her tears on his fingertips. "I love how you are," he said, a deep rumble she could feel vibrating through his massive chest. "If it's no good at all, we won't do it. We'll just be together for a while."

"But I *want* this!" she cried fiercely, her hands fastening to his upper arms. "I *want* you!"

"Go slow," he said softly. "Slow."

"Slow," she repeated, and experimentally lifted and fell, at the bottom of the fall finding the core of her feelings intact.

"No good?" he asked holding her still for a moment.

"No, no! It's all right!" *God just let me, let me!*

He sighed; his hands rippled over her, transmitting such a depth of tenderness and caring that she shuddered as she tracked their passage. He seemed to be reading her through her skin, sensitive to her breathing, to her slightest motion.

She closed her eyes, cradling his head in the crook of her arm, and kissed him in a sudden frenzy of responding as her body—an ally now and not the treacherous enemy it had once been—moved to take her over.

Her hair damply matted against her cheeks and forehead, she lay panting, afire, yet chilled as she began quickly cooling after her almost desperate exertions. It's all right, she thought. And it was good, good. She turned to fit herself to him, her eyes filling, holding him tightly.

"Marry me, Jess." His hand opened and closed in the springy depths of her hair.

"I can't! I'm so fond of you. You mean more to me than anyone ever has, except Sandy. And I know I'll always want to see you. But I can't. I can't even *think* about it. Please understand."

A slight movement of his head indicated he did. "Okay," he said, at length. "But I wanted you to know how I feel."

"I do know. What time is it?"

He reached to lift his watch from the bedside table. "Coming up for eleven."

"Oh!" She sank back against the pillows, still assaulted by the confused inflow of feelings.

"You want me to take you home?"

"I've got to go," she said, reluctant to get up and dress, knowing when she did she'd be returning herself into the guilt.

"Okay," he said and got up. She had no choice but to do the same.

Tying her scarf over her hair, she walked beside him down the corridor toward the elevators. She wanted to hold his hand but, as she'd anticipated, she was so stricken with guilt she couldn't bear touching him now. All she wanted was to get home, go to sleep, and not have to think about anything.

"You sorry now?" he asked, concerned.

"No," she lied. "I'm not sorry." In part, that was the truth.

"I love you, Jess."

"I know that." Torn, she wished she could simply respond with a like declaration, but she was too shaken to think coherently. Guilt lay like a coating on her skin. She could almost taste and smell it.

"What's the matter?" he asked, touching her arm.

"I'll be all right. It's just . . ."

"I know," he said quietly. "And it's okay. We're still friends."

"Yes." Her voice was husky, her thoughts utterly unsettled.

"We'll go slowly, take our time. It'll be okay."

She exhaled and relaxed a little. He was being very kind and most understanding. Perhaps it would all work out. "We'll take our time," she agreed. And hurried into the house trying to convince herself there was nothing disloyal in seeking a bit of comfort, knowing she was going to have to keep reminding herself of that, possibly indefinitely.

◊ Thirty ◊

"I've had it up to here with you!" he shouted, chopping the flat of his hand against his throat. "Take your goddamned kid and get your ass *out* of here! I'm not listening to one more *minute* of this shit!"

"He happens to be *your* 'goddamned kid' too, you know!" Tillie shouted back, not believing he was serious.

"You *listen* to me!" he said, suddenly menacing in his lowered tone of voice and the rigid set of his reddened features. "And listen real good, lady! I never in my life hit a woman, but you don't take your kid and get out of here now, I'm gonna start in a big way!"

"Wait a minute . . ."

"Now! Or I'll *throw* you the hell out!"

"Oh, all right. You're being ridiculous. I can't talk to you when you get this way."

"You're all through talkin' to me, period. It didn't *work*, lady! I'll be damned I'll put any more money into you. And I'll see you in hell before I put any goddamned ring on your stinking finger. Get the kid and get out!"

She whirled around and flounced out, down the hall to Bobby's room. He hadn't yet awakened from his nap and was

386

sprawled on the bed, almost hidden beneath soft toys and learn-to-read books. She cleared a space at the side of the bed and sat down, with her fingertips pushing the hair back from his sleep-flushed forehead, thinking they'd go out and drive around for a while. She'd get Bobby a hamburger and a milkshake and she'd have a coffee or two. By the time they were finished, Big Bobby would be cooled down and start to see reason.

"Bobby?" She reached for his small limp hand.

He stirred. She leaned forward to kiss his cheek, and his face contorted as his arms and legs stiffened and he came up out of his sleep.

"Come on, honey, wake up. We're going out for a while."

He stared at her blankly, his mouth pursed with sleep, then he blinked and asked, "Where we goin'?"

"Out for a while. Come on." She stood up looking down at him. "Go wash your hands and face and make sure you go to the toilet. Okay?"

"Where we goin'?"

"Just out. Hurry up now."

Groggy, he sat up, his thick blond hair tousled and his cheeks very red. The sight of him was always a reaffirmation. She'd lost one child. She damned well wasn't going to lose another. Satisfied he'd get up in another few seconds and do as she'd told him, she left and continued down the hall to her bedroom, the one she shared with Big Bobby. She stopped in surprise in the doorway to see him yanking open the dresser drawers, tossing her things out in a pile on the floor. "What're you doing, Bobby?" she asked quietly, starting to become afraid. Could he really be serious?

"You take your crap with you, too, hear? I don't want you comin' back at me later on for stuff you left here. What you leave gets burned out back with the trash."

"Look, Bobby, I didn't mean it. It's really all right if we just go on as we are. We don't have to get married. And Lew's got it all wrong..."

"No, you meant it all right. And what kinda woman are you, anyhow, you go suckin' up to a man's closest friend, thinkin' maybe he'll give you somethin' I can't? Me and Lew, we're friends," he said, pained. "You think he wouldn't tell me straight? You think he'd get it all wrong about my ole lady offerin' all kindsa wonderful smiles and flirtatious gestures? You're a fool, woman! And that's a fact! Always lookin' out

for a new golden goose might lay bigger 'n' better eggs. I'm
sick to death of you. Five and a half years of you, Tillie, I
oughta get some kind of prize. And that's the God's honest
truth. So, you take your stuff, whatever you want, and get
out."

"I did nothing of the sort!" she lied hotly.

He wanted to hit her; he'd never in his life wanted to do
anything more. But he held himself back.

"What about Bobby? He's your child, too."

"That boy ain't no child of mine. I mighta put him in you,
but what came out sure God ain't no way related to me. He's
a fine boy," he relented. "And he's been no problem to me.
But you take him and good luck to the fuckin' two of you."
Having finished dumping the contents of the drawers, he
stalked over to the closet, threw open the bi-fold doors and
began tearing her clothes off the hangers, tossing them out
behind him into the pile while she stood, speechlessly watching, mentally cursing Lew Franklin and his big, stupid mouth.
Friends, she scoffed. Lew Franklin was a goddamned liar and
he'd only told Bobby because Bobby had walked in and caught
the two of them in the kitchen. It could've been perfectly
innocent. There'd been a party going on, after all. But, no.
Lew jumped like he'd been struck by lightning and rushed out
looking guilty as sin.

She wanted to believe that once this fit was over, Bobby
would be just as sorry as always when he drank too much or
when he stayed out all night playing poker and wanted to make
it up to her.

Finished with the closet, he looked around the room, a slim,
handsome man, made ugly by his rage. Spotting her keys on
the dresser, he walked over, snatched them up and let them
bounce on the palm of his hand.

"What're you doing with my keys?"

"*My* keys," he corrected her.

"But I need the car keys."

"That's *my* car, case you're forgettin'."

"And just how'm I supposed to get out of here if I don't
have the car? Walk?"

"You got it bang on, lady! *Walk!* Might do you some good,
bring you down a notch or two from those high-flown ideas
you got. Thinkin' you can put the sweetness on a man's best

friend. I should've known better. It was how you nailed *me*, come to think of it."

"We can't *walk!* Are you *crazy?*"

"I've *been* crazy," he said, with a scary smile. "Putting up with you, a woman who ain't even good in bed. I don't think you even *like* it, the truth be known. I'm doin' the one smart thing I've done in years, getting rid of you. I'll miss the boy. He's not a bad kid, not by a longshot. But *you*." He shook his head. "You're gonna go to your grave thinkin' it's your right to do nothin' but ask for things, makin' demands on people, thinkin' you've satisfied the askin' by playing the pretty hostess and paintin' your high-toned paintin's and lettin' me bed you down regular. You don't get one damned thing in this here world without *earning* it, lady. And you've sure as hell earned what you're getting. Just be glad I'm not giving you a boot up the ass to help you on your way, 'cause every bone in my body's just itchin' to lay into you."

Giving the ring of keys a final toss, he caught them, walked past her wearing a ferociously self-satisfied expression, and went out.

Dumbfounded, she stood staring at the pile of clothing on the floor, thinking she'd been an idiot, trying that with Lew, but she'd thought...Never mind what she'd thought. A few hours and everything had gone wrong.

From behind her, Bobby said, "How come Daddy threw down all your clothes?"

"Oh." She turned. "He's just in one of his bad moods."

"You said we're going out. Are we?"

"In a few minutes." Think, she had to think. What was she going to do? Where could they go? This was really happening. One little mistake and now it was a disaster. They'd have to leave here, but where was there to go?

Shuffling through her thoughts, she began automatically picking the clothes up off the floor and putting them down on the bed. If they were leaving and he wouldn't let her take the car, they'd have to walk. How the hell were they going to walk and to where? If he really did mean it and they'd actually have to *walk*, then there was very little they could take with them. Because Bobby couldn't get all that far and she'd have to carry him. If she had to do that, she wouldn't be able to carry a suitcase, too.

Suddenly, anger shot through her and she straightened, saying aloud, "To hell with it! Burn it all! I don't care." She could get more things, other places. Going over to pick up her handbag, she opened her underwear drawer for the nest egg she kept hidden there. She felt around, pushing bras and slips and panties out of the way. It wasn't there. Gone. He'd found her money and taken it. More frightened now, she opened the drawer on the other side, relieved to see her jewelry box still in place. But she lifted the lid to find it empty except for her old rings, the ones from Press, and the watch Jess had given her at graduation. Tossing the rings and watch into her handbag, she opened her wallet. Thirteen dollars and some change. She caught her lower lip between her teeth, fully frightened now. He was throwing them out with no money, no car, and just their clothes. Bobby's piggy bank. Clutching her handbag, she ran down to Bobby's room, heading straight for the fat pig on the toy shelf. She was almost sick with relief to find it still heavy. She ran into the bathroom, locked the door and then, on her hands and knees, emptied the contents of the pig onto the bath mat. She counted quickly, her lips moving. Stacks of quarters, dimes, nickels, two singles and a five. Eleven dollars and eighty-eight cents. She scooped up the money and dumped it into her bag.

Her momentum lost, she continued to sit on the floor, trying to think where they could go. Nowhere near here. All the people she knew were his friends. Canada? Back to Canada. Jess. Jess wouldn't turn her away, would she? But twenty-five dollars wouldn't get them to Tampa, let alone Toronto.

She unfolded her legs and sat with her back against the tub, thinking it through. She lit a cigarette, then flicked the match into the toilet. February and it was warm here. But it'd be cold once they got up into Georgia. So that meant she'd have to bring warm clothes and coats. They were going to have to hitchhike north. *I'm so scared. How can this be happening?* How could he do this, all because of one silly mistake? Never mind that! He was doing it. *Think!* All right, all right. They'd hitchhike. Jesus! She'd need their papers, the passports and Bobby's birth certificate. Where were they? Okay, right, she remembered. And one small suitcase. All her things . . . she'd have to leave them. She was scared, but there was nothing else to do. First, she'd get the papers. What else? Think! She should've insisted on her own bank account, or saved some of her money. But she'd been so sure once Bobby was born, he'd marry her. And then she'd have all the money she needed. Why had she thought she wanted to marry him? He was right: she'd hated having him heavy on top of her, pushing into her. She'd hated it with him even more than she had with the others.

What was he doing? She sat away from the tub hearing noises. She stood up, fear making the hair on her arms stand on end. He really was going crazy and if she didn't get herself and Bobby out of there, he might kill them both. He'd certainly looked mad enough to kill, the way he'd thrown his fists into the air when he'd started going on about his "best friend Lew." She darted into Bobby's room and quietly closed the door while she got out his parka, a pair of corduroy trousers, underwear, a shirt and sweater, a pair of sturdy lace-ups and woollen socks. And a hat! Where was the one with the pompom? She found it, looked around the room to see what else there was, then grabbed his favorite teddy bear from the bed.

Back in her bedroom, she pulled a small canvas bag from the back of the closet and pushed in Bobby's clothes, a pair of wool slacks she hoped still fit her—why the hell had she let herself gain so much weight?—a Shetland sweater, a change of underwear, an old plaid shirt, her pea jacket, loafers, and a pair of warm socks. She tested the weight of the bag. Doubtful. It weighed a ton, she thought, reopening the bag, thinking to dispense with the change of underwear, the Shetland and the plaid shirt. But wait! *You're not thinking!* Once they got out of Florida it'd be cold. They'd have to wear all these things and then the bag would be empty. So, she'd leave everything as it was and take along another change of clothes for each of them as well.

When she'd finished the bag was heavy. But she'd manage, she told herself, picking up her handbag and the canvas suitcase. She still wanted to believe he'd get past his temper, pout for a while and then tell her to forget it. But seeing little Bobby sitting on the edge of a chair in the living room watching transfixed as his father attacked his mother's paintings convinced her. Big Bobby seemed deranged in the way he was trying, with his hands, to tear the paintings apart. And she knew there wasn't going to be any changing of his mind. Her hand on Bobby's arm got his attention. She crooked her fingers at him, then held a finger to her lips and he smiled, a willing accomplice, and tiptoed along beside her to the door.

"Where we going, Mom?" he asked, loping along beside her down the driveway.

"It's a surprise," she said, wanting to scream with fear.

"How come you got that suitcase?" he asked, enjoying the mystery of this game.

"We're going for a trip," she said, forcing a smile for him. It's real, it's real, she reminded herself. At the end of the driveway she switched the suitcase to her left hand in order to take hold of Bobby's hand.

"You stay close to me now," she cautioned. "You know how fast the cars come along here."

"But where're we *going*?"

"Canada," she said, then felt a shock wave of memory, for the first time in years recalling how she and Jess had run away from the house in Vermont. "We're going to see my sister, your aunt Jess."

"Oh! The one you told me about?"

"That's right. Jess. I only have one sister, remember?"

"Oh, yeah." He gave her a sunny smile.

What if she was gone, if they'd moved away? Or she might have died. Anything could have happened. Why hadn't she stayed in touch? Please be there. I've got nowhere else to go. You've *got* to be there!

Why are we walking? she wondered all at once, becoming aware of cars passing. They were only a few miles from the main highway. She'd have to put her thumb out, but she was terrified. Anybody could be in one of those cars, any kind of crazy . . .

"I'm going to try to get us a ride," she said, thinking if they could get to the interstate, they'd be able to hitch their way right up I-95.

Giggling, he watched her stop and turn, holding out her thumb.

She felt like a fool, a fat stupid fool, and was angry with the people in the cars that kept right on going and wouldn't stop. Couldn't they see she had a child with her? Couldn't they see she wasn't a thief or a murderer, that they didn't have to be afraid to stop for her? She was furious with them for not stopping, for not knowing she wasn't dangerous. A white, late model Chevy pulled over ahead of them, throwing up the gravel, its right indicator light flashing. Her outrage evaporating, she said, "Come on, Bobby!" grabbed his hand and ran

with him, the suitcase making her run awkwardly, heavily to
one side. They hurried toward the car and Tillie bent, with her
hand on the car door, to see a woman. Sighing with relief, she
smiled as she got the door open, and the woman smiled back,
asking, "How far you-all goin'?"

"How far are *you* going?"

"I'm headin' right the way on up to Jacksonville to see my
mama," the woman, a bleached blonde about Tillie's age said,
keeping her smile. "That far enough for you?" She pulled the
front seat forward so Bobby could climb into the back. Tillie
deposited the suitcase on the seat beside him, then got into the
front and closed the door, and they were off.

The woman's attention remained on the traffic until she'd
steered the car back into the flow, heading toward the entrance
to I-95, then she again smiled over at Tillie, asking, "Where-
all you comin' from?"

"Just back there."

"First ride, huh?"

"That's right. Thank you for stopping."

"Oh, that's okay. You were a fella, I wouldn't of stopped.
But I don't see no harm to a woman with a little boy. Darlin'
little boy, too."

"Thank you."

"So, where-all you headed to?"

"Canada."

She laughed. "You-all plannin' on hikin' yourselves right
the way to *Canada*?"

"That's right."

"Gonna take you *days,* honey."

Tillie went silent, trying to estimate how long it might
actually take, guessing it was about two thousand miles, or
maybe only fifteen hundred.

"If we pick up another ride in Jacksonville, it might not
take so long."

"Be close on midnight, time we hit Jacksonville. Not much
traffic heading north that time of night."

"Maybe not."

"Best thing for you-all to do's stop the night over to Jacksonville, get out on the road real early in the mornin' and start
again. Lotta trucks out early. You'll probably get a ride right
away."

"I think," she said, considering the meager amount of money

in her bag, "we'll try our luck, see if we can't keep going."

"Hard on the boy, that," the woman said softly. Then she asked, "Where to in Canada anyhow?"

"Toronto."

The woman whistled between her teeth. "Say, now, that's close on two thousand miles. I know it cause this one time I drove on up to Buffalo, you know? Had me this boyfriend up there? Drove it all in one go and nearly killed myself, truth to tell. I was so tuckered by the time I got there we just had us a big ole fight, then I slept some, got back in the car, turned round and come on home again. Last I saw of *him* and that's a fact. Didn't even 'preciate my drivin' all that way."

"That's too bad," Tillie sympathized. Two thousand miles. How was Bobby going to keep going for all those miles? How was she? *Why* was this happening? She swiveled around to see Bobby kneeling on the seat, his hands flat against the side window, watching the cars go by. She turned front again and opened her bag for a cigarette, removing the pack to offer one to the woman. "Cigarette?"

"Oh, no thanks. You mind not smokin'? Afraid I don't much like it."

"No. All right. Of course." She put back the cigarettes, laid the bag down flat on her lap and held her hands tightly together over the top of it.

"You-all from Canada?" the woman asked after a time.

"I'm a Canadian, but I was born in New York."

"I thought you-all had kind of an accent."

An accent? *She* had one of those stupid swamp-water drawls.

Another gap. Then the woman asked, "How old's your boy? He sure is nice 'n' quiet."

"He's five. He likes cars." Fall asleep again, Tillie thought, willing him to. If he slept for a couple of hours, he'd be less cranky once they got to Jacksonville and had to stand by the roadside trying for another ride.

"I always wanted me a baby," the woman said, a little sadly. "Had me two husbands and it wasn't 'til a long time after I was done with the second one that I found out I couldn't have babies." She shook her head. "Put me in the dumps for one real long time, that did. All the time thinkin' to blame them, the husbands, you know? And it was me. I was the one. Made me feel just terrible for thinkin' what I had. And terrible for me, too. You know?"

"That's really too bad," Tillie said sincerely. "Bobby is my second son. My first boy . . . he died."

"Oh, honey!" The woman turned to look at her with a grieved expression. "I'm *real* sorry to hear that. I think it must be the saddest, sorriest thing in the whole world to lose a child."

"I've got Bobby." Discovering a new source of sympathy inside her, she said, "I think it must be an awful feeling to find out you can't have children."

"Threw me off real hard."

They fell into a not unpleasant silence that lasted until they stopped for gas. Tillie realized the woman expected her to offer to contribute and didn't know how to explain, without feeling more of a fool, that she didn't have the money to spare. She said, "I'll just take Bobby to the john. We'll be right back."

The entire time she was in the ladies' room, with Bobby picking this, of all times, to have a long, red-faced, groaning bowel movement, she was positive that when they came out the woman would be gone, and she was so anxious to get back she practically screamed at Bobby to hurry.

"Gotta push hard." He gave her a sweet smile. "Almost done."

She rushed him out—he was still trying to do up his fly— to see the car was there and the woman was waiting.

"I'm sorry we took so long." Tillie apologized, lifting Bobby into the rear.

"Oh, that's okay. Bet you thought I was gonna go drivin' off with your suitcase 'n' all, didn't you?" She grinned.

"Oh, no. I just hated to keep you waiting so long." Tillie looked back to see Bobby had the suitcase open and was dragging out his teddy bear. A good sign. It meant he'd curl up on the seat with teddy for a pillow and go to sleep.

"When we gonna eat, Mom?" he asked, leaning across to pat her on the shoulder.

"We're gonna stop real soon now," the woman said, reaching with her right hand to touch his face. "You sure are one sweet-faced child. Sweet-natured, too. There's a drive-in place just off the next exit, about fifteen miles on."

Tillie finally took a good look at this woman. She had

elaborately coiffed, almost white-blond hair, with a pretty face but so much makeup she looked doll-like. She was slim with very uplifted breasts poking pointedly against a cotton-knit pullover, and pedal pushers. She looked like a cocktail waitress, or a hooker. If she washed off all that makeup, combed out her hair and put on some decent clothes, she'd be beautiful, Tillie thought.

"Do you work?" she asked, curious.

"Me?" The woman grinned again, showing twin rows of dainty white teeth. "Sure do, honey. Bet you'll never guess what I do."

"Secretary?" Tillie suggested dishonestly.

"Nope!" She looked very pleased. "Nobody *ever* guesses."

"What do you do?"

"Hairdresser. Got me a nice shop in Hollywood and three operators. Got a manicurist too, and a woman comes three times a week to give massage to the regulars."

"Isn't that interesting," Tillie said politely, for some reason terribly touched by this woman, finding her cheery disposition and pride in her shop almost lovable.

"What-all d'you do?" she asked Tillie.

"I'm an artist. Was," she amended.

"Really? What kinda artist?"

"Well, actually, I taught for a time. And I did some graphics work, and some oils. I haven't worked at it for the last three years. But I'm going to get back to it now." Remembering all her supplies in the spare room, she felt a bit sick at the loss. She should've kept working. She might have had enough paintings for a show. A show! Who was she kidding? "I wasn't bad," she said. "A good craftsman, but not really a creative artist. I've never admitted that to anyone before," she said, looking a little confounded.

"Funny thing about bein' with strangers," the woman said. "It makes you kinda free to talk about things you wouldn't want to talk about with people you know real well. Safe, kind of, I s'pose."

"You're probably right. I've never really thought about it."

"Say, my name's Alma, by the way. What's yours?"

"Tillie. And that's Bobby."

"Tillie. Ain't that a for-sure cute name? What's it short for anyhow?"

"Matilda."

"Matilda," Alma repeated. "Don't know's I care for that. I like Tillie way better."

"So do I," Tillie said.

"Say, listen, if you go on and open up that little draft winda there, I don't guess your smokin' would bother me all that much, and I can tell how you'd really like one. Go on."

"You're sure?"

"Sure. Go on."

"Thank you, Alma."

"Think nothin' of it."

How kind you are! Tillie thought, gratefully lighting a cigarette. If she'd been someone Tillie had never spoken with or listened to or spent time with, she'd never have suspected this woman capable of such kindness and sensitivity.

After they'd stopped for hamburgers, for which Tillie felt obliged to pay, Alma responded with increased friendliness as they drove on. Tillie felt more and more predisposed toward this fragile, overpainted, yet appealingly open woman, so that later, when Alma pulled over, saying, "I gotta let you out here, hon. I turn off just ahead there," Tillie felt uprooted and shaken as she got Bobby and the suitcase out of the car. Before closing the door she said, "Thank you for everything, Alma. I hope you have a good time visiting your mother."

"I hope you get another ride right soon. Good luck. And good-bye, honey!" she called out to Bobby.

"Luck to you, too," Tillie said, her throat lumping. "Take care of yourself." She closed the door and the white Chevy drove off.

"What're we doing?" Bobby complained, rubbing his fists into his eyes. "I'm *tired!*"

"I'm going to try to get us another ride," she said, looking toward the approaching traffic. As Alma had predicted, there wasn't much moving on the road.

"How come we couldn't stay with that lady?" he demanded crossly.

She laid the suitcase down flat on the shoulder saying, "Sit here while I try to get somebody to stop." Disgruntled, Bobby sat, elbows on his knees, fists jammed against his cheeks, stating, "I wanna go *home!*"

"That's where we're going."

"I mean *home!*"

She squatted beside him saying, "Bobby, we're not going

to be going back there, honey. We're going to live in Canada from now on."

"But what about my *daddy*?" he asked, ready to cry.

"You'll be seeing him again soon. You just sit now." She got up and moved to the side of the road, watching the pairs of lights advancing, holding out her thumb.

When the truck slowed, she felt unreasonably frightened. An enormous tractor-trailer, the cab seemed miles off the ground. The passenger door swung open and the driver leaned across the seat to say, "Come *on*, if you're coming! I haven't got all night!"

She got Bobby up into the cab, pushed the suitcase onto the seat, then climbed in herself. "Thanks for stopping for us," she said, feeling something like despair at the sudden fear she might have to pay full fare for this ride.

◇ Thirty-One ◇

"How come Orphan Nannie doesn't have any eyes?"

"Annie. And she's got eyes, darling. She doesn't have any pupils."

"What're those?"

"The black circles in the middle of your eyes."

"If she doesn't have those pupil things, how can she see?"

"She's not real, Belinda. She's a cartoon, she's pretend. She doesn't have to see."

"Even in cartoons, people have to see."

Jess gave up. Todd and Belinda could too often defeat her with their stubborn logic, their ability to ask never-ending questions. To their minds, everything had to happen for a reason. Every question had an answer. And they pursued their questions doggedly, coming back repeatedly until they got some sort of satisfactory answer.

"Maybe," Belinda said thoughtfully, "she's got X-ray vision, like Superman."

"Maybe." Jess hugged and kissed her a final time, put on the night-light and went downstairs.

The boys were in the den watching television. She walked in and went over to turn down the sound. Todd moaned loudly, protesting, "*Mom*! We're *listening* to that!"

"Neither of you is deaf," she said calmly.

"I *told* you it was too loud," Justin said to Todd.

"Don't pick on him that way, Justin," she said for what felt at least the millionth time."And Todd, there's no need to have it so loud everyone all over the house can hear it. I want you both upstairs by nine-thirty. All right? You can say hello to Aunt Flora and Aunt Nelda, then I want you both upstairs, washed and into bed. No reading, Todd. And Justin, no fooling around with the trains. Straight to bed, both of you."

"Why're they coming over? Are you starting your meetings again?" Justin asked. Todd's attention had already returned to Uncle Miltie.

"We have some things to discuss and no, we're not starting the meetings again. All right?"

"All right."

Remembering his promise, Todd dragged his eyes away from the screen and the dancing Texaco men to say, "Mom? Belinda really hates Robert driving her to school every day."

"I know all about it," she said tiredly.

"Well, she really does," Todd said. "We all do. It's so dumb!"

Justin, knowing why their mother had always insisted on Robert's driving them to school, said in exasperated tones, "Todd, you *know* she's explained it a trillion times. I told you not to say anything."

"I promised Linnie I would, so I did." He looked up at Jess hoping for approval.

"All right, you've told me. Next time, please don't make promises like that to her. And Justin, *please* stop jumping on the others because you understand something and they don't."

Looking sheepish, he said, "Okay," his voice breaking with a croak midword.

She stepped over Todd to sit down for a moment beside Justin and kissed him. He turned scarlet, but he kissed her back. Then stepping again over Todd, she said, "I'm not coming down there. Give me a kiss."

He rolled over and grinned at her—Sandy's face shining out at her from behind the eleven-year-old's features—sat up, flung his arms around her shoulders, and gave her a resounding smack on the cheek. She laughed and gave him a slight shove that sent him back to the floor.

"Remember," she told them from the doorway. "Nine-thirty."

They murmured assent and she continued on her way to the living room. Her thinking triggered by Justin's asking if the meetings were going to start again, she remembered how it had all come together for her. Now it was five years later and this would be the last of the meetings because they were going to talk about getting someone to replace Flora.

"At sixty-two, I want to sit around in my nightgown half the day if I feel like it," Flora had said that morning as a preface to announcing her intention to quit. "Or ride the subway all afternoon taking pictures. What I don't feel like doing is dragging my ass downtown to the office. I'll still lend a hand, but I just don't want to do it full time anymore, Jess."

She sat down to await Nelda and Flora's arrival, picking up a copy of Robertson Davies' new book, *A Mixture of Frailties*, then put it down again, unable to concentrate on reading.

She'd been going along feeling she'd made significant gains. She knew how the company was run and the dimensions of her job; she now actually had some expertise in the business. Yet it seemed that every time she got to the point where she felt she might finally settle into her life and its routines, something happened.

Having become accustomed to her career, and to having René as a more or less permanent fixture in her life, and to dealing reasonably with the children, she'd relaxed and started enjoying her independence and accomplishments. Flora's leaving upended all that. She couldn't imagine finding someone new who'd be as good. There was only one Flora, and replacing her was going to be anything but easy.

Between interviews for replacements for Flora, she worried about Belinda, picturing her walking along the street to school, a car pulling alongside, Belinda climbing in to be taken somewhere and raped or murdered. It made her unreasonably panic-stricken and she had to light a cigarette, swivel in her chair to look out the window, and talk herself down. Yet she couldn't shake the fear and was reluctant to give the children permission to walk to school. She wondered if her nervousness wasn't a part of, or due to, the daily growing feeling she had that she was somehow becoming too big for her skin. She might one day erupt through her flesh like a human volcano, she thought wryly. But whatever her personal feelings, she was going to have to get hold of herself because she seemed to be transmitting all she felt to the children. Nightly there was some sort of scene, the children fighting among themselves with what seemed genuine rage.

But Press, over lunch together, said, "Kids're all the same, Jess. We're having the same problems with the girls. You're taking it too much to heart."

"Be truthful with me," she said. "Am I doing a worthwhile job or are you all just being kind and indulging me?"

"Kind?" He looked surprised. "This is a *business* we're running, Jess, not a baby-sitting service. Believe me, if you weren't handling your end of things, you'd know soon enough. You're doing a marvelous job. Those meetings you chaired with the store managers were a big hit. You had your information down pat and you spoke with authority. Why the hell would you think we were just mollycoddling you?"

"I'd hate it if you were."

"Well, we're not, so you can forget it. I'll admit at the beginning I was a little uneasy, but you've worked like a dog, putting in all kinds of time and effort. I think you're letting Flora's leaving get you down."

"I admit that. I've interviewed a nonstop stream of ninnies for the past week. And when I'm not doing that, I'm home with *them* screaming at each other. Last Friday night the three of them had a knockdown fight in the den over who was going to watch what on TV. It's as if they hate each other."

"They probably do." He smiled. "But only sometimes. Kids fight, Jess. They just do. They'll outgrow it."

"Not before they've driven me crazy." She gave him a small smile.

"Are you and René going to get married?" he asked. "Or am I out of line?"

"Oh, I don't know," she sighed, glancing at her watch. She was already ten minutes late for a meeting. "It just seems like another complication I'm not ready for. There are times when I think I'd like nothing more than to stay home and take it easy. But I don't think I'd enjoy it for longer than a week. Right now, though, I think you're right. I hadn't expected Flora to want to go."

"Does that mean you don't intend to marry again?"

"If I do," she said carefully, "it'll be because things are finally settled and I've done everything I want to do and feel like taking it easy, having someone around to relax with me. I feel good about standing on my own, Press. I don't know if I *need* a husband, if I want one, or even if I care enough about René to want him that way."

"But doesn't it frighten you to think of yourself in ten years' time with the kids grown and gone, finding yourself alone?"

"It frightens me. But in ten years it might not. I can't possibly know how I'm going to feel then. I'm working on now. And right now, despite all the problems, I feel most of the time as if I'm doing a good job."

"You are," he concurred. "No question."

"But you think I ought to get married and retire."

"I didn't say that, Jess. And I don't think it. I'm just not used to dealing with . . . female executives, I guess."

Feeling all at once more determined than ever, she said, "I think you're going to have to get used to it. Because I have no intention of quitting."

"Jesus! I wasn't suggesting you should."

"Good! I may decide to die as chairman of the board."

He laughed, then looked away as she signed for the meal. She couldn't help noticing his sudden discomfort. "Don't let it bother you, Press," she said with a smile, collecting her bag and cigarettes. "It all goes on the expense account."

As they were walking back to the office, he said, "I don't want you to think I was trying to raise objections to female executives, Jess. It just takes a little getting used to."

"I'm sure it does," she said. "It takes just as much for me, you know. It wasn't exactly what I had planned."

"No, I know. The thing to do is keep your eye on where you want to get to, not on the obstacles."

"Is that what you do?" she asked.

"It's what every man I know does."

"I'll remember that."

"You'll make it," he said, as they stepped out of the elevator. "You're making it now."

She'd only been in her office for an hour, but she felt like putting on her coat and going home; instead she got on the intercom to ask Sally, "Who's next?"

"I'll be right in."

Jess lit a cigarette, feeling beleaguered now by this search for a replacement. Flora had agreed to continue on until one was found and even to help her get started. As before, she'd photograph the layouts, but the rest of the advertising work—the liaison wrangling, the copy, the media-spot placements—would be done by the new person. Yet no one suitable had shown up to be interviewed. Perhaps, she thought, she was looking for the impossible.

"Mrs. Woodrich?"

Jess turned. Even Sally was beginning to look a little frazzled after almost three weeks of day-long interviewing. Jess smiled, and Sally returned it. Jess was the first woman Sally had ever worked for and, while she'd been nervous and rattled initially, she now doubted she'd ever again be able to work for a man. She enjoyed never having to explain the obvious—why, for instance, a couple of days a month she went around pale and feeling frayed—and the challenge of keeping up with Jess, reminding her of her appointments both for the office and the children, taking her brisk dictation, bartending for the late meetings, and providing coffee and rolls for the early morning ones. At twenty-seven, she considered herself a pretty energetic person, but she could barely keep up with Jess and was constantly amazed by her employer's drive and energy. Puzzled by it, too. It seemed as if Jess had to keep moving fast because if she stopped even for a moment she might never regain her momentum.

"There's a last one waiting," Sally told her.

"How does she strike you?"

"No good. Ten minutes tops."

"God! Another one. What's happened to all the competent, imaginative people?"

"You'll find someone. It just takes time."

"Do you know how many women I interviewed before I hired you? Twenty-three. What's the *matter* with women? Don't they want a chance to test themselves?"

"Did you?" Sally asked without thinking.

Jess stubbed out her cigarette. "No. I didn't have any choice in the matter. What's after this one?"

"You've got a meeting with Hughes in twenty minutes. Then lunch with Mrs. Ames and that woman from the Crest who's after some advertising. Two o'clock with the accountants, and you've got to meet Belinda at Dr. Aaronson's office at four-thirty for her checkup. Also, you asked me to remind you Mr. Thibeault's arriving at Malton at seven-thirty. Oh, and you said you'd call back the St. John's contractor about the completion date. Here's the page." She placed a typed schedule on the blotter. "Coffee?"

Staring at the page, Jess said, "I don't think so, thank you." She sighed again. "All right. Let's see this last one."

"Are you okay?"

"Do you have brothers or sisters, Sally?"

"A younger sister," she answered, taken off guard.

"How old?"

"Twenty-four."

"Are you close? Do you see each other often?"

"Pretty often. Every time she has a fight with my mother, she comes running down to my place to spend the night."

"What's her name?"

"Rachel." She was trying to decipher Jess's strange expression and the reason behind this atypical line of questioning.

"I have a sister," Jess said, lighting another cigarette. "I haven't seen her in almost twelve years."

It was making Sally feel uncomfortable. In the three years she'd worked for her, Jess had volunteered nothing about herself. She'd been friendly, but distant and a little cool. Now Sally knew she was being told something important and it made her feel privileged, but flustered too, as if her status were about to change. "You must miss her. Were you close?"

"All these years," Jess went on as if she hadn't heard, "and I still worry about her. She might be dead, for all I know." Her words fell into a moment of cold silence during which she looked at her hands, then took a puff on her cigarette and said, "I've changed my mind. I would like some coffee. And please send in this girl. What's her name again?"

"Klein." Holding her steno pad to her chest, Sally moved toward the door. The atmosphere was strange altogether today. She had a peculiar desire to go around behind the desk and put her arms around Jess, comfort her somehow. And that was peculiar because, in the past, she'd always felt Jess was so enigmatic and unapproachable that Sally often wondered how she behaved away from the office. She wished she knew more about the person inside the beautiful clothes, behind the dark, haunted eyes.

Sally was right about Miss Klein, Jess thought, and kept

the interview on a purely perfunctory level. After the woman had gone, Jess lit another cigarette, telling herself she was smoking and drinking too much and eating too little. But, thank God, René was coming tonight. They'd have dinner, talk, make love, and she'd feel restored, able to go on for another month or so until he returned and infused her again with energy and optimism. She wondered how he could go on wanting her. She was almost forty-one. Her breasts sagged, the flesh of her belly had gone puckery, and her hair was as much gray as black. At that moment, she felt ninety. And she thought that Flora, at sixty-two, looked younger and more alive than she did.

Her thoughts coming back to René, she felt it wasn't enough seeing him seven or eight times a year, for a night or two. Not nearly enough. Trying to make up for weeks in a night. It was as if she had a sexual tapeworm. She couldn't seem to get enough of him, and when they were apart, all she thought of was René, looking forward to being held and making love.

The intercom buzzed. She stared at the lit-up call light for a few seconds, then extended her hand to pick up the receiver.

"Mr. Hughes is here."

"Give me a few minutes, Sally, then send him in. Ask if he'd like coffee or a drink. He'll probably take a drink."

"Okay."

She hung up, gazing at her hand curved over the receiver. It looked like the hand of an old woman: white and bony, with prominent veins. She pulled back her hand, retrieved the cigarette from the ashtray, and pushed her chair away from the desk to look down at the street.

Rather than diminishing with time, that feeling of growing too swollen to be accommodated by her flesh was getting stronger. And she felt so tired. A career woman, a mother with three children, she got up at six-thirty every morning to have breakfast with them before they left for school. She drank her coffee while waiting for Robert to come back and bring her downtown.

There'd been late-night meetings, and trips to openings. They'd opened nine new stores in the last five years and she'd gone along to cut ribbons and pretend to lay cornerstones and to try not to grimace when the mandatory photographs were taken of these ceremonies. She'd gone, not letting it show that she'd minded the distances or the traveling, to smile and make inane presentation speeches. She felt tired.

And where was Tillie? Was she happy? Jess wondered, having never accepted Flora's diagnosis, or even Sandy's, unable to believe her sister was an incurable opportunist. There was good in Tillie, she believed, and wished she'd telephone, or send a card, something. How could she just stay away for almost twelve years?

She looked at her watch. Time for Hughes and a meeting about the Scarborough stores to get through, before lunch with Nelda.

She waited by the arrivals gate, a tall, strikingly handsome woman in a dark full-length mink coat, her hair coiled into a thick knot at the nape of her neck. Every time René saw her, she made an electric impression upon him. Standing waiting, she was unaware he'd seen her, her long-fingered hand with a cigarette moving to her lips, her eyes caught in the distances of some inner landscape. The open coat was draped over her shoulders revealing a black suit and a white silk shirt with a string of pearls looped low over the neckline. Black suede high heels added to her height. Slim calves, narrow ankles, a faint shimmer of ash-colored stockings. He let the crowd hurry on ahead in order to take a few more moments to study her.

He'd taken years of English lessons in order to be able to talk to her without sounding, as Marie-Claire had said, like a peasant. He'd acquired a taste for expensive, hand-tailored suits and English custom-made shirts, a fondness for the things he believed she liked, remodeling his externals to better fit what he thought were her expectations. And he'd arrived, finally, transformed into a successful man, with some small measure of distinction, he hoped, to complement what she had innately. He stood to one side of the crowd trying to absorb the impact the mere sight of her made on him.

How was it possible, he wondered, that someone like him had, for years now, been the beneficiary of her passion? Their continuing intimacy seemed something of a miracle. He could never just hurry forward expecting everything; rather, he expected very little, and so, each time he saw her, he was filled with a spiraling sense of reward. He watched her walk over now to extinguish her cigarette in one of the sand-filled receptacles, then lift her cuff to look at her watch, her expression clouding as the last of the passengers passed through the gate.

She thinks I'm not here, he realized, and made himself move, his eyes ready for the brightening of her features and her sudden smile.

"I was starting to think you'd missed the flight." She offered herself into his embrace and lifted her mouth to be kissed. He kissed her, then kissed her again, gratified by the slight change in her eyes at this message.

"There's nothing wrong, is there?" she asked.

"I'm just happy to see you, always happy to see you."

"Oh! I thought perhaps . . . As long as there's nothing wrong."

His arm around her shoulders, small suitcase in hand—he never bothered to check his bag, hating to waste the time waiting for it to be off-loaded when he could be better spending his time with her—they moved toward the exit and out to the car where Robert was waiting. Once in the car, he relaxed, urging her over close to him.

"I wish you could drive," he said, his arm firmly around her. "Then," he lowered his voice, "I could say hello the way I'd like to."

Taking hold of his hand, she asked, "How would you like to say hello?"

He laughed, closing the partition between them and Robert. Holding her, he whispered, "We'd get in the car, drive to the service road over there, and make love."

She laughed, nevertheless enflamed by the idea.

"I was outside watching you"—he put his hand to her face, his thumb grazing her lips—"thinking I'm lucky."

"We have a nine-o'clock reservation at Le Provençal."

"I don't want food," he whispered, his hand leaving her face and slipping down over her breast, safely hidden by her coat. "I want to take your clothes off and kiss you all over."

Forgetting Robert, she was captivated by this declaration and sat with her lips parted, feeling him making her real again and female. Immediately female, wet. Her breath stopped in her throat at the softness of his lips against hers and his hand pressing into her breast.

"I'm hungry, René." Her voice came out husky, her senses pleasurably honed so that she really was hungry. The only times she ate with appetite were when he was with her.

"Me, too." He smiled, his fingers stroking the nape of her neck. "I've decided to move here, make company headquarters here so I can be closer to you. No more of this every six weeks, every two months. I want you every week, *every* night. Marry me."

"I can't." Cooling, she sat away from him. "I'll gladly see you. Not every night. But every week, yes. I'd love that. I always feel so much better when I see you. You're not really moving headquarters here because of me, are you?"

"Only some. We'll keep the big office in Trois Rivières. But I see things now I didn't see before. Maybe because I used to be one way and now I'm not that way anymore. All the English lessons," he smiled. "Other lessons too, learning the differences between what I always knew and what I know now. Too many tempers, too much anger in Quebec. Maybe it was always there, but now I feel it, now I see it. And maybe I'm too old for the fighting. I want to be away from that. Here, I'm respected and left alone, not bothered by priests coming to the house or the office wanting to know why I don't come to church anymore, wanting money. Here, when I get to the end of the day, there's no more business, no one phoning up wanting something for the church or for themselves. I'm tired of all that. And I want to be with you."

"Did you rent a car?"

"I did." He grinned. "It'll be at the hotel. What are you thinking?" he asked teasingly, seeing the color rising in her cheeks.

Her hand moved, coming lightly to rest on his lap. The gesture galvanized him. He wrapped her in his arms and kissed her searchingly, aware of her heat and the renewed essence of her perfume.

He released her and she withdrew her hand, letting her head fall back against the seat. She'd have a night of not feeling stretched beyond her capacities, beyond her skin, a night of feeling wanted and needed and well attended to. Then, she'd get up from his hotel bed at three or four in the morning to dress and have him drive her home, where she'd creep into the sleeping house to climb the stairs with shaky legs, her body feeling strained and raw, and bathe before falling into bed to sleep a glutted sleep before, too soon, she'd have to get up again to dress for the office.

"I'm glad you've decided to move," she said. "Very glad."

Before they got out of the limousine, he watched, charmed, as she ran her hand lightly over the back of her hair, then looked down at herself as if to ascertain his hands had left no sign of their slow passage over her.

Throughout the evening, even when she was absolutely still, she seemed to be vibrating. And later, in his room, when he began to undress her, he couldn't help noticing that something about her had undergone a subtle change. Her eyes remained fixed on him and her body seemed barely able to contain the extravagant energy emanating through her skin. Although she remained unmoving as he took off her clothes, she exuded an impatience bordering on anxiety, very like an untamed animal waiting to be released, holding back with barely controlled impulses until completely certain of its freedom. She remained in that state until he took her in his arms. And then she seemed to burst into action, winding her arms around his neck and giving him a deeply urgent kiss while her open eyes gazed unblinking and unfocused into his.

He'd come to know her and the ways in which she liked to be loved, but now he was confused by an entirely new dimension and appetite she was showing him. She was so avid that she was unfamiliar. She couldn't seem to restrain whatever it was that had her visibly quivering, and so energized she couldn't remain still.

"Jess . . . ?" She turned to look at him, her eyes fixed and glossy. "What's the matter?" he asked, noticing, too, that her flesh was very hot and even had a faintly singed scent to it.

"Nothing's the matter!" she said breathlessly, aware of him not as René but as something she had to have at that moment. She didn't feel like herself, wasn't even capable of real thought as she wound herself around him tighter and tighter, a human rope binding him to her.

After a time, resting, he again studied her as she lay gazing sightlessly at the ceiling, lazily smoking, her hair a long thick tangle, her body slickly gleaming from their strenuous efforts, her upper thighs glistening and a deep flush across her throat and breasts. He curved his hand under her breast, relishing the soft weight of her flesh. His skin looked very dark in contrast to her blue-veined whiteness. Her head turned and she stared at him.

"I love you, Jess," he said, feeling her anxiety. "I don't think you know how much I love you."

Her features relaxed and she was herself again and aware

of him. "Oh, René, I *do* know. And I love you as much as I could possibly love anyone."

"Then why won't you marry me?" To his distress, she crushed out the cigarette, covered her eyes with her hand and began to sob, her body heaving. "Hey!" he exclaimed, leaning over her. "Hey! I don't like to see you cry. Don't. What's the *matter*, Jess?"

"I don't know." She kept her eyes covered with her hand. "I don't know!"

"Sure you know." His hand closed over her hip. "You still feel guilty. " She shook her head. "What then?"

"I honestly don't know." She wiped her eyes with the back of her hand.

"Talk with me," he asked.

"I'm *tired*, René."

Looking at her, all at once he thought she did look terribly tired. Her eyes were slightly sunken and there were small lines about her eyes and mouth he hadn't noticed before. And she was thinner than he'd ever known her to be, her hipbones juttingly prominent. He gathered her into his arms saying, "Tonight, you stay. I won't let you wake me up at three in the morning to drive you home."

"I can't do that," she argued.

"You *can* do that. Telephone right now and tell Polly you won't be home. You'll go in the morning so you can be there for the children."

In the past she'd fought him on this issue. But now she sighed shudderingly, wanting to stay, and said, "All right. Yes, all right," and rolled away from him to use the telephone on the bedside table. She didn't care what Polly thought of it, or about anything except being able to sleep for an entire night feeling secure and needed. The call made, she turned back to him. "You won't forget to wake me?"

"I won't forget. Go to sleep." Fitting her body to his, he said, "I'll wake you."

"Perhaps Press and I should review the Quebec stores. If there are problems, we might be wise ..."

"Thinking in the morning," he interrupted her. "Sleeping now."

She smiled, then closed her eyes, and he held her feeling extraordinarily high. She'd just given him something of im-

mense value, entrusting herself to him for the length of an
entire night.

"How far're you going?" the trucker asked her. The sewing
on his lapel read "Joe." He looked hard and sounded hard; his
face was comprised of unrelentingly hard lines and angles.
Even his mouth looked hard.

"We're going to Canada. Toronto."

"I can take you as far as Savannah. Kid looks sleepy," he
observed. "Why don't you put him back there"—he indicated
the deep ledge at the rear of the cab—"and let him sleep?"

"Bobby, would you like to try to sleep?" Dopey with fatigue, the boy nodded and, clutching his teddy bear, climbed
to the rear of the cab and stretched out. He was asleep in
seconds. The cab interior was warm and she felt herself becoming drowsy.

"Why don't you knock off yourself?" he said, looking over.
"Might as well."

"That's all right," she said, reluctant to relax that far in this
man's company. "Do you think we'll have any trouble picking
up another ride in Savannah?"

"Depends," he said, reaching for a pack of Luckies in his
shirt pocket and offering her one.

"No, thank you. They're too strong for me. I've got my
own."

He lit his cigarette, then said, "There's a truck stop just
outside Savannah. Might be someone going north, maybe fix
you up with a ride."

"That would be wonderful." She smiled, at once regretting
it, filled with dread at the idea that she might be committing
herself to something without realizing she was doing it.

He looked over at her again, appraisingly, his eyes squinting
against the smoke.

She didn't want to, but she fell asleep and came awake to
a firm hand on her arm and Joe's voice telling her, "We'll get
out here." She turned to look at Bobby.

"The kid'll be okay," he said. "I'll be leaving the motor
running."

After covering Bobby with her pea jacket, she climbed down
from the truck to look around at the half dozen or so other rigs
parked outside the diner, all of them with their engines running.
Already the air here was much colder, with a bite to it. She

followed Joe. Inside, men lined the counter and a jukebox was playing loudly. There were booming conversations and bursts of laughter. She saw a door marked Women and went through to use the toilet and then wash her hands and face and comb her hair. Back in the diner, she took a seat beside Joe at the counter, ordered coffee, then changed her mind and ordered a Coke, as well as a container of milk and a peanut-butter-and-jelly sandwich to take back to Bobby. Carefully, she counted out the change and added a ten-cent tip. Beside her, Joe quickly put away two wet-looking hamburgers and a plateful of pale French fries. Then he went to the men's room, came back, and stood at the end of the counter talking to another man. The second one glanced over at Tillie, then nodded. The two men paid for their food, then gestured to her to come outside with them. She hated the way they were treating her, like some sort of dumb thing. But she was dependent on their whims and willingness.

"This here's Doug," Joe told her. "He'll take you on to Raleigh."

"Thank you very much." Her voice emerged high and reedy.

Doug went over to open the driver's door of his rig, calling to her, "Come on! Let's get it going! We're all on a schedule."

She ran across the parking lot and maneuvered Bobby down from the ledge and into her arms. She positioned the suitcase on the seat before climbing down from the cab, and nearly fell. Her heart was thudding as she righted herself and reached for the suitcase. The one called Doug was waiting impatiently in his cab.

She got Bobby up onto the seat and pushed the suitcase in after him, out of breath.

"For chrissake, get a move on, huh?" Doug said.

She stared at him for a moment, overcome by loathing for all the men in the world, hating being dependent on them. Doug pulled on the air horn and, startled, she clambered up and in. She swung the heavy door closed and the truck reversed out of the lot and then, with a grinding of gears, nosed onto the service road, heading back to the interstate.

◇ Thirty-Two ◇

Jess let herself through the front door feeling totally transparent, but was somewhat reassured as Todd came flying down the stairs, said, "Hi, Mom!" kissed her cheek, then ran on down the hall to the kitchen. After hanging up her coat, she went to the kitchen to see the children well into their breakfasts. Olga smiled over at her, asking, "Some coffee, eh?"

"Please." She sat down and could feel something like mild hostility emanating from Justin; she looked over to see he'd been staring at her and now hastily lowered his eyes.

"You stayed out all night," he said accusingly, his fork poised over his plate, eyes averted.

"Yes, I did," she answered, thinking both their voices sounded odd and echoey.

"Where'd you go, Mom?" Todd asked, smiling at her around a mouthful of pea-meal bacon and egg.

Olga set a cup of coffee down in front of her, but Jess was too preoccupied with the problem of how to answer Todd's question to be aware of Olga. "It was late and I decided to spend the night with a friend."

"What friend?" Belinda asked innocently, her pink angora sweater somehow accentuating her innocence.

"Just a friend."

"Are you going to stay out nights all the time now?" Justin asked, his face, still turned away, slowly suffusing with angry color.

"No, I am *not* going to stay out nights all the time. What are you trying to get to, Justin?" She could feel her own anger and something else, nameless but significant, building.

"Well, don't you think you should've told us you weren't going to be coming home?" he asked in tones of indignant self-righteousness, finally facing her.

"Perhaps. But I don't think I'm obliged to tell a thirteen-year-old everything I do."

"We have a right to know," he insisted.

"You think so? Why?"

"Just because we should. After all, what if something happened and we needed you?"

"Polly knew where I was."

"I didn't know that."

"I didn't happen to think it necessary for you to know."

Todd and Belinda, and Olga, too, from the stove, were closely following.

"Well, it's not right," he argued, floundering, feeling morally right but unable to locate the proper words and arguments he needed to develop his case against her.

"Not right?" The anger made her head feel suddenly larger and lighter. "What's 'not right?'"

"Just . . . I don't . . . It isn't, that's all."

In a flinty, even tone none of them had ever heard her use before, she said, "It is not up to you, any of you," she looked around to include Belinda and Todd, "to decide for me what's right or not." Returning her eyes to Justin, her fists clenched on the tabletop, she said, "I'm *someone*, Justin. Not just your mother, but a *person*. I have a life of my own, aside from being your mother, and you do *not* have the right to question me unless what I do directly involves you. You remember that! All of you!" She stood up abruptly, causing the coffee to slop over the rim of the cup. Todd and Belinda gaped open-mouthed at her. Justin's face was a hot red. "I'm not just your mother! Think about that the next time you're tempted to pass judgment!" Quaking with the need to say much more and the effort of holding back, she walked out of the kitchen.

Upstairs, she began removing her suit, feeling both guilty and justified, disturbed by the knowledge that she really shouldn't have stayed all night with René, yet wanting to argue her right to a separate life and to some privacy. She absently hung away her suit jacket and was about to take off her skirt when there was a quiet tapping at the door.

"Come in," she said, her voice still deeper than normal with the residue of anger.

Justin opened the door, looking very cowed now, and stood in the dressing-room doorway. "I came to apologize," he said, his voice breaking into a croak so that he blushed, and, seeing it, she softened considerably.

She stepped over and put her arms around him, feeling him holding himself away from her. "Just because I'm your mother," she said, touching his hair so like her own, "doesn't mean you can say whatever you like to me, Justin. I know you said what you did because you care, but you must understand what I told you. I'm *not* just your mother. I'm a *person*, like all of you. You seem to forget that. I wouldn't put up with anyone else saying one tenth the things you say to me."

"I *know* you're a person," he said, still holding himself away but with increasing difficulty. "But I . . . I needed to talk to you and you weren't here. I was *worried*."

"I'm sorry you were worried." She was getting dangerously close to screaming at him to make him understand. "But because you were, do you really think it's your right to get so angry and be so abusive? I'm not the only one, Justin. You do it constantly to Todd and Belinda, too. You've got to stop this! You're making it very hard for us to love you."

"I don't know," he said plaintively. "I don't *mean* to be that way." He unbent the slightest bit and she drew him closer, resting her cheek against his.

"Justin, is there more?"

He stiffened, saying, "You were with René, weren't you?"

She released him and looked penetratingly into his eyes. "And if I was?"

"I don't know . . . I'm not a kid. Why couldn't you *tell* me?"

"I didn't think you needed to know."

"But *I* think I *do*! Sure you're a person. I know *that*. But you're my *mother*, too, and I was worried."

"Don't you like René? I thought you did."

"Sure I like him. Are you going to marry him?"

"Is that what all this is about?"

"Are you?"

"I'm not marrying anyone."

"Then how come you stayed out the whole night with him?"

"I didn't *say* I spent the night with him. Justin," she said evenly, "it's really not your place to interrogate me this way."

"I'm *not*! I'm trying to talk to you, to find out . . ."

"Find out what?"

"Just . . . what you're doing . . . the things you do. I don't know." He felt miserable and wished he'd never started.

"If there's something you want to know, *ask* me! But don't make accusations and start passing judgments, at least not until you've been out in the world and have a bit of experience. I didn't *plan* to be out all night. I'm sorry if you were upset. I am not marrying René. Is there anything else?"

"You're mad at me."

"Yes, I am."

"Why?"

"Because, if you'd asked me, I'd have answered you truthfully. But you *accused*. You're still a child and I am not obligated to explain my actions to you. I certainly don't have to listen to a boy your age telling me what's right and not right."

"I'm sorry," he said, his hands all sweaty, unable to understand how this had turned so horribly wrong.

"You're going to be late and make the others late."

"Will you still be mad at me?"

"No. We'll both put it aside."

"It's just that I want you to . . . confide in me. As if I'm not five years old like Linnie."

Seeing his pain, she embraced him again. "We'll talk," she promised.

He unbent all at once and hugged her hard, shocked and confounded every time by the cushion of her breasts. Then he broke away and ran clattering off down the stairs, leaving the bedroom door ajar. She stood hearing Todd and Belinda bark at him for keeping them all waiting and his subdued voice mumbling some reply. Then the front door opened and closed and the house was silent. She took a deep breath, walked over to close the bedroom door, then got on with changing her clothes.

"I can't see you tonight."

"Why not?"

"Because," she dropped her voice, looking out the window, "there was quite a scene when I got in this morning. I'm not up to a repeat performance. It wouldn't be a good idea for us to see each other tonight."

"So you'll go home? I *want* to *see* you!"

"I want to see you, too," she said, feeling torn. "But I really don't think it's a good idea. Anyway, I've got a very busy schedule today. I'll be tired."

"No!" he said sharply. "I'll come to the house at seven-thirty. You make a big mistake when you put them first, before yourself."

"I don't want to argue, René. It's all I've done this morning."

"Good! We won't argue. Seven-thirty." He put down the phone.

She gazed at the receiver for a moment, then replaced it. Her life suddenly felt horrendously complicated and tedious, but she simply hadn't the time to stop and think about it. The intercom went off. Before she could reach to pick it up, the office door flew open and an infuriated Flora stalked in waving a fistful of tear sheets.

"Those *cretins* ran the wrong damned ad!"

"What cretins?"

"The *Star*. They ran *next week's* copy *this* week."

"Oh, good God!" Jess sighed. None of the Ontario stores would be ready with the specials. "I'll get on it."

"This business is *idiotic*!" Flora ranted. "*Filled* with idiots!"

She looked at Flora's still-lovely face, examining the anger there and thought, I can't take anymore. She bent her head into her hands, breaking quietly into tears.

Flora stood for a moment, then closed and locked the door, threw the papers into the visitor's chair and went around behind the desk to lay her hand on Jess's hair, asking, "What's the matter, sweetheart?" Jess shook her head, struggling for control. Flora perched on the edge of her desk, thinking, not for the first time, how frail Jess seemed lately. She waited until Jess opened the top left-hand drawer of the desk, pulled out a tissue and held it to her eyes, then blew her nose.

"Just what you needed, huh? Another idiot rushing in screaming. I'm sorry."

"You're not an idiot. I feel as if I am."

"What's the matter?" she asked again, and briefly, Jess told her what had happened. "I see," Flora said. "Looks like we've got a little competition going on here."

"Competition?"

"Justin's jealous, sweetheart. Leastwise, that's the way it looks from here."

"My God, Flora! He isn't fourteen yet. You can't be serious!"

"He's been the little big man for the last five-odd years, Jess. Up 'til now, René's been the nice fella who brings presents and takes Mom out to dinner when he comes to town. But you changed the game and stayed out all night, and now Justin feels differently because he's made the connection."

"What am I supposed to *do*? I'm not going to give up the only source of pleasure I have."

"Course not. But I think maybe Justin's got a point. He really isn't a kid anymore. So why not level with him?"

"You mean actually *tell* him about René and me?"

"You don't have to be graphic. Just explain, kind of, the way things are. He's not dumb, Jess. All he wants, from the sound of it, is a chance to understand and feel included."

"Flora, I can't sit down and tell him I'm sleeping with René. My God! That's bizarre!"

"You don't have to give him the clinical details. You just let him know that the two of you have something going, and that it's what grown-ups do. He *is* almost fourteen, after all. All he probably thinks about nowadays is sex, and here's his mother staying out all night. I can just *see* the pictures he's probably got in his head."

"You're saying . . . Are you trying . . . What *are* you saying?"

"You're right about telling him you're more than his mother, sweetheart. But that's not news to him. The whole problem is he already knows that. Now, he's discovered you're a *woman*. The other sex, huh? I'll bet he's got truckloads of sexual fantasies."

"About *me*?"

"Sure. Some anyway. It's only natural."

"How do you *know* that?"

"'Cause I don't think boys that age're any different from girls that age, and I sure as hell remember speculating like

crazy about what my mother and father got up to in that bedroom with the door closed. Boy, the things I imagined!"

"It never happened to me," Jess said, thinking back. "My
mother was dead by then and I was looking after Tillie. Sandy's
not here, so I suppose René's the logical candidate. I think you
must be right. You've got to be. I'm starting to feel better."

"You want a word of advice?"

"What?"

"You need a vacation. You're skin and goddamned bones,
you know that? Why don't you take the kids and go somewhere
for a week or two? Spend some time, just the four of you,
relax and get close again. Seems to me you're taking all this"—
her waving hand indicated the office—"a little too seriously."

"I'd love to. But there's so much to do. And, it's awful of
me, but what I'd like is to go somewhere warm with the
children, and with René, too."

"So do it!"

"It seems so *open*. I'm not sure it feels right." She heard
again Justin saying, "It's not right." "Maybe that would only
make things worse from Justin's viewpoint."

"I don't know about that. Maybe it'd be just the ticket to
straighten it all out." The intercom went off again. "I'll scram."
Flora slipped off the desk. "Let's have lunch, the two of us
and Nelda."

"Let me check the sheet." She pulled over the day's schedule. "I can't," she said dully. "I've got a lunch with the Man-
itoba managers, to play nice and make them feel important
because they're having lunch with the chairman of the board.
I don't know why I'm doing this when Press really should be
the one."

"Then call and ask him to do it. And you come have lunch
with me and Nelda."

"I'll try." The intercom went off a third time. She picked
up, telling Flora, "I'll call you later after I talk to Press."

Flora went out as Sally said, "Polly called. The school nurse
called to say Belinda's running a temperature, so Robert's gone
to pick her up. Polly wanted to let you know."

"All right. I'll call home."

"Your ten-o'clock appointment's here."

"Who's my ten o'clock?" She pushed around on her desk
looking for the schedule.

"Miss Dominetti for an interview."

"All right. Give me five minutes to make a couple of calls. Offer her coffee, would you, Sally? And bring me a cup, please?"

She got an outside line and called home. "It's just a slight temperature," Polly said. "I'm putting her back to bed, but there's nothing to worry about. She's right here wanting to talk to you."

Belinda came on saying, "Mom?" Her small voice filled Jess with guilt and helplessness at not being free to be there.

"How do you feel, darling?"

"Kind of hot and my throat hurts. Are you gonna come home?"

"I can't right now, Belinda. But I'll be home early this afternoon. You go get into bed, and Polly will stay with you."

Disappointed, she said, "Okay, but I wish you could come home now."

"I wish I could too, but it's really impossible. I'll see you later. Okay?"

"Okay."

Feeling thoroughly guilty, she called Press to ask if he'd chair the luncheon meeting for her, then got on to Nelda to ask her to come along to lunch with Flora and herself. Finally, she got back to Sally. "You can send her in. What's her name again?"

"Dominetti. And I've got your coffee."

Sally showed in a small, darkly compact, well-dressed woman of about thirty who came across the room to set her coffee down on the edge of the desk before giving Jess both a smile and her hand. It was a combined gesture Jess liked. Only rarely did female applicants offer to shake hands with her. She warmed to this woman at once. "Do, please sit down," she said. Sally set Jess's coffee and the woman's résumé on the blotter, then went out.

"I've got a whole portfolio full of samples if you want to see my work," Miss Dominetti volunteered.

"Let's talk for a few minutes first," Jess said, lighting a cigarette. Miss Dominetti declined Jess's invitation to smoke, but sat comfortably waiting until Jess asked, "What's your full name?"

"Marina Theresa Angelique Gabrielle Dominetti." She laughed, very relaxed. "An Italian father and a *Canadienne Française* mother. Between them, they gave me more names

than I know what to do with. My friends call me Marina. It's
a lot easier. You're not Canadian, are you?"

"Why do you ask that?" Her attention was arrested. This
was starting out to be anything but a typical interview.

"Your accent. It's almost English, but the vowels are a little
too flat. I've met a couple of people who sound the same.
Boston?"

"New York."

"Been here a long time?"

"Twenty-three years."

Marina smiled. "That's a pretty long time, all right."

Jess took a sip of coffee, then picked up the résumé and
read it quickly. Marina was older than she looked, almost the
same age as Tillie. And she'd graduated from O.C.A. "My
sister was at the Art College about the time you were. Perhaps
you knew her?"

"What was her name?"

"Tillie. Tillie Greaves."

"Oh, Tillie. Sure, I remember her. Really pretty, blond,
right?"

"That's right." For some reason, Jess felt excited. Here was
someone who'd known Tillie. It seemed to bring her closer.

"Your sister, eh? You don't look one bit alike from what
I remember of Tillie."

"No."

"She was good," Marina said with a slight narrowing of
her eyes, as if retrospectively judging. "But unfocused. She
could've been really good if she'd been willing to work at it.
But I thought she was always more interested in being with
the 'right' sort of crowd than in her work. There was a whole
group who were only there because it seemed kind of a defiant
thing to do. Most of them didn't have any talent to speak of,
but Tillie did, though. I always thought it was a big waste.
What's she doing with herself these days, anyhow?"

"I don't know. I haven't seen her in quite a number of
years. You're very outspoken," Jess said. Referring again to
the résumé, she asked, "What did you do at Simpsons?"

"Mainly, I worked on their catalogs. I started out painting
children's clothing, then went over to write copy. After that,
I spent two years coordinating copy and artwork, doing the
mechanicals. Six years on the catalogs and I couldn't go any
higher, so I left and went to work with a small ad agency just
starting up."

"And you worked there until three months ago?" Jess asked, noticing the woman's small features tighten slightly.

"That's right."

"May I ask why you left?"

"They fired me," she answered bluntly, tensing visibly.

"Why?" There was something about this woman, Jess thought, that seemed to radiate competence. Yet combined with her aura of capability was an almost winsome delicacy, perhaps due to her size.

"Look, I'll tell you the truth and we can get this over with. I'm fed up with lying about it. There were two partners in the agency, a man and a woman. Somehow, about six months ago, it got out I was living with another woman. Chuck could've cared less and said so. But Stephanie started putting the screws on, taking it like some kind of personal threat, as if I was going to attack her some afternoon in the washroom. They had quite a fight about it, and Stephanie won. So, here I am. I couldn't have stayed even if I'd wanted to. She was making my life impossible, making me feel like some sort of freak."

"Were you good at your job?"

"I think so. To tell the truth, I was getting a little bored because there wasn't enough of a challenge left."

"What do you see as a challenge?"

For a moment Marina faltered. Then she said, "I want a chance to show what I can really do, to work and feel I'm actually accomplishing something. Designing ads for shoe stores and writing cute copy isn't it. I'd like to be involved in packaging and product development. All kinds of things. I want some responsibility for a change. I know I'm good." Why wasn't the woman reacting? she wondered. "May I ask you something?"

"Certainly." Jess reached for a fresh cigarette, trying to decide how she felt about someone who had the courage to admit to something so potentially damaging, and if hiring her might create a problem they weren't prepared to deal with.

"What's your status here? I mean, personnel or what?"

"I'm chairman of the board of the Riverwood Stores."

"You're . . ." Marina sat back, convinced that having risked the truth was going to hang her. "I thought . . . I mean, there's nothing on your door or . . ."

"I know," Jess said, her expression remaining nonrevealing. "My husband started this company. On his death, I agreed to take over. The actual running is done by Mr. Bocken and Mr.

Ames, but I do the hiring in certain areas. Since the advertising department was my creation, I'm responsible for the senior personnel. There's nothing painted on the door because this was my husband's office and putting my name and title on the door wouldn't change my feeling that it's still his office. This isn't a small job we're discussing, Marina."

"Your job?"

"No." Jess smiled for the first time, having made up her mind. "Yours."

"Mine?"

"I'd like to propose a ninety-day trial. If we're both satisfied at the end of that time, we'll sit down and talk again. If one or the other of us is unhappy, we'll talk in any event."

"You're giving me the job?"

"I believe I am." She smiled, thinking she sounded for a moment like Sandy, certain Sandy would have hired this woman.

"But . . . ?"

"You want a reaction," Jess guessed.

"You must *have* one."

"My only interest is in your qualifications and capabilities. As long as you do your job to everyone's satisfaction, it's no one's business what you do on your own time. I wouldn't, however, expect you to let your preferences become common knowledge."

"You're shocked, though, aren't you?" Marina asked, testing the ground thoroughly.

Again Jess smiled, and Marina glimpsed more substance behind the smile than she'd expected. She found Jess an intriguing woman.

"The only things," Jess said, "that really shock me are the things my children think they have the right to say to me. I have two sons and a daughter who think my life is their domain. Now, why don't I take you down the hall and introduce you to Flora and see about getting you started?"

"But don't you want to see my portfolio?"

"You've told me you're good. If you're foolish enough to lie about it, we're all going to know in very short order. I'd rather take you at your word. You're very truthful and I like that. I think Flora will like you, too. Flora is just as outspoken as you. I have a feeling the two of you will get on very well."

"You won't be sorry."

"Bring your portfolio along," Jess said, coming out from

behind the desk. "Flora will want to see it."

Marina reached for it, then stopped and again extended her hand to Jess. "Thank you. Really. It's the first time I've told the truth this way, and I don't mind telling you I was scared. I thought you'd toss me out on my ear."

Jess shook her hand, then let go. "I wouldn't suggest you make a habit of admitting it generally. Use a bit of discretion. One thing I would like to ask. How did it become known you were involved with this other woman?"

Marina drew her lips inward, bit on her lower lip for a moment, then said, "We had an argument and split up. She telephoned the office—one of those obscene little calls directed to the right ear. I still can't believe she did that. She wanted to destroy me because I didn't like flaunting my 'difference,' and she did. It embarrassed me. I can assure you I'm not about to tell anyone."

"I see," Jess said soberly. She went to the door, pausing to tell Sally, "If you need me, I'll be with Flora. And meet Marina," she said, turning to include her with a smile. "She's going to be working with Flora."

They stood by the roadside on the outskirts of Raleigh for almost two hours before a car stopped. Bobby was whining complaints and when the car, a snappy red Cadillac, stopped, Tillie threw aside her reservations about male drivers and hustled Bobby into the car.

"Where you goin', honey?" the man asked. He was middle-aged, florid, and very fat. Wedged behind the wheel, he smiled widely at her.

"As far as you are," she said wearily, holding Bobby on her lap, noticing he felt very warm.

"Well now, I'm goin' clear the way to Baltimore." He grinned, chucked Bobby under the chin and they were off. "Course I'll be stoppin' the night in Richmond. So I'm afraid that's where I'll have to set you down."

"All right," she said, pressing the back of her hand and then her lips to Bobby's forehead and cheeks. He was very hot, his cheeks flushed and his eyelids drooping. "Bobby? How do you feel, darling?"

He murmured something unintelligible and settled with his head against her breast, the teddy bear crushed against his ear, his thumb in his mouth.

God! He was sick. What was she going to do? She couldn't

keep a sick child out in the cold for hours on end, waiting for rides. Maybe he'd sleep for a while and feel better when he woke up. Please feel better, she thought.

"Boy looks a mite peaked."

"I think he's coming down with something," she said nervously. "My name's Tillie, " she said, feeling as if she, too, had a fever. "And this is my son, Bobby."

"The name's Jackson. Jimmy Jackson." He fished a card out of his inside breast pocket and flipped it to her between his fingers with a flourish. "Wheels're my game. Any kinda wheel you want, my company can make it for you. Rubber, steel, plastic, you name it. You want a wheel, you come see Jackson's Wheelwrights and we'll see you get just 'xackly what you want."

She looked at the card, then opened her handbag and dropped it in. "Mr. Jackson," she began, her heart beating so hard she felt nauseated, "you're going to stop overnight in Richmond?"

"That's right." He reached again into his inside pocket, this time producing a long cigar.

"Bobby's ill. He needs a doctor. And I . . . I don't have any money. I'm taking him home to Canada. I . . . If you'd let us spend the night and get a doctor for Bobby, I'll do anything. *Anything.*"

His face reshaped itself into thoughtful lines while he considered this proposition. He took another quick look at her, thinking it'd cost extra for the room with her along and maybe a tenner for a doctor to look at the child. But the boy, he thought, sure enough looked poorly. And hell! He smiled to himself. He didn't get pretty women very often, and Mary-Sue was getting sicker, more bloated every minute of the day and that was a fact.

"Say, okay," he agreed. "We'll see what we can do 'bout getting the boy fixed up. Don't you worry none now. Ole Jimmy's gonna take care of ever'thin'."

"Thank you," she said tearfully. What difference did it make if one more man made use of her? It didn't matter at all, as long as Bobby was looked after. She had just over twelve dollars left in her bag.

He got them installed in adjoining rooms in the hotel, put in a call for the hotel's doctor, then sat down with the room-service menu, deliberating. He was a big fat man in an ice-cream suit and Panama hat, but, like Alma, surprisingly kind. He helped Tillie get Bobby undressed and into bed, explaining, "Had me three boys and don't I know how worrisome it can be when they're poorly. He'll be just fine, honey. Don't you worry none."

She returned with him to his room and stood watching as he removed his suit jacket and carefully hung it away in the closet, then placed his hat on the shelf.

"Sit yourself down, girl," he said expansively. "Once the doc comes, we'll order us up some food. They gotta call round for him and he's prob'ly at his supper."

He settled his bulk into one of the room's two armchairs and finally lit the cigar he'd been toying with since picking her and Bobby up. Puffing away with satisfaction, his eyes fixed on her approvingly.

"You're one pretty-lookin' woman for a fact."

"Thank you."

"How long you been on the road?"

"Two days."

"You're lookin' mighty uncomfortable. Something wrong?"

"I'd like to bathe," she said, discomfited. "It *has* been two days and I feel . . . dirty."

"You go right ahead," he said. "Know just what you mean. Always like a nice hot bath myself after a day's travelin'."

"Thank you," she said again, getting up. "I won't be long."

The bath made her feel sleepy and only superficially clean. But the change of clothes helped and so did having freshly washed hair.

The doctor recommended a cool bath for Bobby, lots of liquids, and aspirin every four hours, and said he didn't see any reason why the boy couldn't travel after a good night's sleep. "He's just overtired," he told Tillie. "His throat's clear, so're his eyes and ears, and his chest sounds fine. He'll be right as rain come the morning. I'll just leave you these." He gave her a small tin of Bayer aspirin, then went off with Jimmy Jackson, who paid the ten-dollar fee, gave him a cigar, and saw him on his way.

After bathing Bobby and feeding him half a bowl of chicken broth, she got him tucked away and kissed him good night before returning to Jimmy's room to eat the meal he'd ordered.

He ate, she saw, with neatness and precision, but, surprisingly, very little.

"Always have had more appetite than ability," he said. "My daddy used to say I had eyes bigger'n my stomach." He laughed. "Which would be one fine trick, could he see me now. It's not from eatin' I'm so big," he explained. "Mostly, I guess it's from sittin' so much. An' all the drinkin'. I been tryin' to cut way down the past few months. Mary-Sue, she's got one real bad drinkin' problem. Years now, I been keepin' up with her, keepin' her comp'ny, so to speak." He shook his head. "I already dropped near thirty pounds, droppin' more ever' day. But Mary-Sue, she's all puffed out somethin' fierce. They want," he said sadly, "I should have her put someplace, get her fixed up right. But I don't know. I just truly do not know. You sure God are one pretty woman."

He was making her sad. "You've been so nice to us," she said, her appetite gone. "I mean it. Thank you."

"Say now, I injoy havin' a bit of comp'ny, and it's been some long time since I had me the comp'ny of a woman pretty's you. I never did cheat on Mary-Sue, not for years, I didn't, not 'til the boys were growed. But comes a time when a man needs more'n a drinkin' companion. I don't understand what happened to her and that's a fact, one sad fact. Prettiest gal y'ever saw, Mary-Sue. Sixteen and purely beautiful when we married. She's gone so old now, you know? I think it's missin' the boys, havin' them to look after. She don't have nothin' much else to do with herself, says she's 'not interested.' She's gonna die," he said solemnly. "It's why I don't see the harm to lettin' her go on drinkin' now if that's all she wants. Doc says a few more months'n she'll die of it. Her liver, you know? Ain't no way I know to get her to stop. Truth is, I think she wants to go."

"That's really too bad," she commiserated, thinking for a few moments about staying with him until Mary-Sue finally died. Then he'd marry her and she'd have a place again. But, no. No more of that kind of thinking. Now she wanted something of her own that was all hers, that no one could take away. Something, she thought, that feels the way Bobby does to me. She looked over at him, placing her napkin on the table, then stood up. "Have you had enough?" she asked, ready to push the trolley aside.

"Sure have," he said, his thoughts still on Mary-Sue.

She moved the trolley over by the door, then turned off the overhead light. Returning to stand a foot or two away from him, she started to take off her clothes. Time to pay—for the ride, the doctor, the meal, the bed. She felt like a whore doing these things just to get home again. She undressed while he watched, then climbed naked onto his lap, trying not to let her face show her revulsion as his hand closed over her breast and his face loosened with desire.

"God!" he exclaimed softly. "God, but you're pretty." His hand was respectfully gentle on her breast. Why had she expected him to be clumsy and heavy-handed? Hadn't she seen the delicate way he'd eaten and the careful way he'd placed his hat on the closet shelf? She closed her eyes and let him kiss her, trying to pretend he was someone she wanted, someone she knew and cared for, not a fat man in an ice-cream suit with an alcoholic wife and oddly delicate ways about him. She shrank involuntarily as his hand parted her thighs and his still gentle fingers opened her to his inspection. Bewildered, she realized that if he were a woman, even fat, she wouldn't be feeling the way she did. I'm sorry, she thought. I can't help it. You're a nice man, you are. And you've treated us so kindly. But it's your being a man.

She got off his lap to go sit on the bed while he took off his clothes and then, with a heaving sigh, lay down beside her, his belly huge and hairy.

"Would you do it for me, honey?" he asked shyly, clumsily indicating what he wanted.

She sat up on her knees wishing she could die, but she did it, and afterward lay beneath his tremendous crushing weight as he quickly—mercifully quickly—satisfied himself inside her.

"If it's all right with you," she said, taken with a consuming need to wash at once, "I'll go sleep with Bobby and make sure he's all right."

"Sure. You go on and do that. I understand these things."

Feeling tender toward him and wishing she could actually care for him, she kissed him lightly on the lips, then gathered up her clothes and returned to the adjoining room.

As they were nearing Baltimore, he cleared his throat and she looked over.

"I don't much like the idea of you and the boy out in the cold," he said, directing the car onto the shoulder and pulling to a stop. "There's a Greyhound stop bottom of this here exit

ramp." He pointed to show her. "I'd feel a whole sight better
I knew the two of you were safe. So you take this"—he gave
her one of the hotel's envelopes—"and you go get the bus
home."

That undid her. Bursting into tears, she accepted the envelope, then threw her arms around his neck, pressing her face
into his shoulder while Bobby watched with consternation.

"I'll never forget you!" she wept, meaning it. "You don't
know what this means, what we've been through getting this
far."

"You send me a Christmas card sometime," he said, easing
her away, perplexed by his own generous impulses and her
full-blown response. "I remember rightly, there's a bus comes
along on the hour." He consulted his watch. "You got about
fifteen minutes. Bus'll take you along into downtown Baltimore, 'n' you can get another bus there goin' north."

She and Bobby waved good-bye, then hurried down the exit
ramp toward the bus stop. Once there, she opened the envelope
to see he'd given her a hundred dollars. Enough to get them
home. Feeling choked again, she put the money in her bag.
She started to think about Jess, wanting to think about her, but
the bus came along and she flagged it down. There wasn't time
to think.

◊ Thirty-Three ◊

"I wish you were staying for the weekend."

René took a long look at her. It was the first time she'd ever expressed a desire to have him around longer than his intended time. He was inordinately pleased. "Okay," he said easily. "I'll stay for the weekend."

"Just because I said I'd like it?" she asked, starting to smile.

"Just because."

She put her head down on his chest, thinking that René was only a bit older now than Sandy had been when she'd met him. Perhaps the two of them might have ten years together. She wondered if she had the courage to risk more losses. Was it courage or self-concern? she wondered, scrupulously examining this, warning herself against self-indulgence at someone else's expense.

"When will you be moving here?" she asked.

"Next month."

"Have you found a place?"

"I got an apartment today on Avenue Road. A nice place. You can see the castle from the balcony. You want to go see it tomorrow?"

"You rented an apartment today?"

"That's right." He wound one very long strand of her hair around his hand. "It surprises you."

"It certainly does. When you told me last night you were going to move here, I thought it might be a few months, perhaps. Not so soon." She dropped her head, resting again on his chest. "Would you talk to Justin?" she asked. "He needs a man to talk to. That scene this morning was terrible."

"I can't talk to him unless he wants it. It's not good to push talk on people, Jess, if they don't want it."

"I was thinking." She stopped, reaching for the thought. "I'm taking Todd and Belinda downtown tomorrow. They both want new skates and I'd like to treat them to lunch out. I was hoping you might agree to take Justin to lunch somewhere and give him a chance to talk if he wants to."

"I'll tell you what I'll do. Tomorrow, in the morning, I'll talk with him on the telephone. I'll invite him. If he wants to come out with me, we'll go."

"Thank you. I'm sure it's what he needs."

"Me, I'm not so sure. But we'll see. I think maybe next time you should go out with him, just the two of you, so he spends time grown-up with his mother, too."

"Of course," she agreed. "I had that in mind. I've been thinking it would be a good idea to take the children somewhere at Easter. Bermuda, or Jamaica, perhaps."

He nodded, wanting to be included, to be asked to come along. She thought of asking him but decided to wait and see if Justin would agree to have lunch with him and, if he did, how it would go.

Justin walked along beside René, glancing up at him every so often, feeling strange now at being out with this man. He imagined his mother with René, and things the two of them did together, abashed by the realization that everybody, every single person, had full sets of genitalia—including René and his mother. He thought of the naked things they probably did together and felt confused because he'd always really liked René but now that he understood, or at least thought he did, more about their involvement, he wasn't so sure he still liked him—this tall, hefty man in the brown tweed overcoat with his dark skin and booming laughter, his deep voice and sing-song accent. There were all kinds of things he wanted to ask René, to say to him and talk about with him, but he couldn't seem to find any appropriate place to begin.

"Did Mom tell you to ask me out?" he asked, his fists jammed into his coat pockets, feeling uncomfortable but also grown up, dressed for this outing in slacks and a sports jacket, a shirt and tie, and his good topcoat. He felt more like himself in his cords and turtleneck and pea jacket but was deciding he could maybe learn to feel just as much like himself inside the dress-up stuff. These clothes made his legs want to take long strides, made him feel almost jaunty.

"She didn't *tell* me," René answered, turning to look at him. "You're getting real tall, eh?"

"Five ten already. I'm way taller than Mom now." He smiled, then frowned and asked, "What *did* she say?"

"She said maybe you'd like to come out, be without the others for a change."

He thought about that. "Yeah," he said. "That's true. It's such a pain always having Todd and Linnie tagging along. I mean, I love them and all that. But they're *kids*. You know?"

And you, René thought, you want to be a man now. It touched him and revived the feelings he'd had all those years before when he'd felt himself reaching into his own manhood. "I know," he acknowledged.

"I've even got a girl," Justin blurted out, then went red, furious with himself.

René smiled widely. "You have a girl, eh? What's she like?"

Justin shrugged. "Oh, you know. Just a girl. Uncle Press's...Julie. You know Julie."

"I know. This is a nice girl. Real pretty and real smart."

Justin thought about her and could see the way she smiled with her lips closed to cover the braces, and her hair more red than brown. "Of course," he said, striving to be casual, "she's only eleven, and I'm almost fourteen."

"But you like her?"

"Yeah," he said eagerly. "I *really* do. She understands, you know? I mean, when we get together and talk, she knows exactly what I'm talking about." He looked off into the misty landscape of his own future, saying, in his finally broken new baritone voice, "We'll probably get married." He was filled with his first intuitive sense of conviction, knowing absolutely that that's the way it would be.

"Oh?" René refused to make light of this declaration, sens-

ing something deeper than the frail projection of a young boy's
first longings.

"We probably will," Justin said again.

"Good," René said. "It's good to know what you want."

"And," he went on, gaining confidence, "I've definitely
decided I'm going to go into the business. I promised my Dad
I would, you know." René presented an open face, listening.
Encouraged, Justin said, "I think Mom's working too hard.
Don't you?"

"Maybe so."

"I mean, she's always at work and we hardly ever see her
anymore. Except on the weekends. And then she's always
tired. I don't know. I wish she didn't work so hard."

"I think," René said carefully, "the work is important to
her."

"I suppose. But she's so different since Dad died. Really
different. In lots of ways." He thought about his mother in
those suits she wore to the office and about the business dinners
she went to sometimes so that she didn't come home until
really late when everybody was already in bed, and the half
dozen times she'd gone out of town for a new store opening
and stayed away for three or four days and nights, and the time
a few months earlier when he'd wanted to ask her for an
advance on his allowance, so he could go skating with Julie
and then take her to the movies after, and he'd barged into the
bedroom without knocking as he should have done and she'd
been in the dressing room getting dressed. All she'd had on
were her underpants and he'd seen her naked practically, seen
her breasts and got this really hurting kind of weird feeling
looking at her. She'd turned her back on him and put on her
dressing gown, saying, "You really must knock, darling. What
is it?" And he'd forgotten why he'd come charging in in the
first place. But then he'd remembered and had stammered out
how he needed the money and she'd turned around again all
covered up, and he'd felt a little relieved but kind of let down,
too, because he'd have liked to look at her more, longer. Now
he thought all the time about the way she'd looked, especially
when he sneaked into the bathroom at night to do it, feeling
crummy and like a real weirdo doing it. He'd start out every
time thinking about Mom's breasts that time, but it always
turned into Julie and how she'd let him touch her chest when
he'd asked if he could see. She'd made kind of a funny face

and tilted her head to one side, the way she did when she was all serious, asking, "Why, Justin?" sounding just like a grownup. And he'd said, "Are you growing breasts yet?" and she'd said, "I'm starting." The whole thing serious and important. And he'd said, "I'd really like to see, could I?" And she'd thought about it for maybe five whole minutes and then said, "Okay. But you promise never to tell?" And he'd promised. They'd been down in the playroom over at her house and they'd gone into the little washroom down there to lock the door and she'd lifted up her sweater and watched his face very closely as he'd looked for a long time at the slight swellings that would be her breasts. "I'm having periods now," she'd said with pride. "That means I can have babies." Equally sober, he'd readjusted her undershirt and sweater. Then, on some impulse he'd yet to comprehend, he'd put his arms around her and held her, breathing in the nice smell of her and the softness of her hair. And the next time after that when he *did* it, something actually came out, and he thought he understood the kind of pride she'd felt telling him about having periods and being able to make babies, because now he knew he could make babies, too, and it made all kinds of difference.

"Are you sleeping with my mom?" he asked René bluntly.

"Yes."

"Yeah, I thought so."

And that was the end of it. René didn't explain anything further and Justin didn't care to know more. Whatever strain had existed between them disappeared in the course of this question and answer, and they went on to have a companionable lunch, returning to the house together, laughing.

"What did he say?" Jess asked in a moment alone with René.

"He asked me was I sleeping with you."

"My God! What did you *say*?"

"I told him yes."

"René!"

"There was no more. He just wished to know the truth, so I told it to him."

"I really don't know . . ."

"Hey!" He smiled, touching his forefinger to her chin. "*I* know, eh? It's okay. Now, we'll all make plans for the vacation."

"You'd like to come with us?"

"You'd like that? You don't want me?"

"Yes," she said. "I want you."

They got off the bus in the early morning Sunday desert of downtown Toronto with Bobby asking, "Are we here yet, Mom? Boy, lookit all the *snow*!" He scooped some up with his bare hand, exclaiming, "It's *cold*!"

"It sure is cold," she said, hurrying with him across Bay to the streetcar stop, filled with excitement and hope. Please be there! We can't go any further. There's nowhere left to go. "We're going to go on a streetcar, honey," she told him as one came swaying along the tracks. "Isn't this fun?"

"Oh, boy!" he crowed, climbing up into the car.

She sat down with him, feeling ludicrously happy just to be on a streetcar and to see familiar streets. Looking out the window she saw so many changes. The city looked warmer and less forbidding, with many new high-rise buildings, dozens of them. And all the trees. How could she have forgotten about the trees? Or how clean it was here? At Bathurst, they transferred to another streetcar and she wanted, for no reason, to smile at the few other passengers out this early in the morning. Bobby insisted on going up to talk to the conductor, who seemed to enjoy having him clinging to the guard rail, riding along beside him, and even gave him a book of transfer stubs. Tillie kept looking out the windows, elated at seeing people enter a small church, carrying their missals; the city was still filled with worshippers. But how dignified they appeared in their sedate Sunday clothes.

"Look, Mom, what he gave me!"

"Did you say thank you?"

He stared at her wide-eyed for a moment, then turned and ran back the length of the car to pat the conductor on the arm and, having gained his attention, said, "Thank you!" From where she sat she saw the conductor put out his hand and give Bobby an affectionate squeeze on the shoulder.

When they were getting near the St. Clair loop, Bobby said they had to get off at the front of the car so he could say good-bye to the conductor.

"You got one real nice boy there." He smiled at Tillie.

She smiled back, choked yet again at the displays of kindness that kept occurring.

"You have a nice day," he said to Bobby. And Bobby, with a typical display of the spiritual generosity that constantly defied Tillie's understanding, darted back, ducked under the rail, threw his arms around the man's neck, and kissed him on the cheek. The man looked astonished. Then Bobby ducked out again, reached for his mother's hand and jumped down from the streetcar with her, turning to wave as the conductor clanged the bell several times. The doors folded closed and the car moved on.

She led him up to the corner, glad to see another streetcar coming, telling him, "We're almost there now. Four stops on this one and then a little walk."

At Spadina Road she had to stand for several long moments, looking around. The big red house with the gray roof was still there on the northwest corner. And on the northeast was the old gray mansion that had been converted to doctors' offices sometime in the forties. Opposite where they stood, on the south side of St. Clair, was the start of the park that led down to the reservoir and Casa Loma. It was a walk she and Press had taken dozens of times, one she'd take with Bobby first chance she got.

The light turned green and they crossed, heading up into the Village. She recognized every house they passed. There was the little Laura Secord shop on the corner, and the hardware store. Across the street was the ice cream store. She smiled when they passed the Esso station. As they turned into Gleneden Road, Bobby pulled his hand free and ran along through the snow piled back from the sidewalk in front of houses so familiar to her and so unaltered she wanted to cry simply at seeing them. Even the trees either side of the street made her throat ache. Bobby ran on, leaving in his wake deep holes in the top-crusted snow. She'd even forgotten that: the icy surface of the snow and the crunch it made when a foot went through. God! I loved it here, she thought, and I never knew it. She thought to stop Bobby—his trousers and shoes were getting soaked—but couldn't bring herself to destroy his pleasure. He'd never seen snow before, had never been farther north than Roanoke, where Big Bobby's mother lived.

Upon seeing the house, she had to stop again and take several deep breaths. It, too, was unchanged, except for the wrought-iron fencing that entirely enclosed the property. It was still white-painted brick with black shutters, still an impressive, gracious old house, and the sight of it, after all this time, finally enabled her to think about Jess. She was unexpectedly filled with love for this sister she'd taken so for granted and abused in so many ways. I know what you did for me, she thought, feeling physically weakened by the knowledge. I know what you did and how much it cost you. Such a high price to pay, Jess, and I just went on and on, letting you.

Holding Bobby's hand, she approached the gate across the front walk and put her hand out to press the intercom button. She recognized Polly's voice asking, "Who is it?" and was relieved to know that Polly, at least, was still here.

"It's Tillie. Is my sister here?"

"Mrs. Ames!" Polly's voice soared in surprise as the gate clicked open.

Before they were halfway up the walk, the front door was open and Polly was waiting in the doorway to embrace Tillie heartily, exclaiming, "Your sister's going to be *so* pleased." Drawing them inside, she said, "She's upstairs with Mr. Thibeault. I'll just get her."

"She's with René?" Tillie asked, mystified.

Polly's smile dimmed out. "You didn't know?"

"Know what?"

"Mr. Woodrich," Polly said. "He died. More than six years ago."

"Oh, no."

"It's all right," Polly said gently. "I'll take this fellow in to meet his cousins, and then I'll go up and get Mrs. Woodrich." Her smile returning, she asked, "What's your name, dear heart?"

"Bobby," he answered, entrusting his hand readily into hers as Tillie set down the suitcase and removed her coat, all the while gazing up the stairs.

"Just wait one minute," Polly said. "Oh, she's going to be so pleased!" She took Bobby off down the hall, saying, "You have three cousins. Did you know that?"

"I do?"

"You sure do, dear heart. Belinda and Todd and Justin. They're all in here."

Three children? Jess had had another child, Tillie thought. And Sandy was dead. God! What else had changed?

Polly opened the door to the den and the three children

looked up from their game of Monopoly. "This is Bobby, your cousin," Polly said.

"I'm Bobby," he announced. Then, freeing his hand from Polly's, he proceeded to hug and kiss each of them in turn before plopping himself down on the floor asking, "Whatcha playin'? C'n I play too?"

Fascinated, Belinda was unable to take her eyes off this cousin she hadn't known she'd had. "D'you know how to play? It's Monopoly."

"Sure I do," he lied happily.

Polly closed the door, hearing the children laughing as she hurried upstairs.

Tillie waited at the bottom of the stairs, her hand remembering the smooth wood of the curving banister, her heartbeat rapid and her senses in chaos. With something like a thrill she heard Jess's voice—older, deeper, but still recognizably hers—saying, "Tillie?" Her heart racing, she turned to see Jess at the top of the stairs, her face open with surprise as she blindly flew down the stairs. *You came back!* Jess thought, rendered speechless by the sight of Tillie, rushing toward her with no words to offer, an ecstatic cry breaking from her throat.

For Tillie, the contact was like being allowed to sink into all the softness and comfort in the world. Her throat closed, holding Jess, she wanted to say so many things but was unable to speak at all. She could only think about how much she loved this woman, and what Jess had done for her. For the rest of her life she'd be making it up to her. She realized they were both crying and Jess's hands were moving over her as if to reassure herself that this woman she was holding did actually have substance and was real. Jess couldn't make herself let go for a time until her shock was somewhat diminished. Then she held Tillie away, the corners of her mouth lifting in a smile as she thought, I was afraid I'd never see you again, that we'd grown old in our separate distances and never again be close.

As they gazed at each other, Tillie found her head filled with all the words she hadn't yet the strength to say, words having to do with how profoundly sorry she was—for everything.

Jess drew her into the living room, urging Tillie to sit down beside her on the sofa before retrieving Tillie's hands, trying to swallow the clot of silence in her throat, feeling the obstruc-

tion there with each renewed effort to dislodge it and clear the
way for some of the countless things wanting to be said. Finally, she was able only to ask, "Some coffee? Would you like
some coffee?"

"I would. We just got off the bus and haven't had breakfast
yet."

"We?"

"I have a little boy"—her tears started up again—"Bobby.
He's five."

Jess touched her hand wonderingly to Tillie's face. "You
have a little boy. I'm so happy for you." This adult Tillie, this
altered Tillie.

Unable to say any of what she wanted, Tillie thought, It's
only been four days, Jess, but I've learned so much, understand
so many things I didn't see before. And look at you! My sister.
Gray in your hair and lines around your eyes, but so beautiful.
Were you always this beautiful? Your eyes and your hands
touching me.

"Could we stay with you for a while?" she asked, quickly
qualifying it, adding, "Just until I find a job and someplace
to live, get on my feet again."

"Of course you'll stay here."

With what seemed to be an entirely new set of feelings and
values, Tillie leaned forward, her hand on her sister's shoulder,
to press her lips to Jess's forehead. Jess closed her eyes, thinking, It's over. You're home. And you've changed. I can feel
it, see it. You've changed.

◇ Thirty-Four ◇

"It's really a lovely place," Jess said, looking around. "So charming. But then you've always had a great flair for decorating."

Tillie, too, looked around, feeling a strong yet quiet satisfaction in this place, and with her life. It wasn't quite a year and already she'd paid back most of what she'd borrowed from Jess to get started. She'd sent Jimmy Jackson a hundred dollars and had received a sweetly sad letter from him telling her how pleased and surprised he'd been to hear from her, that she shouldn't have bothered with the money, and that Mary-Sue had died a short time before. He invited her to come visit any time, and sent his love to Bobby.

With four more payments, she'd own the sofa and the TV set. But it'd be another year and a half before she owned the car. Thinking about it, she could feel the old impatience building, wishing all of it could be hers right then, that minute, but she carefully tamped it down, reminding herself again that nothing was coming to her. Remember that! her inner voice, silent partner, told her.

"It's funny, coming home sometimes," she said, lifting the coffeepot to refill their cups. "I come up Brunswick and go past the old house and every single time I have this strange feeling—funny and sad."

"Nostalgia," Jess smiled.

"No." Tillie shook her head, setting the pot on the trivet. "Not that. A kind of awful ... *regret*. For wasting such a lot of time and feelings about things. Until I came back last year, I never realized how I feel about this city. It's changed so much, but it's still the same. Sunday newspapers and Sunday movies. I can hardly believe it. Someday they're going to serve booze on Sunday and the last lingering holdouts'll probably die of the trauma." She laughed, spooning sugar into her coffee.

"How's the shop coming along?" Jess asked, picking up her cup, her eyes taking a slow tour of Tillie's face, still trying to accept the fundamental changes in her. She wondered, as she had for the past eight months, what had happened to alter her so drastically, so dramatically, and if it was going to be permanent.

"Some very interesting things are happening on Yorkville," Tillie said with enthusiasm. "It's going to turn into a minor-league Greenwich Village, I think. Honestly! First they were going to tear down some of the houses and clean up the area. Now, coffeehouses are coming in and some new shops are opening, and they're restoring all the old houses. Of course, we've got a ton and a half of beatniks hanging around, but they're just kids and mostly harmless. It's exciting, Jess. You really should come down and take a look around. If I had the money, I'd buy some of the property around Hazelton or on Cumberland. In a few years those houses are going to be worth an absolute fortune."

"What I really don't need is something else to worry about," Jess said. "But if you think it's a good investment, I'll be happy to lend you the money ..."

Tillie held up her hand, saying, "No. It drives me crazy having the payment books I've already got. Anything more ... Thank you, but I couldn't. The shop's doing better and better. I'm even going to have to hire another assistant soon. I know the collages are kind of custom-made junk, but you wouldn't believe how many people are starting to want them. Word of mouth is helping a lot."

"It isn't junk," Jess disagreed. "I think you had a very clever idea. People want a record of ... how they were, I suppose. I'd like to have you do a large one for René, for Christmas.

Not a subsidy," she qualified. "Something I *want*."

"Fair enough. Get together a batch of good photographs and I'll make one for you. How big?"

"I don't know. Good-sized. About this big." She measured the air with her hands, and for a moment Tillie was captured by the sight of her hands and their long-fingered slender grace. Then, turning back in, she said, "You'll need a lot of photographs for something that big. And it'll cost you."

"How much?"

"At least three hundred. There's a lot of work to it, not just trimming the photographs but putting together the glossy clips, and the pen-and-ink work, and whatever else I decide needs to go into it. I'd like to see sealing wax, I think. And a deep blue ink. Some of that fuzzy ribbon." Becoming enthusiastic, she said, "Get me the photographs as soon as you can. I'd really like to get started on it. Any old programs, ticket stubs and letters, too. Get me a whole bag filled with stuff."

"Tillie," Jess asked very softly, "did I do too much, did I stunt you?"

Feeling a cold stabbing in the pit of her stomach, Tillie lit a cigarette, taking her time before trying to answer. For months, she'd been anticipating the conversation she guessed they were about to have. "Maybe," she said after a moment. "I don't know, Jess. Maybe you did. I had the feeling it was all right to expect everything, because as far back as I can remember, what I wanted you got for me. It seems imbecilic to think of resenting someone for doing all you did for me, but I did. I was so *jealous*. I wasn't interested; I never thought about *how* you got it, I was only concerned with the fact that whatever I expressed a desire for you found some way to provide. It was like a crazy contest, my asking for more and more to see if you'd be able to keep up. It makes me sick now, thinking about it. Because I *knew*. I knew years and years ago, when we went to Vermont with Jamieson Land. I went into your room one night. I couldn't sleep and wanted to get into bed with you, but you weren't there. I *saw* the two of you." She looked down at her hands.

"My God! Why didn't you say something, tell me?"

"I couldn't. I didn't even really know what I was seeing. I just wanted you to get us out of there. It felt horrible, *horrible*. I didn't want you there with him. Not because I was jealous. Not then. It was just this feeling . . . like despair. I felt guilty because I knew somehow you were doing it for me. You'd told me you didn't love him and I could tell that was the truth."

"So you forced that whole running-away episode."

"That's right. But you want to know something?" She looked up again. "I still believe it was the right thing to do. If I hadn't made such a fuss, you'd have stayed with him, wouldn't you?"

"Probably. I don't know. Yes, you're right. I would have."

"It was all wrong, Jess. I hated you being with him. Undressing so he could take those photographs. I think they're exquisite, those photographs. I really do. But they were so . . . *expensive*.

"Then Sandy," she went on. "He loved you the way I wanted someone, Press, I thought, to love me. And I was jealous again, constantly comparing what I had to what you had, never being able to measure up because I was getting second best and you were getting best. Oh, Christ! Have you any idea how *corrosive* jealousy can be? I felt as if it was eating me from the inside out. I didn't want to admit that perhaps you deserved someone good to love you or that you'd paid a thousand times over for the right to have it. I wasn't interested in any of that. I just wanted my share. My share." She smiled sadly, taking her time putting out the cigarette.

"Tillie . . ." Jess began.

"No," she cut her off. "Let me say it. I've thought and thought about all of it ever since I got back. I think it's time we talked, but I've got to say my piece first.

"I guess what I'm trying to say is that whatever you did get, you *earned* it. And the hard way. I probably still wouldn't understand if Bobby's father hadn't thrown me out because I finally went too far and made a pass at his best friend, hoping to latch onto someone with even more money than Big Bobby. Bobby's illegitimate, Jess. The only reason I had him was because I thought having him would force his father to marry me, so I'd finally get the things I thought I wanted. Absolutely insane! I didn't even *like* Big Bobby, let alone love him. And I certainly didn't give a damn about Lew; he was just there, so I thought I'd give it a try. But I was still working on what I wanted, what I thought I had coming to me. Bobby threw us both out, took back every piece of jewelry he'd ever given me, and a couple of things other people had given me, too. He tossed all my clothes in a big pile on the floor, took back the car keys and told me to get out, he was sick to death of me.

"You know something?" She looked up, her eyes very wide and very blue. "I actually sat down a few weeks ago and wrote to tell him he'd been right and that I was sorry. It didn't even hurt at all that much admitting it. I told him that any time he wanted to see Bobby, it'd be all right. I know he loves him. Bobby's his son, after all. And he's not an unkind or uncaring man. It couldn't have been an easy thing for him to do, letting Bobby go. Letting *me* go," she said, laughing, "was most likely the biggest relief of his life." She reached for her cup. "He threw us out," she said, the laughter gone. "And all I had was about twenty-five dollars. I'm not going to go into the details. I wanted to get back here. There was nowhere else left to go. So, I . . . did what I had to do." She looked meaningfully, openly into her sister's eyes. "It was so ugly, Jess, so awful. I still don't feel quite clean. But in a way, I'm not sorry that happened either. I discovered so many things. Kindness. There was that. From people I wouldn't't've given the time of day to a month before, people I didn't think looked right or sounded right, didn't measure up to my standards. It all made me start seeing with entirely different eyes. And as for the other . . . I did it. I had to pay with the only currency I had left." She shook her head again, gazing at her cup. "Talk about the hard way," she said without self-pity. "I don't even *like* men. That's something else I found out. I don't have the right to judge people, Jess. I don't have the right to expect things, either. Most of all"—she returned her eyes to Jess's—"I don't have the right to think anything but the best of you. I took everything for granted and never stopped to think about what you were paying, or *how much*. I'm so sorry for that. It makes me feel awful, thinking about it."

"I don't know what to say," Jess said thickly.

"You don't have to say anything. There's nothing to say, really. I'm not going to get it all straightened out in my head overnight. I'm still working on a lot of it. When I first got back, I wanted to be furious with you for not giving me a job. I was angry because Press and Nelda and Flora were there. Your telling me about ruffled feathers and all that. I was filled with resentment. I wanted to shout, 'What the hell do I care about *them*?' I wanted to say all sorts of things, but I had to stop and decide you were right.

"Half a dozen times a day there's something that comes up I've got to stop and think about because my first reaction is, 'To hell with that crap!' or 'Who the hell d'you think you *are*, pulling that shit on *me*?' I'm fighting it all the time. I'm thirty-five years old, Jess. I've got a six-year-old son and a little business I'm trying to make work. I don't want any miracles and I don't want anything that isn't by rights mine." She smiled. "I want it fast, believe me. But I'm reminding myself constantly that nothing happens that way. 'Custom Collages.'" Her smile widened. "It's really an appropriate name for the business. When I start each new one, I have to take a lot of time to lay out the materials and study the photographs and whatever else I'm going to use, see how it all ties together and what piece will fit where. It's what I'm trying to do with my life. Jesus!" She laughed. "I sound like 'Love of Life.'" She touched Jess's hand. "It's really all right. Don't look that way."

"But I never wanted you to have to go through any of that."

"I did, and it didn't kill me. It probably got me stopped in time. I've always learned my lessons the hard way. Like Owen. What happened to him just makes me love and value Bobby more. It's one hell of a way to learn, I know. But better than never learning at all. Press still finds it hard to talk to me, but Nelda . . . I think, I *hope* we're going to be friends. And Flora, after she finished yelling, gave me one of her big hugs and invited herself over to dinner to talk, and meet Bobby.

"There's one other thing, Jess. I don't know how you're going to react, but it's only fair to tell you. It's about Marina."

"I know. She told me."

"I should've known she would. But I want you to know it isn't Flora all over again. I love Marina. We're both saving so we can buy a house and live together, the three of us. I really haven't ever cared for men all that much. I thought it was just the kinds of men I kept meeting. But it wasn't that. And it doesn't have anything to do with you or what happened on the road. It has to do with me. I feel so much easier about myself knowing who I am, and what.

"Flora came over one night a couple of weeks or a month or so ago, rumbling at me, giving me warnings about messing up Marina. I told her exactly what I'm telling you. Those years I spent with Flora were some of the happiest years of my life. I mean that. But I kept feeling guilty and wrong about it. I don't feel that way now. I won't hurt Marina, not intentionally ever, and I'll stay with her for as long as she wants. I hope it's going to be for good. I'd like some things settled, and I'd like her to be one of those things. That's all."

"I have to be honest," Jess said slowly. "You frighten me, Tillie. Sometimes I have the feeling you're like one of those people who suddenly find religion. I admire you for being candid, but I can't help wondering about your motives, and if you're being completely truthful. I honestly don't understand one woman's desire for another. I have to tell you that. It doesn't upset me. I just don't feel altogether comfortable with it. Not with you, and not with Marina, much as I like her and admire the job she's doing, and her candor. It's something I suppose I'm going to have to learn to live with and understand. My immediate instinct, my spontaneous wish for you, would be to find some man you could love. But if you tell me that you can't, I'm going to try to accept that. I simply can't help having doubts."

"Everyone's doubtful about me," Tillie said with a touch of annoyance. "*I'm* doubtful about me, too. But I'm not trying to lie or delude myself. I can't do more than that."

"No," Jess agreed. "I don't think you can. It's just that there are other people involved and I'd like to think you really are aware of all the implications."

"I'm trying to be. And Marina keeps reminding me. She's good for me, Jess. We're good for each other. I feel . . . safe with her. The way I felt with Flora."

"Someone to look after you."

"No, not that. Someone I care for who, first of all, won't hurt me, won't hurt my senses sexually, and second of all, who's important. I want to do things for her, take care of her if she's sick and bring her tea in bed. I just *care*. I know it's going to be a hundred years before anyone believes me, but that doesn't matter because *I* know what the truth is and how I really feel, and Marina does too."

"All right, Tillie. I've got to give you the benefit of the doubt."

"Don't put it that way," she said, looking wounded. "Give me the benefit of *not* doubting."

"I'll try. I want to believe you. I certainly believe what you've accomplished so far. I wonder if you know how much all of us want to believe, because we all do, not just me. But it's hard, Tillie. I'm sure you can appreciate just how hard it is. I love you and I want this new you to be the one. But every so often...I love you."

"Every so often what?"

"Nothing. Just that I suppose I see the battle you're doing with your resentment and I get frightened that other side of you will take over again. And win."

"That's *not* going to happen."

"Good." Jess smiled.

"I love you, too, you know, Jess. If I didn't, I'd hate you for dishing out your truths—as you see them. I don't want to hate anyone," she said somewhat wearily. "I just want to *be*."

"That's all I want for you. Look, I've got to go. The kids specifically asked me to be home by seven-thirty for a family conference and I promised them I would be."

"Sure." Tillie got up and saw her to the door.

Jess turned. "I believe more than I doubt," she said, embracing her. "I'm proud of you and all you've done."

"I know. You just want to be prouder."

"No. I want you to be happy."

"I know that, too. The difference now is that both of us want it for me. You'd better hurry or you're going to be late. And I've got to get Bobby kicking and screaming into the bath. He thinks being dirty is the ultimate way to live."

They kissed, then Jess hurried off. Tillie watched her get in the car and drive away, then she closed the door, breathing hard, as if she'd just run a race with invisible contestants.

Olga cleared away the last of the dishes, brought in Jess's coffee, then left.

Jess lifted her cup, looking around the table at the children. They seemed very sedate, even formal. She smiled at them, asking, "Are we having some sort of ceremony?"

"Mom," Justin began importantly, "the three of us have been talking. And we all agree, so we wanted to tell you. I mean, after all, I'm almost fifteen. Todd's thirteen already and Linnie's nearly seven."

"Come on, Just!" Todd prompted impatiently. "Don't go into all that! Just tell her."

"All right!" Justin replied. "But you don't just *throw* things at people, you know."

Belinda leaned over to lay her hand on her mother's arm, smiling.

"We've talked it over," Justin began again. "And we think you should marry René." Seeing Jess about to say something, he hurried on. "Listen for a minute, okay? We know it's because of Dad the two of you haven't married. But the thing is, that was a long time ago. I mean, Linnie never even knew Dad, and Todd says he can hardly remember him. The one we all know and remember is René, Mom. He's really been great to us and we love him. You do, too, don't you?"

"Yes." She lifted the cup, her hands unsteady.

"What we're saying," Justin went on, "is, if you love him and you guys want to get married, then we think you should. He might as well live here. He's here all the time anyway."

Belinda and Todd were nodding seriously, their eyes on Jess.

"That's it," Justin said. "That's what we wanted to say."

Jess stared at the table for several moments, then took a drink of her coffee.

"Are you mad, Mom?" Belinda asked in an undertone, her hand still on Jess's arm. "We don't want you to be mad at us."

"I'm not mad." She looked closely at each of their faces in turn, thinking.

"Justin said it all wrong," Todd said, worried. He thought she looked unhappy. "We're not trying to decide for you or anything like that. It's just that we thought maybe you weren't marrying René because of Dad and that you thought we'd maybe think you were trying to bring somebody in to replace him. We only wanted to let you know that's not the way we think at all. We all love René and if you do, too, then we'll be glad having him around all the time."

"You're forgetting the other part," Belinda whispered to him. "You promised, remember!"

"Oh, yeah." Todd looked again at his mother. "The other thing is you've got to let us start going to school by ourselves, Mom. We talked about that, too. Nothing's going to happen to us. Boy, you should hear the way we get it from the other kids about Robert bringing us every day! It's making it really hard on us. Linnie wants to walk with Debbie from up the street, and me and Justin can look after ourselves. I mean, you're driving yourself downtown now. We should get to do the same thing, sort of, for ourselves."

"Especially now I'm in high school," Justin threw in with an antagonized expression. "They all think I'm a rich kid snob. It's embarrassing."

"All right," Jess said quietly, feeling in giving her assent that they were starting—and very quickly—to grow away from her. "I'll tell Robert."

Todd and Belinda cheered loudly.

"What about René, Mom?" Justin asked under the noise of the other two.

"I honestly don't know. But I think you're . . . I think the three of you are wonderful. I'm going to have to give it some thought."

"Sure. Well, we just wanted to let you know how we feel. C'mon, gang. Let's clear out and let Mom think."

Noisily, they pushed their chairs back from the table and filed out. She sat on drinking her coffee, still thinking.

Flora said, "C'mon, sweetheart. The kids're right. And you're right, too. They sure are taking the first big steps away. A few more years and Justin will be going off to university. Todd will be in high school next year. You need someone just for you. For chrissake, a couple more years and Justin's going to marry Julie from the looks of it."

"I know. They're very serious. I keep wishing they'd both try seeing other people, just to be sure."

"Some people don't need to make comparisons to know what they want. That's the way those two kids are. They'll wind up together or I'll eat my hat. But what're *you* waiting for, Jess?"

"Flora, I don't need the same things I once did. I'm not really sure I need a husband."

"You're not putting it off on Sandy, are you? The man wouldn't have wanted you to spend the rest of your life alone, mourning for him."

"No, I realize that. And that's not what I'm doing. But things *have* changed. I'm not the same as I was; I'm not willing to settle down and go back to being a wife and mother."

"We all know that," Flora said patiently. "Don't you think René knows that?"

"I suppose he does."

"Hey! What d'you want, icing on it?"

Jess laughed. "I'm thinking carefully," she said. "I want

to be sure I know why I'm doing whatever it is I decide to do."

"Has he said you've got to quit working or anything like that?"

"No. Of course not."

"Have the two of you *talked* about it?"

"Certainly we have. Lately, it seems that's *all* we talk about."

"And you're still thinking," Flora chided. "Don't take too long. You'll wind up missing out on a good thing."

"If I do decide, it won't be because I'm surrounded by people urging me to do it but because it's what I want to do."

"Sweetheart," Flora laughed, "you're kicking a dead horse here. You know you want to marry the guy and all the rest of this jazz is just a lot of stalling."

"I only wish we didn't have to go through all the legalities," she said. "But, really, there's no other way. I do want him around."

"Nuts if you didn't."

"Is that how it looks?" she asked. "If I don't marry René, I'm nuts?"

"You've got other, better offers?"

"No, but my life certainly isn't empty."

"That's because he's around, keeping it from getting empty."

"You sound like his defense attorney." Jess smiled at her.

"The man's got a strong case going for him. You know he's not going to go asking you to make big changes. He's just going to be there."

"I like who I've come to be, Flora. I feel as if I fit my skin."

"Sweetheart, you're not going to lose that."

"No, I suppose you're right. I really am stalling."

Flora just grinned.

She parked the car in one of the visitor's slots at the rear of the building and got out to stand for several moments looking up at the building, feeling the autumn cold in the air. The sky was very clear and she breathed deeply as she pocketed the car keys and walked back down the driveway to the front entrance. On Avenue Road there were quite a lot of people walking and the traffic was fairly heavy.

A couple was just coming out as she entered and she caught the door and went through the foyer to the elevator. She felt exceptionally calm as she waited. As she went down the hall on the seventh floor she was smiling.

She knocked and waited.

There were footsteps and then the door swung open and René's face broke into a delighted grin. "Hey! Jess!"

Still smiling, she asked quietly, "May I come in?"

MS READ-a-thon—a simple way to start youngsters reading

Boys and girls between 6 and 14 can join the MS READ-a-thon and help find a cure for Multiple Sclerosis by reading books. And they get two rewards — the enjoyment of reading, and the great feeling that comes from helping others.

Parents and educators: For complete information call your local MS chapter. Or mail the coupon below.

Kids can help, too!